DOUBLE DRIBBLE

LAS VEGAS RAMBLERS

BOOK THREE

DOUBLE DRIBBLE

LAS VEGAS RAMBLERS

BOOK THREE

Kasha Thompson

WEBSTER AVENUE PUBLISHING
SACRAMENTO, CA

DOUBLE DRIBBLE

Paperback ISBN: 979-8-9862679-8-2

This edition published and arranged by Webster Avenue Publishing.

Printed in the United States of America. First Edition October 2025.

Character Illustration: Mary Rudkovskaya

Cover Design by: Webster Avenue Publishing

Interior Layout by: Webster Avenue Publishing

Editing: Courtney Driver of Whoproofedit.com

BLACK LOVE NOV·EL

/blak/ /ləv/ /nävəˈ

noun

1. a novel, with Black main characters that examines the complexity of falling and staying in love.

2. a story centered around Black love with just the right amount of sweet, savory, and spice.

For anyone who ever wondered "what if?" And still believes that sometimes happily ever afters require a do-over.

CONTENT NOTES

Please note Double Dribble discusses topics which could potentially trigger certain audiences. Some readers may consider the following as spoilers.

Addiction
Physical & Emotional Abuse
Moderate coarse language
Several sexually explicit scenes

ALDRIDGE

I'D JUST TOUCHED DOWN IN LAS VEGAS THE NIGHT BEFORE, and the last thing I wanted to do on a random Wednesday was view houses. But I was officially a Vegas resident after accepting a trade to the Las Vegas Ramblers. The season would begin in a couple of weeks, and I had no place to live. My furniture, which was being driven here by Rover's Rover from Kansas City, was lost in transit. How exactly does one lose a semi-truck loaded with furniture and personal belongings?

My personal assistant, Nori Booker, worked for weeks to make the transition as easy as possible for me. I was posted up in a cushy hotel on the Strip. When I walked out of the airport, an SUV was waiting for me, courtesy of Nike. And my hotel suite was stocked with my favorite everything right down to the toiletries.

Growing up I wasn't catered to. I was making my own dinners, mostly franks and beans, by the age of seven because my mom worked and my dad was either drunk or MIA. Entering the NBA as the top draft pick changed everything. If I'm being honest, it all started at Grand Summit University. The solo dorm room, the gift cards to restaurants, and shopping trips to luxury stores my mother would walk past when we were younger and wistfully sigh, "One day."

The only thing that wasn't secured was a place to live and that was mostly because I didn't know what the hell Vegas had to offer. "How many places are we checking out today?" I turned to Nori who was driving us to a private gated community called Canyon Gate.

"We just have one lined up today. The real estate company wanted you to meet your realtor. You'll tour the property and then the realtor will pick your brain as to what you're looking for. When they asked me all I could say was your ass was very particular."

"I just like what I like. Does this realtor know what they're getting themselves into?"

"Luxe Desert Dwellings comes highly recommended; they are the premier real estate agency in Vegas. They only serve the elite in Nevada. I'm talking about politicians, insta-millionaire entrepreneurs, celebrities, and of course athletes. Trust me you're in good hands."

It was a silly question. Nori didn't leave much to chance. She was efficient and discreet. At thirty-five she was the oldest assistant I'd interviewed but her résumé was stacked. She'd been a personal assistant to musicians, actors, and sports figures. If she could handle the crazy lifestyle of rapper XYZ Baby than my requests were no doubt mild in comparison.

She stopped at the security gate exchanging pleasantries with the guard on duty. "Hello my name is Nori Booker and I'm meeting a realtor from Luxe Dwellings to view one of the homes." She handed over her driver's license.

The guard walked back to his air-conditioned booth and did God knows what before returning to our SUV. "Go straight ahead for a mile and then turn left. Your realtor is already there." He shifted his head to inspect the inside of our vehicle, more specifically me, before tapping the side of the car and moving back.

"Look at that, twenty-four-hour security so you won't have to worry about undesirables." I nodded unimpressed. As we made our way through the grounds, the streets were lined with mature palm trees solidifying the fact we were no longer in Kansas City. For some reason palm trees signified wealth to me. Maybe because they were so foreign from where I grew up in Philly. Shit like palm trees and police protected communities tucked behind gates was unthinkable when I was a kid. At twenty-six it was still hard to believe this was my life.

"This is the type of neighborhood a brother would get pulled over in, for just existing."

"A six-foot five brother like yourself is kind of hard to miss," Nori teased. "Listen, I know you hate change, but this is a good thing. Vegas is going to take you to the next level."

"You sound like Art." Art Fischer was my manager, and he'd negotiated one hell of a deal to get me traded to the Ramblers.

"Promise me you'll be nice."

"I'm always nice."

"No, you're not. The minute you ain't feeling something or someone you shut down."

"I can't help it if my attention span is compromised. I blame social media."

Nori pointed to a home that was way too much house for one man. "I think that's the place."

"I hate it."

"You haven't even seen it."

"The neighbors are too close. And I bet you they'd call the police at the first sound of loud music."

"This home is over ten thousand square feet no one is going to hear you bumping Elton John at two in the morning."

"Don't disrespect the Rocketman."

Nori pulled into the curved driveway behind a BMW.

Exiting the vehicle, I examined the facade. I was too focused on this trade and my new team to give much thought to where I wanted to live. But like a knockoff Gucci belt, you just knew it when you saw it. And this home while massive, was giving cookie-cutter. "Come on, let's get this over with."

At the front door, Nori rang the bell. It took several minutes for a response. Probably because the floor plan was so huge you had to hoof it so as not to miss visitors who, after waiting for five fucking minutes, would no doubt assume you weren't home. When the front door opened, my jaw practically unhinged. "Danessa?"

Her eyes moved past Nori and up toward me, the smile on her face faltering. "Aldridge, what are you doing here?"

Nori's head was on a swivel. "You two know each other?"

"We went to college together," I said, my eyes still transfixed on Danessa. She looked so grown-up in her sleeveless, flowy cream dress. Her naturally curly hair was silk pressed and swayed side to side as she stepped back from the entryway to let us in. I wanted to retreat. I'm talking full out sprint down the tree-lined street until I put some serious distance between me and this woman.

"Small world." Nori chuckled.

Wasn't shit funny. Danessa standing inches away from me was the worst-case scenario. As the new kid on the

Ramblers, I would be navigating the complicated inner workings of an established team. Huge egos, lazy players, and a "this is how it's always been done" mentality. I was prepared to diffuse some bombs, but Danessa was a land-mine under my feet. "You have no idea." Turning to Danessa, I said, "So you moved back home after law school?"

"Yeah, that was always the plan."

"I remember." I nodded thoughtfully, reminded of Danessa's last words to me.

"You're a native. Then it sounds like we are in good hands," Nori said.

Danessa shook her head, probably shaking loose old memories. "So did you find the place alright?"

"Yes, the directions you provided were very helpful."

"Great, well this is 4207 Timberline Way in the Canyon Gate community." Danessa guided us deeper into the living space. Her mouth was moving, but I was finding it difficult to focus on the actual words. I hadn't seen Danessa in over five years. We spent most of the summer together after graduation and then things deteriorated quickly. "Canyon Gate is in the southwestern part of Las Vegas, providing close proximity to the Strip. Which a lot of our younger and childfree clients appreciate."

"So, you're a realtor now?" I blurted out, clearly still stuck on her and me sharing the same air.

"Yes."

"Your mother was a realtor?"

Her chestnut eyes sparked at my memory. "That's right. I started Luxe Desert Dwellings with my mother and sister."

"Wow, putting that business degree to use."

Danessa offered me an *are you okay* smile. "At Canyon

Gate you're also close to the airport. But the best thing about this place is you never have to leave the property because this is a little community all its own with restaurants, a grocery store, gym, and other amenities."

"I noticed a golf course when we drove in," Nori said.

"Yes, that's right, do you golf Aldridge?"

My nose wrinkled at the way she spoke my name. It was empty and devoid of emotion. I was just Aldridge, no longer *her* Aldi. My name hit differently on her tongue when we were in love.

"I don't." And she already fucking knew that.

"Maybe you can learn," Nori suggested."

"This property has seven bedrooms and six and a half baths." In the kitchen she pointed out the newest appliances and unique features and my eyes followed her hand, mainly her ring finger, confirming there weren't any diamond adornments. The thought of running into Danessa and then finding out she was married was a blow I would never recover from. Luckily, she was ringless.

"The backyard is massive," Nori said.

"Yes, great for parties. You have a pool, a spa, outdoor kitchen and a volleyball court that could easily be converted to a basketball court if you prefer."

"Do you hear that Aldi?" Nori asked in hopes of getting me to engage.

"Yep. Danessa, would you say this is a family friendly neighborhood?"

"Yes, lots of established families live in the community."

I tsked at the confirmation. "I don't see it for this place. I appreciate the tour and your time. Thanks, but no thanks." I prepared to head back the way we came.

Danessa's lip torqued upward. "Thanks, but no thanks?"

"Yeah, I've seen all I need to see."

"With all due respect, Aldridge—"

"Stop calling me that."

"What would you have me call you?"

I blinked rapidly. It wasn't that she was saying my name, but the *way* she kept saying it that bothered me.

"Aldi, this was just the meet and greet. I'm sure once you and Danessa get to know one another, she'll have plenty of places lined up that meet your specifications."

Once we get to know each other? I knew Danessa intimately. This client-realtor shit wasn't going to work for me. "I don't think this is a good fit. No offense."

"I'm sorry, but I take all the offense."

"Excuse me?"

"As your assistant stated, this is a meet and greet. The purpose of this meeting was for you to tell me what you were looking for. Your list of non-negotiables, nice to haves, and dislikes. As your realtor, I would compile that information and only show you listings that meet your requirements, neighborhood, price point, amenities. You've signed a twelve-week contract. Walking away now would be like throwing money into a blender."

My jaw tensed. Danessa knew I hated to waste money. Growing up I clipped coupons and helped my mom make food stretch until next payday. I was the kid who wore the off-brand Air Force 1s from Budget Shoes and my brother's hand-me-downs.

"Do you want to tell me what you're looking for?" A different realtor. "Let's sit in the backyard and chat. Nori, feel free to continue to look around." I followed Danessa to the backyard. She was right, it was great for entertaining.

"It's quiet back here."

Danessa pulled out a portfolio to take notes I could only imagine would be added to my client file. "So, you like a quiet setting."

I hopped my shoulders. "I don't know. It's nice to have a place to get away from all the chatter."

"What else are you looking for?" Her tone was even and relaxed.

"Are you seriously going to pretend like this isn't awkward?"

"It's not. You're the client and I'm your realtor."

"I'm not your client, I'm your ex."

"And that makes you uncomfortable?"

I tensed. *Did she think I was bothered?* Because I'm not. I released a chuckle that was more nervous than confident. "I'm not uncomfortable, I just thought you might be because of the way things ended."

"I ended our relationship."

"Yeah, and I'm sure now you see what a huge mistake that was. I'm not trying to toot my own horn but ... rooty tooty fresh and fruity."

"What is that supposed to mean?"

"I'm just saying I'm a world-famous basketball player pulling in millions."

"The word *famous* is doing a lot of the heavy lifting in that sentence."

"Wow. I'm about to be the face of the Ramblers."

"Remind me again when's the last time you won a championship?"

Rude. She was rude. Last year wasn't my year, the Pioneers made it to the Playoffs last year but unexpected teammate injuries stalled our advance. Moving to the Ramblers would either be career defining or career ending. I was taking a real risk, but I believed in my ability to turn water into wine. "Do you treat all your clients like this?"

"Some clients are more stubborn than others." Danessa leaned forward in her chair. "So, I'll ask you again, what do you want?"

I wanted a time machine to alter the past. I'd return to my senior year of college and dump Danessa first, so she never had the chance to break my fucking heart. Or better yet, I'd go back to freshman year and drop out of Econ 101, preventing me from ever meeting Danessa Irwin. Shit, if I was being real I'd have gone back to the day she ended us and begged her to reconsider. She wasn't the first woman I'd loved, but being with her rewired my brain, making it difficult to move past us.

"I want a place to lay my head. With a big closet. It doesn't have to be fancy."

"Lying isn't going to make this process any easier."

"What makes you think I'm lying?"

"Because you have an opinion on everything. Since you were twelve and drafted a plan to get into the NBA. So, claiming you don't know what you're looking for in a property just doesn't ring true."

"I want a home. A place I can make my own. I don't want a cut-and-paste house. I want to walk in and feel my presence. Aldridge lives here."

"Character and good bones."

"Yeah, everything in Vegas lacks charm and individualism. It's like the homes were designed by AI."

"Okay, I'm not going to lie, that's a difficult ask but it's not impossible."

"Well, you have twelve weeks to make it happen."

"So you're not canceling our contract?"

"Like you said, that would be like burning money. No bueno."

Danessa shut her portfolio. "I'll line up some listings and schedule availability with your assistant."

"Great." I stood with a stretch.

"I look forward to helping you find your next home." Standing, Danessa extended her hand.

I looked at her gesture as if it was a snake ready to strike. Reluctantly I claimed her hand, which was dwarfed when enveloped by mine. Danessa gave a soft squeeze to seal the deal. Like I feared, goosebumps freckled my arm and my heart shifted into a familiar pitter-patter. Danessa's touch was my first addiction. Her soft skin making contact with mine put my sobriety in jeopardy.

DANESSA

"DID YOU KNOW?" I BURST INTO MY SISTER ANIKA'S OFFICE.

"That Mom loves me more than you? Yes, I've always known," she said, not bothering to look up from her paperwork.

"Anika, this isn't a joke." I slapped my hand onto her desk.

"I can't help it that you're a disappointment." Anika was four years older than me, but you wouldn't know by the way she was acting or based on the choices she made. We were complete opposites, and although I loved my sister to death, she often gave me heartburn.

"My client today?"

"What about them?" She finally met my gaze. "Oh my God you look like you bumped into a ghost."

"I did. Today's client was an oldie but a goodie from my past. And a heads up would've been nice."

"I didn't schedule your client today so I'm not sure why you're coming at me all hot."

"Aldridge Mosley," I spat out.

Anika's smile faded and I had her undivided attention. "Aldridge was your one o'clock?"

"Yes."

She raised her hands in surrender. "I didn't know

anything about that. I'd heard he'd signed to the Ramblers, but I didn't have a clue he was our new client. I thought you were meeting with someone named Norah or Nancy."

"Nori is Aldridge's assistant or something."

Anika leaned back in her chair, her eyes pinging from my head to my toes. "You wore that?"

I ran my hand over my dress. "What do you mean?"

"It's just kind of milquetoast."

I blinked owlishly at her dig. This dress cost me two hundred and fifty dollars. Sorry I didn't want to wear a skintight bodycon dress while selling houses.

"How'd he look?"

"Grown." Aldridge was always tall but now his muscles were more defined, and he had an earned swagger to him. In college he was a big deal, but he always felt like an impostor. It would appear the impostor syndrome was replaced by confidence times ten. When we dated, I'd remind him how amazing he was at least once a day. Apparently, he just needed to remove the braces and pad his bank account to finally believe it.

"Grown and sexy?"

"He's always been sexy. Time wasn't going to change that." Most attractive men just got better with age and Aldridge was no different.

"What did he say?"

"He tried to fire me."

"Excuse me?" She lifted her watered-down latte to her lips.

"I think he was irritated by my presence."

"That tracks, I mean you did dump him."

"I didn't dump him; I just ended something that was bound to fizzle out."

"Most women would kill to meet a basketball player in college. Lock him in early."

"I'm not most women."

"Yeah, you're stupid," My mother, Jemini Irwin, said entering Anika's office. "You could have been a basketball wife searching for a new home with your husband who just inked a multi-year contract for millions of dollars."

"I'm doing just fine on my own. Thank you."

"Yes, but spending someone else's money is one hundred times more rewarding than spending your own," Anika said.

"You would know." On more than one occasion Anika's clients turned into her next mark. Relationships were transactional to her. She got that mentality from my mother.

"So, I'm assuming you talked him out of firing us?" my mom asked.

"Yeah, I appealed to his pockets. You know he was always financially focused."

"Yes, that's why I liked him so much. How you let that man get away I'll never understand."

Here we go again. The last thing I wanted to do right now was defend my decisions. "I didn't let him get away."

"You're right about that. You pushed him away." This was our MO, we bickered. Sometimes it was jovial, other times it was a bloodbath with one or all of us saying the worst things in hopes of inflicting the most pain. Trust, I knew we were dysfunctional when at eight years old my mother had me entertain some random man while she changed. We talked about sports, and he mentioned on more than one occasion that I was filling out nicely.

"Did you know Aldridge was our new client?"

"I did." Shame wasn't an emotion my mother was familiar with.

"And you didn't think it was something I needed to know?"

"If I told you, you would've found a reason to back out of it."

I threw my hands in the air. "Aldridge being my ex was reason enough."

"I'm sure he was pleasantly surprised to see you."

"He threatened to fire me, remember. Not exactly rolling out the welcome wagon."

"That sounds like a man who still has feelings," Anika said.

"Are you two listening to yourselves? Aldridge hasn't been secretly pining for me all these years. We've moved on and so should both of you."

"It didn't work out five years ago, but maybe this time it will be different," my mother said with a straight face.

"I'm going to sell Aldridge a house because I'm a professional and this could potentially be a fat commission, and after escrow we are closing the chapter on Mr. Mosley." Pushing past my mother, I exited Anika's office, heading to my own.

When Aldridge and I split up, my mother told me I was stupid. She didn't suggest it, she fixed her lips and pronounced it loud and clear. In her mind Aldridge was supposed to be my ticket to domestic bliss. After meeting Aldridge for the first time one winter break, she virtually sunk her claws into him. Inviting him to every family event and holiday. We weren't wealthy but in comparison to Aldridge and his parents, we were well off with a cute house on a street lined with foliage. Aldridge mused that my life was something he'd only ever seen on television.

For my mother the break up meant letting go of her dream of sitting courtside at her son-in-law's games dripping in diamonds and the newest designer handbag. *"How could you be so stupid, Danessa? He was right there, and you fumbled the ball."* I didn't go to school for a husband like some of my White counterparts who were more concerned with getting their MRS rather than a BS. The last thing I wanted was to coast off Aldridge's success. I wanted to make a life based on my own merit. While being a realtor was never the dream, I was good at it and the money was great.

My mother was a realtor, when I was younger, she would sell modest starter homes to young families, and she did pretty well. Making enough to purchase a home of her own in a quaint working-class neighborhood. She made friends with some of the wives in the community, and even though she was a divorcée they welcomed her into their circle. Which ended up being a mistake because my mother quickly made the rounds fucking their husbands.

Opening my laptop, I pulled up my search engine and entered Aldridge's name. A ton of hits popped up. Aldridge Mosley's net worth, Aldridge Mosley's college basketball stats, Aldridge Mosley's girlfriend. I'm ashamed to admit I clicked on the last entry first. The screen populated with various images, but the picture of him with a blonde-haired, blue-eyed stunner caught my attention. I knew absolutely zero about her, but a pang of jealousy tugged at my heart. Clicking on the article, I learned her name was Ashley Castellanos, of course, and she was a fitness influencer. Was Miss Ashley also making the move to Vegas? Don't get me wrong, I was completely over Aldridge, but seeing who he'd moved on with just confirmed what I'd always known.

Closing each open tab, I reached for my dinging phone. It was Anika texting me instead of walking over to my office.

Anika: Sorry about mom.

Danessa: I don't need you to apologize.

Anika: I know but she was wrong not to tell you.

Danessa: She was.

Anika: I think she meant well.

Danessa: She didn't and that's okay.

Anika: Are we still on for tonight?

Anika snagged tickets to the Anjeni concert at the Sphere. And when I say snagged, one of her benefactors gifted them to her.

Danessa: You're still driving right?

Anika: Yep.

Danessa: Then yes, because I need a drink or two.

THE SPHERE WAS A VEGAS attraction I told my clients about but never visited myself. Singer Anjeni was having an immersive concert, and the place was filled with Hollywood elites. Anika's suga daddy must be someone very important to score premium tickets like these.

"So why didn't your gentleman caller come with you?" I asked, as we settled into our seats.

"It conflicted with some sports thing for one of his kids."

"He has kids?" I was never good at hiding my feelings, so she was getting my unfiltered reaction. At least when we were on the phone and she was recounting some scandalous story, I could make all the shock and awe faces I wanted.

"Yes two."

"Have you met them?" My voice was pitching higher with each new detail.

"I don't think his wife would appreciate that."

"Wife?" My eyebrows were racing toward my hairline.

"It's an open marriage, she's cool." Anika pulled out a gold compact with her name engraved on the back and reapplied her lipstick before smiling at her reflection, no doubt pleased with what she saw.

"Did he tell you that?" Because men be lying.

"No, she did."

Did I mention we were polar opposites? Wives were a hard pass. Kids were even questionable. I was twenty-six and not interested in taking some know-it-all brat to mommy and me classes. Dating was already difficult enough without adding in other people. But Anika wasn't exactly looking to settle down. She was interested in having fun. Which I could respect, men did this shit all the time. Why couldn't the fairer sex join in on the shenanigans?

As the show started, I had a hard time figuring out where to look. The screen was one hundred and sixty square feet and wrapped around the venue. Our seats vibrated from the bass in the music, causing my breasts to jiggle. Then there was the screaming. The Anjeni fandom was hardcore and when the queen graced the stage descending from the rafters, she was celebrated. I thought the grown ass man next to me was going to pop a capillary the way he was carrying on. After thirty minutes I was feeling a bit overwhelmed. "I'm going to go get another drink. Do you want one?"

"Girl, we're not in the nosebleed section, we can use the app to order more drinks." Anika shook her phone.

"I also need to pee. Is that in the app?"

My sister shooed me away, turning her attention back to the stage.

In the lobby, I hit up the restroom followed by the concession. The space was packed with people running about, taking pictures, or purchasing tour merch. My last concert was Usher, and I secretly wished I was the one he was feeding the cherry to. For Mr. Raymond, I was prepared to act a plum fool. In line it was clear I wasn't the only one who was in need of something to distract me. When I made it to the front, I ordered a Paloma, one of the overpriced specialty drinks.

"Thirty dollars for some liquor is obscene," a deep voice called from behind me.

Turning, I was confronted with my reason to drink, Aldridge in a black knit top—that if you squinted was borderline see-through—and black pants to complete the look. He was wearing sunglasses indoors, which was pretentious. And he was clutching a T-shirt with Anjeni's face on it. She was so famous even actual famous people stanned her.

"What are you doing here?"

He removed his sunglasses, slipping them into the open collar of his shirt. "Not so nice when people show up to your spot unexpectedly."

"The Sphere is not my spot any more than that house this afternoon was yours."

"Well since I'm a Vegas resident now I thought I'd see what the city was hitting for."

"And you managed to score yourself tickets to this exclusive concert?" Being wealthy must be amazing. The ability to go anywhere, with damn near anyone, fuck the price. I wasn't struggling for money, but I still cringed when I checked the price tag on a Ferragamo purse. Don't get me wrong, I swiped the card anyway, but not without a moment of silence for my bank account.

"I'm Aldridge Mosley, all I have to do is ask. Shit sometimes not even that."

"Looks like some things never change."

"Ma'am, that will be $37.50," the bartender called."

"I got it." Aldridge stepped up to pay.

"No, I can buy my own drink."

"I know you can. But I'm not going to let you."

"How do you intend to stop me?" I searched my small purse for my bank card but stopped when the distinctive chime of payment being rendered sounded. "Send me your Cash App and I'll repay you."

"Don't insult me."

I pushed out a resigned sigh. "Thank you."

"Don't mention it."

Moving off to the side, I took a sip. It was worth the thirty-seven dollars. "Are you enjoying the show?"

"Uhm, I think I was experiencing vertigo."

"Oh my God, I thought I was the only one. It's ginormous."

"When they said it was immersive, they weren't kidding. If I sat in there for any longer my ears and nose were going to start bleeding." Aldridge looked around. "Did you come alone?"

"No, I'm here with my sister."

"Anika?" His face brightened. He thought my sister was a hoot.

"Yeah."

"How is she ... still scamming brothers out of their money?"

"How do you think we got the tickets," I joked. What about you?"

"I'm here with my Ramblers buddy."

My head jerked back. "Your what?"

"The organization assigns new players an accountability buddy to help with the transition."

"No kidding? Who did you get?"

"Deion McCabe."

I grimaced.

Aldridge scratched at his beard. "Yeah, he's been a bit of an asshole. Letting me know he is not my babysitter. And if I kill someone under no circumstances should I call him."

"He's not willing to help you bury a body?"

"I know right. We're teammates."

"Sounds like he's trying to avoid being your bunkmate in jail."

"If we got caught, I'd take the fall."

"The fact that you've thought this out is actually disturbing."

"You should always have someone on reserve in case you need help digging a hole."

He was right. I knew exactly who to call if I were ever in that situation. "Anika is my first call, hands down."

"Shit, Anika would be pissed she missed out on the kill."

We shared a laugh at my sister's homicidal tendencies.

"Runner up, my mom."

"Why is your family all good with a shovel?"

"Never cross an Irwin woman, few live to tell the tale."

"I guess I'm one of the lucky ones."

I found my straw and took a long sip. "How are you liking Vegas?"

"This is my second day, and I've seen a snooty neighborhood, the CTE-inducing Sphere, and you." That didn't sound like a compliment. Was he including me in his underwhelming experience thus far? "But you're my realtor so hopefully you can change my mind about the city."

"I'll do my best. You know Vegas is so much more than just the Strip. We have pockets of communities that are just as eclectic and interesting as anything you'd find in Philadelphia or New York. And the people are really friendly and welcoming. I think because most of them were transplants themselves at one point in time."

Aldridge's phone dinged and he checked the screen. "That's my accountability bud asking where I'm at."

"Wow, he's taking his role very seriously."

"He can probably sense I'm in danger."

"Am I dangerous?"

"Being this close to you is hazardous to my mental health."

The AC in this place was on full blast but, somehow, I was overheating. "God, I hope that's not true."

He shrugged. "You know what they say, high risk can often equal high reward."

Did he consider interacting with me a risk? And if that were the case, why would he continue to do it? Where was the reward in that?

"I gotta run. Remember if your nose starts to bleed during the second half of the show, pinch the soft part of your nose."

"Thanks, I guess."

"Have a good night, Danessa." He took a few steps backward as if sneaking one last look before turning and walking away.

A chill coasted down my spine. Aldridge was right, we were in danger.

ALDRIDGE

TODAY WAS MY FIRST OFFICIAL PRACTICE WITH MY NEW TEAM. I opted to be traded to the Ramblers because in Kansas City I was the third biggest player. The spotlight was harder to triangulate when you had to share it with two other people. Ramblers CEO, Sariah Thornton and Coach Justus Chappel assured me I would be the new face of the team. Currently Colin Pratt was considered the star player, but he was getting older and had done little to move the needle on a championship. Just consider me the David Ruffin to his Otis.

It was very clear I was being hired and granted a huge contract and signing bonus because they believed I could do what Pratt had not … deliver a championship. To be honest, it felt like the Ramblers organization was more confident than I was. Sure, I knew what was required to win and I was willing to sacrifice everything else for a chance at a championship. But at the end of the day, just like the Temptations, shit would fall apart quick, fast, and in a hurry if the team wasn't on the same page. My expertise was ball handling, not interpersonal skills. We had a great coach and some really talented players and while I didn't have a plan per se, I had concepts of a vague plan and it was simple. Win more games than you lose.

"Hey newbie, pass the ball," Colin Pratt yelled.

I wasn't a newbie. I'd been in the NBA for over five years. And Colin Pratt didn't get to tell me what to do. If I allowed this motherfucker to son me on my first day that would be our dynamic the entire season. The only thing Pratt had on me was years. Neither him nor these other players were going to determine my fate. I was more than capable of being an asshole right back. Dribbling the ball, I walked further away from the hoop until I was well beyond three-point range and took a shot. A shot that circled the rim before sinking into the basket.

"Shit the newbie is locked in," Deion said.

As an accountability buddy, Deion seemed alright. His tongue was sharp, never holding anything back, and he wasn't looking to make a new friend. He kept me under his wing because that was part of his job. And upon first meeting him, he let me know there were in fact dumb questions and I shouldn't be asking him any of them. I get it, no one wanted to babysit the new kid. So I tried to stay out of his hair.

"Practice ain't real life. And when you have twenty thousand fans booing and jeering you, I bet your hand isn't as steady," Pratt claimed.

I cleared my throat. "Basketball is what I do. So, whether it's a three-pointer …" I drilled another three. "A jump shot." I drifted to the left before surging to the right and dropping another basket. "Or a slam dunk." Palming the ball, I backed up to give myself a runway before launching myself into the air and pushing the ball over the rim. "The results are going to be the same every single time."

I believed in respecting my elders, but one thing I wasn't going to allow was the disrespect. Pratt saw me as his replacement and felt a way about it, but that didn't have shit to do with me. He could work with me or against me. And if it was the latter, he would find himself riding the bench this year. I didn't need new friends. I needed a championship ring.

Coach Justus rapped his hands together from the sidelines. "Okay, stop goofing off and let's start with conditioning drills. Up and down the court fifteen times. Mosley a word."

I jogged over to where Coach was standing. "Yes, Coach."

"Stop playing with your food. No one likes a showboat."

"I wasn't showing off, I was just giving them a preview of what's to come."

"Cocky players lose games."

"Kobe was cocky."

"Motherfucker you're not Kobe." Coach Justus didn't mince words, and he wasn't looking to hold a brother's hand. From what I'd seen of him thus far, he seemed firm but fair. He was also driven, when he visited me in Kansas City to discuss a possible trade I was impressed by his passion and love for the sport. Coach being a former player and ring holder was also appealing because it meant he understood what it would take to win.

"So shut up and dribble. Got it."

"I'm not telling you to take everything on the chin, but you could try to make this transition easier."

"And what does Pratt have to do?"

"I'm having similar conversations with him about his current attitude. You let me handle Pratt and you focus on the game."

"Alright."

"Now go run."

When practice wrapped, I was greeted by several missed calls from my mother. The Ramblers Training Facility was massive with large spaces that produced an echo when you spoke. I located a discreet area and ducked into an empty conference room. Upon entering, the lights flickered on and the projection screen displayed the Ramblers logo, a basketball ablaze in flames. Dropping into one of the oversized leather seats, I returned my mom's call.

"Hello?"

"Is everything okay?" Calls from my mother always wrecked my nerves because I never knew if she was just calling to say hello or tell me she needed bail money for my father, uncle or brother. Shit if I'm being real, a call like that could be about any man in my family and a few of the women.

"Of course it is, baby. How's Vegas?"

Despite being exhausted, I couldn't help but smile. "Hi Mom. Vegas is Vegas."

"Have you found a place yet?"

"I haven't even been here a week."

"So where do they have you staying?" I could tell she was doing several other things while talking to me, washing the dishes and moving in and out of the house.

"I'm staying in a hotel at the moment."

"Have you met the team?"

It was clear this conversation was going to be heavy on the questions. "I did and they all love me," I teased.

"What's not to love? I raised my baby right." She tsked and then under her breath she said, "Why is this man lying to Judge Mathis."

"How's work?"

"You know Denise, my new coworker? She just told my boss she felt uncomfortable around me because I never engage in small talk."

"No, she didn't."

"Yes, she did. She's lucky I'm a God-fearing woman because my tongue and these fists stay ready."

"Momma, you can't go around beating people up."

"I didn't, but I wanted to. She needs to mind her business. I get my work done and don't bother nobody."

"Well once I'm settled in here you can tell nosy Denise to suck it." This new contract elevated my tax bracket big time. I was making decent money in Kansas, but my Ramblers contract was the kind that created generational wealth. We grew up poor, I'm talking me and my brother sleeping in the living room because we could only afford a two-bedroom apartment, and the rooms were reserved for my parents and sister.

So poor I could never participate in the Scholastic Book Fairs at school. Except for that one time when my fifth-grade teacher, Ms. Hammel, gave me ten dollars to buy a book. I purchased *Diary of a Wimpy Kid*, and an eraser shaped like a boom box. Money was always tight, some months we'd gone without water or electricity. But my mother always found a way to get us through.

I'd been working since I was ten doing odd jobs around the neighborhood. When I turned thirteen, I started working as a bicycle delivery person for a local Chinese restaurant. The only reason they hired me was because I lied about my age, and my height allowed me to look a convincing sixteen. They paid me in cash, which meant I could keep some of my money before handing over the rest to my mother for household bills or groceries.

"I wanted to tell her my son was a famous basketball player."

"Okay Mom, we talked about this. You can't start every conversation with the professional ballplayer card."

"Why not? Parents whose children are doctors or lawyers do it all the time.

"Yeah well, they shouldn't either.

"So, when can your father and I come to visit?"

My mother was always welcome. My father, however, could jump off the Girard Point Bridge and I wouldn't shed a tear. Problem was, my mother refused to travel without him despite him being a useless piece of shit. I wasn't up for visitors, not right now. I'd be a horrible host because of practice, my time in the gym, and this house search. "Once I'm settled, we can talk."

"Well have you started looking?"

"Yes, I met with the realtor the other day. Funny enough—" I stopped short, deciding against mentioning Danessa. When we were dating, my mom loved her. Honestly, I think she was just glad I'd brought home a Black girl. Once we broke up, Danessa quickly went from future daughter-in-law to the one that got away for both me and my mother.

My phone dinged with an incoming message from Nori. "Mom, I have to go. Talk to you later."

"Okay, don't forget to call your uncle and wish him a happy birthday."

"Sure thing." I was not going to call my uncle, but to appease my mother I would shoot off a HBD text.

I pulled up Nori's series of text messages.

Nori: Updates, the moving van has been located and should be here by the end of the week.

Nori: The hotel wants to know if you would like a personal butler.

Nori: You have an interview with ESPN next week. More on that later.

Aldridge: Is the butler free?

Nori: No, there's an additional fee.

Aldridge: Then the answer is no. And what exactly do I need a butler for?"

Nori: Make dinner reservations, drop off your dry cleaning, purchase tickets to the latest show.

Aldridge: That's what I pay you for.

Nori: I know but you're in Vegas now. I'm sure these athletes' assistants have assistants.

Aldridge: Don't get any ideas. We are not like these other rich folks. We are on a budget."

Upon hire she took one look at my household and whipped that shit into shape. Nothing moved unless she greenlit it. She kept me on schedule, fixed any inconveniences, and made sure I linked up with the hottest designers. Nori touched everything but my finances, which were exclusively handled by me and my accounting firm. I would be damned if I ended up like some of these other celebrities who at the end of their reign had nothing to show for it.

I didn't play about my money mostly because I wasn't the only one depending on that check each month. Even though I was grown and my mother worked, I still supported my childhood household. And by support I meant I paid the mortgage, car notes, school fee, and college tuition. I couldn't fuck this up because if I did, the impact would be so much bigger than just me.

Nori: One last thing. I heard back from the realtor, and it sounds like she's been busy. She has a bunch of homes lined up for you.

Aldridge: Great.

Nori: Was that a great I'm so excited or a great one more thing to do?

Aldridge: Maybe a mix of both.

Nori: When do I get the story about you two?

Aldridge: You don't.

Nori: Do you want me to hit pause on the home search?

That was an excellent question. I needed a place. Staying at a hotel was a waste of money and was not sustainable long term. It wasn't the house hunt that was the problem. It was who the hunt was with, Danessa. Seeing her again after all this time caused some feelings to resurface. Like what gave her the right to be walking around Vegas clearly thriving and acting like she'd leveled up since me. She was finer than I remember her being. She didn't have any business looking that good. And her smile … was there a man in her life who was being treated to that smile and phat ass every day. I'm not implying she wasn't allowed to move on, but it made it hard for me to pretend she regretted her decision to leave me when clearly she didn't.

Aldridge: No, the sooner I can find a place the better.

Nori: Got it. Then I'll tell Danessa it's a go for Saturday.

Aldridge: Great.

DANESSA

I NEVER GOT NERVOUS WHEN MEETING WITH CLIENTS. I'D represented politicians, dignitaries, celebrities, and one time a Saudi prince. But this afternoon I was running around the property like a chicken with its head no longer attached. Fussing with pillows, opening and closing doors, and I was torn between retracting the hideaway slider or keeping them shut as a mini surprise.

This could probably be considered normal behavior when one was about to tour a house with their ex. Oddly enough this wasn't the first time we'd walked through real estate together. In college we lived on campus all four years. But during our senior year, Aldridge drove up into the hills and stopped in front of a home with an open house sign out front. Inside we pretended we were engaged and looking for our million-dollar starter home.

I don't know who we were fooling because we stood out like sore thumbs among the real million-dollar bank accounts. In the backyard of this well-appointed home, Aldridge vowed to buy me a house just as big as this one when he made it to the NBA. This wasn't an empty promise. Aldridge had a gift, and he was on the shortlist to be drafted in the first round. Some people were even saying first pick.

It was at that moment in the type of yard I'd only seen online, I knew I needed to get off the Aldridge Mosley ride. I didn't want to be a basketball girlfriend and eventually a spouse. The thought of spending the entirety of my life chasing his dream while deferring mine turned my stomach. Looking back on it now, it felt a little silly. I was a realtor, a profitable one, but still a realtor all the same. Was this the life-changing future I'd envisioned for myself?

I'd graduated with a degree in business with the hopes of going to law school. I ultimately wanted to work for the Innocence Project which worked to get individuals who were wrongfully convicted out of jail, but life had other plans. A bell ringing brought me back to the present. Before answering the door, I fussed with my hair and swept any possible eye boogers from the corners of my eyes.

Swinging the door open, my composure was shaken. Damn did this man not have an off day? He was outfitted in a white T-shirt, black shorts, and a baseball cap and he looked effortlessly pulled together.

"Is my car going to be safe out there?" Aldridge joked.

"I know what you're thinking, but this is an up-and-coming neighborhood."

"Meaning?"

"Meaning, in a few years this place will be a hot commodity and you'll be able to get three times what you paid for it."

"Gentrification at work." He entered the space and when he walked past me, I was greeted by the scent of him and it stirred my soul, causing a bit of longing to rise to the top.

"Is your assistant joining us?"

"No, she's dealing with a moving truck crisis we thought was fixed but apparently the universe got jokes."

"Who's your moving company?"

"Uhm … I don't know, something about a truck, a guy and his dog."

"Rover's Rover?"

Aldridge snapped his fingers. "Yep, that's it."

"I know the owner, I'll put in a call."

"Really?"

"Consider it done."

"I'll let Nori know." Aldridge took note of the high ceilings.

Did he just wake up fine and ready to ruin some innocent woman's life? His deep flawless skin had to be the work of a dermatologist because there was no way this man had a better skincare routine than me. And then there were his long lashes which I'd always been jealous of. Men did not need full long lashes. What he had naturally; I was paying Natalia two hundred and fifty dollars a month to maintain.

"So what am I looking at? Because it looks like a Vegas lounge act."

"It's ultra sleek and modern. It's also industrial. The architect was Bovine."

"Is that name supposed to mean something to me?"

"If you had any culture it would."

"Ouch."

"He's a renowned local architect. His properties rarely come on the market."

"What I'm hearing is a bidding war."

"Not with me as your realtor."

"Cocky."

"I'm just saying."

"No, I appreciate it. Talk your shit." He walked over to the kitchen. "Where are the appliances?"

"They're hidden."

"I do not want to play hide and seek in order to put away my groceries."

"The fridge is right behind you."

Aldridge reached for the handle opening the refrigerator door. "It's big."

"Sub zero. It's considered an entertainer's kitchen."

"Okay," he scoffed.

"You're new to town you might make new friends. Or maybe your girlfriend likes to entertain."

His head swiveled in my direction. "My who?"

"Your girlfriend, Amber … Alison … Alica?" I pretended like I hadn't spent hours Googling him.

"Ashley."

"Yeah I think that's it."

Aldridge flashed me a look that told me he wasn't walking into my hastily crafted trap before entering the living room. "I hate the way this place is decorated." *Please note my question regarding a significant other was deflected.*

"You're not buying the furniture."

"What is it about rich people and taste? It's like the richer you get the shittier your sense of style becomes. Gold toilets, imitation Roman sculptures, and those ugly colosseum columns. It's a home, not Caesar's Palace for God's sake."

"You said you wanted something with character."

"Yes, elegant, refined, not cartoonish."

"The toilets can be changed and the column is not part of Bovine's original design."

"It feels like we stepped into a time machine. Is that

why his properties are so popular because once you cross the threshold you are back in the seventies?"

"It's not that bad."

"The living room is sunken."

"Okay tell me what you do like about the place?"

Aldridge looked around trying to come up with something nice to say. "I like that the sliding glass door slides all the way out of view. It makes the area feel open and extends the living space."

"And the cons?"

"I bet if we did our research we could locate a porn movie from back in the day with this house featured in it. A housewife gets a knock at the door and it's the horny repairman with tight pants and a handlebar mustache."

"Wildly specific." I laughed.

"And he'd say, 'What seems to be the problem?'"

Aldridge looked to me like he was waiting for me to deliver the next line. I decided to play along. "My washer is on the fritz."

"I have the tool that can fix that."

"I bet you have a lot of useful tools." My cheeks heated up at this silly game.

Aldridge took several steps in my direction, causing the heat to morph into a steady burn. "Sweet cheeks, you have no idea." His eyes were smoldering. *Was he still playing around?* "And then the cheesy music would start up and the washing machine wouldn't be the only thing getting a tune up." Aldridge's face was normal and he appeared completely unbothered.

I, on the other hand was able to identify a distinct throb in my pleasure center. "Why was the music so corny?" I turned on my heels and walked out of his eyesight.

"Should we head upstairs?"

"Yeah, you go ahead and I'll be right up." Aldridge brushed past me and took the steps two at a time. *Would you stop being ridiculous,* I ordered myself. It was just Aldridge. There was no need to get spun like a top. *He has a girlfriend which means the last thing he's checking for is you.* My heart seized up with the realization I was selling him a house he was going to fuck another bitch in. Not that it mattered because I was completely over him. I hadn't thought about Aldridge in years, and when I happened to see him on TV or online, I was just glad he was doing well. He deserved to be happy. Just because we didn't work out didn't mean his life needed to go to shit. I mean it would've been better in this moment if he'd gotten traded to Bulgaria rather than Vegas. Was that possible, international trades?

Clearly this house was a bust. I needed to find him his forever home and close this deal and then I'd never have to see Aldridge again unless it was at a basketball game. On second thought, I could just forgo basketball for the next three to five years or at least until he was traded to another team.

I made my way to the stairs but Aldridge was already heading down. "Save yourself the trip. The second floor is worse than the first."

"That's because you're seeing how it is and not how it could be."

"It has a smell."

He wasn't lying. I'd hoped the air fresheners I'd plugged in earlier would mask the distinct smell but no such luck. "It's been loved."

"How much is this monstrosity going for?"

I swallowed hard preparing myself for Aldridge's dramatic reaction. "Four point five."

"Million?" He tilted his head and shouted.

"Yes."

"Is it crack? It has to be crack."

"It's a seller's market."

"For four point five I want all the amenities, an AI butler, and a happy goddamn ending every fucking night."

"Are you done?"

"No. For four point five million I want Elvis himself to jump up out of the grave and sing 'Love Me Tender' between bites of a peanut butter, banana, and bacon sandwich."

"So what you're saying is you'd like to pass on this property?"

"I want to erase the existence from my memory."

I chuckled.

"Why did you show me this place?"

"To help you with your expectations. And to see if you could make out a diamond in the rough."

"You're saying this place is Aladdin?"

"Every home has potential. It just takes the right buyer to see it."

"This home would take a considerable amount of money, a sanitation crew, and possibly a séance to make it livable."

Fucking drama queen. I'd forgotten how over the top he was. "Okay, let's check out the neighborhood."

ALDRIDGE PUSHED THE PASSENGER SEAT OF MY BMW ALL THE way back and it was still a tight squeeze. Touring the neighborhood was just as important as touring the house. You could hate a home but love the surrounding area. If you were on the fence about a property, the vibe of the neighborhood could tip the scale. I found neighborhood tours especially helped clients who were new to Vegas. How do you decide where to live if you don't know anything about the area?

With Aldridge in tow, we headed to the heart of the neighborhood just minutes from the Bovine house. I parked in a nearby lot next to the local coffee shop Brewed Awakenings. Exiting the car, I pointed in the direction of travel. "Before you commit to any house, you always have to try the local coffee shop. If you hate the coffee, you'll end up hating the home."

"Are you dropping realtor secrets?"

"I think it's common sense."

"You may be right. I didn't test out my local coffee shop in Kansas City. And the day after moving in I tried it and the coffee was bitter and the staff was rude. Needless to say, I never went back and would often have to drive to a different café several miles away."

"And that's an inconvenience. Most people are looking for walkable neighborhoods. If you have to hop in your car for a coffee and bagel, it sort of defeats the purpose."

Aldridge held the door open for me. When we walked inside, we were immediately slapped in the face by that distinctive coffee bean smell. The vibe of the shop was eclectic with a mixture of booths and tables. There was even counter seating like you would find in a diner.

"So what's good here?"

I'd only been to Brewed Awakenings once before, but I knew Aldridge enough to provide a drink recommendation he would most likely enjoy. "I think you should try the cortado."

"Never heard of it."

"Do you still love lattes and flat whites?"

"Yes."

"Then trust me, a cortado is right up your alley."

Aldridge offered a slow nod while still examining the menu. At the register he took my suggestion going with the cortado and I ordered a forest matcha. We found a corner booth and waited for our names to be called.

"So where are you staying right now?" I fidgeted with my napkins and extra sugar packets.

"I'm at the W hotel on the Strip."

"Wow, that hotel is very interesting." Whoever was responsible for the design of the hotel really leaned into the fact that it was a Vegas property. There was nothing subtle or understated in the design choices. I'm talking gold antler chandeliers, God awful wallpaper which featured a Victorian lady whose eyes followed you around the room.

"You're not lying. When I checked in it was very clear I was no longer in Kansas City."

"Aldridge," the barista called out.

He jumped up to retrieve our drinks. When he returned, he placed mine in front of me.

"Thank you."

"No problem." He reclaimed his seat. "I will say that being on the Strip these past few weeks has erased any thoughts about buying a place on Las Vegas Boulevard."

"For most people it seems like fun but more often than not it loses its appeal really quickly."

"Why do you think that is?"

"It's like being in the middle of one big party every single night. It tends to get old."

Aldridge took a sip of his coffee and smiled. "Where do you stay at?"

My breath hitched. Up until this point I was doing my best impression of someone who was unbothered. Trying to act as if sitting across from Aldridge and casually chopping it up was completely normal. We hadn't spoken in over five years. Nothing about this was normal. Him being in Las Vegas. Me having to pretend his scent of sandalwood, lavender, and basil wasn't triggering my desire. The fact I had to hold myself back because all I really wanted was one of Aldridge's strong full hugs that told me I was safe and everything was going to be okay.

Having coffee with my former college sweetheart, now world-famous basketball player, was not something I thought I'd ever have to endure. But when my mother said life had a funny way of humbling you, she wasn't lying. I thought I was fine. After all these years Aldridge rarely ever crossed my mind. I'd had plenty of exes since him. But Aldridge was the type of man who left a mark. He was the litmus test for all other men I dated. Settling for the bare minimum wasn't a viable option. I knew what real love felt like and if a man couldn't love me the same or better than Aldridge, I wasn't interested.

Aldridge snapped his fingers in front of my face. "Earth to Danessa?"

"Oh I'm sorry."

"Where'd you go?"

"What do you mean?"

"You did that thing you do when you're here but not."

"I'm here." I offered a strained smile.

"I know I'm not the most interesting conversationalist, but try to stay with me." He winked. "So what area do you live in?"

"Uhm … I live in a condo off the Strip. Man-made lake, all the amenities."

"That makes sense because you loved being catered to."

"Look, I make no apologies for demanding what I want. I know my worth."

"I'm not disagreeing with you. You deserve nothing but the best. I know when we were together I tried to provide you with that."

"You would always let me size up on my quarter pounder meal," I teased.

"Shit I was poor, so a large meal was the equivalent to the Hope Diamond for me. I mean sometimes I'd even let you add on some chicken nuggets. Do you remember that?" He flashed his bright smile.

"And you demanded they provide extra sweet and sour sauce."

"Only the best for my baby." Aldridge cleared his throat. "I mean—"

"No I get it … past tense. No need to explain." I took a long sip from my cup. "So how is your family doing?"

"Still in Philly. Not much has changed. Duane was released from jail. He's working as a cook at some diner."

Duane was Aldridge's older brother and one of the reasons he went as hard as he did. Duane getting locked up kinda scared Aldridge straight. Before Duane was arrested Aldridge was on a very different path.

"I'm so happy to hear that he's doing well."

"Yeah, he's keeping his nose clean and it seems like he's really trying to turn the page on the past. I think it helps that my folks don't live in the same area anymore."

"When did they move?"

"I bought them a home the year I was drafted. It's not a mansion or anything like that, but it has four bedrooms, three and a half baths. But most importantly the neighbor-hood is safe and in a good school district."

"That's amazing. You always talked about relocating your mother."

"You should have seen my mother's face when we pulled up to the house. That made it all worth it."

Providing for his family had always been a priority for Aldridge. His mother often worked two jobs, and his dad's employment was spotty at best. But with five mouths to feed, money didn't stretch quite as far. And as one of the oldest, the responsibility of supplementing his parents's income fell on Duane and Aldridge. Duane took to the streets and Aldridge focused on basketball. Both were essentially long shots. Most drug dealers end up going to jail or worse, and most basketball players never make it to the NBA.

"I can hear your mother's reaction. 'Aldridge, what have you done?'" I imitated his mom's distinctive Philly accent.

"Pretty much just like that."

"She must be so proud."

He hopped his shoulders. "I'm trying."

I could sense there was shit he was holding back, and I let him have it. It wasn't my place to pry. "So how do you rate the coffee?"

He examined his cup. "Mmm, seven out of ten."

"My spot back home is hard to beat." Hearing him call Kansas City home was jarring because it reinforced there was a whole life I knew nothing about. That I knew him, past tense.

"I'm sure I can find a place that will make you eat those words."

"Coffee isn't my thing. I used to drink whatever, but

then Ashley put me on to this one spot and I fell in love. Like I finally get why people are so serious about their cup of Joe."

After he mentioned Ashley, I tuned everything out. The way he casually dropped her name in the conversation. Like she was family or a longtime friend. I didn't give a fuck about Ashley, and if he said her name one more time I would ... okay I wasn't going to do shit, but I was fucking pissed.

"It just takes one good cup to turn you out." Or one mediocre social media influencer.

"Yeah, I'm addicted." Aldridge chuckled at some inside joke I wasn't privy to.

"Okay, we'll move on to the next house and a new location."

"No more porn houses."

"No, I've made a note. Client would like to avoid homes that could be featured in extracurricular videos."

ALDRIDGE

I was drafted right out of college to the Kansas City Pioneers. During my four years in Missouri, I was able to establish roots. Make friends and become a local at some of my favorite restaurants. Missouri wasn't my first pick. I'd hoped to get drafted to a city like New York, Los Angeles, or Chicago. Looking back now, Kansas City probably saved me. I was twenty-one coming off a breakup and I was ready to be on demon time.

There is trouble to be had in Missouri if you go looking for it and I did a deep dive into the seeder aspects of the city. The first two years I was a reckless asshole looking to fill a void. If there was a party, I was usually in the thick of it surrounded by beautiful women. I was getting more pussy than I could manage and experimenting with drugs I had no business trying. Looking back on it now, I don't know how I was able to maintain the late nights and early practice times. I was moving at a breakneck speed, but I always knew I couldn't fuck up my golden ticket.

So I showed up to every practice on time, sometimes with sunglasses and a raging hangover, but I was there, and I ran those drills until I was ready to puke. There's a reason we are warned that everything should be tried in moderation because overconsumption gets old and eventually you have to fuck weirder, indulge harder, and ignore your morals.

When I ended up at a party snorting coke, I knew I'd lost the plot. Eventually, I fell all the way back from the party scene and worked on me. I was straight as an arrow, I cut out sex, started saying no to drugs, and learned to enjoy the company of an intimate circle of friends. I'm not saying I'm a choir boy now, but I'm choosy when it comes to who I give my energy to.

I'd been in Vegas for barely two weeks, but I knew I needed to go to an NA meeting. Shit was coming at me fast and I couldn't do this sobriety thing alone. It was seven in the morning, and I was at Clean Slate Collective, a narcotics anonymous group held inside of a storefront church. This was the part I hated the most because the anonymous never really benefited me. People knew who I was. And if they didn't, they could guess from my six-foot-five frame I was a ballplayer. In Missouri everything seemed removed, no paparazzi or celebrity vloggers looking to break the next big story.

"Welcome in," a man in a tan short-sleeved plaid shirt called out. "Find a seat anywhere. There are plenty open." He wasn't kidding, it was just me and him.

"Am I early?"

"No, I'd say you're right on time." His voice was rough, and his face lined. He was probably in his fifties but if he told me he was older, I wouldn't bat an eye.

"Is it usually this well attended?" I joked, taking a seat across from him.

"On Monday people have to work."

"Do you want me to come back?"

"That's up to you. But if you prefer, we could just talk. I could use the company. Name's Pete by the way."

I scanned the empty room with its wood paneling and folding chairs. "I'm Aldrid … Al. People call me Al." No one called me that, except my dad. I hated that name.

"Nice to meet you. What brings you here?"

"I'm new to town. Just moved here for work. I thought it would be good to establish a routine. In Missouri, that's where I came from, they told me finding a group and attending a meeting was critical to my sobriety."

"So, you've attended meetings in the past?"

"Yeah, once a week, sometimes more when needed."

"You know there are other meetings in nicer neighborhoods."

"I'm aware and I've been to some of them in the past."

"And?"

"And I hated them. The people didn't seem real. I couldn't relate to their problems. And I found myself judging them, which is crazy because I'm in no position to think I'm better than the next addict."

"When's the last time you used?

"A year and a half ago."

"When's the last time you wanted to use?"

"What time is it?" I joked. "Are you a pastor or something?"

"No, me I'm a meth addict. Recovering, but if my mother heard you confusing me for a man of God she would be tickled pink."

"I'm sure she'll get a big laugh when you tell her."

"She's dead."

"Oh God, I'm sorry." My face flushed with embarrassment.

"It's been years now. She passed long before I got clean. I was so fucking high I didn't make it to her funeral."

"Again, I'm very sorry."

"It's hard choosing to be clean every day."

"The alternative is worse. I didn't like who I was when I was high."

"Shit, I did. I was funny mostly because I didn't take shit seriously." Pete took a sip from a paper cup.

"How long have you been clean?"

"Nine years. I've been choosing myself for nine years."

"Congratulations, that's great."

"I tried and failed so many times I stopped counting. But my mom's death was a wake-up call. Don't get me wrong, I didn't immediately check myself into rehab. That took months but the seed was planted."

"I went to rehab after an overdose." Leaning forward in my chair I asked, "Is the group good about discretion?"

"I can't speak for everyone who walks through that door. But the groups I host take that shit seriously. We're all just addicts in here."

"Do you think I could get a list of the groups you host?"

"Sure." Pete rose with a groan, his knees popping. After rummaging through a backpack in the corner, he returned arm outstretched with a flyer. "Everything you need to know is on there. Do you have a sponsor?"

"Not in Vegas no."

"I'll pitch in until we can find you a more permanent solution." With that we exchanged phone numbers. I liked my sponsor in Missouri; in truth I was kind of attached to him. The people that hold you up and support you when you're at your lowest leave an impression. Jimmy didn't have to go so hard for me. But he never missed a call. Listened when I wanted to use. And provided a safe space when everything around me felt hostile and unfamiliar.

"Thanks." I didn't budge from my chair.

"Do you need something else?"

"Uhm." I looked to the front of the room with the picture of Jesus staring back at me with a benevolent smile. "Is it okay if I just sit here for a little bit longer?"

"No problem at all." Pete sat back down taking a sip of coffee.

I didn't really have anything I wanted to say. I just wanted to be in this space for as long as possible. And Pete had gained my trust. Being from Philly, I was a good judge of character. I could point out the users, the bullies, and the people it was best to avoid if you want to continue breathing. Pete appeared to be a straight shooter, and he would never piss on my head and tell me it was raining. And if I rang him in the middle of the night telling him I was thinking of calling a dealer he would listen, allowing me to vent before offering alternatives.

For his part, Pete just sat in the chair across from me. He could have left or scrolled his phone, but he just sat staring out the window humming. And that small gesture meant the world to me.

MOVING TO VEGAS AND JOINING THE RAMBLERS FELT LIKE THE first day at a new school. All of my safeguards were gone as I tried to navigate this new city. You had people who were trying to test me, people who wanted something from me, and people who seemed cool but one could never tell if there were ulterior motives. When my teammate, Dante Caldwell, suggested we hangout I reluctantly accepted his offer. I had zero friends in this town and Nori insisted I couldn't sit up in my hotel room like Brandy forever.

Dante was twenty-eight and we had similar interests. That was a lie, all I knew about this man was he was the loudest one in practice, and that was saying a lot with the cast of characters on this team. When he approached me on the second day of training, he seemed cool enough. Dante was always on ten which could be a little annoying, but I considered that a plus. He'd always advance the conversation even if my responses were "uh-huh" or "Wow, that's crazy." It took the pressure off me. I was in Vegas with no home and zero friends. It was time to test the waters in my new city and see what it was hitting for. And if I had to stare at the creepy Victorian woman on my hotel wall for one more night, I might start to crack.

Dante planned our whole evening. First, we hit up a lounge for pregame drinks, I had seltzer water with a wedge of lime. Afterwards, we made it to Enclave, which Dante claimed was the place to be on a Saturday night in Vegas. And from the looks of it he wasn't lying. Enclave was packed with scantily clad women and men in wife beaters. The music was my speed, some Hip-Hop like XYZ Baby and Future, fused with Dru Hill, Aaliyah, and Jodeci. Everyone was in a good mood, which boosted mine. Dante secured a VIP booth, so the bottle girls were making the rounds. When I told our waitress I wanted a Shirley Temple she looked at me like I was lame. Alcohol was never my drug of choice, always opting for stronger substances. Pete would probably be disappointed if he saw my current situation. Surrounded by people who were all intoxicated in some form or fashion.

But when you were in your twenties going out and getting wasted was what you did. Twenty-somethings were not interested in sober game nights or picnics. If you got invited anywhere, there was a pregame at someone's apartment. Most of the time you were already feeling the liquor working through your system and you hadn't even left the house. Then you'd hit up the bar or club and it was shots, then drinks, followed by more shots. And if you were in your twenties with a little bit of money there was no limit to the shit you could get into.

"This is what life is about," Dante said, pouring something into his cup. "Do you know in college I got zero play?"

"Really?"

"Yeah, I wasn't a starter, and I wasn't as swole as I am now. But shit, cut to the present and these bitches are practically fighting each other for my attention. And I always say, ladies why fight when you can share."

I chuckled.

"What about you? I bet you got a ton of bitches in college."

"Nah, I was in a relationship most of college."

"A what?" Dante leaned in.

"I had a girlfriend," I shouted.

"Shit, how do you spell that? *Girlfriend*?" He said the word like it was foreign to him. "Hopefully you don't still have that problem."

"Don't tell me you're anti-relationship?"

"I like options. Relationships limit them."

I nodded thoughtfully. Not going to lie, that was sound logic. I'd found myself single again after being with Ashley for over a year. Ashley was fun. She was an influencer, and she was a girly girl. Her nails were always done, her fit was always right, and when she stood next to me we looked impressive. I liked Ashley, but that like never quite transitioned into love. For all her good qualities she was also self-centered, and her physical beauty was her best asset. She was rude to waitstaff, housekeeping, shit she was crappy to her friends.

I was never going to marry Ashley. It was about a good time but in the last few months it stopped being fun. She started asking real fucking questions, like where were we headed. Could I see myself married in the next five years? The answer to that was yes, just not with her. I actually said that out loud. As you can imagine a fight ensued, she started to cry, and I said we should end shit now before I hurt her any further. That made her cry harder.

The funny thing is until that moment I didn't know she cared so deeply. But maybe the tears were less about me and more about the loss of access my presence provided. Let's not pretend dating a ballplayer didn't come with built-in perks. Courtside at the games, entry into all the hottest parties just off the strength of my name, and the boost to her social media which included men who were fans of me and wanted to live vicariously through Ashley's posts of us together.

"Excuse me?" I was pulled from my thoughts to find a Black woman with wicked curves in front of me.

My head jerked back when my brain made the connection of who she was. "Hold up, Anika?"

"You didn't think you'd be in my city and never run into me did you?"

Dante nudged me. "Who's this?"

Dante and I both stood. "Uhm, Dante, this is Anika Irwin." The two exchanged fuck-me eyes and a bit of bile crept up my throat.

"Nice to meet you." Anika extended her hand and Dante kissed it before literally sucking one of her fingers into his mouth. And to my surprise Anika squealed in delight.

"Could we not." I inserted myself in between them. "Is Danessa with you?"

"No, you know she can't be out past her bedtime." I was unable to hide my disappointment. "But I could call her and convince her to meet us at the … Waffle House maybe."

"I'm down for the Waffle House. I have alcohol that needs to be sopped up," Dante said.

I pulled Anika aside. "Do you think she'd actually come out if you asked?" Anika was like family, and she was always good at sniffing our bullshit, so I wasn't going to try. Yes, I wanted to see Danessa again.

Anika smirked. "I know what to say to convince my sister. You just make sure your fine ass friend is there."

"Dante? Done." I swallowed hard. "Uhm also … maybe you could throw on a jacket because I can see your areolas," I said as delicately as possible.

Anika thrust her chest forward. "Are you slut shaming me Mosley?"

"No, I would never." My eyes were focused on everything but Anika. "I just … you look cold."

Anika laughed. "You haven't changed Aldridge. I see why she still likes you."

My brain stretched from the new information. Locking eyes with Anika, I asked, "Did she say that?"

"Do you want me to call her or not?"

"Yes, please."

There were hundreds of bad bitches at the Enclave, and I was only thinking about one. And truthfully, she was all I could think about since arriving in Vegas. Before our first meeting I'd seriously contemplated texting her with the "I'm in your city," message. When she opened the door to the property in Canyon Gate, part of me thought I willed her there because she was steady on my mind. I'm not saying I wanted my old thing back. But we weren't just lovers, we were also friends and that is what I missed the most. Okay, I also missed the way my dick felt when I was inside of her, but I was trying to keep it classy.

I WAS STUCK IN A BOOTH WITH DANTE AND ANIKA WHO'D quickly shifted from flirting to all out freak nasty talk. Matching freak levels was cool and all, but I was literally sitting next to them while Dante loudly explained the physical mechanics of The Screwnicorn. *Trust me, do not ask.* This is what I get for trying to be friendly. A few days prior, Nori claimed I wasn't making an effort to get to know the other players on the team. I disagreed, stating I was pretty familiar. Deion tolerated me, Colin Pratt despised me, and all the other players were reserving their opinions of me until our first game.

I wasn't antisocial, far from it, but the last thing I was going to do was beg someone to sit with me in the cafeteria. Every day at lunch I was joined by a player from Serbia who only spoke to me in his native tongue although I knew he could speak English. Dante extending an invitation to hang out was my only olive branch, and if this was going to actually work, I had to at least have a few allies. He wouldn't have been my first choice, but he was the only one trying to connect.

But now I was regretting my decision and seriously considering docking Nori's pay. Listen, I was in no way a cockblocker if you liked it, I loved it. But Anika was like a sister to me. And watching her stick her tongue down Dante's throat was a visual I could have done without. I was about to call the night a bust and head out when Danessa entered the Waffle House and changed my whole perspective. *Stick with it for the plot, I told myself.*

Danessa didn't immediately spot us, giving me a chance to linger over her frame. She was dressed casually in sweatpants, a cropped graphic T-shirt, and sneakers. The outfit was basic, but the bracelets, multiple rings, and brown lined and glossed lips really took the fit over the top. It was two in the morning and with little effort, this woman was the finest person in the room. And I know what you're thinking, that's an easy title to claim at a Waffle House but trust me it didn't matter the setting, Danessa would always take the prize.

Anika's sing-song laughter drew Danessa's attention in our direction. Her face telegraphed her surprise to see me. That surprise quickly morphed into anger which I hoped wouldn't be aimed in my direction. Approaching she cleared her throat to pull Anika from out of the crook of Dante's neck.

Anika pushed Dante out of the booth jumping up. "You made it."

"I thought you said you didn't want to eat alone?"

"Oh them? They were here when I got here. Aldridge and I were just catching up."

"I can see that." Danessa's eyes bounced from me to Dante.

"Dante Caldwell, it's a pleasure to meet you. And might I add you are just as fine as your sister." His eyes tripped down the length of Danessa's body stopping at her ass, causing the muscles in my jaw to flex.

"Nice to meet you, Dante. Anika, can I talk to you over there for a minute?"

"Sure."

The two sisters went to the other side of the diner, and I used that time to draw some boundaries. "Hey, just so we're on the same page. Danessa is off-limits. No leering, no crude jokes, and absolutely no suggestion of an after-party orgy."

"Listen, I'm happy with the chick I'm with. I know for a fact I'm getting laid tonight. Can you say the same?" Dante tagged me on the chest.

I wasn't trying to get laid. I just wanted to see Danessa again.

When the ladies returned. Anika didn't bother reclaiming her seat. "Dante, could you walk me to the restroom?"

"Why the hell would I do that?"

"Because I'm a lady and if you're trying to get active tonight it would be in your best interest." Dante didn't need any additional convincing. He tossed his arm around Anika and they were off.

Danessa slid into the booth opposite me. "So did you and my sister plan this?"

"No, why would you say that?"

"Because I get that it's a small world, but it ain't that small." She perused the menu.

"We ran into one another at Enclave, and she suggested we grab some food."

"And how did I get dragged into this exactly?"

I expelled a breath of air. "That I really don't know."

Danessa bit down on her full lips. "You are and have always been a horrible liar."

"I may have mentioned your name."

"Umm. So who's this Dante guy?"

"He's my teammate. And he seems to have taken a liking to your sister."

"Poor bastard." She reached for one of the full glasses of water on the table and thought twice, pulling her hand back.

"He can take care of himself." I placed my untouched glass of water in front of her.

"So I see you've taken my advice."

"Which is?"

"Getting out and experiencing Vegas." She took a long sip.

I scratched my beard. "Something like that. So what do you do for fun?"

"Not the clubs."

"I know you're not acting uppity?"

"Clubs are great for special events. But every weekend is madness."

"I agree with you there. Most people don't know when to hang it up."

"Exactly and that's when you get the Uncs in the club doing the Cabbage Patch or some other ridiculous shit."

"Watch out there now." I tried to imitate one of my uncles.

"Don't hurt yourself." Danessa mimicked in a raspy voice. Fuck matching my freak, I needed a woman who could match my funny. A person who got your sense of humor made even the most mundane day memorable.

"So were you just up jonesing for waffles, or what?" I wanted to know if she was already out when she got the call.

"I'm used to Anika calling me in the middle of the night. I'm like her unofficial designated driver."

"You could always hit her with the do not disturb."

"Have you met me? I'm a pushover for that woman.

She's my big sister and I still idolize her even though I recognize she is deeply flawed."

"Sounds like me and my dad." I didn't idolize him, that ship had long passed. But I did still seek his validation even if I wished he was dead every other business day.

"Have things not gotten better?"

"He sees me as a threat to his manhood. So no."

"Well, it's the father's job to provide but your dad seemed content to defer to Duane and you for financial support."

"He tried."

"Did he?"

"I am too hungry and sleep-deprived to have this conversation. Let's just call it a tie, we're both simps for our family."

Anika and Dante returned, and they looked disheveled like they got to groping one another in the restroom. When I pictured hanging with Danessa in the Waffle House, I didn't include Dante and Anika who both just said the first things that popped into their brains. There was no assessing the table and deciding maybe you should save the story about the time you got an anal plug stuck in your ass and had to be taken to the hospital. Mind you, that was Dante sharing this story. I was all for sexual liberation and God knows I'd tried all manner of sex toys, but gotdamn that was an image I could do without.

By the time the food arrived I was starving. I got the lumberjack special with pancakes, bacon, sausage, ham, home potatoes and scrambled eggs with an added slice of cheddar cheese on top.

"So when are we going to get tickets to a game?"

"Baby the season hasn't even started yet," Dante said in between forkfuls.

"I believe in staying on ready."

"I guess your seats will depend on you."

"Really what do you want me to do for them?" I was convinced Danessa and I were invisible because Dante and Anika were acting as if we weren't there.

"I could think of a few things. Do you want me to name them?"

"Do tell, daddy."

"You two are ruining my appetite. Some things don't need to be shared," Danessa said.

"Sounds like you need to work through some of that pent-up energy. I could talk you through it."

One minute you're enjoying your cheese eggs, and the next white hot rage had you shoving Dante out of the booth, knocking him to the floor. Towering over him, I screamed, "Do you think I was joking when I said don't fucking overstep?"

Dante's hands were up indicating surrender. "Aldi, chill out I was just playing."

"Save your jokes for your motherfucking momma."

"Now why does his mother gotta be a motherfucker?" Anika said.

Dante stood up, fists clenched, his eyes narrowing at the corners. If we got to bustin' in the Waffle House, it wouldn't be the first time this place saw that kind of action. And if I'm being honest, I had a ton of pent-up energy I could easily unload on his face, one punch at a time. Normally, I didn't care about shit. You could say whatever and it would just roll off my back. But I did not play about Danessa, not now or ever. You would find your ass airlifted to the hospital over her.

"Bruh, you're tripping. Order a drink or something to mellow the fuck out."

"I already told you I do not play like that, so stop pushing me." I was yelling and everyone in the restaurant was staring at us, cameras were out, TMZ had probably already been contacted, but I didn't care. If Dante couldn't catch a clue, we'd for sure end up on the local news.

"Aldridge, I'm not offended. It's cool. Let's just enjoy our waffles." This was Danessa always the voice of reason. I was already on ten, so it would take very little for me to dial it up to fifteen and squabble up.

"I'm not really understanding what the problem is?"

"What it is is disrespectful." I spat the words out. "And that's all you need to know."

Anika chimed in, "Dante he's not gonna do nothing. Danessa's his ex and he feels a way about—"

I turned to Anika, she could catch my wrath too. "Feels what way? I don't feel shit." Turning back to Dante, I continued, "This is about the fucking principle of the thing. My friend ... and I use that term real loosely ... should not be trying to push up on my ex-girlfriend. Negro, this is simple bro code."

"I didn't know she was your ex, damn. Now that I do, I'll move differently." Dante wasn't a punk and if it came to it, I knew he'd get a few licks in. An altercation was not worth the headaches that would follow, both online and from the Ramblers organization. I could hear Coach Justus now. "Boy you ain't been in town for two solid weeks and you're already showing your ass."

"That's all the fuck I'm asking." Did I just have a temper tantrum in this late-night diner? Yes, yes I did.

"And this is exactly why I don't do the Waffle House at three in the morning." Danessa chugged her Diet Coke.

60

IN THE PARKING LOT, THERE WAS A BIT OF CONFUSION ABOUT who was going where. Dante was my ride but he was too preoccupied with Anika. "You still driving me home?"

"Umm, my girl is hot and ready and I'm not trying to let that simmer."

"Wait Anika, I thought *I* was driving you home," Danessa said.

"No, I didn't need a ride home, I needed someone to split the blueberry pancakes with."

Danessa released an agitated breath. "Anika, I was at home, in bed before you called."

"I know, isn't this so much better?" Anika flashed a glance at me before grabbing her sister's face and planting a kiss to her cheek. "I love you both. And welcome to Vegas Aldi." She claimed Dante's hand and the two didn't look back.

Fake fucking friend.

"I'm going to have to drive you home aren't I?" Danessa asked, irritation laced in her voice.

"I mean I could order a RideX, but what if my driver is a stalker fan who ends up locking me in a warehouse and cobbling my feet so I can't get away? How would you live with yourself?"

"Ugh, get in but absolutely no comments about my driving."

"You won't hear a peep out of me, Speed Demon."

I climbed into her passenger seat, relishing the role of passenger princess. The seat was positioned all the way back from the last time I rode in it. Which was a good sign, if you know you know. Danessa exited the parking lot and turned onto the street. At the light she said, "Dante's a character."

"This was my first time hanging out with him outside of work and will probably be my last."

"Well, it's not all bad. Seems like Anika and Dante made a love connection."

"That ain't love. That's pure unadulterated naked lust." I opened her glove compartment, not looking for anything in particular. I was just nosy.

"I mean that could be fun too."

Flashing her a quick glance, I said, "I'm sorry we pulled you out of bed for an X-rated peep show and fist to cuffs."

"You really were going to beat Dante's ass?"

"Absofuckinglutely.

"Anika didn't surprise me. When she's near a rich eligible man, I don't exist. But you, caught me off guard. You might want to slow down on the vodka cranberries."

"I did that shit sober."

"Principle, it that what you claimed?"

"Yep, without order there is chaos. So when someone is talking grimy to your ex. You might need to realign shit with a tap to the jaw."

"You know if push came to shove, Anika and I would've had your back."

"She's selfish that's for sure, but at the end of the day if anyone fucked with you she'd rip their throat out with her teeth."

"She would." Danessa chuckled.

"Anika is that for you and Duane is that for me."

She nodded. "Duane was always so proud of you. I imagine that hasn't changed."

"Yeah, when he'd call from prison the one thing he'd always say before hanging up was, "Don't end up like me Aldi. You're better than me.""

"He was right."

"Nah, I was never better, I just had some lucky breaks." Having a big brother was like having a blueprint of what to and not do. Duane made all the fucked up choices before I could with varying success. Duane stood up to his bully, so when I was in second grade, I did the same. People knew not to fuck with the Mosley brothers. Duane got a job selling drugs. I opted for food delivery. Duane got his sixteen-year-old girlfriend pregnant. So, I wore a condom every time in high school.

"You shouldn't feel guilty about that."

"I know. Rationally I know, but I still do."

Danessa reached for my hand and gave it a quick squeeze. The contact was brief but enough to get my heart to accelerate. It's weird how something once second nature, a hug, a hand squeeze now felt foreign to us both. "I'm excited to report I think I've found some pretty good homes for our next outing."

"You're batting O for two right now. So, you'll have to really bring it."

"I plan to."

"Don't get me wrong, hotel living has its perks like twenty-four-hour room service."

"I'd imagine. Once a month I wake up in the middle of the night craving pork dumplings. It would be so nice to just press a button and have it delivered to my door."

"The pros of being in transit."

"Is Ashley going to make the move to Vegas?"

"Why do you keep bringing up that woman's name?"

"She's your girlfriend. It's a fair question. It may impact the types of houses I show you."

"Ashley and I have been broken up for months now."

"Oh, my bad. I didn't know. I mean that's not what people are saying online."

My brows hiked up my forehead. "Online? Have you been Googling me?"

"No, I mean yes. But only because I was trying to check out your home in Kansas City. For research."

She was full of shit.

"So your research led you to my past girlfriends?" The side of my mouth ticked upward.

"No, not all of them. I mean I didn't come up. Look my bad, I didn't know Ashley was a sore subject."

I hated it when people put twenty on ten. At no time did I hint at being upset about my split from Ashley because I wasn't, and any suggestion to the contrary only pissed me off. "Who the fuck said that?"

"You're getting defensive."

"Yeah, because I don't like people making assumptions. Sometimes relationships end and it turns out to be *the best thing* for all parties involved."

Her eyes quickly landed on me with irritation. "What the fuck is that supposed to mean?"

"I don't know Danessa. You broke up with me and claimed it was for the best. Do you remember that?"

"I'm not doing this with you." She turned her attention back to the road ahead.

"Doing what?"

"Relitigating the past."

"I didn't bring up the past you did. With Ashley this and Ashley that."

"I was just trying to make conversation."

"Well don't."

Danessa's features turned sour as she turned up the music to drown out the awkward silence. Leaning back, I focused on the billboards zooming by me. If I was ever in need of a lawyer, Vegas has me covered. My favorite sign was for Big Greg Esquire "Call me before your ex does." A lawyer who went by the name Big Greg would never see a dime of my money.

Glancing at Danessa, whose mouth was in a tight wad, I turned back to the window. I was on one tonight. But you can't have shit both ways. We'd been over for a long time so she didn't get to ask me questions about who I was dating, fucking, or entertaining. And why did she care? One of the last things she said to me was, "This has been fun, but you can't seriously think it's a forever thing." Maybe I was dimwitted because I didn't see any of the signs that our relationship had run its course. Loving Danessa was my endgame. It was the ace in my back pocket. No matter how hectic our lives would get with her in law school and me playing in the NBA, we would always have each other to keep us grounded.

A T-Pain song came on and I couldn't help but tap my fingers against the center console. When he started singing about the bartender, Danessa joined him and in spite of myself, I couldn't help but sing too. Do you know how hard you have to be to stay mad when a T-Pain song comes on? It's impossible.

Danessa's body grooved from side to side. "You're an idiot," she casually said in between shoulder shakes.

"Yep," I agreed as we belted out the chorus at the top of our lungs.

After exiting the freeway, Danessa took a back street I didn't even know existed to avoid the traffic on the Strip. Pulling into the hotel valet and drop-off area, she placed her car in park.

"Thanks for the ride."

"My pleasure. I love pretending to be a taxi driver on a busy weekend."

"Well if you want I can give you some gas money like we did back in college."

"Back then you didn't have a car."

"And gas money was my way of paying it forward."

"It's on the house. I might not have signed a multi-year contract for millions of dollars, but I'm doing alright for myself."

Exiting the car, I squatted down so I could see her through the passenger window. "Text me when you get home so I know you made it there in one piece."

"You're acting like my mother."

"You and I both know that's a lie." When it came to maternal instincts, Danessa's mother was hit or miss.

"True, my mom is more likely to call me and say don't wait up."

"From one latchkey kid to another, text me to confirm you got home." I placed my hand over my heart. "As a courtesy, please."

"Okay."

"Goodnight, Miss Danessa."

"Goodnight, Aldridge."

DANESSA

Anika took the walk of shame the next morning and ended up at my place. "How was your night?" I asked.

"That Dante has a dick on him." Anika's hair was piled on top of her head. "He knocked the Sonic coins out of this pussy. What about you? Did you and Aldridge get along okay?" Her face lit up. "Were we both on our knees slobbing knobs last night? Twinsies."

"No. I did not slob Aldridge's knob."

"You're no fun." She opened my fridge looking for God knows what.

"He's my ex."

Anika hopped her shoulders. "I fuck my exes all the time. It's not unheard of."

"I know, but it's never a good idea to spin the block."

"Shit, the way Aldridge was looking at you last night he clearly wanted you to hop on top and go for a ride." She rolled her hips.

I had to agree he did give me his full attention. At least he did when Dante and Anika weren't making everything uncomfortable. And then he almost came to blows with Dante over me. I'd never known Aldridge to play about me, and it would appear some habits hadn't died. If a man looked at me sideways, he was always ready to defend my honor. When a guy in my Health and Diversity class tried to get too familiar one time, Aldridge showed up to the next class and set him straight. Despite all of this, I didn't want to acknowledge Anika's statement. "I'm still mad at you by the way."

"For getting you out the house?"

"For conspiring with Aldridge."

"He asked for you and I just made things happen." After examining the fridge and pantry, she closed each one, coming up empty-handed. "Why yes, Danessa I would love a cup of coffee."

"You are capable of making it yourself."

Anika plopped onto my couch. "I've had a rough night and you're nice and rested."

I added a fresh pod to the coffee maker and set a mug underneath. "Do you want the cinnamon coffee cake creamer or the caramel macchiato?"

"Caramel, please."

Pulling the creamer from the fridge, I added a generous serving to her mug.

"So, I'm just going to state the obvious here. Aldridge is looking real sexy. The baby face is gone and his lineup is on point. Shit even his arms were glowing and well moisturized."

"Do you have a point?" I swatted at her feet so she'd sit up before handing her the mug and taking a seat next to her.

"My point is that man is like fine wine."

"I honestly hadn't noticed. When I see him, I still see the same old Aldi."

"Liar, liar, pants on fire. He even walks differently, probably to compensate for all that dick."

"Excuse me?" I'd never really discussed Aldridge's penis or his proficiency in the bedroom.

"I've conducted thorough testing on all manner of men. And the ones with big dicks just have a certain walk. Aldridge has it, Dante has it. That dude from that New York cop show has it."

"Stabler?"

"Yes, Stabler. I'd fuck Stabler."

My face lit up. "You know who'd I'd fuck?"

"I'm all ears." Anika crossed her legs, getting cozy.

"Now just hear me out. The lead singer from the rock group Void with all the tattoos."

"The one with the topknot?" She cringed.

"I know, I know but take away the topknot and he could fuck me on the kitchen counter."

"Sometimes I find it hard to believe we're sisters."

"Shut up." I gave her a playful shrug.

"So when are you going to fuck Aldridge?"

If anyone else asked me that at nine o'clock on a Sunday morning, I would be surprised but my sister rarely shocked me any longer. "Been there, done that, had the pregnancy scare."

"Don't act like you don't want to do it again. You were gone off of that man."

"That's only because he was my first. But I've added some miles to the pussy since then."

"When it comes to sexual experiences it's Mary, mother of our Lord and Savior, that nun I met once, and then you."

Don't listen to Anika. She had me sounding like a born-again virgin. I'd dated many men and was involved in all types of carrying on. But in the last year or so I felt burnt out. Tired of meeting a guy who pretended he liked all the things I did only to have them turn out to be flakes once they hit a few times. Men saw me as a conquest. I didn't kiss on the first date, and I required several interactions before we became physical. Most men were in it for the thrill of the chase, not because they saw me as unique or appreciated the value I could add to their lives.

"I'm sorry if I'm more reserved than you."

"Reserved, bitch you could've been a basketball wife, and if the marriage didn't work you would've had numbers of rich players and celebrities from one end of the country to the other."

"You sound like Mom."

"Sometimes Mom is actually right."

"Mom thinks we should marry for money and not love."

"Tons of bitches marry for love and end up broken-hearted with a negative balance in their bank account."

"Look, I completely understand wanting someone who is able to provide. No one wants to struggle. But if I had to choose love and struggle or money and unhappiness, I'm going for love."

"You know for a college graduate you are hella dumb."

"You can always give me my coffee back and dip."

"I'm just saying you had love and Aldridge's upcoming payday, and you walked away."

"Because I didn't want to be a basketball wife. I've heard stories about wild parties and infidelity. And fame changes people. I didn't want to watch Aldi, my Aldi became unrecognizable."

"He seemed real regular degular to me last night."

Anika was right, not much had changed. Maybe he was a bit more confident and yes he was finer, but he didn't seem jaded by fame or out of touch with the real world.

When I was near him, he felt like the man I fell in love with. If he hadn't gotten traded to Vegas we would never have crossed paths, and I could live in the delusion he was a womanizing asshole. Being around him was like returning to a childhood home where so much was familiar, the creak of the stairs, the tile in the kitchen, the sound of the wind against the vinyl siding. So much remained the same, but there were hints of change you didn't quite recognize.

"I'm just not built like you and Mom. I'm sorry I don't want to be the Thelma to your Louise when it comes to sexcapades."

"I swear favor is wasted on the good girls. You do know you can't take your low body count to heaven with you, right?"

"I don't care about stuff like that. I have to know a guy before we have sex and most men end up eliminating themselves, because the more I get to know about them the less I like them. You do realize the bar is in hell when it comes to dating."

"Yes, I'm out here too, but that's why you have to move like the guys do."

"I don't have the energy to play games. I just want to meet a man who's funny, loves his mother, and fucks me within an inch of my life."

Anika's tone became serious. "I want that too, but until the right man comes along, I'm going to keep scamming and ghosting these fuckboys."

We both shared a laugh. "Is Dante a fuckboy?"

"He's King Fuckboy. An arrogant know-it-all who thinks he is God's gift to women. I'm going to have so much fun breaking him."

"He's Aldridge's friend, so maybe go easy on him."

Anika shook her head. "No mercy, every rich jerkoff can get it."

"HOW MANY BEDROOMS?" ALDRIDGE ASKED AS WE TOURED the primary bedroom. This house was in Sunrise Manor; an area considered the best kept secret in East Las Vegas. I chose this neighborhood because it was very different from the previous one. It had a homey family feel and some impressive pieces of real estate. The curb appeal was there. This was the type of neighborhood where people actually waved hi when you passed by. Kids riding their bicycles outside while neighbors gossiped.

"Seven."

"Seven bedrooms all to myself."

"You live in Vegas now, I'm sure you'll have tons of family looking to visit."

"They can stay in a hotel. I'm not going to be their personal tour guide. I got shit to do."

In the bathroom he took note of the floor. "I like the marble."

"They're heated."

"No shit."

"Take off your shoes."

"No, you take off *your* shoes."

Kicking off my heels, I hit the switch that controlled the floor. "Now you."

Aldridge released a loud sigh but he complied, removing his slides and socks. "So, when does the magic happen exactly?"

"Give it a chance to heat up." We stood in the middle of the massive bathroom, our toes wiggling on the tile that was quickly transitioning from cold to warm. Even his size sixteen feet were attractive. He must get biweekly pedicures.

"I think it's kicking in." He stepped from side to side.

"And just look at the view from the bathtub." I bit down on my lip. This home was surrounded by mature trees and offered tons of privacy.

Aldridge walked over to where I was standing, hovering inches behind me. If I just scooched back a smidge, my ass would probably brush up against it. And by it I meant his dick, something I'd been thinking about a lot lately. The weight, the girth, the warmth it emitted when resting in the palm of my hand.

"It's nice," he said.

I turned to face him. "The view or the floors."

"The view, the floors, the company." He leaned in bridging the height gap between us. "I like this place."

"Shut the fuck up." I beamed.

"I didn't say I was ready to put in an offer. But I like the vibes."

"The vibes are immaculate."

"Danessa?" When he spoke my name, it felt weighted like my moniker was a sacred vow.

"Yes."

"I think I'm going to need heated floors. It's a nonnegotiable."

"I'll add it to your file." He stepped back suddenly, and a tingling swept up my back and across my face, my stomach dropping at the sense I was exposed. I didn't know what to do with my hands, and I was now fully aware I was sans shoes in some stranger's bathroom.

"Can you believe this? If you told me when I was sixteen my basketball dream would have me standing on heated marble floors in a bathroom as big as my childhood home, I would never have believed it."

"You really came up with a plan and executed it. You deserve all the good things."

"We, we deserve all the good things."

"I'm still trying to figure my shit out." I stepped back into my shoes.

"You own a condo, a business you started, and don't act like the bottoms of your shoes aren't red. You're doing great."

"I'm doing okay."

"Don't play with me. I will not accept any Danessa Irwin slander. You deserve the world and it's clear you're claiming it for yourself."

One thing about Aldridge, he'd always been my biggest supporter. If I told him I wanted to pull the moon from the sky, he wouldn't tell me it was impossible, he'd ask if I wanted company. Growing up I didn't have that kind of support. My mother's love always came with conditions. I was a straight A student, class president, on the debate club, prom queen and my mother didn't care. Correction when I told her I was crowned prom queen you'd have thought I'd told her I'd won Miss America or something. I don't think I'd ever seen her prouder.

Second correction, I think she was beaming when I brought Aldridge home for the first time. Aldridge didn't notice, but I could distinctly make out dollar signs behind her eyes. For my mom he was our meal ticket. Which is one of the reasons I ended things. Aldridge had enough people to support within his family. He didn't need three more grown adults leeching off him.

"Do you want to see the wine cellar?"

"I don't drink wine, it gives me headaches. While I like the house, I don't love the location."

"You don't know diddly squat about this area."

"It's far as hell."

"Allow me to change your perspective."

"I'm a stubborn man who isn't easily persuaded."

"Grab your shoes and follow me."

ALDRIDGE

Danessa decided she was prepared to play tour guide. Seeing how I was perpetually down on this city, I was game to have my perspective shifted. I know I just got here but the results were already in. Vegas was hot and there was nothing interesting to look at, just desert landscaping and various shades of browns and orange, Turkish coffee, coriander seed, rustic pottery, and the nightlife was a bit too balls to the wall for me.

Vegas was a place that celebrated vices, the freakier the better. And seeing how I was keeping my vices PG-13, I didn't exactly fit in. Don't get me wrong, I loved a good party but most of them always spiraled out of control with too many strangers, random beautiful women, and drugs … tons of fucking drugs.

Once my recreational use switched to a morning bump, my life started to circle the drain. I was fucking up at work, avoiding my mother's calls for fear she'd be able to hear the desperation and need for a hit in my voice. Anger was my new default temperament. I'd forget things, appointments, birthdays. It was easier to push my old friends away while replacing them with new ones who shared my destructive hobbies. I knew better, I lived through this shit with my dad. And yet, I let it happen anyway.

"First stop." Danessa pointed to a fragrance store called The Scent Lounge.

"Really?" My lips pressed together as I fanned my face. *Why the fuck was it so hot?*

"Yes."

Holding the door open, I then followed her inside. The cool breeze helped but not by much. How did people live in warm weather cities like this? I just wanted to be inside a dark room with nothing but my boxers on and an insulated tumbler filled with ice and crisp water.

The clerk welcomed us in with a wave. "Let me know if I can help you with anything."

"Hello, I think you can. We're interested in making our own fragrances."

"What?" I thought we were here to sniff. I wasn't expecting to be put to work.

"Of course, let me get you set up with trays." The clerk walked over to a shelf, returning with two wooden trays topped with an index card and baby pencil. "You'll find all our fragrances along these walls. I always encourage visitors to walk around and get a feel for the scents they like, and then I can help you hone your preference." She handed us the trays. "My name is Clara if you need anything."

When the clerk walked away, I leaned in and whispered. "I don't know how to make cologne."

"Neither do I but Clara's here to help us." Danessa dipped a test strip into the nearest glass bottle.

"When you said you were going to show me the neighborhood, I thought you meant another coffee shop."

"We can do that too." She brought the strip to her nose and frowned. "Smell this?"

"No, it clearly smells disgusting. I saw you turn up your nose."

"But your reaction could be different."

"I'll pass."

"When did you become a party pooper?"

"Party pooper? I'm the life of the party. I walk into the event and people cheer and shout, "Aldridge is here.""

"That's never happened."

I grabbed the strip from her hand and took a whiff. "It smells like a wet dog and not in a good way."

She giggled. "I know right." Danessa lingered over the display, sniffing every bottle, her reaction to each varying greatly. If I closed my right eye and squinted, I'd confuse this for a date.

"So do all your clients get this level of attention?"

"Yeah, pretty much." She said it so matter-of-factly, it made my head jerk back.

"And here I thought I was special." One hundred percent I was fishing for a compliment or some indication that being with me meant something. I wasn't looking for declarations of love because that would be crazy. But a hint she was also finding it difficult to breathe and her palms were humid due to our proximity would be nice.

Danessa moved on to the next bottle.

"Hold up. You're really not going to acknowledge that. The least you could do is affirm my uniqueness."

"I'm your realtor, Aldridge. I'm not treating you differently. I'm just doing my job."

Fuck this perfume shop, fuck this neighborhood, and fuck her. *Aldi, chill don't ruin this vibe. You're right ... but I absolutely have to.* I wasn't a random dude looking to purchase a house. We had history so I *should* be treated differently. She wasn't dealing with just anybody. I used to belong to her. And since I was now uncomfortable, every motherfucker in this shop was fittin' to be too. Danessa, Clara the fragrance guru, and the unsuspecting mother and daughter on the other side of the shop perusing atomizers. "You're telling me you take every fucking client to the fragrance shop?"

"Sometimes it's Pilates, other times a brewery. My goal is to help you envision yourself as part of the community." She was talking to me like a fucking realtor. Her voice was even different. It was polished, less casual, one thousand percent fake.

"So we could have been eating hot wings right now but instead we're here?"

"Don't act like you don't like to smell good. And you hate wearing the same cologne as everybody else."

"I discovered Light Water Intense before any of those other motherfuckers at college, and a few months later everybody and their uncle was wearing it." I bit down on the inside of my cheek. *Shit she was right, a fragrance shop was very on brand for me. Why hadn't I gone to a place like this before?*

"Are you done Christopher Columbus?"

"No, no amount of fragrance shops or hand-pressed coffee is going to make me magically fall in love with this place. It's not Kansas City."

Danessa finally looked at me, sensing from my tone I was actually upset. "You didn't even wanna go to Kansas City. You were pissed when you got drafted."

"Yeah, well things change. I grew to enjoy a slower paced life."

"Stop acting like you were out there baling fucking hay. KC is a major city."

"Well at least in KC they're not handing out pornographic materials on every corner." Yes, I was shouting, Yes, I was making a scene. Yes, I was an asshole.

"That's just on the Strip."

"Do you think that makes it better? This place is literally Sodom and Gomorrah."

Danessa rolled her eyes. "When was the last time you actually entered a church? I'm talking boots on the ground."

"I attend church virtually every Sunday. Thank you very much."

"If you hate Vegas so much then why are you here?"

"For my fucking job, duh."

"Then just rent a condo and be done with it."

"Done with what?"

"Annoying me," she snapped back.

"If you're annoyed imagine how I feel. Having to tour ugly ass houses in weird ass neighborhoods."

Danessa didn't like scenes. She preferred to blend in, not stand out. Her mother was good for causing chaos in unexpected places. By the way she dialed up a fake smile while sneaking glances at the others in the shop, it was clear I was taking shit too far. But the thing about me was when I got this way, I didn't know how to stop. It was scorched earth or nothing. She dropped her voice, hoping to disarm me. "I'm basing my searches on what I know about you."

"What do you know about me? We haven't been in one another's company in years. So, what you used to know or think you know no longer applies."

"I know you'll need several bedrooms for visits from family. I know you love the water and always said when you bought a home it would have a pool and a grotto. I know you don't do anything without music and your place will need good acoustics and thick walls. So, unless you've fundamentally changed, the places I'm showing you are close if not spot on based on what you're looking for."

Damn she had a good memory.

"My priorities have shifted." That was a lie, I still wanted all those things. "And *Vegas* is really disappointing me right now."

"Is it Vegas, the homes, or me you're taking issue with?"

"Maybe it's a combination of the three." I pinned my arms across my chest.

"Wow, one minute I think we're making headway and the next you're basically calling me a stranger and shitting on my hometown."

"I mean technically I'd consider us acquaintances."

A slow disbelieving head shake was her initial response. My stomach knotted and I could barely fill my lungs with air. I'd hurt her. My words did that. I wanted to apologize, tell her I was scared of disappointing my team, myself, and her. In so many ways I wasn't the man she fell in love with, and her presence drove that point home.

"Wow, glad to know exactly how you feel."

"Like you said, you're my realtor. I'm just trying to keep shit professional."

Once again Danessa scanned the virtually empty store in which the three other individuals tried to pretend they weren't invested in the argument as much as Danessa and I were. "This was a bad idea," she whispered.

"The fragrance shop?"

"No this." She waved her hand in the space between us. "Me being your realtor."

Heart palpitations seared my chest. "What do you mean?"

"Clearly this isn't working for you. You hate the houses; you hate my tours of the neighborhood—"

"No I don't. I liked the last house. You're reading way more into this."

"Don't do that. I'm not misconstruing things. I'm picking up what you're putting down."

"Well, I'm glad one of us has a handle on things because I don't know where all this is coming from."

"Aldridge, you've been berating me for the past ten minutes. I think it would be best if Anika worked with you from now on."

"Let me get this straight. You're dumping me?"

"I'm not dumping you. I'm just stepping back."

"No, you don't get to dump me twice in a lifetime. I'm dumping you. You are officially fired."

"You can't fire someone after they've already quit."

"I'm the client, and what the client says goes."

"Fine, whatever helps you sleep at night."

"I have a sleepy girl mocktail each night and rest like a baby."

"A what?"

"You've never heard of a sleepy girl mocktail? A little cherry juice, some magnesium, sparkling water over ice, maybe a sprig of rosemary as garnish. Chef's kiss." Danessa stared at me in silence, like I'd sprouted wings. This was my MO of late, I was sour and then switched to sweet when I realized I'd fucked shit up. "Nessa?"

"No, no." She wagged her finger at me. "I'll transfer your file to Anika. You'll be in good hands."

"I think you're blowing this out of proportion."

"Don't fucking try to gaslight me. If you're so unhappy,

get someone else to find your persnickety ass a house." I knew she was pissed because she was pulling out SAT vocabulary words. She backed away, never lowering her silencing finger. Turning, she exited the shop leaving me alone.

Imploding my life was what I was good at. When things were going well, I'd find a way to ruin it. This move, a chance at a championship, and seeing Danessa again were all good things. I think it was a form of survivor's remorse. Making it out of North Philadelphia wasn't possible for everyone. And now I was looking at houses in the millions of dollars. I was grateful but questioned whether I was worthy.

"Excuse me, are you Aldridge Mosley?" Correction: I was semi alone with the exception of a fellow shopper.

"Yep."

"Can I get a picture?"

I'd just had a fight with my realtor ex-girlfriend. Who, as hard as I tried, no longer found me charming. I was in a city with zero friends. I had a new job where everyone was calling me the great shining hope while secretly wishing I failed. And my allergies still thought I was in Kansas City and had not recalibrated for the desert weather. But let's squeeze a selfie in. With a deep exhale, I agreed, "Sure."

***

"WHAT ARE YOU DOING?" NORI ASKED.

She had a key card to my hotel suite and carte blanche to come and go as needed. This wasn't the case in Missouri because in Missouri I had a life and friends. But now that I was in Vegas my phone was strangely dry. And I had to live vicariously through my friends' social media, witnessing all the fun times I was missing. It was Sunday and if I was in Kansas City, I could be taking a quick run with Rhythm and Roots, the local all Black run club. Instead, I was adding my sneakers to my gym bag so I could workout alone.

"Is that coffee for me?"

"No."

I strolled up to her while she was still putting her bag down and stole the cup from her hand, taking a long sip. "Thanks, you're the best assistant ever. Oh, by the way, the realtor you hired quit yesterday."

Nori frowned. I don't know if it was because of the theft of her coffee or the news of Danessa severing ties. "What did you do?"

"Me?" I pointed to my chest.

"She quit for a reason."

"She quit because she's not a good realtor." *Duh.*

Nori eyed me suspiciously. "What's the story with you two?"

"Excuse me?"

"It was clear at our first meeting with her that you two have history. Did you sleep with her and never call her back?"

"No. I mean yes but I called her back." I'd gotten very little rest last night and might have sent some late-night texts to Danessa that were inappropriate and ignored by her. "We used to be a couple."

"When was this? I know every woman you've ever dated." She followed me to the living room, taking a seat.

"No you do not. I don't tell you everything."

She pursed her lips at my blatant lie.

Nori was like a big sister. There wasn't much she wasn't privy to. She'd witnessed me slowly spiraling downward. Nori suggested I get help and for months I ignored her until one day she found me passed out on the bathroom floor, face down in my own vomit. That was my rock bottom.

"When did you two date?"

"College. We met freshman year and started dating the year after. You know how college is. Everything feels more intense. It was my first time being away from home and living on my own. Danessa was beautiful and smart. She was prelaw and was so passionate about the political system, social injustice, and defending the little guy. Danessa taught me things I never really thought about. We had deep discussions. She loved to debate and present a controversial counterpoint. On the flip side, she was never the life of the party. But she was popular. People wanted to be close to Danessa, and all she wanted was to be next to me."

Nori gasped. "She's the one that got away?"

"What? No." I pushed her words away with a wave.

"Aldridge, it's all over your face."

I couldn't refute that so I pivoted. "This coffee sucks by the way."

"That's because it's mine and not yours. So, why'd Danessa quit?"

"I don't know. We were in a perfume shop—"

"What does that have to do with showing you houses?"

I snapped my fingers. "That's exactly what I said. Next thing I know she's upset and claims I'm not taking shit seriously and that we're a bad fit."

"As a couple or as a client?"

"As a client. This had nothing to do with our past."

"Sounds like you fucked up." Nori bit into my half-eaten granola bar on the coffee table.

"Excuse you. That's the conclusion you draw after you hear she blew up at me for no reason?"

"With you there's always a reason."

"I resent that." Grabbing my phone, I pulled up Danessa's contact and prepared to send her another text message. "I'm going to text her." As I typed, I spoke the words aloud so Nori could give feedback. "Danessa, this is Aldridge. Stop fucking playing with me and respond to my messages."

Nori snatched the phone from my hand and deleted my unfinished text. "Have you lost your mind?"

"She's ignoring me."

"And I'm sure you deserve it." Nori shook her head in disbelief. "What did you mean by messages? Have you been texting her?"

"No." I sounded like the cat who ate the canary.

She scrolled up and read through the thread of unanswered text messages I'd sent in the early hours of the morning. "You told her she was overreacting and she needed to calm down. A phrase women just love to hear. And then you claimed she was the worst realtor to ever realtor. Those were your exact words. Next, we get to the section when you trip down memory lane. I'll spare you the details because it's embarrassing for you. And lastly you closed it all out by once again insulting her and stating her ears were too big for her head. And I quote, 'Proportionately it just doesn't work.'" Nori stared at me waiting for answers.

"I stand by the last statement. Because she always had big ears and I just thought eventually she'd grow into them. Adults keep growing well into their twenties but nope, they're still very pronounced."

"I'm convinced your frontal lobe hasn't fully developed. In college I learned your frontal lobe should mature by age twenty-five, but in some cases, it can take longer, up until the age of thirty. So hopefully you make leaps and bounds in the next four years."

"I will admit that maybe some of those messages were poorly thought out."

"You called her the Mayor of Fartville."

A smile crept over my face. "Listen, that's a high honor."

"Aldridge!" Nori screamed.

"I was vulnerable and scared. And my father never loved me." I threw out buzz phrases in an attempt to excuse my behavior.

Nori planted her face into her palm. "So we need to find a new realtor."

"No, I have a realtor, we just need her to change her mind."

"Maybe she would've before but after your text tirade I'm not so sure."

"Have you met me? I'm a—"

"Asshole?" Nori interrupted me.

"I was going to say charmer."

"Your plan is to beg for forgiveness?"

"I'm going to apologize like it's 2004 and I'm Ruben Studdard."

DANESSA

"WHY DO I GET STUCK WITH ALDRIDGE?" ANIKA ASKED while rearranging items on my desk.

"Because he's a client of the agency and one of us has to service him."

Her expression turned mischievous. "He wants you to serve him up that ass."

"Shut up. That's not what this is about." I shuffled papers across my desk.

"Nessa, I know men. Aldridge isn't over you. The fact that you can't see that is alarming."

"I know you believe everyone is in love with you, but I live in reality."

"I don't think everyone loves me, but I do think everyone should."

"Just think of the commission we'll get to share." When I wanted my sister to do something I led with what was in it for her, and splitting a potential million-dollar commission was a huge incentive.

"Yeah, about that. If I'm showing him the homes, I should get the full commission."

"Not after I did all the reconnaissance. Fifty-fifty that's the deal."

"So, I sell him a house and then what, you never see him again?"

"That's the plan."

"You have the worst plans. Aldridge is back in your life for a reason."

"It's more of a coincidence, a fluke." I reached for my iced coffee which practically melted by the time I got back to the office because it was as hot as the devil's balls out there.

"Lying to me is one thing, but lying to yourself is a whole other level of lunacy."

No one was lying. Two weeks ago I wasn't thinking about Aldridge Mosley. He was just one of my many exes. The only reason I quit was because it was clear my presence was making him uncomfortable. So I decided to put us both out of our misery.

My mother entered my office hidden by a bouquet of white roses. "Someone has an admirer." She set the vase on my desk.

"Who are they from?" My eyes narrowed as I examined the arrangement suspiciously. I couldn't think of one suitor, past or present, who'd be sending me such a beautiful bouquet.

"I don't know, you'll have to read the card." Jemini was lying; she was always in our business. I can guarantee you she'd already read the card and pulled three or four stems to make herself a smaller corsage. Locating the card within the massive arrangement and opened it up.

I hate having to admit when I'm wrong, but this is one of those times.

AJM

My face often betrayed me, but this time I managed to look unfazed. "It's from Aldridge."

"I knew it." Anika snapped her fingers.

Jemini fluttered closer. "What did the card say?"

"Stop acting like you haven't already read it." The last thing I wanted to talk about was Aldridge because my mother would always choose his side. You'd think she'd birthed him and not me the way she sanctioned everything he did. Our front door chimed, indicating someone entering the office, and Jemini went to the lobby to respond.

I handed the card to Anika. "What do you think that means?"

"Sounds like he is looking to make amends."

"It's going to take a whole lot more than some flowers and a generic non-apology to fix things."

Anika leaned in to smell the roses. "The flowers are a nice touch."

"Hello, delivery for Danessa Irwin." Standing just outside my office was a man with another massive bouquet."

"I think there's some type of mix-up. I already received a bouquet." I pointed to the arrangement already taking up half my desk.

"Well this must be your lucky day," he said, setting the flowers on the other side of my desk. Before he left my office, another arrangement of flowers arrived, and then another.

"I'm here for this type of carrying on." Anika kicked her feet from her perch on my credenza. "Rich men apologize different. That's why I'm always picking fights." Three more bouquets were delivered, turning my office into a florist shop. "You're going to have to let him have this round."

"Because of a few flowers?"

"By my count, there are eleven vases in here. Ain't nothing few about em."

The final bouquet was delivered by the tallest delivery man I'd ever seen. Even though his face was concealed by the blooms, it was easy to tell it was Aldridge. In the split second it took for him to put the vase down on a side table, I swept my tongue over my teeth, smoothed my hair, and checked for eye boogers.

"I think that's the last of them," Aldridge said.

"What are you doing here?"

"I was in the neighborhood."

"With dozens of roses?" Anika asked.

Aldridge gestured toward the exit. "Anika could you—"

"No, no I can't."

He looked at me hoping I'd back him up, but I didn't bat an eye.

"Listen—"

"Aldridge is that you?" Just what we needed, Jemini stirring the pot.

"Ms. Irwin, how are you?"

"Jemini, you can still call me Jemini. And I'm not doing as good as you with your hundred-million-dollar contract." She walked into Aldridge's chest, offering a warm hug.

"It's nice to see you again."

"When I heard you were moving to town, I knew it was only a matter of time before you and Nessa crossed paths again. You're looking good, Aldridge." Jemini caressed his arm. I loved my mother, but rarely did I like her. She was a habitual line stepper. Aldridge was off limits. I'd already set a hard boundary around him years ago. *Danessa you can't be implying your mother would try to fuck Aldridge?* Yes, that's exactly what I'm saying. She'd slept with my boyfriends in the past. Aldridge would never, but Jemini Irwin most certainly would.

"Mom could you—"

"What? Aldridge came all the way over here. The least you could do is apologize for not having his back."

My face contorted with disgust. "I don't have anything to apologize for." Jemini was not a girl's girl. Often taking a man's side over her own daughters. That shit irked the fuck out of me.

"Actually, I'm here to offer apologies," Aldridge said. Despite our differences, he would never allow my mom to throw me under the bus. He'd fall on his sword whether he was in the wrong or not.

"I'm sure you didn't do anything wrong. You know how Danessa can be." My mother flashed a cold look in my direction. *Mothers are their daughter's first bullies.*

"Mom," Anika chimed in. "I think we should let Aldi and Danessa talk without an audience." I gave Anika a silent thank you.

"I was just trying to help," Jemini said. All she knew how to do was make things worse.

"They're grown and don't need us butting in."

My mother grabbed one of the vases before leaving, and Aldridge closed the door behind her.

"Some things never change." I attempted to excuse her behavior.

"You know your mother just wants the best for you."

"In her opinion, the best always requires me to forgive some man who fucked up."

"I'm still just some guy to you?"

Standing, I threw a stress ball in the shape of a rainbow at him which he caught in his hand. "You're an asshole, Aldridge."

"So, I've heard. I thought I was a lovable goof but now I realize it's reading more assholeish. Asshole adjacent. Bordering lovable goof and asshole. Skirting the vicinity of assholary."

I laughed in spite of myself and immediately regretted it. "You do know this was all part of my mother's plan. She concealed your identity and hoped us seeing each other again would stir something up."

"I'm not going to act like your mother's plotting didn't work. Being around you again got me thinking about what I missed out on."

Neither my brain nor heart were prepared to have a conversation about missed opportunities and what could have been. I revisited that topic periodically and always settled on the same conclusion. If I hadn't ended things with him … time, temptation, and travel would have done it for us. "Aldridge—"

"I'm talking about our friendship."

I released the breath I was holding. My life was complicated enough without my ex-boyfriend pining for me. But just to be clear was he friend zoning me? Me!

"You were my best friend and then you were gone. I'll admit the first few months … shit the first few years without you were pretty bad. There were so many times I just wanted to call and hear your voice or honestly, cuss you smooth the fuck out. But as time passed, I accepted not hearing from you was probably better as long as you were happy, that's really all that mattered. So suddenly being confronted with the one person I secretly hoped to never see again was daunting."

My heart sank from my chest. "You never wanted to see me again?"

"No, Danessa. You hurt me … real bad."

I moved closer. "I never meant to hurt you."

Aldridge held up his hand silently asking me to stop. "I'm over it. I moved on years ago. But the thing I've never stopped wishing for was you as my friend. Did you know white roses signify new beginnings?"

He moved on? "No, I didn't." *When did he move on?*

"Yeah, white is linked with honor and reverence which is how I remember us."

"So you got me hundreds of roses because you want to try to reestablish a friendship?" I should be relieved, but my heart dropped another two feet.

"Yeah, I'm in your city and we've both matured since college, and I was just hoping we could hit the reset button and be friends."

I blinked sheepishly. I've never wanted to be Aldridge's friend. *Don't get me wrong, he was my best friend in college, but I loved him. Not right now. I don't love him right now.* But I still held a deep affection for this man. Friends was a big ask. Friendship required no jealousy when he eventually met someone he liked better than me. It also meant no messy dumb shit which us Irwin women were known for.

"You sent me some disturbing text messages." I'd woken up on Sunday morning to a barrage of texts from Aldridge. They started out benign but with each unan-swered text, Aldridge got more aggressive.

"Not my proudest moment. Much of it was said out of frustration."

"Like the dig about my ears?"

"I love your ears. I think they accentuate your head. And without them poking out like that you wouldn't have such keen hearing. In school we were in the back of the lecture hall and you caught every word."

I smooshed him in the head. "I know you're not talking about imperfections with that unibrow situation you have going on."

"I get that waxed now." He pointed to his brows. "I'm practically an Adonis." He was joking but there were no lies detected. Aldridge was the type of brother who turned heads when he entered a room. His skin was rich mahogany and always seemed to glow. His voice was deep and when he spoke, the bass rattled my chest. His large hands could palm my ass guiding me over his dick when we fucked.

"Much improved." I managed to squeak out.

"So can we shake on our rekindled friendship and to you being my realtor again?"

"We can be friends but I'm still not your realtor."

"Come on, be serious. If I'm going to find a home, I need your expertise."

"So now I'm an expert. I thought I was the worse realtor to ever—"

"Stop referring to the text messages." He threw his hands up in frustration. "You wanna play hardball. Okay." He huffed out a breath before pulling out his phone.

"Who are you calling?"

"I didn't want to do this, but you've left me no choice." My face was a puzzle while Aldridge tapped on his phone screen. Luther Vandross's "A House Is Not a Home" began to play. He swayed side to side and when Luther started singing so did he.

Aldridge was halfway through the song when my initial shock finally dissipated. "What's happening?"

"It's a concert with songs about home I personally curated for this occasion. Because I need you … to help me find a home. Up next is 'Take Me Home, Country Roads' by John Denver." When the guitar strings from the next song started to play, Aldridge danced along like he was at a rap concert. His movements were robust but weirdly enough, still matched the beat of the song. I was certain no one had ever done the Dougie to a John Denver song.

"Do you have no shame?" I yelled, doing my best to hold back a laugh.

"When it comes to you, no."

Grabbing his phone, I scrolled through the songs settling on "Coming Home" by Leon Bridges. When the melody started to play, Aldridge's movements stalled, and his gaze meandered over my features. My hips swayed from side to side and he mimicked my motion.

"Can I?" He was asking for permission to touch me.

"Yes." His hand gently landed on my waist, and I was now following his lead. We swayed back and forth in a small circle. Sneaking a peek at his face, I quickly dipped my head. His eyes were intense and rather than decipher them, I preferred to lean in, resting my head on his chest. Friends. I could do this. I could be his friend.

ALDRIDGE

AT TWENTY-SIX I WAS COMING TO THE REALIZATION I DIDN'T know how to make friends. During school, people gravitated toward me with little effort. I never had to overextend myself or travel too far out of my comfort zone to find individuals I clicked with. In Minnesota shit was easy because I was from Philly and a basketball player, and people found that interesting. I stood out because most folks had *normal* jobs.

In Vegas everyone was a celebrity, all the men were gym rats and played in a band, and all the women were sculpted and drank lattes with oat milk. No one was checking for me like they were in Kansas City and that's why against my better judgment, I was at a party. Who was throwing this party? I wasn't entirely sure, but the home was impressive, and half my team was in attendance.

I was holding up the wall, nursing a ginger ale trying not to stand out like a sore thumb. Everyone seemed to know one another already so it felt weird trying to insert myself into conversations. Like what was I supposed to contribute? The trendiest restaurants in town, I didn't have a clue. Casinos with the best payout? I wouldn't even know where to start. GPS was needed to find this place because each street still looked the same to me. Was being here looking like a lame better than just cutting my losses and dipping?

The few people I did know weren't checking for me. When I first arrived, I caught the eye of Dante with two drinks in his hand. He tossed me a nod but then fled in the opposite direction. *Can I ask you a question? Taking into consideration all you know about me, would you consider me cool? No, on second thought, don't answer that. If I had to ask the question the answer was no.*

I spotted Colin Pratt moving through the crowd with his entourage. The more I got to know him, the more I hated him. As a Ramblers veteran, he believed his superstar status was solidified. But he was a ball hog who assumed the team was only there to make him look good and if we weren't supporting his inflated ego, we were useless.

Basketball teams were no different than a regular nine to five. You had employees who showed up and did what they were asked. They didn't make waves or expect any fanfare. Then there was the office manager who'd been with the company for years and gathered a clique of minions who did their bidding. That was Colin. And then you had me, the new hire who questioned everything. I didn't give a fuck if this is the way it's always been done. If shit isn't working, you don't keep doing more of the same thing.

Okay Aldi, you just can't stand in one place all night. You have to say hi or initiate a conversation. I searched the crowd for another lonely loser. If I just had a drink, a few sips even, it would really take the edge off. *Hi, I'm Aldridge. How about this weather we're having? Is it always this hot? What's up, I'm Aldi. Do you want to go somewhere and suck my dick?* You laugh, but that has actually worked in the past. *Did you know Pope John Paul the II was named an honorary Globetrotter?*

I glanced at the sun-kissed blonde standing next to me, dancing offbeat to the Ying Yang Twins. "Hi, did you know they're not twins?"

"What?"

"The Ying Yang Twins. They're not twins, not even related."

"Okay?"

"I'm Aldridge by the way."

"Persephone." Her handshake was weak.

"Like the Greek goddess, I dig it. My name, Aldridge, means alder tree or village."

"Cool." She turned, giggling with her friend.

I felt like the old man in the club who didn't know everyone was laughing at him, not with him. Heading to the backyard, I hoped for better luck. This yard was just as impressive as the house with a covered patio and a pool and hot tub combo in the middle of the yard. Past that, there were tons of places to branch off and have intimate conversations. To the left there was cornhole, large-scale Connect 4, and Jenga.

"I know that's not who I think it is." Colin Pratt's voice called out. "Newbie, thanks for gracing us with your presence." I wasn't interested in a dick measuring contest, so I attempted to head in the opposite direction. "Where the fuck are you going?" Colin stood, pushing a woman who wasn't his wife off his lap.

"It's a party. You should learn how to chill out," I said.

"It was a party until your bitch ass showed up."

"Why, are you scared I'll steal all your hoes?"

"Ain't nobody checking for a brother who still has the taste of Similac on his tongue."

"You know Colin, this ole G hating ass behavior is wearing thin."

"What do I have to hate about? I'm living the dream. Look at my wrist, check out my whip in the driveway, not to mention the bad bitches on my arm and no bad bitches on yours. I'm who you're trying to be."

"Ain't nobody trying to be a washed-up ballplayer, with a bad back, and two, maybe three salvageable years left."

"You hear this guy?" Colin shook his head, getting support from the random clinger ons around him. "If it wasn't for me, you wouldn't even be here."

"Trust me, I know. If you were doing your job they wouldn't have hired me. But don't worry, I'll get you a championship ring as a parting gift."

Colin literally stepped over people to get at me. "You think you have it all figured out don't you?"

He was inches from my face. Colin was trying to provoke me into doing something stupid. I wasn't taking the bait. "Not all. But I definitely have your number."

"You want to talk about what you know? Well let me jump in. I know you're just another hood baby trying to make good. I know your brother's a felon and your father ain't much better. I also know you're not ready for prime time." Colin leaned in close so only I could hear him. "I mean are you going to make it through the season without a trip to Cirque Lodge Wellness?"

The fact Colin was so pressed he'd decided to dig up dirt on me meant he was more shook than I first thought. Yes, I'd gone to rehab in Utah. Fortunately, I had a coach in KC who did all he could to shelter and support me. Only a handful of people knew about the extent of my addiction. The Pioneers organization closed ranks around me to shield me from exposure. In the off season I voluntarily admitted myself into treatment and got the help I needed. After successfully completing rehab, I went on to take us all the way to the finals.

Colin was a bitch for bringing it up. But I was well versed in the art of playing dirty. I offered up a dry hand-clap. "You did your homework, congratulations. So did I. I know about all your little proclivities and vices. And boy do you have a fuck ton of baggage. So maybe you should watch your mouth before I implode your picture-perfect life … Bucking Bull." That was his username on some back page hookup site for people who were into freaky shit. My assistant, Nori, was also an unofficial private detective. Before I dated someone, she took it upon herself to search the web for reasons I shouldn't. When I asked her to look up Colin, I was hoping to find a talkative side chick not that Colin liked rope play and being peed on.

The muscles in his jaw tightened and ruminated. "You fucking piece of shit. Someday I'm going to knock that smug smirk off your face."

"Why not right now? I dare you. But we both know you ain't gonna do shit. You talk but you can't back none of that shit up. Now me on the other hand, I'm just waiting for you to test me so I can shift your fucking jaw."

Fuck playing nice and making friends. If Colin wanted to test me, I would make his life a living hell. It sucks because I was actually excited for the chance to play with him. He was a talented veteran who would eventually be in the Hall of Fame. But you know what they say, never meet your idols because you always end up disappointed.

Colin leaned in expecting me to flinch. I'd been hit

before and could take a punch. If he swung on me, it would be rockabye-baby. The last thing he'd see was my fist before his body hit the grass.

"Hey, we're all here to have a good time. Let's cool out." Dante inserted his body in between us. When Dante was the voice of reason, you knew you were tripping. Colin and I both backed away, but I didn't take my eyes off him until he went inside the house.

"He's an asshole," Anika said. I hadn't been here long enough to notice she was here. My eyes widened as I canvassed the area. "She's in the bathroom. And you're welcome."

"For what?"

"For convincing her to come out yet again so you could have another shot."

"Who are you, my matchmaker?"

"I'm just a former faux sister-in-law with a soft spot for you."

"Well Danessa and I are just friends now so—"

"Okay, sure sparky." She patted my shoulder like I was pathetic.

When it came to Danessa, my radar was always active and it started pulsing erratically when she entered the backyard in a scoop neck tank top and cutoff jeans. She was dripping in gold. Her ears, her neck, her wrist and her fingers. Her hair had that just styled bounce to it. A group of women nearby were throwing frosty looks in her direction with the realization tonight's competition for baddest of them all had crowned Danessa as the winner. Danessa's head was on a swivel clearly searching for her sister. She was probably regretting being here and already ready to leave. When she spotted me next to Anika, she shuffled back a step or two as if she wanted to retreat but thought better of it.

"You're here?" she said on approach.

"I mean it is a basketball party and I'm … checks notes … a basketball player."

"Per usual you missed all the action," Anika said.

"There was action?"

"Yeah, your *friend* almost came to blows with Colin." Dante gripped my shoulder.

"Colin?"

"Colin Pratt the point guard for the Ramblers." Dante's clarification caused me to roll my eyes.

"You need a drink." Anika pointed to me.

"No, I'm good."

Anika ignored my protest. "I'm gonna get you a drink." Dante followed behind her, apparently they were now attached at the hip.

"I don't drink," I called out after her.

"It'll be a light pour," she said before heading inside.

Danessa took a sip from her cup, her silky hair framed her face before cascading over her shoulders. The party was loud between the music, buzz of conversation and guest carousing all around us. I'd never been a fan of big crowds and was often posted up in the corner. Danessa and I had that in common. We'd be in our own little world, laughing at inside jokes or singing songs word for word. Too caught up in one another to care what anyone else was doing. Anika was the life of the party, but Danessa was better in smaller settings. That's when she let her guard down and when she locked eyes with you, you felt like the only one.

People made assumptions about who I was but very few took the time to get to know me. And I'd let the surface shit slide because I wasn't trying to go that deep with most people. But with Danessa I trusted that no matter how vulnerable I got, she'd still get me. Or at least that's how it used to work.

"I didn't expect to see you here."

"You know Anika, she begged me to come. Actually, she and Dante teamed up on me."

"Are they a couple now?"

"Uhm, I think they're still just having fun."

"I wish I could turn my brain off and just say fuck it every once in a while."

"Anika's ability to ignore responsibility is both a marvel and a source of frustration."

Another Ying Yang song came on. The DJ clearly had a preference. "Did you know the Ying Yang Twins aren't twins?"

"Yeah, they're not even fucking brothers or related. Neither is Omarion and Marcus Houston."

"Yeah, just a bunch of fucking phonies." Fuck Persephone. She didn't get it. "Are you having fun?" I was so bad at this. I never expected I'd have to make small talk with the woman I once thought I'd marry.

"It's crowded and I think I interrupted a group of people doing drugs in one of the bedrooms."

"Really?" I hoped my tone came off as nonchalant and not slightly interested. Parties were usually off limits for that very reason. I wasn't anti-social; I was a drug addict and places like this made me want to use. While Danessa told me a story about the ride to the party. My mind tried to calculate how I could discreetly excuse myself so I could head upstairs. I just needed a pill to take the edge off.

The thing about being an addict was it was a lifelong condition. For the rest of my life, I would have to choose sobriety. If for one minute I thought I was smarter and stronger than the addiction I was toast. Relapsing was a real possibility, especially if I kept putting myself in situations like this.

"Are you okay?"

"Yeah, why wouldn't I be?"

"Because you're sweating profusely."

I mopped my brow, which was dotted with perspiration. "I just need some fresh air."

"We're outside." She tilted her head examining my features, which only made me sweat more.

"Fresher, less congested air."

"Do you want company?"

"Yeah." Danessa followed me through the yard and out a side gate. "Better?

"Uh-huh." I took several deep breaths. My heart was trying to bust through my chest and my skin felt like it was infested by ants.

"Anxiety?"

"Something like that." I sucked in rapid, stuttered breaths.

"Just close your eyes and count backwards from ten."

"No, I'm good."

She claimed my clammy hands and it did nothing but disrupt my nervous system further. "Close your eyes." I did as I was told. "Ten."

I hated myself.

"Nine."

I was never going to be normal.

"Eight ... seven."

I was no better than my father.

"Six ... five."

I should call Pete.

"Four."

Was it always going to be this hard?

"Three … Two … One."

Opening my eyes, Danessa greeted me with a reassuring smile. "It happens to the best of us. I was in Whole Foods a few months ago and broke out into a cold sweat. My cart was full, but for some reason the thought of being in the store one minute longer wigged me out."

"What caused it?"

"Stress, life, too many people. I don't really know."

"I think for me, it's trying to solve problems that haven't even presented themselves yet."

She checked her phone and smiled. "This party is a bust. I think I know a place that will provide the wide-open spaces you're seeking."

"I'm down." Anything to get away from this den of iniquity.

After a quick twenty-minute drive, we were back downtown and pulling up to a chain linked fence. Pushing the call button, we waited for what felt like an eternity before the speaker crackled. "Who is it?" an aggressive male voice asked.

Danessa draped her body across my lap to be closer to the speaker. "It's Danessa." She leaned further out the window so she could wave toward the camera, her ass perched in my face. It was perfectly positioned for a quick smack or a naughty love bite. There was another brief pause and then the gate rattled open. Danessa made her way back to the passenger seat and said, "Take the first left."

Once inside we stopped at a guard station and parked next to the only other car in the small lot.

"Danessa, what are you doing here?" An older gentlemen exited the guard shack with a limp.

"I know it's late Earl, but I was hoping I could show my friend around."

When I exited the car, Earl's face lit up. "Oh shit it's number four."

"Earl, this is Aldridge Mosley, he's a client."

"Damn, you're tall." Earl accepted the hand I extended, and we exchanged daps. "Welcome to Vegas."

"Thank you."

"I see you've met one of our finest resources … Miss Danessa."

"We actually went to college together," Danessa said.

"Is that right? So you got to witness his meteoric rise from the bottom up."

"I don't know about all that." Normally I wasn't shy, but something about Earl's down-to-earth nature made me want to be modest.

"Shiiiiiit, you brought your team to the finals in your third year. That team was a mess when you were drafted. They went from dead last to contenders in the span of three seasons. Hopefully you sprinkle some of that magic on the Ramblers."

"I'm sure gonna try."

"If it isn't too much trouble, could I get a picture for my son?"

I posed for a picture and grabbed a basketball from my gym bag in the backseat. Signing it, I gave it to Earl.

"I appreciate it."

"Anytime."

"Do you remember your way?" Earl asked Danessa.

"Yep, just follow the lights."

"Alright, I'll leave you two to it."

I watched Earl walk away. He was bowlegged and each step looked painful. "Where are we?"

Danessa pointed in the direction of travel, and I fell in step with her on the dirt path. "We are at a Vegas staple. It used to be a hidden gem, but now everybody and their momma knows about this place."

Although it was well after one in the morning, the area up ahead was bright with a flicking light source. When we rounded the corner, my feet stalled and my mouth unhinged.

"Welcome to the Neon Museum."

"Are you shitting me right now?" In front of me was a metal Hard Rock guitar standing over eighty feet tall, all lit up in red and white lights. Next to it was a Stardust sign in a funky vintage font.

"This is the place where old Vegas signs are retired. Which is cool because it gives them a second life." Danessa had always been a history buff. She loved digging into the story behind forgotten things.

"This is impressive. When you said you had a place, I wasn't expecting this."

"I like to keep you on your toes." She offered a casual leg kick.

"My footing is always precarious when I'm around you."

"Let's go. This is your VIP tour."

"How do you know Earl?"

"He used to date my mom."

My left brow lifted to signify my skepticism.

"He may not look like much now. But back in the day he was a professional wrestler. He was super strong and could lift both me and Anika at the same time."

"And now he works as a security guard?"

"Life comes at you fast. You know how it is, people come into a ton of money and start spending. Fuck the future when you need a Rolex and a Mercedes right now. He got injured and was never on top again, and after that he blew through his cash pretty fast."

"Damn." A chill overtook me. You hear about stories like this and think that could never be me. But a bad investment, health issues, or a greedy accountant and all you could be left with are the memories.

"A common Vegas cautionary tale."

"And when the money was gone, so was your mom?"

"You know Jemini. She doesn't do broke."

"I respect your mom for her honesty."

Danessa's mouth bunched into a dubious pucker. "She's transactional. I don't know if love should ever be that."

"I don't know, at the end of the day we all want something. Men want sex and a baddie on their arm. Women want a provider and a man over six feet tall."

"I don't believe that. That's what people say because they're afraid of being hurt. But when you peel back the layers at the end of the day, people want to be loved … sincerely." I looked at her as if she'd just beamed in from another planet. "Don't tell me you've become jaded."

She had to break into a slight jog to keep up with my long strides, so I switched direction, walking backward in front of her. "I'm not jaded. I just live in the real world. People are not looking for love. They're more interested in status, likes, and views."

"Not everyone."

"Danessa you are the exception, not the rule."

"Well, I still believe in love and that each of us has our own person."

I forced a smile at the realization she didn't see me as her person if she was holding out for someone better.

"What?" she looked at me.

"Nah, you just said a mouthful." I turned forward, needing a minute to hide my disappointment.

"So did you leave the party because of your confrontation with Colin?"

No, because I'm an addict in a new city with no support system in place. "It just wasn't my scene."

"Because of Colin Pratt?"

I jerked my shoulders. "I think Colin Pratt hates me."

"Well technically you're his replacement. It would be a shock if he didn't." She hooked her arm in mine and our steps synced.

"You're right but I didn't expect him to be so vocal about it. I thought he'd be passive-aggressive. That I could handle. It would be like talking to my dad."

Her features darkened. "How is your dad?"

"I'd rather we talk about Colin." My father was a lot of things and one of them was my biggest hater. My mother made excuses for him, claiming he had a rough childhood and despite his lack of enthusiasm, he was very proud of me. He wasn't proud, he was jealous. You don't expect that from your parents, but that's what it all boiled down to. His son was living the life he wished he could. I could see it in his bloodshot eyes, he would sell his soul for a do-over or a reset button. But the thing about that is a reset wouldn't change the fact he's a gambler and an alcoholic who would rather spend his last dime at a casino or race-track before using it to provide for his family.

Danessa knew about my history with my father and the disappointment and anger that clouded our relationship. "How do you plan to coexist with Colin?"

"I plan to perform and once I start solidifying wins, all that bravado Colin is carrying around will dissipate."

"He's still the starting point guard."

I scanned the area. The museum was closed and there was no one else around. "Actually, I'm going to be starting."

"What, the Ramblers are going to bench their star player?"

"I don't even think Coach has shared that with Colin yet. But yeah, I'll be replacing him in the starting lineup."

"No pressure."

"Pressure I can handle. I came out of the womb feeling the pressure." According to my mother, I was born with the umbilical cord wrapped around my neck. The doctor had to resuscitate me.

"When Colin finds out—"

"He's probably going to be looking for a fight."

"You could pull him aside and have a conversation man to man."

"That's not my responsibility. I'm here to win and if Colin stays out of my way, we'll all go home with a ring."

"Being an athlete requires balls of steel. Because I could never."

"Don't act like you're not competitive. Miss Delta Phi Omega … cheerleading captain … debate team co-chair … Black Student Alliance president."

Danessa held a hand up like she was warding off my words. "That was a long time ago."

"I hate when you do that."

"What?"

"Sell yourself short."

"It's just hard to explain."

"I'm listening."

"Everything has just come easy to you."

My face crumpled. "I grew up in the hood with a mother who worked two jobs and a father who barely kept a job because he was always drunk."

"I know and that sucked. I'm not trying to downplay that. But you've always been smart, handsome, and athletic. It's like God endowed you with the tools to be successful despite your circumstances."

Stopping, I looked at her straight on. "Danessa you're way smarter than me. And far better looking."

"I had to study every night to maintain my GPA. While you barely cracked open a book and aced every test."

"That doesn't mean that God didn't … What did you call it? Endow you with gifts."

"According to my mother my face card and phat ass are my gifts."

"I mean … that shit doesn't ever decline. It's like you have no spending limit shit is always getting approved."

"I don't want to be just a pretty face."

"I don't see you that way."

"You have to say shit like that. You're my friend."

Anytime she said that word it was like being inflicted with a thousand paper cuts. Yes, I was her friend. But the concept of being only her friend was taking some getting used to. "Are you calling me a liar?"

"No." She drawled out the O and ended her statement with a pout.

"Nooooo," I mimicked, nudging her with my shoulder. "So what's it been like being back home?" We took to walking again.

"When I first came back, I had to move in with my mother. Anika was shacked up with some soccer player at the time."

Frown lines creased grooves around my mouth. "Oh no."

"Yeah, it was enlightening to say the least. I stayed with her for six weeks, and each one of those days I imagined burying her in the yard."

"So you found your own place?"

"It was a studio. Tiny. But it was all mine. I own my place now, but I'm still so proud of that first apartment. The shower leaked and the landlord was creepy, but I got to make my own rules. And I didn't have to bump into strange men on my way to the bathroom at night."

"I can respect that. You've never been one for handouts."

"In Jemini's opinion, that is a moral failing."

"She just wanted you to be her scam partner," I joked.

"Do you know she's currently dating a linebacker from the Raiders?"

"I mean … your mom is fine as hell."

"Eww." She shoved me hard. "I've heard that all my life. She's forty-seven dating twenty-year-olds."

"Momma's gotta live too."

Danessa pretended to throw up.

"You didn't have to leave the party because of me."

"Kinda did, you were freaking out over Colin."

"I wasn't freaking out."

"You were all sweaty and zoned out."

"Nah, that was about something else."

"Did one of your exes show up unexpectedly?"

"No, you were my only ex in attendance."

"Well, whatever it is, just know that if you ever need to talk I've got you."

"I appreciate that." I wasn't prepared to see the disappointment in her eyes when I told her about my past.

There were still hints of the young man Danessa fell head over heels for. The kid that was just happy to be out of his city and was using basketball as a means to escape. In my mind I was good at sports, and it allowed me access to some of the best schools in the country. Shit, these institutions made billions off the free labor of athletes. So while they were using me for NCAA championships, I was using them for an education and networking that could serve me in the future.

"You know ... you're not alone."

"Really, cause I'm feeling like a one-man show right now."

"That's because you push people away."

"I don't."

"You do. Even when we were dating you would go MIA on me."

"You don't know everything."

"You're right, I don't."

"It's not like how it was when you and I were in college. You'd think with all this money and fame shit would be easy. But it's harder and the stakes are higher. And if I fail, I let a bunch of people down."

"You could run away from it all and become a first-grade teacher."

"I'd actually love that."

"Sounds like buyer's remorse."

"Look, I'm the last person who has a right to complain. I've gotten almost everything I've ever wanted."

"What's missing?"

She was missing. Everything was bitter after she left. My success was overcast by a shadow because all I'd ever wanted to do was share my happiness with her. Sometimes love can wreck you. Shatter you into a million little pieces.

I've tried to put myself back together, but I've never been the same. It's like gluing the pieces of a broken vase, it may still function, hold water, house flowers but it's different. Losing Danessa permanently altered how I saw myself.

I looked behind us, realizing the past few minutes all passed in a blur of twinkly lights. "You are the worst tour guide ever."

"I'm a multitasker."

"Less talking, more flashing lights."

DANESSA

"What's this?" Anika reached for a college brochure on my kitchen counter. I should start charging her rent. Since she lived five minutes away she was constantly over at my place stealing my food and shoes.

"Why are you always snooping through my shit?"

"If it was a secret it should be hidden like my vibrator."

I snatched the brochure from William S. Boyd School of Law from her hand. "I'm thinking about going back to school."

"Law school?" Anika took a bite of her everything bagel loaded with cream cheese.

"Yeah." I don't know why she was acting so surprised. After college the plan was to go to law school. It had been on my vision board since I was ten. I wanted to be a prosecutor or work for one of those organizations that help get wrongfully convicted individuals released.

"How exactly are you going to do that and sell homes?"

"Plenty of people work and go to law school."

"I thought there were internships and tons of homework?"

"There is."

She flipped through the pages of the course catalog for a school in California. "So once again, how are you going to do both?"

"I've been saving my money. So, I have my expenses covered for the first year."

"Wait, you're serious." Anika pushed her bagel aside, no longer interested in eating.

"Yes. It's something I've always wanted and being a lawyer could be beneficial for the business."

"That may be true, but you have criminal law classes dog-eared." She pointed to the open course guide in front of her.

"I'm just weighing my options." I gathered the brochures and admission packets from various colleges and universities and stuffed them into a nearby drawer.

"And how are you going to pay for tuition?"

I bounced a lazy shoulder. "Loans, a part-time job."

Anika's face lit up. "You could ask Aldridge."

"Aldridge, my client?"

"Aldridge, your ex who's still in love with you."

I sipped from my coffee mug, convinced my sister was being paid under the table by the Aldridge fandom to push this agenda. "As many times as you say that it's never going to make it true. We've both moved on."

"He's single, you're single."

"The doorman is also single. Should I try for a love connection there too?"

"Not the same. Nessa, don't make me call you out."

"I have no idea what you're talking about."

"Just because you moved on doesn't mean you're over the past. Have you dated? Sure. Has anyone compared to Aldridge? No."

Anika was acting like I'd been stuck in purgatory since the breakup. I had a robust dating life. There was an adjustment period, but I'd successfully moved beyond my college sweetheart. "I was engaged to Marcus. Remember him?"

"I remember you getting cold feet and calling it all off three months before the wedding day." She picked a seed from her teeth.

I didn't really have a comeback for that. Marcus held a special place in my heart, but marriage was a big commitment. It made sense on paper, he was a restaurateur with a string of successful properties in Vegas, California, and Portland. Jemini loved him, mostly because of his portfolio and proximity to the rich and famous. We were damn near a perfect match. Despite all that, I could never shake this nagging sense something was missing.

"And do you remember what you said to me the night before the shit hit the fan?"

Swallowing hard, I fessed up. "I said I wished Marcus were someone else."

"Not someone else, Aldridge."

"To be fair I was hormonal, tipsy, and an emotional wreck."

"Excuses, excuses."

Anika was trying to use my statement a few years ago as a gotcha moment. Did I miss what Aldridge and I had? Of course. I've been fortunate than most. I'd dated several men who were emotionally intelligent, self-sufficient, and good in bed. However, it was difficult to find a connection like I'd had with Aldridge. He just got me from day one. We could communicate through silence. And when we did speak even the ordinary chitchat had a way of making me feel safe and seen. I could be my authentic self with Aldridge, something I couldn't do with Marcus. The thought of donning a mask for the rest of my life was exhausting.

"Look, can we talk about something else?"

"Okay." Anika wasted no time redirecting our conversation. "Let's go on a double date."

"With who?"

"Dante, me, you, and one of Dante's homeboys."

"Ugh, no that sounds like a horrible idea."

"What? Dante knows tons of eligible bachelors with deep pockets."

"You and I don't have the same taste in men."

"I know what you like. I'll make sure he ticks off all your requirements. Strait-laced, handsome but not pretty, tall—"

"He doesn't have to be tall." I returned the creamer to the refrigerator.

Anika rolled her eyes at my blatant lie. "Smart, good dresser. Shall I go on?"

"No, you've covered the basics." If we weren't sisters, I'm not sure we would be friends.

"You need to trust me. Anika knows best."

Anika never knew best. My sister was the type who jumped before considering the consequences. She was the person who banged on my door at two in the morning and demanded I pack a bag because we were going on a road trip. I cannot even begin to list all of the sticky situations she'd gotten us into. Some which left me fearful we wouldn't make it out alive.

"Why can't you and Dante just chill together?"

"Because lately your phone has been a bit dry."

"I have plenty of men hitting me up. If I wanted, I could call any one of them and be wined and dined tonight."

"So text one of those men and ask them to hang out with us. Feel free to drop Dante's name if that helps."

She was calling my bluff. I was confident I could find someone who was willing to take me out, but I wasn't into making the first move. "Why am I always letting you talk me into things?"

"Because I'm your big sister. Besides, a little male attention will remind you that you're that bitch. I see the way men look at you, and you are totally oblivious.

"I'm not oblivious, I'm just not interested."

"You are too beautiful to not be getting your back blown out on a regular basis. Maybe you don't find a love connection, but maybe you find a brother to realign your spine."

Not going to lie, sex would be nice. Great sex would be life changing. But I'd take a mediocre dick down over a silicone one any day. Toys were great but an actual dick thrusting and making me cream was ideal. "Okay, but no fuckboys."

The corners of Anika's mouth curved into her signature mischievous smirk. "Your pussy is safe with me."

"I don't remember you being this picky," I said after walking into the last home I had scheduled to show Aldridge that day.

"I'm not picky. I have preferences, yes."

"Well this home is more contemporary than the last few I've shown you. The builder did a really good job of curating the space so the flow makes sense and is efficient."

"How big?"

"Fifty-five hundred square feet. Which is also smaller than some of the previous places we looked at."

"I noticed kids playing outside."

"Yes, this is an established neighborhood so you're going to get a good mix of older residents and new families who have upgraded from their starter homes."

Clients like Aldridge were the worst. It was clear he wasn't really sold on Nevada and so the thought of planting roots made him hesitant. Settling on a place would make everything real and I don't think he was ready to commit to Vegas as his new home. I totally understood Vegas was an acquired taste. Either you loved it or you hated it. And because it was a transient city with thousands of people from all across the globe coming and going every day, it was difficult to get a true sense of the city's culture.

Aldridge circled the floor plan in silence, opening closets and testing the height of doorways. I dreaded showing him these houses because long after we parted ways, the scent of him would linger in my car and on my clothes. The other day I returned home from a tour and was frozen in my closet for fifteen minutes just inhaling my blouse like I was auditioning for one of those detergent commercials. He didn't wear the same scent as he did in college, and I think I preferred his new cologne better. It made me want to bury my face into the crook of his neck while I stroked his dick.

"The half bath is big."

"There are five bathrooms in total."

"The fireplace?"

"It's gas."

He frowned. We both knew he didn't give two shits about a wood-burning fireplace. He opened windows and examined baseboards like he was a home inspector looking for a reason to issue a negative report.

"There's a mother-in-law suite in the back. And while there isn't currently a pool, there's more than enough yard to install one."

"Good to know."

A shiver ran down my spine with the memory of his deep baritone voice telling me I was a good girl while he stretched me out. Fuck Anika for planting this seed in my head.

Aldridge nodded, walking around the kitchen island. "I'm just a visual person and it's hard for me to imagine a space with no furniture or decor."

"It's a blank slate which means you can make this place whatever you want."

"I guess." He scratched at his beard, looking less than enthused.

The key to closing the deal was helping your client envision themselves in the space. This could be difficult when a home was vacant and unfurnished. It lacked warmth and personality. I knew I should've staged the home to offer the best presentation. Grabbing Aldridge by the hand, I pulled him toward the backyard.

"Where are we going?"

"Trust the process." Outside I stood in front of the grill attached to the outdoor kitchen. "Could you hand me the plate with the burgers?" I tapped on my phone and Frankie Beverly and Maze's "Before I Let Go" began to play.

"What?" His head swiveled as if he was looking for answers.

"The grill's ready, so can you hand me the plate with the burgers?" I pointed at an imaginary plate on the long counter.

"This plate?" Aldridge gestured tentatively in the same direction.

"Yep."

Complying, he pretended to grab hold of a heavy plate and handed it to me.

"Do you still like your burgers medium well?"

"Yes." He stared dubiously at my sudden game of make-believe.

I shook imaginary salt and pepper over the grill, pointing to the lush backyard. "Looks like your mother started the electric slide."

"She did?" Aldridge squinted into the space beyond the covered patio.

"And your Uncle Sully is hitting on my sister."

"He needs to abort that mission right now."

"I think it was smart to go with the slide on the pool because your niece seems to love it."

"Yeah, I'm … glad … I listened to your advice."

"You should always take my advice." I tossed a smile over my shoulder.

Aldridge pointed to the ghost guests on the grass. "Who invited Dante?"

"Well, you know Anika and him are practically sharing a shadow now."

"Wow shit is moving fast." Aldridge canvassed the space. "Where's your dude at?"

We traded a glance. "You know very well I don't have a dude. Can you pass the hot links?"

"Why is that?" We pretended to trade a platter.

"Because I'm busy, dating is similar to dancing on hot coals, and men are dumb. Just take your pick."

"Men are dumb?"

"Yeah, just a plastic bag for a brain floating around in their head."

"Harsh."

"Not all men. But most."

"You might want to flip the burgers."

"Good looking out. There's cold beer in the fridge." I pointed to the refrigerator a few feet away.

"I don't drink."

"Since when?" Aldridge could drink most men under the table in college. Mostly because of his massive size.

"Since … we have a lot of catching up to do."

"Well there's also ginger ale. The brand in the glass bottle that you like."

"You remembered?"

I remembered everything about this man. To the cloud-shaped birthmark on his back, his aversion to walking barefoot, and the curve of his dick. Aldridge's hand moved across my waist as he passed behind me to check out the fridge. And I was acutely aware of my heartbeat.

"Wait, there's actually drinks in here." He pulled out the ginger ale bottle.

"I offer an immersive experience."

Opening two bottles, he said, "Let's make a toast."

I accepted one of the ales. "Okay go ahead."

Aldridge tilted his head back and licked his lips. "To the past catching up to the present and shaping the future."

I raised a disbelieving eyebrow. His toast seemed to

capture the moment. The past was definitely bleeding into the present. "To the past, present, and future."

He took a long sip. "I can't believe you found these."

"When you submit a contract on a house, I'll buy you a case."

Aldridge downed the remaining ale and waved his hand over the grill. "Why are you manning the grill by the way?"

"Because men don't know how to grill any more. Back in the day someone's daddy or uncle would be in his brown sandals cutting up but times have changed."

"Well I'm here and the grill is man's work so you can go take care of the potato salad or something."

"You're not going to burn them like last time?"

He narrowed his eyes. "That was years ago and my song came on." He casually tossed his arm over my shoulder. "It's nice to have our families all in one place. We should do this more often."

Aldridge's cognac eyes locked on to mine. What started out as make believe was beginning to feel real. In another reality this could've been our lives. Cookouts with the family. Me wrapped in his arms next to the grill. Laughter as Jazzy Jeff and the Fresh Prince filled the air. I knew Aldridge well enough to know he was holding back. There were words on the tip of his tongue that would remain unspoken. In leu of speaking, he leaned in and kissed me on the top of my head. To be honest, the sweet gesture wasn't enough. What a sick and twisted world to be this close to Aldridge and unable to experience him fully as God intended.

Backing away, I pretended to be engrossed in picking the next song. Breathing was difficult and my mind released memories of the weight of his body overtop of mine, my legs wrapped around his waist, his dick so deep it made me lightheaded. Each memory was a little serotonin boost. It hit me like a ton of bricks. Anika was right, partially anyway. When it came to Aldridge, I didn't know what the fuck I wanted. "So is this place a contender?"

"I like it. But the gas fireplace and lack of a pool is a deal breaker."

"You never once mentioned a fireplace."

"True, but if the home has one it needs to be real."

Mental note, real working fireplace. "Got it," I said through gritted teeth. I'd probably shown him over twenty homes and every one he took issue with. In one home the closets were too small, the next home they were too big. Another house had an outdoor basketball court which was a no because he couldn't use it year-round. Then when I showed him one with an indoor court, he complained of a weird smell. He was like a six-foot-five Goldilocks.

"This is close but no cigar. The grass … I don't know, is it just me or is the color off?"

"So the grass needs to be greener?"

"Yeah, something like that."

"I'll add that to my *extensive* notes."

"Sounds like you're suggesting I'm difficult?"

"Did I do that?"

"Yeah Urkel, you kind of did. There was a tone."

"I had a tone?"

"Okay so you're leaning into the innocent real estate agent bit."

"I'm just here to help you find your *perfect* home."

He pointed and snapped in my direction. "There it goes again. The way you emphasize the word perfect."

"I do not know what you are talking about."

He flashed me an okay signal.

"In other news I reached out to the moving company. They located your items, and they should be at the drop-off location by midweek. I emailed your assistant the details."

"Really, just like that."

"Well, I did drop your name and told them if the moving truck wasn't in Vegas by Wednesday we would take to social media and drag them for filth. And if one item was missing their little family-owned business would cease to exist."

"You threatened to ruin a mom-and-pop business for me?"

"I did."

"Wow, you are the most gangster realtor I've ever met."

"Sometimes you have to crack some eggs."

"Dirty dozen."

"What does that mean?"

"Uhm, eggs come in a dozen. You're not playing nice. Shit … I don't know, I just wanted to contribute to the badassery."

"Nice try. A for effort."

"So as a thank you for getting my belongings squared away, what about tickets to the first home game of the season?"

"I don't need to be compensated."

"No, I know. Honestly this is more for me than you. It would be nice to have a familiar face in the crowd."

"You want me to be your cheerleader?" I teased.

Aldridge claimed hold of my hands. Yes, whatever he wanted … it was a swift yes. He wants a gas fireplace; I would rip out the old one and build anew. He wanted me among the throng of twenty-thousand fans cheering him on, consider it done. If he wanted to rub the tip of his dick over my clit until we both exploded. Sure, I'm game.

His tone was earnest and his voice a bit shaky. "I want you to be there as my friend."

"Of course. Yes." How could I say no when he was being vulnerable? If he needed to see my face to help him acclimate, I would be front and center with a huge smile and a number four jersey.

ALDRIDGE

DEION'S HOUSE WAS EXACTLY WHAT I EXPECTED IT TO BE, modern, sleek and masculine. Shit, why wasn't Danessa showing me places like this?

"How much you pay for this place? If you don't mind me asking."

"I don't remember, around six."

"Six million?" My eyes fled to my hairline.

"Yeah.

"Million?"

"It's probably worth ten now."

I wasn't paying six million on a gotdamn thing.

Following Deion out to the backyard I had to admit it was money well spent. The yard was manicured with perfectly symmetrical bushes and a waterfall attached to the pool. It was like an oasis, the tranquil gurgle of the water cascading into the pool could make you forget your worries. Shit, I was tired of hotel living. I needed a space all my own.

"What happened the other night?" Deion asked.

"Huh?"

"You, Colin, heated exchange." Deion reached for a nub of cheese. If you told me I'd be hanging out with *the* Deion McCabe in his backyard noshing on a charcuterie board …

shit, if you told me Deion McCabe ate charcuterie boards, I would not have believed you.

"Is that what Colin said?"

"That's what everybody is saying. They thought you two were going to come to blows."

"I know Colin's your friend and all, but he's an asshole. And he instigated that situation."

"You could've just walked away?"

I blinked owlishly. Was Deion "Bust You in the Head Until the White Meat" McCabe suggesting being the bigger man. "I'm from Philly, we don't walk away."

"And that's why nobody likes you."

My head jerked backward with surprise. "Excuse me?"

"Colin may be an asshole, but so are you."

"I was defending myself."

"You have a slick mouth, and you don't know when to shut the fuck up."

"I know you're not talking about slick mouths." A female voice from behind us rang out, stealing the words off my tongue.

"A and B conversation Sloane, so—"

"Nope, I have thoughts." This beautiful woman with wild hair sat down next to Deion.

"Aldridge, this is Sloane. Sloane, Aldridge."

"Nice to meet you." I extended a hand she didn't bother to shake.

"Mmm, normally any time someone meets Sloane, nice isn't the word they use," Deion said.

"What? I'm a joy to be around. A joy."

"You're my joy. I'll give you that." Deion smirked and the two shared a wordless exchange that made me feel like an intruder.

Sloane swept her big curls from her eyes. "So, you're having problems with Colin?"

"Nothing I can't handle."

"Colin talks a tough game, but he's a private school kid who had everything handed to him."

"So am I," Deion said.

"Yeah, but you were raised differently." Sloane grabbed hold of his chin and gave it a shake.

I nodded in agreement. "I've known plenty of guys like Colin, all bark no bite."

"I think someone needs to slap the shit out of him one good time and he'll tighten up."

"I like her." I smiled so big it split my face.

"It's never easy being the new kid in town. But your game will speak for itself. If you're really as good as Deion says you are, that will silence the haters."

I turned to Deion. "You think I'm good." The thought caused my stomach to trill with excitement. Joining the league allowed me the opportunity to play alongside veterans and the experience had been a mixed bag.

"You can shoot a ball. Don't read too much into it." Deion's tepid compliment still meant a lot. Despite what my teammates might think, I wasn't trying to be an agitator. I wanted the Ramblers to succeed. I wasn't stupid enough to truly believe I could make that happen alone. "Look, you could be the second coming of Jordan but if the team isn't behind you, you'll flounder."

"What do you suggest?"

"Learn to play nice in the sandbox. Stop acting like a one-man show. Most of the guys understand their role and if you show them some respect, they will fall in line."

"When have I been disrespectful?"

Sloane looked up from her plate of assorted meats and

cheeses. "You're a cocky little shit and it's written all over your face."

"Listen, I'm an elite ballplayer. I've worked hard to perfect my craft, and I'm not going to dim my light to make others feel comfortable."

Both Sloane and Deion broke into uncontrollable laughter.

"Did he say dim his light?" Deion wiped away a tear.

"Sounding like he read one too many self-help books." Sloane rested her hand on her pregnant belly which jiggled as she laughed.

"Okay, well fuck you Deion. And on a lesser more respectful level, fuck you as well Sloane."

"Don't shoot the messenger," Sloane said.

"Look, I've been in this game far longer than you and I've worked on teams with all types of personalities and big egos. The times I was happiest were when I was vibing with my teammates. You don't have to be BFFs but there needs to be mutual respect."

"If I didn't respect the players, I wouldn't have agreed to join the team."

"Then show it motherfucker."

"How exactly do I do that?"

"I'm glad you asked. Each month we have a team-building function. The players take turns planning the event and the others show up."

Shit, I didn't know I'd be leaving with homework. "What type of event?"

"It can be whatever you want. But no strippers, no drugs, no gambling. I'll add you to the rotation."

My voice elevated in pitch. "What does that mean?"

"That you need to plan and coordinate an event for the team. Damn are you dense?" My eyes must have bulged from my head because Deion added. "You can have your assistant make the arrangements. You do have an assistant, right?"

"Yes."

"Just checking because you have no friends, no place to live, and zero bitches."

"I have bitches."

Sloane and Deion both flashed me a dubious look.

"I can plan something, no problem."

"Aldridge, no corny shit. This is your chance to make a good impression."

"I understand the assignment, don't worry about me."

DEION'S WORDS STUCK WITH ME. MOSTLY THE PART ABOUT having no social life. So, when Dante reached out and suggested we go on a double date, I actually agreed. Well first I said no because other than Danessa I didn't know any other women in Vegas. Dante shut me down with the offer to set me up with one of his lady friends. I immediately said no again because I did not want Dante's sexual hand-me-downs. He assured me he wouldn't do me dirty.

I finally agreed on the following conditions, no MILFs don't get me wrong, older women were great, but I was looking for someone I might be able to vibe with long term. No kids. Eventually I wanted kids, but I wasn't ready to date a woman who came with an insta family. Situations like that required you to come correct, and I wasn't interested in anything serious just yet. No friends of Anika. I loved Anika as the sister of my ex, but she was not remotely my type. How she and Danessa were raised in the same house was beyond me because the two couldn't be more different.

After attending an NA meeting, I rushed home to shower and change before heading out to meet Dante at Sin City Playland, an arcade facility with food, drinks, and popular top forty hits so loud you could hear it from the parking lot. Tonight was my first date since moving to Vegas and I felt a bit out of practice. First dates were always awkward, so I would rely on my pro basketball player status to do the heavy lifting tonight.

Checking in on the main level, I walked up the stairs which opened up to the first of three gaming floors. The music and people laughing and shouting were in competition. It was a bit of a sensory overload with ringing, dings, and chimes going off every other second. I didn't have to find Dante, he found me piecing the noise with a shrill whistle. Turning in the direction of the noise, I spotted him waving me over.

"You made it." We exchanged daps.

"I said I'd come and I did."

"I bet ten dollars you'd flake on us," Anika said.

"Excuse me?"

"You're a flake, don't act surprised."

"Speaking of flakes, where is my date?"

Anika and Dante exchanged a glance. "She's loading her gaming card."

Rubbing my hands together, I peppered them with questions. "What's her name? Where's she from?"

"Aren't you eager? I know it's been a hot minute since you had any pussy but calm down," Anika said.

"Why does everyone think I'm hard-pressed for sex?"

Anika patted my arm like I was a pathetic loser.

"When's the last time you experienced a nut that wasn't self-induced?"

I snatched my arm from her touch. "I don't have trouble in the woman department, thank you."

"Says the man who needed me to set him up on a blind date," Dante said.

"So, I'm a lame for trying to meet new people in this city?"

Dante and Anika consulted one another. "Yes," they said in unison.

This was the last time I hung out with these two. I didn't need to be ganged up on. If this mystery woman wasn't a ten, we'd all be brawling cause I wasn't going to subject myself to insults and a five in the face. The crowd around us seemed to part like the Red Sea and there was Danessa. It took me a few beats to make the connection this wasn't an extreme coincidence, Danessa was my date for the night. Did she willingly agree to this?

When Danessa caught sight of me, her face crumbled. Got it, she'd been hoodwinked like me. Knowing Anika, she'd probably straight up lied to get Danessa here. Danessa's face transitioned from surprise to irritation to clenched-fist rage. Turning to Anika, she unleashed her fury. "Are you fucking kidding me. You promised."

"I know, but I lied."

"Fuck you, Anika. I am so tired of your shit." Danessa shoulder checked her sister on her way past me and down the stairs.

"Danessa wait," I called after her, shooting the disastrous duo an angry look.

I caught up with Danessa almost halfway down the block. "Hey, can you slow down?"

"I'm done with her. Everything is an opportunity to

embarrass me or make me uncomfortable." Danessa shifted her weight from side to side as if she couldn't contain the hostile energy flowing through her body.

"You were ambushed too."

"I explicitly told her not to play matchmaker when it came to you and me, and she did the complete opposite."

"I should have known Dante and Anika would find a way to turn this into a shit show."

"Do you know she actually thinks you're still in love with me?"

My half strangled laughter rang out. "That's crazy." Why would I still be in love with my ex who I haven't seen or thought about in over five years? It's not like I was secretly stalking her social media pages and practically had an aneurysm when she was briefly engaged. No, no I was definitely not in love.

"It's delusional. Some fairytale about second chances and fate." She rolled her eyes and waved her hands like the thought of a do-over was nonsensical. I was all for redos, reheating leftovers, replaying songs, retracing my steps, reporting for duty. Okay that last one didn't make sense, but you get my drift.

Danessa didn't get mad often so when she was angry, you knew you'd fucked up. And Anika clearly fucked up because the thought of being on a date with me was so unsettling, Danessa was shaking with rage.

"Dante is just as bad. He claimed he was setting me up with one of his homegirls. Now I'm over here looking stupid for believing him because I don't think he has any friends who are female. I'm pretty sure this plan was to hook us up all along. Why Dante is so invested in this little charade, I'll never understand."

"Because he's balls deep in my sister and he'd probably wrestle an alligator if she asked him."

"Okay, I didn't need that visual."

"Wrestling an alligator?"

"No, the disturbing graphic balls deep visuals."

"When did you turn into a pussy?"

I clutched my chest. "Wow, ma'am it's nine o'clock. I don't feel comfortable talking about ball sacks and pussy until well after midnight."

"So demure."

"I'm a gentleman and I expect to be treated as such," I joked.

"A delicate six-foot-five flower."

"I'm in my soft guy era." I kept my composure for as long as I could before cracking up and Danessa followed suit. Laughing with her was my favorite pastime. She had two laughs, her soft dainty chuckle and then her maniacal Joker on steroids life. That was the laugh I loved the most. It was like she was an evil genius who'd just hatched her next plan for world domination.

Danessa unfolded her body as the remaining laughter waned. "I wasn't even interested in going on a date, but you know Anika, she guilted me until I agreed."

"Yeah, I was apprehensive too. But everyone's been telling me you're not going to make friends locked in your hotel room. And it's hard to disagree with them."

"I'm sorry. You probably thought you'd been hooked up with a baddie and then you saw me."

"I was surprised, yes, but don't act like you don't clear the baddie category."

Now that her frustration was dissipating, I was briefly treated to an appreciative smile. "You know what? I blame myself because what the fuck was I thinking trusting my sister."

I checked my watch. "Do you want me to walk you to your car?"

"No, I'm not trying to ruin your night any further."

"For the record my night wasn't ruined because you're here."

"Yeah right, I'm sure you had high hopes for a very different ending to this evening."

My brows climbed my forehead. "Are you talking about sex?"

Danessa hitched an uncertain shoulder.

"I did not have plans on having sex tonight. You know me, I'm a bit of a prude. I need at least three or four dates before I give up the cookie."

"You are definitely a slow starter but when you warm up, you get to cooking."

When it came to Danessa I'd been preheating for weeks now. All I needed was the green light and I'd be ready to slide inside and make her cream. But we were just friends, and I needed to remember that so I didn't end up with a broken heart part deux. *How many times do you think one could survive heartbreak?* I'd been through one and it was similar to a death. Not only did I lose Danessa, but I lost my plans for the future. Everything I thought I knew about myself and the life I wanted was turned on its head because one woman stopped loving me. The fact we willingly gave people the ability to destroy us was madness.

"Let's make the most of the unexpected. I mean I got a fresh cut and all dressed up for the occasion. This place looks like fun. And I'm always up for some friendly competition."

"You don't have to be the glass half full guy."

"I'm not. I could think of far worse things than spending time with you. I saw a Need for Speed game that was just begging for you to play it and ram your souped-up car into a wall."

"I'm better on the straightaway. Curves are more challenging."

"You never slow down."

"If I slow down, I'll get passed by the other cars," she shouted. Danessa was serious about her failed strategy.

"So, your plan is to scrape your car on the side of a mountain instead of … oh I don't know … learning how to drive?"

"You play your way, and I'll play mine."

"So, what do you say? Let me dust you on the course and show you how a real professional handles a curve."

She craned her neck, looking around me. "Is the professional stopping by later or—"

"Mofo, I'm the professional. I went to Disneyland, they had a *Cars* racetrack attraction. I got certified and everything."

"Trust me, it's not going to help. I'm way better than I used to be."

"I sincerely doubt that."

"You're going down."

DANESSA

ALDRIDGE EASILY BEAT ME IN EVERY NEED FOR SPEED race. But I redeemed myself on Pac-Man and we came out even in head-to-head Mortal Kombat rounds. We were now at the Skee-Ball machines, and Aldridge was making a big show of stretching before we started to play.

"If I win this game, I need a new title like Gamemaster," he said.

"I will not be calling you that."

"All this dominance needs to be recognized."

"I could call you Lil Big Head. Because your ego is getting out of hand."

There was a gleam in his eye. "I'll admit I have a big ego, but everything I say I back up tenfold."

"Do you need to trash talk at every conceivable opportunity?"

"If you're afraid to lose, just say that."

"I don't lose."

"You were literally so bad at Need for Speed the game malfunctioned and couldn't read your card. I think it had secondhand embarrassment for you."

"Did I or did I not bitch slap the shit out of you and then slice you in half on the last game?"

"My hands were sweaty."

I shoved him. "No, you can't make excuses."

"I got a finger cramp. I'm out of practice."

"You need to add finger conditioning to your workout routine. My fingers stay ready."

"I'm sure they do." Aldridge simulated finger banging.

This time I swatted his arm aggressively. "I have other tools for that."

"Love a woman who stays suited and booted."

Hinting at sex acts with my ex was not something I'd have predicted. But flirting was kind of fun, and I was so good at it. If they were giving out medals for best flirt, I'd at least win a silver. Flirting was entertaining because there were no real expectations for anything more. You could test the water without getting wet. Not that I was testing things out with Aldridge. We were friends, old pals, comrades, homies. He was the lil homie, lil big homie. Extremely fine homie. The homie that walked with a slight limp because his dick was so big.

Aldridge swiped his card to activate our game. I started out rough but quickly caught my stride and sunk three balls worth fifty each. He talked smack the entire time. How he could hit fifties and hundreds consistently was maddening. Like I said, shit just came easy to him. When the game ended, it was clear I'd been dusted and I begrudgingly accepted defeat.

"You had an unfair advantage because your arms are so long."

"I can't help it I don't have T-Rex arms like you."

"My arms are perfectly proportioned like everything about me."

"You are perfect in every way except when it comes to arcade games."

"Excuse me, are you Aldridge Mosley?" A young man asked standing among a group of friends.

"Yeah."

"See I told you." He spat out to a friend before turning back to Aldridge. "I knew it was you. We're so hype to have you in Vegas bro."

"Thanks, I'm happy to be here."

"Can we get a picture?" a girl with braces asked.

"Of course." Aldridge seemed in his element as if being approached by strangers was perfectly normal. But I guess for him it was. I often forgot how much of a big deal he was, not just in Vegas but in the NBA.

"I got it." I grabbed the girl's phone and took several photos.

"I can't wait to tell everyone we met you," another guy with red hair said.

"I appreciate the love."

"You have no idea. I know you're gonna bring us a championship."

Aldridge flashed his signature smile. "I'm hoping."

"You got this bro. Thanks again."

"Have a good night." He waved to the group who were all smiles and excited chatter as they walked away.

"Wow, talk about pressure," I said.

"I'm used to it. The organization talks about me in interviews like I'm the second coming of Christ. Expectations are high."

"But at the end of the day you're just one man."

"When we were together, you seemed to think I was up there with the greats McCabe Senior, Jordan, LeBron."

"And I still do. That hasn't changed. But people can't expect you to deliver a ring in your first year with the team."

"That's what I was brought here to do." He nodded and we walked back to our table. Taking our seats, the waitress appeared to check if we wanted more drinks or appetizers. Aldridge ordered truffle fries.

My chest tightened at the thought of all these expectations being laid at his feet. Ramblers Nation could be fanatical. And their love came with conditions and the minute Aldridge didn't deliver they would turn on him. "But what if you can't?"

"I'll disappoint a whole lot of people."

"And that's why I don't like sports. It places undue pressure on players that no one can realistically live up to."

"They aren't paying me millions of dollars for my sparkling smile and winning personality. What would you tell me before each game?"

I paused to recall our many pregame conversations. In college it became quickly apparent Aldridge was a phenom. There were banners with his face front and center. Anywhere we went in our small college town, business owners would comp him. I don't think he ever paid for a meal the four years we were there. He also experienced an immense burden at nineteen with grown adults looking up to him like he was their idol. "Try your best but if you lose, you're still a winner to me."

"While you were telling me to do my best, which I appreciated, I was telling myself winning is a habit, and I'm in the habit of winning."

"You've already accomplished so much and I'm sure you're going to do much more, but I just want you to be realistic."

"World class athletes aren't realistic. If I train hard and I'm disciplined, I will reap the fruits of my labor."

I slipped my hand in his. "No matter what happens

this season, I want you to know I think you're an amazing human. And your value isn't just derived by how many games you win."

Aldridge released a nervous chuckle.

"I mean it. I'm really into self-care and positive affirmations. I always keep a self-help book on deck."

"This is a real reach coming from the woman who always had several irons in the fire."

"And you know where that got me? Burnt out. I'm just offering up some friendly advice. I know this is going to be an exciting season filled with ups and downs. But just remember even when things are down, you're still important and loved."

His right eye twitched and he let go of my hand. "You love me?"

"Aldridge I've always loved you. That never stopped because we ended. I'm sure you feel the same."

He swung his head in a no. "I was mad at you for a really long time, so my feelings are kind of muddled."

"Oh." My lungs constricted making it hard to breathe. Breaking up with Aldridge was the hardest relationship decision I'd ever had to make, because there wasn't an inciting incident. He never cheated, he put me first, he was a gentleman, he didn't ignore me to hang out with his friends, he'd text back almost immediately, he was genuinely supportive, and in his eyes I walked on water. Our breakup was a case of the right person at the wrong time. Or the right person who just happened to pick the worst career.

He rearranged the condiments on the table. "Danessa you have to know there was nothing I wouldn't have done for you." He met my gaze, and his brown eyes were layered with regret and pain. "I honestly don't understand why I wasn't enough."

My heart bowed at the thought he'd been carrying that belief around all these years. "No … Aldi—"

Anika came walking up to our table dancing like she was Mary J. Blige, kick and all. "Dante just asked me to marry him."

The blood drained from my face. "What?" Aldridge and I said in unison.

"I know. He just dropped to one knee and proposed." She flashed her ring finger with a fake ruby ring you get from one of those candy machines. It barely fit her finger, but she was beaming with pride.

I went into problem solver mode. "You can't get married, you two barely know one another."

Dante smacked my sister on the ass. "I know I can't live without her."

I popped out of my seat and yelled, "Are you out of your fucking mind?"

Aldridge stood standing in between us. "Danessa, chill."

"No, I will not chill. My sister just got engaged at an arcade with a plastic ring."

"You need to get over this because you're going to be my maid of honor."

I grabbed Aldridge's arm and pulled him to my eye level. "I don't have the bandwidth for this right now."

"Do you wanna leave?"

"I want to jump off of a bridge."

Anika tossed her arm around me. "Nessa …" Her voice was a song. "You need to take some deep breaths. Dante's going to be your brother-in-law. And eventually you'll love him as much as I do."

"Bitch you better be fucking joking."

She looked to Aldridge for congratulations. "Are you happy for me Aldi?"

"If you like it, I love it."

Anika gasped. "You can give me away. It's going to be a family affair."

I shrugged Anika's hand from my shoulder. "Can you walk me to my car?"

"Sure." Aldridge nodded.

I collected my things and headed toward the exit. "Don't tell Mom I want to break it to her in person," Anika called out.

We walked in silence through the outdoor mall for several minutes. "You're pouting."

"I'm not pouting."

"Why are you so upset?"

"Because that's not how this is done. Love is just not that simple."

"Are you mad or are you jealous?"

I stopped in my tracks. "I don't wanna marry Dante."

"I think you know what I meant."

"Okay, I feel like I've done everything right and Anika has done everything wrong and she always comes out on top. I've followed every fucking rule and made sacrifices, and I have zero to show for it. A few years ago, I was the one engaged. I was the one getting married."

"What happened?"

Aldridge is what happened. "That's not the point. I do think marrying Dante after just a few weeks is a bad idea. But at least Anika is living. Me on the other hand, I'm just stuck in place. Shit, I'm probably regressing. No man, a law school dropout, with a job I'm not over the moon about, back in the city I grew up in."

"Wait, you didn't finish law school?"

His question helped to feed my sense of inadequacy. "No, I quit because it was too hard, and I didn't know anybody."

"Okay, that's okay. Everybody's journey is different."

"That's the thing everyone is on a journey, but my mode of transportation is broke down on the side of the road."

"So, get out and walk."

"Stop, stop." I held up a silencing hand.

"Stop what?"

"Stop trying to be sensible and let me vent."

"Okay you've got this, the floor is yours."

"I didn't realize my life was going to be this fucked up." Aldridge's jaw clenched; it was clear he wanted to object. "Don't speak. I just thought I'd be further ahead at this point. I'm not happy ..." I covered my eyes with my hands. "God, I don't know why I'm telling you this." My attention was drawn to a couple across the way who appeared lost in love. I barely remembered what that felt like. "I'm not happy with the choices I've made. I feel like my feet are in quicksand and when I make the slightest movement, I just sink further.

"I know objectively someone looking in would envy my life. I own a business, I drive a nice car. I have beautiful hair and a wardrobe most women and some men would kill for. But I feel like I'm wasting my potential. I don't want to be the pretty, cool girl. I want to be a boss bitch who grabs her dreams by the fucking balls and just clamps down on it." I made my hands look like claws to drive home my point. "You know just ... ugh."

I couldn't have these types of conversations with Anika. She was too easily distracted and would just tell me

I was being ridiculous and put on her bad bitch playlist as a rallying cry. "Say something."

"You told me not to speak, dear."

"Yeah, but I'm over here pouring my heart out and you're giving me radio silence." I tapped on a pretend microphone. Bueller, Bueller?"

"I … understand … where you're coming from."

"How could you?"

"You don't think I feel inadequate?"

"No … you're Aldridge Fucking Mosley. You are a big fucking deal. You have endorsements with Nike and Powerade."

"And Lexus."

In spite of my mood, I couldn't help but giggle. "You just had to slip that in there."

"Just want the record to be accurate."

"You're proving my point. You have everything you could ever want."

"Danessa, I don't think you realize how difficult these past few years in the NBA have been for me."

"What do you mean?"

"Nice try but we're talking about your problems not mine."

"I know what my problem is, it's me."

"I think you're being too hard on yourself. You're twenty-six, that's young. Do you know our frontal lobe may not even be fully developed yet?"

Rubbing my head I said, "I didn't know that."

"So how are you going to be hard on yourself when you most likely still have a hole in your head?"

"Well, when you put it that way."

"Our twenties are for figuring shit out. If you don't like the path you're on, pivot. You are not stuck, you're paralyzed, there's a difference. Get out of your fucking head and stop comparing yourself to others. You do not want what Anika has because those two are going to end up in jail or in front of a judge."

"Don't jinx it."

"You were the one who was saying what a horrible idea it was."

"Yes, but I don't want to put any bad juju on it."

"Danessa you own a company you built from the ground up. Not many people can do that."

"Yes, all true but I just saw myself someplace else at this age."

"What did you think you were going to solve? World hunger?"

"I had a plan."

"Mmm, yes your plan."

"Real estate pays the bills, and it feels really good to watch a couple's faces light up when they find their home. It's funny no matter how rich the person, there's always that moment of excitement as the possibilities for that house and their future kind of flashes before their eyes. And I think seeing that hopeful look year after year just made it more apparent I didn't have anything to be excited about."

"You have your entire life ahead of you. That should make you excited."

"Every day giving tours of houses I could never afford. It's not very challenging. It's not open heart surgery.

"You're squeamish."

"Okay it's not basketball. You get to wake up each day and do something you're passionate about. I don't have that."

Aldridge hooked his thumb under my chin, bringing

my eyes to meet him ensuring he had my full attention. "You can start over at any time. Danessa you are the smartest woman I know. You don't settle for anyone, not even me. Your drive, your passion that's what made me fall for you. You used to be Team Never Scared, and now you're getting spooked by a potential plot twist."

"You have to say that. You can't say you know what Danessa, you're right. Your life is really unfulfilling."

"Okay first I don't sound like that."

"And second?" I giggled.

"If you believed in yourself just a quarter as much as I believe in you, you'd be unstoppable. Life doesn't always give you what you need, but it will always give you what you settle for."

"Damn, that was a word."

"I've been attending church virtually every Sunday, so I'm damn near an ordained minister."

If Aldridge was my man this would be the part where I sucked his dick on the ride home until his eyes rolled back and we veered into oncoming traffic. And then when we got to the house the shit I'd let this man do to every orifice of my body would be obscene.

"Danessa?"

"Yes." I spoke that word entirely too breathy.

"Did I make you feel a little bit better?"

"Yeah, thank you for listening."

"Of course."

He opened my car door. "Aldridge, I missed this. Being able to talk to you."

"Me too."

"I'm glad we decided to give the friend thing a go. Are you glad?"

"Uh-huh."

"Well, that isn't a ringing endorsement."

"My bad. Being your friend is good. I planned on giving you a friendship bracelet the next time I saw you to solidify how dang stinking happy I am to count you as a friend."

"Okay you put too much on it. Dial it back."

"Do you remember that big headed doll back when we were kids with the bowl cut?"

"The My Pal dolls?"

"Yeah, I wanted one of those dolls but my dad said, 'No son of mine is walking around with no damn doll.' Which was dumb because the kid in the commercial was a boy. And him and the doll were going down the slide together and drinking out of juice boxes—"

"Get to the point."

"The point is you're my real life My Pal doll. Friends till the end."

"That was Chucky."

"It still applies. But if you prefer, you're the Sinclair to my Overton."

"They were a couple."

"Not at first but point taken. You're the Max to my Khadijah."

"Wow you are such a dork?"

"Yeah, but I'm a cute dork. I'm a 'Here me out' type of dork. Anyway, I had fun. Maybe ... we ... should do this again." Aldridge was probably stuttering at the realization he'd just lightweight asked me on a date. "Not, not like a date ... but on some friend zone type vibe. You don't have to wear makeup or dress to impress, and I will try not to look so devastatingly handsome. And when the check comes, we just split that bad boy right in half like King Solomon. Because friends don't make friends pay for their app, entrée, and dessert."

"And after the meal we'll just go to our respective homes. Because that's what friends do," I added on.

"Sometimes, occasionally friends have sleepovers." I had to fight off the laugh bubbling in my chest. "You know with the face mask and pajamas, maybe a good rom-com."

"And then in the morning they go to brunch at that trendy spot everyone's raving about."

"Cut to twenty years from now and they're picking out wallpaper for the guest bathroom. Because friendship."

"I should go."

He plunged his hands in his pockets. "Text me when you get home. It could be a quick 'I'm home,' message or a photo. I don't … I don't know. I'm going to let you figure that out."

I laughed so loudly passersby several rows away looked in our direction. "Goodnight, Aldridge."

"Drive safe."

ALDRIDGE

THE RAMBLERS PLAYED A HANDFUL OF EXPOSITION GAMES BUT today was the first official game of the season. Preseason allowed us to get accustomed to playing together as a team and anticipating what our teammates would do. I appreciated that our first game was in Vegas. It was nice to have your city rooting for you.

As the lights dimmed, Colin Pratt leaned into me and said, "Don't fuck up newbie." I didn't respond, he was just trying to get into my head. But the fact I was starting, and he would be sitting on the bench spoke volumes. The announcer introduced the visiting team, the Portland Trail Blazers, first. I shook out my limbs and rolled my neck while he did.

During our warmup I spotted Danessa, my mother, and Anika in the crowd. I'd offered to fly my mother out for the game, she always attended my first game of the season. It was like my one superstition, well that and tapping on the locker room door three times before the start of every game. What I didn't expect was for my father to also be in attendance. My mother kept that part a secret, probably because she knew I would've told her he wasn't welcome.

Panning over to my father he had a drink in his hand, it probably wasn't his first of the night, and unlike my mother who appeared excited my dad looked pissed off. As if my mother dragged him to this game and he'd rather be anywhere but here. If I were an unemployed custodian with a son playing professional ball I'd be beaming from ear to ear. But the only time my father bragged about me was when he thought he could get something out of it.

The announcers' tone enlivened, and the crowd started to stomp their feet. "And now the starting lineup for your LAS VEGAS RAMBELERSSSSS!" The instrumental version of Nipsey Hussle's "Grinding All My Life" played loudly in the background.

"At power forward, standing six foot eight, with power, finesse, and the heart of a lion, from UCLA … number seven, CAMERON 'THE TANK' BRADLEY!!" Bradley pounded his chest, flexing to the crowd as lights swirled around him.

"At the shooting forward position, a man who can do it all, the Swiss Army knife of this squad, standing six foot two, from the University of Kentucky, number eleven, TYLER WILLIAMS!!" Williams threw up three fingers indicating his triple-threat versatility as the crowd roared.

And at center, the six-foot four beast in the paint, reigning from the heart of New Orleans, the man who owns the rim … number twenty-three, DARRRIIIIUS JOHNSON!!" The crowd erupted as the spotlight flashed over Darius, who pumped his fist toward the fans in the stands.

At the shooting guard, a sharpshooter from deep, a defensive nightmare for opponents… Standing six foot five from Duke University, number twenty-seven, DEION 'DECK' MCCABE!!" The arena literally shook as Deion coolly strolled to center court, nodding to his teammates.

"At point guard, standing six foot five, hailing from

Northeast Philly, a man with speed and court vision like no other, he's the playmaker, the spark plug … number four ALDRIDGE 'THE TOWER' MOSLEY!!" Making my way to center court I raised both arms, hyping the crowd, ready for tip-off.

"Your Las Vegas Ramblers, ladies and gentlemen! Make some noise."

The next forty-eight minutes of gameplay were a blur. Playing basketball was kind of an out-of-body experience. You know at the end of the day when you get in your car and then next thing you know you're in your driveway; it was sort of like that. My body relied on muscle memory to make the three-pointers. Even though I couldn't see him, I knew McCabe was nearby, so I passed the ball to a fixed point behind me and Deion drove to the hole.

I ran to the other end of the court, setting up a screen that denied the Trail Blazers' center from making his basket. At the free throw line I locked in, sinking both baskets to widen our lead. When I stole the ball, I drove to the basket with nothing but red shirts behind me. With a spin, I threw down a double-handed dunk. Celebrating with a roaring scream. McCabe and Dante dapped me up before Coach Justus called me to the bench. With five minutes left in the game, we'd secured the win and I was allowed to rest. I passed by Colin who was coming into the game to relieve me.

"Don't fuck up our lead," I said under my breath. Petty? Yes, but it felt good.

After the game and press interviews, I met up with my parents in the members only lounge. You either had to be a player, staff, or extremely rich to get in. When my mother spotted me, she shot up. "There's my baby." She pulled me into an embrace and we swayed side to side. There was just something about a mother's hug that fixed what ailed you.

I looked around hoping no one overheard. "Mom please, not in mixed company."

"Well, I haven't seen you in months and I'm just so happy for you're doing well. That was a heck of a game."

"Thank you."

"Your father and I are so proud. Aren't we Lamonte?" She looked to my father. This was normal, my mother speaking for the both of them and my father grunting in agreement.

"Hmm." My father was already looking for the waitress to refill his glass.

Taking a seat I said, "I'm glad you could make it out. I wish you'd told me you *both* were coming."

"You're so busy, I didn't want to be a bother. Your assistant, Nori, helped me get everything squared away."

"Did you tell Nori Dad was joining?"

"No, we paid for his ticket on our own. Didn't want to spoil the surprise." More like didn't want to ask for permission and risk me saying no.

My phone dinged with an incoming message.

Nessa: Great game. Thank you for inviting me.

Aldridge: Where are you?

Nessa: Stuck in traffic.

Aldridge: I was hoping to see you tonight and thank you personally for coming.

Nessa: Your folks are here, we can connect some other time.

> Aldridge: The thought of seeing you after the game was kind of the highlight of my day. Don't get me wrong my mom is great but she ain't you.

> Nessa: …

> Aldridge: Turn around.

> Nessa: …

"What does a man have to do to get a fucking drink?" My dad yelled.

Looking up from my phone, I casually said, "I think you've had enough."

My father's eyes flashed with anger. If I wasn't a grown man who now towered over him, he'd be ready to slap the piss out of me. Lamonte Mosley loved hitting defenseless women and children. I think that shit actually brought him joy. Making others feel small and afraid. "Did I ask for your opinion? You're the child. Don't tell me shit. I do what the fuck I want. Mind your fucking place." My dad's voice was elevated and drawing attention. "Where the fuck is my drink!"

"I'll get you another one. It's fine." I headed to the bar. This is why he wasn't invited. He was always an embarrassment. My dad assumed I was trying to show him up when I offered to pay for a meal or cover a flight. Fake offended but when he needed a little spending money or help paying a bill, he had no shame about forcing my mother to call and ask. My mom would say it was for her to get her nails done or that Tootie, my sister, needed new shoes because she was growing like a weed.

My phone dinged again. It was Danessa and instantly my mood was lifted.

Nessa: Where do you want to meet?

Aldridge: Are you hungry?

Nessa: I'm always hungry.

Aldridge: Meet me in thirty minutes at the Bites and Brews Plaza.

Nessa: Okay.

My mom came up behind me leaning her head on my arm. "He's just tired."

"No Mom, he's drunk."

"Your father likes to celebrate." She would always defend him so there was no use fighting it. "I saw Danessa, she's still as pretty as ever."

"That she is."

"Are you two—"

"No, just friends."

"I like the thought of you making friends out here. She's a nice girl. Good influence."

"Yep."

My mother shifted so we were facing each other. "Are you okay?"

"I'm good."

"Are *you* okay? I pointed to the bruise on her arm.

"You know me ... I have two left feet. It's good laying eyes on you. Let's not wait so long between our next visit."

I drove my folks back to their hotel. Nori had the foresight to book my mom into a hotel other than the W. After dropping them off, my father stumbled with each step and my mother insisted she didn't need any help, I hightailed it over to the plaza which was an open air food truck court with seating and music.

Danessa was sitting on a bench near the entrance so she saw me coming from the parking lot. "Born and bred in Northeast Philly, give it up for number four, Aldridge Mosley," Danessa imitated the Ramblers announcer from tonight's game.

"Please, please hold your applause." I approached with a side hug.

"You were amazing tonight. On fire. Unstoppable."

"Thanks," I whispered because she was drawing the attention of lookie loos.

"Are you embarrassed? Am I embarrassing you?"

"No, I just want a laid-back night. No autographs, no pictures, no platitudes."

"I'm down for a night of just food and good conversation."

"I'm going to get a burrito the size of both of my hands."

"That's a very big burrito."

"What about you?"

"Actually, a burrito the size of your hand sounds really appetizing. It will help sop up all the beer sloshing around in my stomach."

"Oh so you and Anika had a time tonight."

"The tickets you gave us came with free beer and wine. Which your dad also appreciated."

I rolled my eyes. "Let's order." After getting our food, we headed to a small vacant area with two Adirondack chairs separated by a table with a fire pit in the middle.

Danessa took one bite of her burrito and broke out into her happy dance. "This was a good choice."

"You're not the only one who knows about hidden gems in Vegas."

"This place is hardly a hidden gem, but it's a nice way to spend an evening."

"Don't be a hater because I'm becoming well versed in all things Vegas."

"Really, do tell me more of what you've learned."

"Vegas has a rich history, you know Elvis … Tom Jones … the Rat Pack … the Bunny Ranch."

"How do you know about the Bunny Ranch?"

"Are you kidding, that's the reason I agreed to join the Ramblers."

"I thought Vegas was a shit hole?"

"I never called it that. It's hot as hell and the residents tend to stare, but I'm learning this city has some redeeming qualities."

"You're Aldridge Mosley of course people stare."

"Someone should tell them it's rude."

"I thought you'd be used to people asking for autographs and singing your praises." She pushed the foil from her burrito, taking another bite.

"I don't ever wanna get used to that. It's weird. I'm just a guy who's good with a ball. The Stan culture is disarming."

"You handle it well."

"Because I don't wanna be the headline story on SportsCenter. First rule of being an NBA player is, keep your nose clean."

Her brows inched up her forehead. "I don't think I could willing surrender my privacy for wealth and fame."

"Fame takes for sure but it also gives back when you have talent to go with the celebrity."

"Sounds like the cost is worth it for you."

"This job allows me to support my family. If I get stopped in the mall or at the grocery store so be it."

"The love from the fans is also a great motivator."

"There's nothing like locking eyes with a kid in the crowd with my jersey on. That's something you never get used to." I could never afford to attend professional sports games as a kid, but I did stand outside and arena waiting for my favorite player to make an appearance, and was rewarded with a signed basketball from Deion McCabe.

"It's cool knowing you're out here inspiring the next crop of young ball players."

"I don't know about all that." The thought of being someone idol was unsettling.

"Well, I do. Some kid is out there right now with your poster on their wall watching the highlights from tonight's game and taking notes." While I wore blinders singularly focused on my next goal, Danessa was always thinking about the bigger picture and my legacy. I was just manifesting a championship, but Nessa was already envisioning my number getting retired and me being inducted into the basketball hall of fame. I'd missed having her in my corner.

We both focused on our food and looked to the crowd for entertainment. I took the time to workshop the logistics behind a do over. There was a reason Danessa was back in my life. Maybe there were lessons we still needed to learn. Or perhaps it was the universe's way of telling me Danessa was my person, which was something I'd started to doubt the longer we were apart.

"I'm tapping out. I can't eat anymore."

"Lightweight." My burrito was already gone. "So did Anika go home?"

"No, she went to celebrate with her *fiancé*."

"That is still so bizarre. I mean he's a fuckboy, she's a fuckgirl. What could they possibly have in common?"

"The fuckary is the common thread. They're both chaotic and spontaneous. Just like their whirlwind romance."

"I say we place an over-under type bet on the union because there is no way."

"He gave her an official ring."

I gasped. "Shut up."

"Five carats, pear-shaped, flawless diamond."

"Oh shit, her pussy be talking."

"That's my sister you're referring to."

"Your sister got that good good. That Sergio Mendes 'Never Gonna Let You Go' type of pussy."

"I don't know who or what that is."

"Oh it's a classic song. It will give you all the feels."

"Right. Anyway, I think this wedding just might happen."

"I'm gonna get them a toaster oven but like from Williams Sonoma because your sister is bougie. Don't even ask me to include your name on the card. My gift is going to kill. And every time they reheat a Hot Pocket, they'll think of me."

"That's thoughtful."

"They'll probably be able to pass it down to their kids and shit. Generational wealth."

"I'm glad you think this is funny."

"What did Jemini have to say?"

"Jemini wants to invite five hundred people to the wedding. She thinks it should be a destination affair, and she's looking into the possibility of John Legend performing."

"Pfft, John Legend does not perform for players who

come into a game from off the bench. They're not getting John Legend. Maybe Johnny Gill."

"Wait, is John Legend on your wedding vision board?"

"What? I … I don't know what you mean. What's a vision board?"

"You're lying."

"I don't care who Mr. Legend performs for."

"Sure. So what else is on your wedding vision board?"

"Shiiiit I don't really know." I scratched my head acting like I didn't know exactly what my dream wedding would entail. I'd only considered marriage one time with Danessa and you know how that ended. "Let me think … okay so boom, beach wedding, lilacs, my wife will have three dresses, one for the ceremony, another for the reception, and the last one for the kick back after the older folk have gone home. Something a tad bit more racy, short, ass cheeks abundant. Cigars, mocktails that are so good you don't even notice the liquor is missing. My best friends from childhood all hyping me up. Bridesmaids all tens. Food immaculate, vibes top tier. Wedding night sex … scandalous."

"You've given this some thought."

"Nah, that was just off the top of my dome. I was freestyling that shit. What about you?"

"Small, intimate. Like a micro wedding. Just close family and friends. No great-uncle Lester's. No random lady who used to know me when I was little, asking me if I remember her. I want it to be one hundred percent authentic to the love me and my husband to be share. Maybe some food trucks like this or In-N-Out Burger. A cotton candy machine. A private moment right after the ceremony, just him and I."

Shit, sign me up. "That sounds dope."

"Really?

"I hope I'm invited."

Danessa leaned over the arm of her chair. "I hope you are too."

I don't know exactly what was happening. But this woman was my future wife, and I was prepared to beg, borrow, and steal to make that my reality.

Danessa turned her attention back to her margarita. "Did you know your father was coming tonight?"

"No." I wasn't in the mood to talk about parents, but I understood it's been forever since Danessa had seen my mother.

"It's nice to see the first-game tradition is still alive."

"She's been to all my first games."

"Your dad was less talkative."

"That's Lamonte Mosley, the life of the party."

"I'm surprised your mom is still with him."

"That's the thing. I don't know if my mom is scared or if she just actually loves him. We've talked about her leaving and she'll listen, but she also makes excuses for him. And it just pisses me off because how do you love someone more than yourself, more than your kids? Like he broke Duane's arm. Tootie peed the bed until she was twelve."

Danessa's expression was solemn. I wasn't telling her shit she didn't already know. When I was in college my sister, Tootie, would call me bawling her eyes out because our dad had come home drunk and looking to pick an argument. Duane was in jail, I was away at school and Tootie was left alone to deal with the broken pieces. And my emotions were mixed because while I was free of the drama, my sister was smack dab in the middle of it.

"I love my mom, but I swear for God I hate her just as much."

"She's a victim too."

"Yeah, but she was the adult. Like at seven I knew our family dynamic was fucked up. We could never have friends over. We had to lie about obvious bruises. At ten I was telling teachers who asked about my black eyes that I fell off the top bunk bed, I'm just clumsy and accident prone. I hate him. And I don't ..." My throat was tight and my chest was heavy and I needed to pause so I didn't lose my shit. "I hate him. And in the same moment I want him to say 'Good job, son. I'm so proud of you. I'm so proud ...'"

"Have you tired talking to him about this?"

My mind went back to the bruise on my mother's arm. "I try not to think about it. Sometimes Tootie will mention an argument or Mom crying and I just don't acknowledge it. Distance is a luxury because I can pretend that shit doesn't exist. I can go to sleep every night and just act like it's not happening anymore. What do they say? Out of sight, out of mind. But every time I get a call from an unfamiliar number I think, this is it. This is the call where the cops or a hospital tells me my mom is dead."

"Aldridge."

"I can't make my mom leave him. I can't want it more than she does."

"You have to remember your dad was significantly older than your mom when they met. And he did what abusers do. He isolated her, he groomed her. He made her believe that she wouldn't survive without him. Even now with a rich and famous basketball playing son. I'm not trying to make excuses for her but it's so complicated and deeply ingrained. They've been together for almost thirty years."

"I don't presume to know what my mom is thinking or what she went through. I just wish she made different choices. And not for me but for her. Because she deserves to be happy and the thought of her living a lifetime of sadness doesn't sit well with me." Danessa had moved from her chair to kneeling in front of me with her hand on my knee. "I wish he hadn't come to see me play."

"You know your mother loves you right?"

"I know that my father ruptured my eye socket and at the hospital my mother said I was hit with a baseball bat while playing outside."

"I don't have the words to make this all better. I just wish I could take away your pain."

"You can't fix something you didn't break. But you did show me I was capable of having a mature loving relationship. Until I met you, I avoided commitment because I feared I'd be just like my dad. Nurture versus nature, you know. I learned how to love with you and for that I'll always be grateful."

Danessa's bottom lip quivered, and tears streamed down her cheeks. I stood pulling her to her feet. "Please stop crying. Cause if you continue to cry then I'll start crying and get a headache."

Danessa's face brightened slightly as she wiped away the tears. Her shoulder brushed against my arm as we watched the water in the large fountain a few feet away shoot upward, swaying in synchronization with the music. The evening was warm, the kind that made the city feel like it was holding its breath.

It had been years since we'd been together, but time hadn't dulled the magnetism between us. If anything, it had become sharper, more potent. Every glance, every brush of skin sent electricity crackling through my body. I could feel her now, just inches away, the heat radiating off her. Her familiar and intoxicating floral vanilla fragrance pulled me closer.

Danessa turned to face me, the shadows of the lights scattered across the plaza danced across her delicate features. My heart thudded against my chest, louder than the music and commotion from the bustling crowd. It was impossible to deny the way my body reacted to her presence, the way my pulse quickened when she looked up at me like that, as if we were the only two people in the world. She took a step closer. Her movements were slow, almost hesitant. Her eyes searched my face as if trying to gauge whether she was crossing a line. I held my breath, unable to move, unable to break the invisible thread between us.

Then, so gently it almost hurt, she reached up and cupped my cheek, her thumb brushing the edge of my jaw. The simple touch sent a shockwave through me, and I leaned into it, into her. I closed my eyes for a moment, trying to steady my breathing, but the moment I did, the warmth of her breath against my skin forced them open. Leaning in she paused, lingering just inches away from my face. The anticipation was excruciating, the tension like static in the air between us.

With a slowness that only heightened the longing, Danessa pressed her lips against my cheek. It was soft, but the emotion behind it was anything but. Her kiss lingered, as if she was savoring the moment, pouring years of regret and desire into that single touch. Danessa's lips were warm, but the contact still sent a shiver down my spine, making my knees weak.

She pulled back and her eyes met mine, everything around us was moving at normal pace but it seemed like in our little bubble the world stood still. The air between us thickened with the unspoken things we'd left unsaid for far too long. I could feel the heat of her body, the barely restrained desire simmering beneath the surface. Her lips parted, but no words came out.

Instead, she let her fingers slide down my arm, my muscles tensed beneath her touch. Was it really that easy to just pick up right where we left off?

With her initial kiss still burning my skin, I stepped back. "Thanks for coming to my game." My voice was light as if my DNA had been sprinkled with a dash marshmallow fluff.

"I appreciated the invite. Even though I watched most of the game through my fingers."

"You just need to trust the process. I can feel a championship in my bones." My instincts were rarely wrong. The Ramblers were going to win it all this season, I was going to find the home of my dreams, and Danessa was going to remember why she fell in love with me.

DANESSA

"SORRY, I'M LATE." I JOGGED UP THE DRIVEWAY IN MY HEELS. "My other showing ran long and then I had to head back to the office for a closing."

"Wait, you have other clients? I thought I was getting an exclusive service."

"Ha, ha very funny. This place just dropped on the market, and it won't be there for long. You are one of the first people to see this home."

"Love the area."

"Up until now we've been pretty conservative with staying within your budget. But I thought I'd show you what you could get if you bumped it up just a smidge."

"How much more?"

"I want you to view it first ..." Aldridge rolled his eyes. "Keep an open mind and we'll discuss price at the end." Typically, when people knew the price point right off the bat their financial bias kicked in. We've all done it, you go shopping and you spot a beautiful pair of leather boots, but they cost two thousand dollars. Knowing the price up front is like dumping cold water on the fantasy that you could be a showstopper on a night out with friends.

"Sounds expensive."

"First look at this outdoor entrance. It's impressive, opulent but understated."

"It's nice."

"At night when it's all lit up, it's perfection." Unlocking the front door, we walked inside. "Upon entry you are immediately greeted by this living room. The walls and floors are neutral which allows you to determine the direction you want to go in aesthetically. High vaulted ceilings lead to the dining room in this open floor plan."

"I can see that."

I went about ticking off all the unique and interesting features of the home. It had been a long day and I was hoping to wrap up this showing, head to my condo and crawl into bed for the remainder of the weekend. "The property is wired with surround sound throughout. The chandelier over the dining table is custom-made and imported from Italy. And you have these big, beautiful sliding glass doors which lead to the courtyard."

"Are you okay?"

"Yeah of course. Why?"

"Because you're being real formal, real professional right now."

"I'm working." Even after all these years it was difficult to fool Aldridge, he knew me. When I was upset or worried, I tended to shut down and just stick to the facts. Today was no different. If I could have canceled this showing I would've, but like I said there would likely be multiple bids on this house by the end of the weekend.

"Yeah, but it's me and you're over here pointing out wall sconces and surround sound."

"I'm not here to entertain you."

"I know that Danessa; the vibe is just off."

"Are you here for the vibes or are you here for the house?"

"Look if you're having a bad day we can pin this for another time."

"I'm not having a bad day. I'm trying to do my job and you want a comedy show." I dropped my purse on the dining table. "How many real estate agents does it take to change a lightbulb?"

"I don't know."

"None, the lightbulb and wiring are in perfect working order and bright enough to illuminate an entire city block. You could search a lifetime and never find a lightbulb brighter or more energy efficient."

"That was a horrible joke."

"Moving on to the kitchen."

Aldridge grabbed my arm, stalling my steps. "Did I do something? Are you mad about the other night?"

"No, no, no." I pushed out an exasperated breath. "I received an email."

"Oh okay … like about … was it about me?"

Narrowing my eyes I searched his face. "No, it was from UNLV's law school."

"Are you in legal trouble?"

"No, I applied, and the email has a link that will determine my future." I was serious about needing a change. In the past few months, I'd submitted applications to several law schools. William S. Boyd was my top choice because it was local. After college, law school was my next step. Aldridge was on board with me attending law school at the University of Missouri. It wasn't my top pick, but it would allow us to remain together. We had it all planned out. We'd even been to Missouri apartment hunting. Our breakup stalled all those plans.

I'd already committed to Mizzou's school of law and had to deploy plan B with zero preparation. I ended up moving to Chicago to attend law school. The first semester was tougher than I'd anticipated and when my grandmother passed, I used that as my excuse to leave, claiming I needed to be closer to family. It was just supposed to be a year hiatus and then I'd apply to schools closer to Las Vegas. During that time, I got my realtors license and started making really good money. Then a year turned into two and the rest is history.

"Why would they reject you? You're Danessa Fucking Irwin an icon, a legend, a fashionista."

"I should have put that on my application. I'm Danessa Irwin. If you don't know, you better ask somebody."

"I'm just saying you had one of the highest GPAs in our graduating class."

"It's been five years."

"Doesn't change the fact you were top of your class and are currently a successful business owner. Those are all positive desirable qualities. You're working yourself up over an email you haven't even opened."

"Yes, because William S. Boyd is the only law school in Vegas. And if I don't get in, I'd be forced to look outside of the state and that comes with a host of other problems."

"What's the worst thing that could happen?"

"I don't get into Boyd. I spiral into a deep depression. I stop showering and start to lose my hair. I become a social recluse whose only friends are a trio of birds who hang out on my balcony. Even though they are only there because I feed them nuts. And then—"

"Oh, there's more." His eyebrows climbed his forehead.

"Then my condo gets foreclosed on because I haven't been working and now me and the birds are out on the street. I'm a twenty something single mother to three wild birds. Who's going to take care of Alvin, Simon, and Theodore," I yelled.

"Maybe you could put them up for adoption?"

"I'm all they have in the world." How could he seriously suggest I abandon them.

"How about we just rip off the Band-Aid. Obviously, I'm not going to let you go unhoused."

This conversation wasn't about him solving my problems. I had a sizable savings and if I was ever in a jam, I wouldn't ask my ex to bail me out. "It's not up to you. It's up to Wells Fucking Fargo."

"Danessa, I'm going to hold your hand when I say this. You are deeply troubled." I snatched my hand and swatted him away. "Let's just look and if it's a rejection I'll read Boyd Law for filth and if it's good news I tell you how amazing and dumb you are to ever think it would be any other result."

I clutched at my midsection. "My stomach hurts."

"Well this is a million-dollar home so you can't shit here."

I sputtered out a laugh. Aldridge was probably right. I'd received this email hours ago and was too chicken shit to open it, instead allowing myself to obsess over the possibilities and ruin my day. If I didn't get in it wasn't the end. It may feel like a chapter closing but there were other avenues I could pursue. But not getting in would be a resounding confirmation I wasn't good enough and perhaps this was all there was.

"Okay let's just do it." Pulling my phone from my purse, I located the email. Aldridge stood next to me intently focused on the screen. When I tapped on the email link I was directed to Boyd's admissions website and had to provide my name and the last four of my social. Pressing enter, a new window popped up and I read the message aloud, "We are happy to inform you that you have been accepted into William S. Boyd School of Law starting winter of next year." The phone dropped from my hand as I squealed. "I got in. I got in!" This moment felt momentous and waving my hands wasn't enough. I jumped into Aldridge's arms wrapping my legs around his waist. His huge hand rubbed my back as he spun us around.

"Congratulations. I never had any doubt."

I loosened my grip and landed with my feet back on the floor. "Thank you for believing in me."

"I believe in you because you're always a sure thing."

Swallowing hard, the reality of the moment hit me like a ton of bricks. "I think I'm going to throw up."

"No, we're not doing that. Today is about celebration. Tomorrow you can spiral into a new hypothetical doomsday scenario about your major, class size, and preferred professors but today we celebrate."

"You're right. It's time to pop bottles, blow up balloons …" My face lit up. "Or get a cake. I could definitely eat an entire sheet cake."

"So let's go celebrate. Let's make the rest of the day all about you."

"Okay." I couldn't help but smile from ear to ear.

"Do you want me to call your sister to join us, or you could invite some friends?"

"No, I just want it to be you. You know, small, intimate."

Aldridge's smile faded and he stared at me as if he were solving a puzzle or connecting dots. "I'm so proud of you."

His words tickled something deep within and tears fell from my eyes. "Thank you."

He cupped my face wiping away my tears with his thumb. "Happy tears, right?"

"Happy tears."

"Okay." Aldridge let me go and clapped his hands. "Let's get into some shit."

ALDRIDGE DROPPED ME OFF AT HOME WITH INSTRUCTIONS TO pack an overnight bag, and be prepared to leave in an hour. That allowed for a quick shower, outfit change, and frantically tossing clothes into my weekender bag with zero clue what I was packing for. We couldn't be going far, maybe one of the casinos for a bit of fun and a spa treatment.

When he picked me up, we were in a premium RideX and Aldridge was sporting a goofy smile.

"Well, this is very covert ops. Where are we going?"

"You'll find out when we get to our next destination."

"I don't like surprises."

"You're just going to have to cope."

"Is it—"

"Don't try to guess."

We ended up at North Las Vegas Airport a smaller airport reserved for helicopters and private planes. "It's a helicopter ride isn't it?"

"You're warm but still cold."

The car pulled alongside a jet parked on the runway with the passenger door open and boarding stairs in place. On the tarmac everything moved very fast, the driver transported our bags to the plane. A flight attendant greeted us at the bottom of the stairs. "Welcome to Zeppelin Air Mr. Mosley, once you are settled onboard, we can prepare for takeoff."

"We're flying?"

"Yes." He placed his hand on my back guiding me up the stairs.

Onboard my head was on a pivot. I'd never been on a jet before. It was spacious and we were the only two passengers. "Who else is joining us?"

"No one. Small and intimate, remember?"

"We can't just do this. Hop a plane to God knows where."

"Mexico."

"Mexico," I gushed. "No one knows where I'm at."

"That's what makes it exciting."

"I'm supposed to have brunch with Anika tomorrow."

"She'll understand."

"Aldridge?"

"Are you going to hem and haw the entire flight?" He dropped into the roomy leather seat.

"No."

"Great, buckle up, buttercup."

This wasn't my life, flying in private jets to beach front resorts. Shit, I hadn't packed a swimsuit, the thought of us leaving Vegas never crossed my mind, but thankfully I always kept my passport on me. I could be spontaneous given time to plan. Buckling my seatbelt, I leaned into the seat taking a few deep breaths. This was fine. This was perfectly fine. It would allow Aldridge and I a chance to spend uninterrupted time together. Just him, me, and his cognac eyes that could access my soul.

"Can I get you something to drink?" the flight attendant asked.

"Champagne? Is that possible?"

"This is a non-alcohol flight but I can prepare a delicious mocktail."

"That would be lovely. Thank you." Wow, Aldridge really took the no alcohol thing seriously. I'd heard of athletes with strict diets and exercise regimes. I guess this was just part of his conditioning.

I turned to Aldridge and demanded answers. "Are you going to tell me how you pulled this all off?"

"When you went home to go change, I made good use of my free time."

"You did all this?"

"Keep in mind I also have an amazing assistant who knows how to get shit done."

"Aldi?" My eyes probably took up half my face. When I went home to shower and change it took me an hour, maybe an hour and a half tops, and in that time he'd hired a private jet, secured a place for our stay and no doubt had other surprises in store. Anika was right, wealthy men did give better gifts.

"I know it's not much, if I had more time, I could've flown us to Italy or something."

I pressed my hand to his chest. "It's perfect, no notes."

On the ground in Mexico, we were met by another private car that escorted us to a house so impressive I had to pinch myself to confirm I wasn't dreaming.

"Welcome to Luna Del Pacifico. My name is Marisol, I will be your valet for the duration of your stay. We have you reserved for one night. How was your flight?"

"Like a hop, skip, and a jump," Aldridge said.

"That's what we like to hear. Follow me."

This was the type of place from an architectural magazine. Open spaces, that still managed to feel intimate. A kitchen with a walk-in fridge any chef would swoon over. The pantry was stocked with snacks and beverages and there were five bedrooms, two of which were primary. Both spacious with jaw dropping views and a bathroom I was going to enjoy getting ready in later tonight.

"For madam this will be your room. Feel free to settle in, I will be returning with refreshments shortly. Mr. Mosley please follow me."

This room was bananas. There was luxury and then there was whatever the fuck this was. Plenty of men had offered to fly me out to Paris or Bali and each time I declined. But this was something a girl could get used to. With the stunning views it felt like a nature retreat surrounded by trees. The ocean, which I could see from my window, sang a calming song. I was going to sleep like a baby tonight.

If I told Aldridge this was too much, and I'd have been cool with pizza and cold beer, he would brush my objections aside. He said we should celebrate, and this was definitely the better way to do it. A knock at my door pulled me from my thoughts.

"Ingresar," I called out.

Aldridge opened the door and was already in his swim trucks and nothing else. His thick muscular thighs were obscene. I'm talking explicit content. His shorts were well above his knees, showcasing his strong legs and from the waist up it was just sculpted muscle starting with the deep-set grooves just under his abs. I found myself zoning in on the tattoo of my name on his chest. He'd gotten it claiming he wanted me close even when we were apart. Why he hadn't covered it up years ago with a lion's head or the Liberty Bell was beyond me. If the roles were reversed, I wouldn't want a reminder of the person who broke my heart.

"I thought we could go swimming. We can walk to the beach or hit up the pool."

I sucked in air, cringing. "I didn't pack any swimsuits I thought we were going to a casino."

"It's all good. If you want to swim in your birthday suit, I wouldn't object, but there's brand-new swimsuits in the dresser. Just take your pick."

"You thought of everything."

"Meet me outside when you're ready. No rush."

———

It would appear Aldridge had settled on the pool. There were tapas and a pitcher of tamarind pineapple quencher. Marisol had already brought a glass to my room while I was changing.

"I can't believe we were in Vegas just a few hours ago," I said. Aldridge pulled his attention from the ocean in front of us to look at me and performed a double take. Friends didn't look at each other the way he was staring at me. His eyes tripping over my body like he was taking inventory or a mental picture to be called up at a later date. The swimsuit options were plentiful and for my part, I chose the tiniest one. My cups runneth over and my ass was on display.

"A place like this can really shift your perspective."

"Have you been here before?" I dropped into the queen-sized lounger next to him.

"Yeah, I came here for a few days before I landed in Vegas. Just needed to get my mind right, you know."

"I imagine this place tunes you right up." His lips twitched with a ghost of a smile. "What?"

"This is just nice. You, me, paradise."

"I can't thank you enough for this."

"Stop, you deserve to be celebrated."

"You could've just gotten me a cake."

"There's cake." I returned his goofy smile. "So just sit back, relax, and have a good time."

"Done and done." Putting on my sunglasses, I melted into the cushion. I'd been on edge all morning over that email, so to finally be able to breathe and have it be in a practical nature preserve was very satisfying. A random thought popped into my head and I needed confirmation. "Did your moving truck ever show up?"

"Yeah, it came just like you said."

"Great, I was just wondering because I never got a thank you card."

Aldridge chuckled. "You want a thank you card?"

"It's usually customary when someone does you a solid."

"Okay, here's your thank you card." He flipped me the finger.

"Wow, who raised you?"

"Katherine Mosley from Northeast Philadelphia and she ain't spending five dollars on a funky thank you card."

"We used to be a society. When I scratched your back, you returned the favor with a card and money inside."

"You sound like Jemini."

"I'm offended and gravely injured." Waving my hand over the space I continued. "I'll just consider this the thank you note."

Aldridge returned to his phone checking out Sports-Center's newsfeed, so I decided to check my missed messages. Nothing out of the ordinary, final closing documents, clients with questions, and a text from some guy I didn't remember giving my number to asking me on a date. Ignoring all of that I texted Anika.

Danessa: Guess where I'm at?

Anika: Three guesses, the gym, Trader Joes, or that Thai place we love.

Danessa: Nope. Mexico.

Anika: Excuse me?

I loved it when I could shock my sister, it was usually the other way around.

Danessa: Aldridge took me. A quick overnight trip.

Anika: What happened to being just friends?

Danessa: We still are.

Anika: So are you going to fuck him in Mexico?

Danessa: What? No.

Anika: A man. A fine ass man takes you out of the country for a spontaneous trip and you're not giving up the head.

The thought hadn't crossed my mind.

Danessa: Is that customary?

Anika: I've been flown out both domestically and internationally and each time I showed up and showed out.

Danessa: You sound like an escort.

Anika: And you sound like a prude. Girl, stop playing dumb and fuck that man. You know you want to.

I one hundred percent did. But if he brought me out here because he thought I'd feel the need to reciprocate he was dead wrong.

Danessa: We're just enjoying each other's company.

Anika: You can do that with his dick in your mouth.

I glanced at Aldridge to make sure he hadn't noticed the blush taking over my face.

Danessa: I can't.

Anika: Good girls have the worst stories in the nursing home. No one wants to hear about Patricia who married her high school sweetheart after he returned from the war. Now Bessie who was busting it open for Billy Dee Williams or Nat King Cole. That's a story I'd pay to hear.

Fuck I didn't have any stories. My whole life had been PG-13.

Danessa: What if he's not interested?

Anika: It's Aldridge we're talking about, he's interested.

Danessa: What do I say?

Anika: Tell him you haven't been stretched out in a while and ask him if he could help. You say that and Aldi will do the rest. You'll come back from Mexico with a limp and a concussion from him fucking you through the headboard.

I dropped my phone releasing a nervous chuckle. "I'm hot I'm gonna go for a swim." Not waiting for his response, I jumped into the pool.

When I finally came up for air Aldridge was wading into the water. "This water is perfect."

"Uh-huh."

He floated over to me. "You okay?"

"Yeah, I'm great."

"Have you been to the Greek islands yet?"

"No."

"Is it still one of your dream destinations?"

"Yes."

"What do you say we make a plan to visit this summer?"

Making plans would mean spending more time together and that was proving more difficult than I first assumed. Plus, a trip to Greece would probably require back door action or pissing on him, both of which I wasn't up for. "I can't plan that far out. I have work and now school."

"I can plan it, you just have to show up."

"And when you end up with a girlfriend in three

months what is she going to think about your vacation with your ex?"

"I'm gonna have a girlfriend in three months?"

"Probably sooner. Women in Vegas love men like you."

"Rich?"

"Don't sell yourself short. Rich, tall, handsome, Black." I whispered the last word like it was taboo. But sometimes it seemed like dating Black was trendy and one of those nursing home stories Anika talked about. They could tell all the old bitties about their summer fling with a Black dude.

"She'll just have to be cool with it."

"I don't know any person who'd be okay with you cozying up to an ex."

"See that's the difference between you and me. I'm not a jealous person."

"Bullshit, you practically curb stomped Dante over words."

"It was the principle not jealousy." He flashed me a smile before plunging his head under the water.

Maybe it was the balmy weather or sweet drinks, but I was going to fold like a cheap card table. It was getting harder and harder to pretend I wasn't feeling Aldridge. And my thoughts of him were damn near pornographic, Deborah Cox was right, we couldn't be friends because I wanted to fuck him. You know what they say, if you give a bitch some dick, she is going to want to suck it before bedtime. And if you let her suck it before bedtime, she might slip it inside and cream on it. And if she creamed on it, she'd have to put it back in her mouth to lick it clean. It was a vicious cycle.

When Aldridge popped back up to the surface, I blurted out. "Anika said I have to sleep with you?"

He sputtered out a cough. "Excuse me?"

"She said it was like a silent quid pro quo."

"Exchange for what exactly?"

"For this, bringing me here. And that in turn I should thank you with my vagina."

"Do you wanna sleep with me?"

"No … no because … we're friends."

Aldridge giggled far too long, and I hated I wasn't in on the joke. "Danessa, I expect absolutely nothing. I just wanna be here with you."

An unexpected release of tension lightened my shoulders. "I am really appreciative."

"I know you are, and you don't have to pop pussy for it."

"Whew." I pretended to wipe my forehead. "I'm gonna get another drink." Well, that was a relief, I swam to the stairs climbing out. There would be no exchange of goods or services. Wait, he asked if I wanted to sleep with him, but the real question was did he want to sleep with me. Turning, I stared at him in the pool. Aldridge waved and winked before swimming away.

ALDRIDGE

Rubbing my eyes I rolled onto my back. We'd been out
in the sun for hours and settled on a siesta before dinner. I
hadn't even climbed into the bed, just collapsed on the
duvet. Sitting up I gave my body a stretch, dinner service
was in thirty minutes. The sun had already dipped beneath
the horizon. In the shower I resisted the urge to jack off.
Images of Nessa's curves in that swimsuit, the way the
triangles of her bikini top barely covered her nipples that
turned to high beams when she came in contact with the
cool pool water.

I didn't bring her here with any preconceived notions.
The goal was for her to feel special and valued. Swear for
God sex wasn't a part of the equation when I hastily
planned this trip. Hopefully I'd successfully assuaged her
fears that I was expecting us to fuck. I'd never been that
guy, if I invited you somewhere or treated you to something it never came with strings. After my shower I moisturized liberally because no one liked an ashy brother and
spritzed on some cologne.

A gentle knock on my door was followed by a steward
appearing in the doorway of the bathroom with a mocktail
on a tray. "Ms. Irwin is enjoying a drink on the deck."

"Thank you, I'll be out shortly."

I loved this place, they took pride in catering to you. When booking my first visit, Nori provided the instruction of zero alcohol or drugs on the premises. And they'd honored that with delicious mocktails and smoothies. Not only was this a private resort, but the place was focused on wellness, with spa treatments, hiking trails, and holistic practices like sound therapy and breath work.

Danessa was on the veranda in a dress that dusted her curves with an open back. When she spotted me, her face lit up and my heartbeat stuttered. The candles scattered on the table illuminated her skin, making her appear ethereal.

"Hi." I leaned in offering up a respectable hug before claiming a seat next to her

"Did you get enough rest?"

"I slept like a baby. Opened the sliding door and listened to the ocean."

"I woke up drooling, that's how hard I slept."

"Well, you can't tell, you look beautiful."

"Thank you, you look really nice too."

"Are you hungry? Cause I'm starving."

"Yeah, let's eat."

Dinner was red snapper with rice pilaf and an assortment of sides. For the first twenty minutes or so the only words uttered were to compliment the food. With Danessa I didn't feel the need to fill the silence. We could say multitudes with little to no words. And right now, I was giving full and content.

"Tell me what you've been up to these past few years," Danessa asked, setting her fork down, her stomach finally catching up to her eyes.

"Basketball, all day every day."

"You had to be doing more than that."

"I've been working on Hoop Legacy, my active and

loungewear company. It really took off in the past few years, so a lot of my energy is focused on that. And then there's the businesses, I have a few laundromats in Philly. And that shit is mostly passive cash for me."

"Smart to have secondary streams of income."

"I'm not going to end up a fucking cautionary tale. This money I make today is going to send my great, great, great grandchildren to college. This isn't just about me. It's so much more."

"It's something to be proud of, not many people succeed as loudly as you have. Positive press, your own shoe, sold-out jerseys before your first Ramblers game."

"You heard about that?" I beamed with pride.

"Yeah."

"The Ramblers have definitely crowned a new king."

Danessa squinted. "Ouch, I think I got something in my eye."

Leaning forward, I was ready to investigate. "You okay?"

"Yep, it's just your ego. A bit flew in my eye, but I got it … here you go." She pretended to hand me back a chunk.

"Motherfucker, I was about to blow the hell out of your eye socket." Danessa, indulged in an extended giggle. Picking up a dinner roll, I threatened to throw it at her.

"Don't you dare."

Ripping the bread in half, I said, "Tell me about this law school?"

Her eyes flickered, excited to talk about the news. "It's local, which is a major plus. Boyd is the seventy-ninth best law school overall. I know that doesn't sound like much but being in the top one hundred is impressive. It has a respectable criminal law program. But I'm still torn between criminal law and property law.

"Did you apply to any other schools?"

"Yeah, like a dozen but Boyd was my top choice. I'd love to go to Stanford or Yale, but I'm not fresh out of college and my priorities are different. So, Boyd just makes the most sense."

"Have you told your mom or Anika yet?"

"Nope, only you and I know."

I put my hand over my heart. "That makes me feel special."

"If I told Anika she wouldn't have taken me to Mexico, maybe the Jalisco Grill for half-priced drinks. She probably would've even splurged for guacamole made at the table."

"I love when they prepare it fresh in front of you. It's like dinner and a show."

Danessa looked off toward the pool and I took a moment to admire her. I loved how relaxed she was in this space and with me. She had demanding clients and a ton of responsibility, so being able to get away even for twenty-four hours was important.

"What should we do now?' she asked.

"I think we need music."

Back inside, Danessa acting as DJ selected a song by a popular female rapper from the south. She gyrated and rolled her hips while singing word for word about being a bad bitch, with pussy wetter than Niagara Falls, and how she was prepared to ride dick like a BMX bike. I would've joined in, but her hips had me in a trance. However, when Alicia Keys's "If I Ain't Got You" came on we both sang horribly off-key in homage. If we were left in an empty room, she and I would find a way to have fun. We didn't take ourselves too seriously, and Danessa would never make a snide remark about me acting my age.

"You need to stay hydrated." I handed her a bottle of water.

Opening it, she downed the water in one long chug. "Have I told you I'm happy you're here?"

"You may have mentioned it."

Danessa paused the music. "No seriously, I'm happy you're in Vegas. At first, I wasn't, but now I am."

"You weren't happy to see me?" I half joked.

"Were you? There's just so much stuff between us. You know."

"Yeah."

"And I was worried that being confronted with the past would ruin my memories of you. Cause I really value the time we spent together. So I feared seeing you again would somehow corrupt how I remembered us. Does that make sense?"

"Yes. There's what happened and then there's how you process what happened. And maybe my presence would reshape how you felt about the relationship."

"Yeah, exactly that." Other than the end, our relationship was amazing. Don't get me wrong, we had fights, but we preferred to talk things through. Danessa was too important to me to allow hurt feelings to fester. So, when I did something that upset her, she'd tell me and vice versa. She continued, "I think we're placed in the spaces we need to be. We could be anywhere tonight with anyone but we're here together, and I think that's kind of special."

"Agreed. I know I feel lucky to have your attention."

"You make it hard to ignore you."

I stepped back instinctually, just enough to feel the pull between us stretch tight like a wire. Her eyes locked onto mine, soft and unreadable, then dropped to my mouth with such focus it made my breath hitch. The space between us sizzled, thick with the weight of every unsaid thing. We just stood there, close enough I could feel the heat radiate from her skin, close enough the scent of her perfume vanilla, coconut and something spicy wrapped around me like a dare.

Danessa tilted her head up, lips parted slightly, and my pulse hammered in my throat. My hand was near her waist, fingers twitching as I resisted the urge to pull her in and end any doubt that it was her, then, now, and always. Instead, I leaned in slowly, deliberately, until our noses brushed and she could sense my lips ready to devour hers. "Danessa—"

"We should go for a swim."

It felt like I'd just been kicked in the face by a horse. "What?"

"A night swim it'll be nice."

I know I said I wasn't interested in sex, but a kiss … I was kind of hopeful. "Okay, I'll go change."

Danessa reached for my hand stopping me. "Can you unzip me?"

"Of course." Grabbing her waist, I spun her around. With a tap on her hip, I let her know I was done.

Danessa backed up toward the sliding doors and shrugged out of her dress. "I think we should swim au naturale."

"Get the fuck out of here." The silhouette of her curves caused my blood to race downward.

"Okay." She pulled off the pasties covering her nipples and stepped out of her panties before jumping into the pool with a cannonball. "Come on in the water's fine!" she yelled.

Outside Danessa was swimming laps. I walked to the shallow end because I never jumped into pools. You could sprain an ankle or break your neck. Tossing my clothes into a pile, I descended the steps with Danessa's eyes all over me. I wasn't shy and relished the attention. *Yes, this is the dick you walked away from as thick as ever and it's not even hard.* "Someone is feeling naughty."

"I just wanted to swim."

"Naked?"

"Clothes are overrated."

I extended my hand. "Hi, I'm Aldridge. Who the fuck are you?"

"I'm the same Danessa from dinner."

"Nope you can't be, because my Danessa would never do this."

"I'm not *your* Danessa."

"Fair enough. So what are we doing?"

She piled her curly hair into a messy bun. "I hadn't really thought further than this."

"Why are we naked in the pool?"

"Because earlier Anika implied, I was boring. And she's right. I don't take chances. My instinct is always to say no. But saying no to every new or strange thing has gotten me nowhere."

"Wait a second. Hold up, hold up, hold up. Are you looking to get turned out? Because I will fucking *decimate* that pussy."

"No, we're friends," said the woman whose nipples were playing peekaboo in the water. You know it's to a point where I just have to ask. Am I reading this all wrong? We were naked in a pool, for what reason, what purpose?

I scooped up a wave of water and splashed her with it. "What the fuck, Danessa?"

"I just wanted to have a fun story to share. I'm always

the one listening to the stories and I never have any of my own."

"You don't need crazy stories."

"If Anika were here, she'd fuck Marisol. Or have a three way with a guy and his father. And all I have to share is how delicious the snapper was."

"It was really good. Best I've had."

"Nobody wants to hear that shit."

"Just lie. Tell her I fucked you on the beach, and you squirted all over the place."

"Eww."

"Excuse the fuck outta me for offering solutions."

"Lying is pathetic because it's not real. Life is passing me by with no significant meaning. Every day is exactly like the last. Wash, rinse, repeat. The highlight of my day is going home and scrolling social media to watch other people live their lives, go on trips, graduate, get engaged, or married, and start a fucking family. And I'm so far removed from any of those things ever happening for me."

"You're not boring?"

"I'm like lactose-free vanilla ice cream topped with the little ball shaped sprinkles everyone hates."

"You got me to ditch my clothes and join you in the pool."

"I never said I was ugly, I said I was boring."

"Let me think." Danessa wasn't dull, she was cautious. She didn't need to experience shit firsthand to know it wasn't beneficial. After watching her mother and the revolving door of men, she learned to guard her heart and avoid unnecessary risk. Her life was "boring" by design. But playing it safe could only carry you so far. "Okay, come with me." I climbed out of the pool.

"Where are we going?" She reached for my hand, and I

helped her out. I tried my best not to let my eyes dip below the top of her head.

"To the beach. It's semiprivate, which means there are homes spread out to the left and the right of us. We're going to head down to the beach butt booty naked and run in a few circles and head back up. And you can tell your sister you went naked on a public beach."

"Is that sexy enough?"

I snapped my fingers in front of her face. Since we'd exited the pool, she'd been affixed to my dick. "Hey, eyes up top, pervert."

"Where exactly do you expect me to look? Your dick is out."

I covered my junk with my hand.

"I can still see. Like I can see it."

"Tilt your head up. Do you see my head … up so I can't see anything. Be respectful."

"It hurts my neck," she shouted.

"Do you want to do this or not?"

"Okay."

"That's what I'm talking about. On the count of three, one, two …" I slapped her ass right before three and she squealed. We both made a mad dash to the shoreline and in the sand, we frolicked and skipped with Danessa laughing the entire time.

"This is damn near scandalous. I bet you someone can see us." She gasped in delight. "We could get arrested for public indecency."

There weren't any other homes on this stretch of the beach, this villa was one hundred percent secluded. But if the possibility of getting caught made Danessa feel like she was living then it was worth it.

DANESSA

"THERE YOU ARE. YOU READY TO HIKE?" ALDRIDGE ASKED.

"Is anyone ever really ready for a hike?" Squinting at the sun, I gave my body a stretch.

"We've been lazy, and my muscles are mad about it. I need to get some exercise in."

"Yeah, but what does that have to do with me? I could stay behind, and you know, snack."

"That's not an activity."

"You like uphill hikes to waterfalls, and I like finger foods. Both are restorative."

"Did you drink your smoothie?" He reached for my Camelbak to confirm it was filled with water.

"Yes, dad."

"When we get back we'll have a big breakfast."

"You're lucky I already ruined my silk press."

We headed off to hike to a waterfall Marisol claimed would take our breaths away. After last night I kind of wanted to bury my head under the covers and hide out. What was I thinking stripping naked in front of Aldridge and jumping into the pool? It was so far out of character for me. While I was embarrassed, I couldn't help but admit it was fun. Doing something, I didn't plan. I mean I'd planned the skinny dipping, but the beach antics were unscripted.

Anika was probably stalking my apartment, waiting for signs I'd return. Once I did, she'd want a play-by-play and at least I had a story to tell. It's rough being the rule follower in a family that considers rules as loose suggestions and not tips to live by. Jemini and Anika were similar in how they viewed life. While I was drafting pros and cons lists, they were screaming FUCK IT while jumping from planes.

"Do you miss Missouri?" I huffed behind Aldridge.

He slowed so I could catch up. "Parts of it. I had friends and a routine I loved. But Missouri was never the endgame."

"Is Vegas the endgame?"

His shoulder hunched. "Don't know."

The contents of my stomach sank like a stone. Possibly losing Aldridge a second time was not something I'd considered. But players get traded. Damnit, why'd I let myself get attached? Was this destined to be our lives, wrong place, wrong time, for the next thirty years? When Aldridge suggested we try our hand at friendship, I knew deep down inside we were both hoping for more. I didn't want to admit it, but I liked having him around and I liked who I was when we were together.

"It must've been hard leaving your friends?"

"Yeah, we all promised to visit and stay in touch, but you know how it is."

"You should reach out and make it happen. People get busy but I'm sure they'd love to hear from you. Just like you can fly to Mexico, you could easily hop on a plane for a quick weekend in Kansas City."

"Have you been since we visited our senior year?"

"No." Kansas City was strictly off limits because Aldridge lived there. Sure, the chances of running into him were slim but there was a chance, and I wasn't strong enough to casually be confronted with the man I loved. Used to love. Shit when I opened the door to that home a few weeks ago and he was on the other side, I was thrown for a loop. Viola Davis ain't got shit on me because I delivered a masterful performance of a chick who was unbothered when in fact I was crashing the fuck out internally.

"We should go."

"We?"

"Yeah, I'd love for you to meet my friends." I don't know if it was the elevation or the ease of his words, but pressure was building at my temples. This is how it happens, a person just elbows their way into your heart, taking up space and rearranging things. And when it's over it's damn near impossible to move on. This was a mistake attempting to be friends. "Do you want to take a break?"

"What?"

"You're sweating a lot." He pointed at my face.

The air was humid, and my mind was racing. We stopped at a clearing that looked out on to a crop of lush green trees. I'd made a sincere attempt to move on from Aldridge, but he crept into my thoughts. The memory of him so vivid it was impossible to ignore. I compared men against him. And some of them were really great, like Marcus, but they weren't Aldridge and in the end that caused me to second guess. Taking a long gulp of water, I decided to implode my life. "I have a friend, her name is Tamara and I think you'd really like her."

Aldridge wiped at his mouth with the back of his hand. "Excuse me?"

"She's really pretty, and fun, and you two would probably hit it off."

His eyes narrowed as he scrutinized my face. "Where's this coming from?"

"Just thinking about what you said and want to help you make new friends. Plus, I owe you a blind date after Anika and Dante pulled the switcheroo on us."

"Do you listen to the things you say before saying them?" His tone was pinched letting me know he was annoyed.

"Always."

"I don't need to be hooked up by my ex-girlfriend."

The emphasis on the "EX" part threw me. "Just trying to help."

"Don't."

"Fine, forget I ever mentioned it." I stomped away in a huff.

"You're an idiot," he called after me.

Spinning around I asked, "What did you call me?"

"An idiot."

"Excuse me for trying to help you get laid."

"Why is everyone so concerned about who I'm fucking? If I wanted to have sex, I could've fucked you in the pool last night."

"No, you couldn't." He could've if he'd applied the slightest effort instead of being a gentleman. He could fuck me right now on this dirt path if we wanted to.

Aldridge chuckled. Approaching, he stopped inches from me. "You're a bad liar."

I removed my sunglasses from my head, securing them over my eyes. "And you're full of shit. How much longer?"

"Fifteen maybe twenty minutes."

"I hate this." I stomped and pouted like an unruly toddler.

"It's worth it. Trust me."

He was right, the waterfall was stunning. The pain in my legs and my wet sticky skin took a back seat to the visual wonder before us. The roar of the water drowned everything out, including my muddled thoughts. The crystal-clear aquamarine color let you know you were in paradise. Next to the water it was at least ten degrees cooler. Aldridge stood with his hands on his hips admiring the view while holding back an I told you so. "We getting in?" he asked.

"Hell yeah we are." We both stripped to our bathing suits and climbed in. The water was cold but refreshing after our hike. Aldridge floated on his back, Mexico agreed with him. I felt silly bringing up Tamara, not because she wouldn't be a good match for him, but if they met and hit it off she wouldn't know a minute of peace because I'd constantly be looking for ways to steal my man back. Aldridge with another woman was the last thing I wanted.

He motioned me forward and we swam to the massive falls. I held my breath as we passed underneath. It took a few seconds for my eyes to adjust but when they did I was treated to a cave, the water was still and clear allowing me to see all the way to the bottom.

"I like to think of the space between a waterfall as a pocket in time." In this tiny alcove with the water thundering around us his theory seemed to hold true. From here we were hidden from the world and its expectations. "Here in this little sweet spot, we can be unapologetically who we are. So, I have to ask. Who do you want to be in this moment?

"Fearless." My eyes shamelessly landed on his full lips.

"Let me help you with that."

I nodded, not one hundred percent sure what I was agreeing to.

His firm yet tentative touch was all the encouragement I needed. Aldridge claimed my hand placing it over his chest and it rattled against my palm, the beats fast and erratic. I found comfort in the knowledge his nervous system was off-kilter just like mine. Bending to meet me, he dusted his lips across mine before devouring them whole. Our kisses left me possessed as every memory we ever shared came flooding back.

The soft smile he'd offered on the first day of class. A kind gesture to a stranger who was in way over her head. His body drifting into mine when we shared a laugh as if we were trading secrets. Aldi's focused determination when he was inside me drawing out ever scream and spurring uncontrollable tremors. It all rushed back to me, memories I'd banished to the recesses of my mind were now vivid and bold. But more than that, it was the now. The way he tilted my head slightly like he wanted more, and the hitch in my breath just as my lips grazed his skin.

As I released a soft moan, I could feel his dick grow as if I'd uttered the magic words. Aldridge's hands cupped my ass squeezing tight. His strong grip grounding me and making me feel safe. I wrapped my legs around his waist and my hips worked to give him a preview of what could be possible if we pushed past our fear. His lips took up residence in the softness of my skin. My jaw, neck, and collarbone all receiving special attention.

Approaching voices pulled us from our all-consuming desire. Aldridge released me back to the rocky surface before plunging his head under the water. When he popped back up his eyes were clear and his tone even. "We should head back."

"Okay?" I didn't know if I'd make it back my legs were hollow and my pussy was a wet throbbing mess. Passing back through the waterfall felt like a reset. Whatever transpired in the dim alcove was washed away by the rush of water. Aldridge helped me out and we dressed in silence. Halfway back to the villa he turned and asked. "Are you okay?"

"No."

"I didn't plan for that to happen. I don't know what I'm doing Nessa."

"And you think I do?"

"I'm just trying not to make shit complicated."

"It's too late for that."

"When I said I wanted us to work on our friendship I meant that."

"So, did I." I wanted to scream, *"What are we doing?"* Aldridge's expression was unreadable, but it felt like regret. If he thought kissing me was a mistake, then it was one that would never happen again. "Let's just get back to the villa. I'm tired, hungry, and ready to go home." I purposely brushed past him hoping he'd grab my arm, press me to his chest and smash his lips into mine. None of that happened. The remainder of the trek back I lagged behind solely focused on not bursting into tears.

ALDRIDGE

It was my month to plan a team building event for the Ramblers players. I'd taken Deion's words to heart and thought long and hard about the best activity. When the bus I rented pulled up to the building, I held my breath, now uncertain of my choice. The driver opened the doors, and the team filed out. The only direction the invitation provided was to dress comfortably and be prepared to move.

On the sidewalk I rallied the troops. "Thanks for showing up. I wanted to pick something that would allow us to relax while still providing a new experience for most. So I asked myself, Aldridge, what activity would a bunch of men in peak physical condition enjoy but also be challenged by, and I decided on Pilates."

There were audible groans from various people in the crowd. "Are you kidding me? The last team event was ax throwing and now you're saying I have to stretch for the next two hours?" Paxton complained.

Okay not the reaction I expected but I wasn't going to let a few negative remarks get me down. "Yep, Pilates is actually proven to be great for professional athletes because it helps with core strength, range of motion, muscular balance, and it can help prevent injuries by increasing flexibility."

"Did no one tell you the rules for these events?" Colin Pratt hissed. "We're trying to have fun not whatever the fuck this is."

"Yeah, well I'm sorry this event doesn't include an open bar and a bunch of barely legal women for you to run game on."

"I'm a married man so what the fuck is that supposed to mean?"

"I don't know ask your wife." Colin was a known womanizer and although he had a wife and kids at home, he moved like a bachelor. Normally I didn't give a shit what another man was doing. But I'd met his wife, and she was bubbly, outgoing, and oddly enough one of the few people who talked to me at the preseason party for staff, players, and their families. Maybe she was gauging my temperature to see what type of time I was on and how that would impact her husband which in turn would directly affect her and her family. In my book it was fuck Colin Pratt for life and any team expectations of allegiance. Because if his wife ever asked me to my face if her husband was cheating, I was snitching and offering her the contact number to a good divorce lawyer.

"Hold on, wives are off limits," Powell said.

"This fucker wouldn't understand that shit because he can't keep a bitch. What happened to the influencer model chick you were dating. Did she dump you when she realized you're a scrub who's ideal of fun is Pilates and Scrabble game nights?"

"Well when I'm no longer feeling a relationship I end things. Unlike you whose over here collecting side chicks like infinity stones."

"I think he's trying to say your dick is for everybody," Dante always leaned into an opportunity to instigate some shit.

Deion interjected. "You two are acting like some bitches. I'ma need y'all to wrap this shit up … bickering back and forth like two old biddies."

My eyes telegraphed surprise. "Old biddies? That's not a word you hear every day."

"It sounds like something my grandma would say," Dante agreed.

Deion's jaw ruminated. "It means annoying nags."

"Oh I know what it means. I'm just wondering why you're saying it," I teased.

Some of the other players chuckled. "Sorry Deck even I have to admit you should drop that word from your vocabulary." Colin chuckled.

Deion rubbed his beard. "Can we just go inside and start stretching?"

Inside the studio reformer machines were set up for all fifteen players. I chose a one in the back away from Colin. Our instructor an outgoing blonde welcomed us to class. It was a private session just us and the trainer.

"I heard you lot were basketball players." Her British accent caught me off guard. "My name is Stacy and I'll be your instructor this afternoon. You all look big and strong but make no mistake this class is about to kick your ass."

"Doubt it, sweetheart," Colin shouted out to a smattering of laughs.

"I'm looking forward to breaking you."

"Wait what?" Dante asked.

"Now remember this is a safe space so if you have to tap out or need to cry feel free." She hit play on her remote and ambient music filled the room. "First we're going to start with some footwork. Follow me, legs together toes on the bar." She jumped on her machine.

The footwork was simple enough, the goal was to get us acclimated to the repetitive motions. I took Pilates classes regularly and was excited for us to ramp shit up. I'll admit I chose this class because I knew most of the guys weren't flexible and I wanted to humble a few of them. Yes, the purpose of the team event was to build camaraderie and what better way to do that than to watch each of them tap out one by one.

Halfway through the class and grumbles rang out from various players. We were tasked with holding the high bridge position. The position required us to bend backward with one foot on the bar and the other straight in the air. Players were quitting left and right. I turned my head and next to me Deion was in perfect form his eyes closed. This shit was light work for him which didn't surprise me. He seemed like a man who appreciated that strength conditioning was more than just weights.

"Continue to hold." Stacy's voice was soft and calm.

Closing my eyes I released a deep breath pushing out the bullshit and accepting peace. My quickie getaway with Danessa was supposed to be Zen and relaxing but for most of the trip I was on edge. Mexico made me realize I was still madly in love with her. Okay let me stop lying, I knew that shit when she greeted me at the door of that first property several weeks ago. I'd had a couple of relationships since her but everyone else was just keeping her seat warm. Our kiss under that waterfall erased any doubts.

I loved her and I needed her to know it. But I was also terrified because she literally destroyed me. The breakup hit me hard. She changed her fucking number, blocked me on everything, and moved the fuck on. I had to have a few screws loose if I was ready to spin the block on heartbreak. Honestly, it should be fuck Danessa for life. Who was I kidding, if someone said I needed to wrestle a bear to get my girl back, I would douse myself in baby oil and get in position for a double leg attack.

Stacy's voice interrupted my thoughts. "Great job guys. Even the ones who tapped out." I surveyed the studio and found Pratt huffing in the back of the room. Pussy. "There are healthy snacks and drinks in the next room. Thank you so much for coming to Body Flex."

After thanking Stacy for the excellent class I joined the others for refreshments. When I walked into the room, there was a round of applause. "That shit was hard as fuck. I loved it," Dante shouted.

"That's because Pilates works different muscles. This was a good class." Deck gave the event a compliment and by extension he was complimenting me. I wanted the team to be pushed out of their box but I also wanted to pique their interest so maybe they'd check out another class on their own.

"Glad y'all enjoyed it. I've been attending these classes for a while now and it's not about brute force, but it still requires strength and patience. You should have seen me at my first class, my legs got tangled in the machine. But look at me now … growth."

"Sign me up. I'm down for another class," Dante announced. I don't really understand how Dante became my best friend on the team, but here we were.

"Me too," Deion said checking his watch before brushing past me. Deion's words shifted the energy in the room, and players buzzed about the next time we could get together for more stretching. Colin Pratt did not join in on the excitement. He just loitered in a corner, flashing me a dirty look.

Dante pegged me on my chest. "Anika said you went to Mexico."

"Yeah, with Danessa."

"No invite? I would've been down for margaritas by the pool."

"Well then you would've been disappointed because it was a dry resort."

Dante's voice dropped to a whisper. "So did you two …" He inserted two fingers into a hole in his other hand.

"What did Anika say?"

"That you two were on some voyeur shit. Running around naked on the beach." So, Danessa had shared our exploits. I thought she would chicken out and just rave about the snapper and the views. "Just so you know, I'm all caught up. Anika told me about college, and Danessa stomping on your heart to go to law school in Chicago which she ended up dropping out of a few months later. I'm firmly on your team. Shit, so is Anika. You know women and that independent I don't need a man bullshit they be spewing. Anika said she still loves you, so there's that."

"What?"

"Danessa she's still fucking in love with you. And when you guys ended, she immediately regretted it or some shit. But she had to stand on business."

"Anika said that?"

"Not word for fucking word but yeah."

Anika was an unreliable narrator, you couldn't believe most of the shit that came out of her mouth but if half of it was true, Danessa and I needed to stop being polite and have a real fucking conversation.

"Wow this is you?" I asked as I made my way through the entry hall which opened into Danessa's living space. Her condo looked exactly like I'd pictured. Light colored furniture, art by Black artist, zero clutter. I'd only been here for a minute, and the space already felt like a place I'd like to kick off my shoes and hang out in for a while.

"Yeah."

"I see why you like it, views of the city at night, nice high rise building with what I can only imagine is all the amenities."

"All the perks of homeownership with none of the responsibilities."

I leaned in towering over her. "You trying to be neighbors?"

"No, I'm not suggesting you move here. But I wanted to give you a feel of the condo option since we haven't explored that yet."

I looked out the window at the area below. "Is that a lake?"

"Manmade, yes. There are running and bike paths and a picnic area. Sometimes they have concerts at the amphitheater."

"I like the way you decorated the place."

"Thanks, let me show you the rest."

A few days ago, we were at a private resort enjoying drinks with umbrellas in them, and now back in Vegas we were pretending like shit hadn't shifted between us. I'd seen Danessa naked for the first time in a long ass time, and it wasn't something I could just push away into the murky recesses of my brain. In Mexico I was respectful, but all I could think about was her smile, tan lines, and naked ass. I wanted more. More access, more time.

Danessa led me to the second bedroom she was using as an office and then to the primary which was spacious with large floor to ceiling windows. On the way to the bathroom, I scanned the walk-in closet for size 14 shoes or a rack of men's shirts.

"And this is my bathroom." The word bathroom was an understatement. It was like a wellness getaway in here with candles, a soaker tub, and eucalyptus in the shower.

"The tub is huge."

"I checked, it should be long enough for you to fit." Was that an invitation? I absentmindedly opened up the medicine cabinet and was quickly chided. "Mind your business."

"My bad. Can I open the linen closet?"

"Knock yourself out." I scanned the neatly folded towels and labeled bins with toiletries and hand soap. We needed to talk about Mexico and my feelings. I couldn't be a good friend to Danessa if I was constantly thinking about fucking her. She wanted to be friends, and I was willing to fall in line and be the best friend she'd ever had. But not before she knew I still had feelings for her. That for me this wasn't over.

"How'd your event go yesterday?"

Closing the closet I rolled my eyes. "Colin tried to start some shit, but—"

"You should just bop him one good time."

That seemed to be the consensus. "Danessa, I thought you were all about protecting your energy."

"Yeah and sometimes you just need to let motherfuckers know you are not the one or the two. I bet if you did, he wouldn't test you again."

"Colin is all talk and the minute he wants to stop flapping his gums and square up, I'm ready. I ain't been in a fight in a minute and I would love the chance to brush up on my combos." I playfully swung in her direction. "Right hook, left hook, jab, cross, uppercut."

"Sweep the leg … nut stomp."

"Whoa, not the nuts."

"I don't fight fair."

"I remember." I opened a bottle of perfume from her bathroom counter giving it a whiff.

"What's that supposed to mean?"

"You're the woman who picked up a chair and threw it in a room full of people."

"Don't act like the situation wasn't already out of control."

"How did throwing a chair help?"

"Everybody was fighting. I just put something extra on it."

"I had to defend you."

"Yeah, and it was exciting. You the tall, strong brother jumping in to rescue me, the damsel in distress."

"You had a taser in your hand, you weren't that distressed."

"I was ready to stun anyone who tried it."

These damn Irwin women. "And I've never been on a dinner boat since."

Danessa exited the bathroom, and I followed her into the kitchen with commercial-grade appliances. The only reason I knew that was because she always pointed it out on our house tours. I could clock an eight-burner Nostalgie oven from a mile away.

"Thoughts."

"Listen, I love condos."

"Their low maintenance and secure which is great for individuals who travel often."

"I agree. I'm just thinking about the trajectory of my life long term."

"Meaning?"

I hitched my shoulder. "A few years from now I may get married and start a family, and a condo doesn't really support that." This wasn't something I'd given much thought to, but it was a possibility. For the longest I thought I'd be a married man by now. The plan was to move to Kansas City and start planning our wedding. But Danessa decided to break my heart instead.

Danessa's head jerked. "Married?"

"Don't screw up your face like that. I am very much in demand. I think they call me a high value man."

She rolled her eyes. "I hate that phrase."

"You said it yourself people our age are pairing off and getting married."

"Yes, but you don't even have a girlfriend."

"When you meet the one, shit moves fast."

"So you plan to meet the one and be married in two years."

"I don't know maybe less. Maybe I'll pull a Dante and Anika."

Danessa clapped her hands. "Wow. Dante and Anika are not the standard, they're an anomaly."

"Why are you so pressed?"

"I'm not. If you want to marry some chick you bumped into at a pool party, be my guest."

"Wait are you mad about a hypothetical baddie at a fake pool party?"

"No, this tour is over." She tried to shove me toward the door.

"Are you jealous, Danessa Irwin?"

"Of what, your bad taste in women?"

"I picked you."

"No, you didn't. I did the picking."

"Could you stop trying to push me it's embarrassing?" She'd even leaned into it but I didn't budge. "If you want me to leave, I'm gone." My feet remained planted.

"Great."

"Are you hungry? Because I could feed you." I was lightweight talking about my dick.

"Umm ..."

Shaking my head vigorously I finally backed up toward the door. "You know what, never mind."

"Wait why?"

"Because anytime a woman says 'Umm' the way you just did she's not interested."

"I'm interested in dinner and we could stream a movie. But shouldn't you be outside looking for a wife who's okay with you referring to yourself as a high value man?"

"You're not going to let me live that down, are you?"

"It's a stupid phrase. Are you staying or not?"

"I don't need a pity invite. I need an enthusiastic yes."

"I'm not going to beg."

"I'd love to see that." My eyes briefly dropped to her mouth, but I quickly reset. "Are we ordering or are we cooking? Because I could probably eat an entire baby cow right about now."

"I don't have much in the fridge."

"Danessa, I grew up poor. I know how to work magic in the kitchen." Opening the fridge, I found a whole uncooked chicken, celery, half an onion a bag of frozen vegetables, and some unidentifiable soupy sauce in

Tupperware. In the pantry I scored with three potatoes. "I can make you dinner, but you have to help."

"Why are you acting like I can't cook?"

"Because when we were together you couldn't."

"Yes, I could."

I slammed a can of mushroom soup on the counter. "You gave me food poisoning."

"That was one time."

"How many times have I poisoned you?"

"Zero," she whispered.

I leaned in pointing to my ear. "How many?"

"ZERO!"

"Okay just wanted to get that on record."

"Noted. Now what can I do?"

"Wash, oil, and salt the potatoes."

"I can handle that."

"You better because if you fuck up baked potatoes, I'm going to have questions."

We moved past each other going about our respective tasks. Danessa would occasionally brush past me on her way to the pantry. And I think she may have washed her hands at least twenty times in the process. Cooking together wasn't foreign for us. When we dated, I'd cook almost every weekend, in the shared kitchen in my dorm room. Danessa would drink wine and supervise because she was a shit cook. While other guys my age were going out to the club on Friday nights, I was at home in my happy place with my girl and good food.

I was working on seasoning the chicken when Danessa came up from behind me. Her hand landed on my back which caused me to flinch before relaxing into her touch. "It already smells good."

I was tempted to kiss her like I'd done so many times in

the past. Suggesting we cook together was probably a bad idea. Shit being around Danessa for any length of time was a bad idea. Her presence warped my reality, blurring the lines between our blissful past and the cold realization that what we had was most likely gone. Ruined by time and hurt feelings.

"I could get used to having a personal chef."

Why was she standing so close to me? "Don't."

"I have a salad bag I can put together."

"Sounds good."

Put a finger down if you moved to a new city and your realtor is your ex from college. The one who got away, broke your heart, and never looked back. But after all these years you two decided to try to be friends and now you're in her kitchen making dinner, but all you can think about are her teardrop breast and the voracity in which she used to suck your dick. Please note that I've put a finger down.

We settled into eating and watching a scary movie Danessa selected.

"See and that's why you can't go on a vacation with just anybody." I gestured toward the television.

"What do you mean?"

"They heard a noise in the cellar and this dude is talking about let's check it out."

"It could be an animal."

"Or it could be a homicidal killer ready to gut them like a fish."

"They paid a lot for the house rental."

"Fuck that house rental if it were me, I'd already be in the car and on the highway to the nearest civilized city."

"You'd just leave?"

"I can guarantee you everybody in this movie is about to die. But not me, cause my ass would already be home."

She licked sauce from the corner of her mouth. "I think you're overreacting."

"Danessa we are Black, we don't do creepy cabins in the woods."

"What if I wanted to stay?"

"Shiiiiiit, I'd be on the eleven o'clock news talking about, 'I always liked Danessa she was a nice girl. I tried to get her to leave but she said what happens in a remote cabin stays in a remote cabin. And I guess she was right because they ain't found her body.'"

Danessa shoved me. "Jerk face."

"At least I *still* have a face." We both shared a laugh.

"Do you remember our last vacation together? Not Mexico."

Nodding my head I slowly recalled our road trip. "I remember it fondly."

"I'd always wanted to go on a road trip and one day you came home after your last final and said we should hit the road the next day."

"And you thought I was bullshiting."

"It was just so unplanned which I think made it that much more fun."

"We didn't plan shit we just jumped in the car and drove. No itinerary no reservations just the open road."

"We didn't even have a proper playlist."

"During that trip I learned you were directionally challenged."

"That's what GPS is for."

"What was your favorite part of the trip?" I asked, tossing my napkin onto my plate.

"Visiting all the national parks and walking the trails and seeing that huge cowboy boot. And do you remember the tiny cabin?"

"My legs were hanging off the bed."

"That's right and we ended up sleeping on the floor. But the roof was made of glass, and we were able to look up at the stars as we drifted off to sleep. What was your favorite part?"

"That's easy, being with you."

"Be serious."

"I am being serious. Being with you, sharing those experiences with you meant everything to me."

"Me too."

"You can't change your answer now it's too late."

"I'm not changing my answer I'm amending it."

"So you liked the hiking trails, the huge boot, and—"

"You."

Do you know the saying "Decide what you want and then act as if it's impossible to fail"? That shit always resonated with me but never more than right now. I was practically rubbing elbows with the woman of my dreams. The woman who was the bane of my existence because from the minute I met her, she occupied every square inch of my brain matter. There was not a day that went by in which I didn't think of her, wonder if she was okay and perhaps was thinking about me too.

I brushed her hair from her shoulder. "You know every day I tell myself, Aldridge the window of opportunity has passed. And that's okay because what we're creating in this moment can be something new, perhaps something better."

Danessa shook her head as if she was attempting to lock things in place. "Are you still joking?"

Muting the television, I stared into her eyes. "Nah, I'm dead fucking serious."

"I don't …"

"I just want you to know this can be whatever you want it to be. And I will play my part to perfection. Whether that be as your friend or something more." If she offered me crumbs, I would gladly take them.

"I don't know if we get do-overs."

"Maybe this isn't a remake but a sequel."

"Most sequels suck."

"Mmm … we're the exception, not the rule."

"So how does it work?"

Hell if I knew. I just wanted a second chance, a rematch. "We both know how this works." With me worshipping the ground she walks on and basking in the glow of her affection.

"With you kissing me? I don't know, just exploring suggestions."

My heart was beating so loud I'm surprised she couldn't hear it and offer to call an ambulance. "Act one, the kiss. I like it. That's a hell of a way to start a sequel."

"Maybe we could add some moderate groping for good measure."

"Excellent fucking suggestions." Grabbing her arm, I pulled her onto my lap, so she was straddling me. The weight of her ass pressed against me, causing my temperature to rise and my dick to expand. She was so close now, and the look in her eyes held a promise that made my pulse pound in my ears. It was difficult to catch my breath because the room felt smaller, the air thicker.

The seconds right before a kiss can define the course of history. A good kiss could lead to exchanging vows. Bad kisses could dash hopes and build walls. Right now, with Danessa searching my eyes for confirmation I was ready to write a new chapter, my heart was filled with so much uncertainty. *Is this a huge mistake? What if our chemistry has faded? Was I setting myself up to be hurt again?* But just past the uncertainty, there was hope. Hope, that every decision, every ending, every relocation, every failure over the past five years was preparing us for this.

I could feel the heat radiating off her. Every nerve in my body was alive, aware of the way Danessa's gaze moved from my eyes to my mouth and back again. Leaning forward slightly, I drank Danessa's familiar scent. The soft whisper of her breath was like a siren song drawing me closer. Danessa's timid smile matched what I was thinking, *Are we really doing this?*

My thumb traced the line of her jaw, slow and deliberate, and she leaned into my touch. Landing on her mouth, I outlined the fullness of her thick lips. Her hand slid to the back of my neck, and she gave my curls a tug. I couldn't breathe, couldn't think. All I knew was I wanted her closer, needed her closer. My face hovered just inches from hers. Her breath brushed my lips, warm and steady.

Danessa parted her lips, barely, which caused me to hesitate, wanting to savor the moment, draw it out. I wanted to let the anticipation build until she thought she might come undone. She wasn't deterred, she leaned forward, just enough that our mouths were a breath apart, so close I could almost feel the kiss, feel the way her lips would press against mine, shy at first but becoming increasingly more possessive the longer we kissed. Her eyes fluttered shut, surrendering to the ache, to the longing she'd been holding back.

And in that suspended second, before our lips met, the world fell away, leaving only her, only this. I slipped my tongue past her lips and indulged in her. Framing my hand at the base of her neck, I secured my claim intending to be locked in this moment for a while. Warmth bloomed in my chest and spread to my extremities as if Danessa was uploading her essence into my soul. Her lips were soft and determined against mine.

When Danessa moved her hips back and forth over my very erect penis, I unsuccessfully tried to suppress a moan. With assured movements she circled my crotch. I stared directly into her mink eyes trying my best to convey I was down for any and everything. The look in her eyes was a mixture of surprise and determination. If Danessa was trying to come, I'd do everything in my power to help make that happen. My hands grasped her waist offering an assist so she could glide over my member.

Thank God I was wearing these thin ass shorts because I could feel her pussy print against me. The friction had my dick on swole and I started to recognize the gravity of what we were doing. Danessa had given me a green light and I was going to reward her. With her body still rocking, I stood. Danessa clung to my shirt, uneasy with the change in position. Lying on to my back, I gestured for her to climb back on top. Danessa stepped out of her panties, and although her tennis skirt still concealed her bottom half, the thought of her naked underneath made my heartbeat flutter.

Climbing on top and with very little words we both understood the assignment. I was here to be used as she saw fit. From this vantage point, I watched her rock across my lap occasionally rubbing her breast or squeezing a nipple. Before I'd even processed it, she was pulling down my shorts and underwear causing my dick to bob back and forth when released. We both looked down at it, probably each considering the next move.

Danessa floated down so our faces almost touched.

"Aldridge, I need you to fuck me right now. Can you handle that?"

"Yeah, uhm, yes I can definitely do that."

"I wanna feel you inside of me."

"I would like that as well." When I woke up this morning, I didn't realize this would be the best day of my life. It's funny how you could workout, run errands, go to a work event and then hours later be on the precipice of fucking the hottest woman you'd ever met. My dick was now in between her legs surrounded by her warmth and wetness. Danessa controlled the tempo. Leaning back she slid her pussy lips up and down my shaft. I wasn't inside of her yet but we'd moved from dry humping to wet humping and I was quickly unraveling.

Wrapping my hand around her neck, I pulled her back down so we were eye to eye. "Hey?"

"Yeah," her voice was breathy and a full octave deeper.

"I want you to know I'm about to fuck you so thoroughly your neighbors are going to call the cops to conduct a welfare check."

Danessa smashed her lips into mine while still rubbing her pussy against me. She started to nibble on my ear, but my attention was drawn to the entryway and the sound of the lock opening. "Is that your door?"

"What?" She tugged on my ear with her teeth.

"I think someone is opening your door."

Danessa jumped up, tripping several times on her way to the entry hall. "What are you doing?" she shouted. I hopped back into my shorts ready to fuck someone up. But relaxed when Anika's voice filled in the blanks.

"Where have you been?" Anika responded back.

"You just can't barge into my apartment whenever you want."

"I called and texted you an obscene number of times. I thought you were dead."

"Well, I'm not so can you leave now."

"No, let me in." Anika pushed the door open, brushing past Danessa. "Why do you look like that?"

"Like what?"

"Disheveled and your eyes are all shifty."

"I was working?"

"At nine o'clock at night?"

"Yeah."

"Hmm, God you're so weird. Sometimes I can't believe we're related. I just need to borrow your burgundy dress, the one that makes me look snatched."

"You were going to break in and steal my dress?"

"Borrow." I could hear the voices getting closer. By the time Anika entered the living room, I was sitting upright with a pillow on my lap. "Well, what do we have here?"

"I told you work."

Anika looked from Danessa to me and back again. "Have you two been fucking?"

"Eww, Anika be so fucking for real right now. How gross, absolutely not."

Damn, she was putting a whole lot into that denial. Gross, me? "Hey Anika."

"Aldi." Anika examined the room for evidence. "Dinner for two, ambient lighting, candles. This is a sexual crime scene if I ever seen one."

"Get the fucking dress and go."

"You seem uptight, so I'm guessing the penis has not broken the seal yet."

"Go get the dress," Danessa said through gritted teeth.

"Okay chill out." Anika disappeared into the bedroom.

Danessa turned to me. I thought she was going to apologize, instead she said, "You need to leave."

I jumped up from the couch letting the pillow fall to the floor. "What?"

"Can you do something with that?" She pointed to my dick which was still sporting a very prominent chubby.

"Why do I have to leave?" I whispered.

"Because I need to talk to my sister before she tells everyone she knows that we're getting the band back together."

"Will you at least call me later?" God we hadn't even fucked and I was pussy whipped.

"No." The woman who just moments ago had lust in her eyes and was ready to make my dick disappear was gone.

"I'm leaving town tomorrow for work." Danessa was wrangling me toward the front door. "I won't be back for a week." She opened the door and pushed me out. "Danessa?"

"Sorry, have a safe trip." She offered a cringe-filled smile before shutting the door in my face.

DANESSA

I HADN'T EVEN LOGGED INTO MY COMPUTER AND ANIKA WAS already in my office. "Are you ready to talk about this weekend?"

"Good morning, happy Monday."

"Bump all that. I let you stonewall me the other night because Dante was waiting for me in the car, but I have nowhere to be today." Anika claimed one of the chairs in front of my desk, crossing her legs.

"There's nothing to talk about."

"Okay, so I see I need to treat you as a hostile witness."

"What?"

"Ms. Irwin were you and Mr. Mosley on a date on the night I stopped by to pick up the burgundy dress that had my man taking it off of me with his teeth?"

"I want that dress dry cleaned before you return it."

"Objection, the witness will answer the question."

"No."

"So what was he doing there?"

I clicked on an email attachment because unlike Anika, I actually had work to do. "Like I said it was work. I was giving him a tour of my apartment."

"Your apartment and your pussy because—"

"Stop it."

"So you gave him a tour of your apartment and then you two had dinner?"

Hitching my shoulder I said, "We had to eat."

"Hmm, I'm sure you kept his mouth full."

"Objection."

She pointed a wagging index finger in my direction. "Overfuckingruled."

"I'm requesting a mistrial."

"Bitch you're about to be sentenced to life without the possibility of parole if you don't answer my questions. Did you fuck him? And look me in the eyes when you answer because I know when you're lying."

"No."

Anika leaned in. "Were you about to fuck him?"

"No, nah, nope."

"Swear on Pudding Paws's plushy life you're telling the truth."

Pudding Paws was the stuffed teddy bear I slept with for way too long as a kid. I named him Pudding Paws because his paws reminded me of tapioca pudding. And he may or may not be on one of the shelves in my closet as we speak.

"This is ridiculous. What I choose to do ... or not do is my business."

"We're sisters, we tell each other everything. Like I've consumed so much cum this weekend I think I'm getting a sore throat."

I aggressively gagged. "No one ... no one needed or wanted to hear that. I could have gone my entire fucking life without that information. God you are such a fucking oversharer."

"And you're not a good sister. I gave you something now you have to give me something."

Fuck, I know in Mexico I was whining about not having interesting stories, but Aldridge was off limits, sacred ground. But if I didn't acquiesce, Anika would keep bringing him up. "Aldridge's penis is still perfect."

Anika gasped. "Did you put in your mouth?"

"No."

"Did you wanna put it in your mouth?"

"I plead the fifth."

"So are you guys back together?"

"No, it's not that. I honestly don't know what we're doing."

"Ask him or better yet, tell him. Tell him you made a mistake and that he's your man again. Then suck the meat off his bone to seal the deal. A good dick sucking is like a promise ring, only wetter with a fifty-fifty chance you get a little something in your eye."

"What if that's not what I want?"

"To be with Aldi?"

"I mean I don't know."

"Well, you better get to figuring it out because he's going to come back from being on the road with an erection and a dream. Do it for the culture."

"What the fuck does that mean?"

"There are millions of women who would love to fuck an athlete. Shit there's probably a couple thousand that want to fuck *your* athlete. So do this for the women all across the country who will never know the thrill of having a man in peak physical condition fuck her until her walls collapse. And I know Aldridge can fuck because when you two were together, you did not play about that man. When them college girls would try to holler at him you got real froggy."

"Because he was my man. Play dominos, bitch, play in

traffic but don't play with me or mine." Back in college a lot of women ignored the fact that Aldridge was taken. He always shut them down immediately, letting them know he had a girlfriend but some of the remedial bitches needed an additional reminder.

"You're awfully heated about a man you claim to no longer want."

"It's the principle of the thing."

"Send him a nude pic."

"What?"

"Send Aldridge a picture of your wet pussy. Let him know you're about that life and you're calling dibs."

"Why would I need to call dibs?"

"Because he's a basketball player on the road. During the game he's throwing the ball and at night pussy is being thrown at him."

"You give the worst advice."

"Do what you want, but Aldridge isn't going to stay single for long." Anika stood, took several of my pens and headed down the hall to her office.

Normally I listened to my sister's advice and did the opposite. Her life choices were not ones I wanted to necessarily emulate. Of course I was attracted to Aldridge, time was never going to change that and seeing him again it was inevitable I'd be conflicted. But I ended our relationship for a reason. Nothing had changed, he was still a basketball player in high demand. I noticed the way women looked at him when he entered a room or walked past them. Why would I open myself up to that type of drama?

However, I'd be lying if I didn't admit the possibility of seeing him with one of those other women would piss me off. Yes, he was my ex, but I still felt connected to him and a tad bit possessive. Did I have a right to feel this way? No. When he wasn't in my city, the chance of me seeing him with a beautiful woman on his arm was slim to none. Vegas, however, was a small big city in which you could connect anyone by seven degrees of separation. The thought of Aldridge dating, fucking, or falling in love with someone else was enough to make me crash out.

Grabbing my phone, I typed a quick text message.

> Danessa: I'm calling dibs.

Aldridge: What?

> Danessa: DIBS!

Aldridge: On what?

> Danessa: Everything.

Aldridge: Can I get a vowel because I don't know what you're talking about.

> Danessa: I know you're on the road and there are plenty of women and opportunities and I'd appreciate it if you didn't entertain anyone until we've had a chance to speak.

Aldridge: Oh shit are you putting my dick in your cart?

> Danessa: No this isn't about your dick this about you.

Aldridge: Danessa, I'm a singularly focused man so you don't have to worry about me or my dick doing anything you wouldn't approve of.

Danessa: I just think we should talk ... about stuff and things.

Aldridge: Things and stuff.

And where he could stuff his thing.

Danessa: So we both agree to put a pin in any extracurricular activities?

Aldridge: Yep, I'm going to ask the woman I met at the club to go home now.

I knew he was joking. Right, that was a joke? There wasn't a woman in his room. Right?

Danessa: Tell her Danessa Irwin has already licked it and so you're mine.

Aldridge: I'm gonna go find a Sharpie and write your name on it.

Danessa: You better not I want that dick returned to me in pristine condition.

Aldridge: Gotdamn, yes ma'am.

ALDRIDGE AND THE RAMBLERS RETURNED TO VEGAS AT ONE IN the morning and since we had a house showing the next day, we decided to wait until then to talk. I was currently pacing the hardwood floors of the home I planned to show Aldridge. My confidence had waned considerably since our text message exchange. What if Aldridge was looking to get his lick back? Perhaps he was lulling me into a false sense of security and then once he'd gotten the cookie he'd dip, ghost me, or worse break up with me in an attempt to hurt me like I'd hurt him. I'd never known him to be malicious, but time and heartbreak can change people.

Despite my best efforts, all I could think about were all the ways this could go horribly wrong. All the ways I could end up in misery. My life wasn't in the best place right now but at least I wasn't nursing a shattered heart. The past could only hurt me if I let it.

Today's house wasn't on the market yet, but I knew the realtor and she gave me a heads up that an estate sale was taking place in the home over the weekend. So, I thought it would be smart to use that intel to get a jump on the competition. Desirable homes in Vegas were scooped up quickly so sometimes you had to go above and beyond to get a leg up.

When Aldridge walked in he appeared frazzled. I waved and he made a beeline in my direction. "I had to park a block away. Why are there so many people here?" His hand found my waist and he pulled me into a hug.

I quickly pushed him away and scanned the room. "It's an estate sale."

"Why are we at an estate sale?"

"We are touring this house which is also the backdrop for this estate sale. Try to ignore the kitchen wear, jewelry, and clothes and focus on the bones of this house."

"Got it." Aldridge's hand found mine.

"What are you doing?" I politely removed my hand from his.

"I ... I just ... I thought—"

"I'm at work. I'm working. We should tour the house." Shit was already feeling weird. Or maybe it was just me acting weird. Me suggesting we circle back to the good old days was stupid. "First, we have the living room ..." Aldridge pinned his arms across his chest. He didn't verbally object, but his body language was speaking volumes. I believed in the separation of business and personal. I'd worked hard to garner a reputation as a realtor who was both professional and knowledgeable. The last thing I wanted was to be seen holding hands and making lovey dovey eyes at a client.

Aldridge and I had a lot to talk through and truthfully, my persistent second thoughts made me want to say sike real quick. We were not the same people we were in college, and it was silly to think we could just pick up where we left off. Maybe what I was feeling for Aldridge was just a spark that would fizzle out given time.

Upstairs I showed him the first of four bedrooms. "This would be a great room for a office or kids' room."

"So, are we just going to act like nothing happened?"

I shot him a look which I hoped conveyed this wasn't the time or the place. "Let's check out the next bedroom."

Aldridge planted his feet, blocking the exit. "Fuck the next bedroom Danessa, I wanna talk now."

I flashed a pained smile at the couple in the corner of the room flipping through records. "Can you keep your voice down?"

"No, I can't." The volume of his voice was even louder and echoing off the walls. "You said you wanted to talk, so let's talk."

"Talk about what, the herringbone floors?"

"No, not the floors. The fact that you were grinding against my dick the other—."

"Okay, shhh. We are in mixed company." I surrendered my hand in the air. "What do you want me to say?" I whispered inches from his face.

"I want you to acknowledge it happened and it wasn't all some fever dream."

Exhaling an aggravated breath, I grabbed his arm and proceeded to search for a room we could escape to. I found a small alcove adjacent to the third-floor landing and shoved him inside, closing the door behind us. "I know I said we'd talk but I didn't mean in a house full of strangers."

"Fuck these people. I don't know them. Danessa, all I've been able to think about is what happened last week and your text messages—"

"I think we may have let things go too far," I blurted out.

"Really because in my opinion it didn't go far enough."

"Aldridge."

"I could go further." He walked over to me, forcing me to retreat until my back was confronted with the solid wood door. "Tell me what you're thinking?"

"My brain is like soup filled with what ifs."

"Goddamnit Nessa when I said I was cool with being your friend, I meant it, I really did. But if I've unlocked a side quest in which I get to fuck you, I'd like to explore that."

"There is no scenario in which us sleeping together would be a good idea. It would only make things complicated." I knew I was giving mixed signals. A few days ago I was all in and staking claim, and now I was acting like a punk ass bitch. But I'd had time to think and all I could see were the cons.

"I can do complicated. What I can't do is pretend."

"Pretend?"

"Pretend like every time you're near me I don't want to grab your face and kiss you. Pretend like I wouldn't prefer to hear you say my name a few octaves higher and out of breath. Pretend like I don't imagine how my entire body thrums when I'm inside you. Danessa I—"

"I'm not the same person I was in college. I've changed and some of it isn't for the better."

"You don't think I've changed? I would never expect you to be the exact same girl I met in college. I'm down to get to know the new and slightly improved Danessa."

"What if you don't like her?"

"Nessa you're like … this house. There may be stuff everywhere, and a few design choices I wouldn't make but when you step back and take it all in it's easy to see this place has good bones. That's you. You were built on a strong foundation so no matter what, you're capable of weathering any storm. Maybe there are cracks, a flickering light or a door that squeaks when you open it but in my opinion that just adds to the charm."

My chest was tight, and I could easily hyperventilate at any moment. "I don't even know where we'd start."

"How about with a date. That's usually how most relationships begin."

"A date?" It seemed slightly absurd to go on a date with a man who'd seen the star-shaped birthmark on my right ass cheek.

"You, me, a dimly lit restaurant, appetizers, entrées, and dessert. I pay, you smile at me adoringly. Maybe you let me hold your hand, possibly a good night kiss."

"That was a very thorough definition."

Aldridge licked his lips and his voice deepened. "I really like your style and your energy, and I was wondering if you'd be down to link up tomorrow night?"

A huge smile overtook my face. Those were the exact words he used to ask me out our sophomore year of college. I was in the cafeteria studying, as usual, Aldridge passed by my table, and we exchanged silent head nods. A few minutes later he walked by again but this time he took a seat, asked me what I was studying for, and the rest was history.

"I'd like that. Just to be clear you're asking me on a date?"

"Yes, one hundred percent."

"You'd be surprised how many guys ask me out and then want to split the bill or send me a cash app request to pay my half for a slice of pizza and soda."

"I'm not like other guys."

"I think I'll be the arbitrator on whether you're more of the same or a new breed."

"Fair enough."

It tickled me we could recreate our conversation after all this time. Aldridge chuckled. "I don't think us being here is a coincidence. I believe in the grand design of things. This isn't a mistake. So, stop waiting for the error message and just let whatever this is happen."

"This isn't some sick revenge long game … is it?"

"I'm a lover boy. I'm not into getting payback."

Heartache was one of the pillars of any romantic relationship. But I was willing to suspend my disbelief and just float in the pocket for as long as God allowed.

ALDRIDGE

FIRST DATES WERE A BIG DEAL BECAUSE THEY WERE THE DAWN of something new. A great first date could change your life. I'd made reservations at Nobu. The restaurant had the dark, moody vibe I was looking for. I wanted something grown and sexy, and this place fit the bill. I'd hoped to pick Danessa up but practice ran long, so I sent a car to fetch her.

We'd come a long way from our first date at the pizza shop on campus. I ordered a large pizza half cheese, half meat lovers for us to share. Danessa wore a pleated skirt that hit just above her knees and a stack of gold necklaces which she fussed with the entire time. The total meal was probably less than twenty-five dollars. After dinner we just strolled through campus and chatted about any and every-thing. I was struck by how easy it was to talk with her. She got my sense of humor and would often add to the joke until we were both in stitches.

At the end of the date, I'd already secured another. By date three I'd asked her to be my girlfriend. And I waited patiently until she was ready to have sex. To make her first time special, I booked a three-star hotel because dorm rooms didn't really allow for a romantic experience. Danessa made me feel seen in a way being the star athlete didn't. I walked the campus, and people would shout out my name or pat me on the back because of a good game, and none of it mattered if I didn't have Danessa's approval. Getting an education and drafted were my primary goals but after that, my mission was to consistently fill Danessa's cup so she felt loved, heard, and safe enough to be vulnerable with me.

Cut to present day and our second first date I was just as nervous but also optimistic. Her agreeing to this meant I wasn't the only one wishing for a second chance. I wanted my girl back real fucking bad, and I was going to do everything in my power to make it happen.

As Danessa walked toward the table, my knees felt hollow. I had to brace myself against the booth to prevent myself from falling to the ground in worship of this goddess. Danessa was rocking a long, form-fitted black dress with white ruffle detailing at the bottom and the straps were tied in big bows. That dress hugged her curves and accentuated her round, plump ass. Her skin shimmered in the light, radiant and smooth. I peeped as men's heads turned as she breezed past and the fact that her final destination was my table caused me to straighten my back.

Her smile was a gift. "Hi."

"Hello." I leaned in with a hug and couldn't help but inhale her. She smelled like sex in its purest form, black currant, orange blossom, pralines and a hint of musk. I waited for her to sit and then followed suit. "You look amazing by the way."

"Thank you. Honestly my bedroom is a disaster area. I couldn't settle on what to wear."

"Well, I'm glad that dress won the battle of the outfits. I'm mean cause you just … ten out of ten, new high score, four plus four … ATE."

"I love it when you hype me up."

"Don't even get me started. I could write a one hundred-thousand-word dissertation on all the things that make you beautiful. I'm talking three hundred pages, single spaced with a methodology, discussion points, research objectives, and a glossary to define and identify each freckle and mole on your body."

"Stop it, you're embarrassing me."

"You should be embarrassed. When God created you he must've had a heavy hand because you were blessed with extra doses of beauty, brains, and booty. You are literally shitting on everyone in this restaurant including me.

"I don't know about that, but you look really handsome as well."

"I can clean up when I have to."

"I hope you weren't waiting for long?"

"No, I got here early, and I've waited years for this so what's an additional fifteen minutes?"

My heart was pounding in my ears. Even though this was Danessa sitting across from me, I couldn't shake my nerves. We'd spent a bunch of time together in the past few months, but I never had any expectations. Tonight was different because I was hoping for so much. After perusing the menu Danessa suggested we order drinks.

"I like the way you think." We ordered a white wine, and a guava ginger punch. "I have a confession to make."

"What?"

"I'm nervous as hell."

"It's just me."

"Yeah, and you're kind of a big deal. I could be sitting here with anyone else. My coach, Ms. Thornton, the Ramblers owner, shit even my dad and I wouldn't have butterflies performing laps in my stomach right now."

"Take a deep breath." Without hesitation I complied, breathing in through my nose and out through my mouth. "I was nervous too on the drive over, but then I saw you and it all just melted away." The waiter returned with our drinks and took our order. When he left, we each savored our first sips. "Is it good?"

"Yeah, it's delicious. Try it."

Her fingers brushed against mine as we exchanged the drink. Danessa took a timid taste. "Oh, wow it is really good." She slid the drink across the table placing it in front of me. "Why'd you stop drinking? Is it because your body is a temple?"

A first date wasn't the right moment to delve into my addiction and recovery. Even though alcohol was never really my struggle, I'd decided to give it up because drinking in excess could lead me to make poor choices and my sobriety wasn't something I was willing to gamble on. "Umm something like that."

"I think it's great. So much of our socializing as a society revolves around alcohol and the whole party culture."

"Exactly if you can't have a good time sober, I think that's a problem. But I'm never going to be the liquor lieutenant. Fuck all that, people can do what they want."

"Well, whatever you're doing is working because the Ramblers are on a winning streak. My social media feed is filled with highlights from the games, and the comments are all positive. Of course you have your occasional hater, but for the most part people are loving the new direction and you."

"It's been going better than I expected. But I can't help but feel like the press is building us up to knock us down."

"Why do you think that?"

"Because that's what they do. Feel good stories don't get engagement. People live for the drama. If I see one more article about the rivalry between Colin and me I'm going to lose it."

"But you two hate each other."

"Hate is putting a little too much on it. We don't fuck with one another but we're also professionals and know when it's game time, all that shit falls to the wayside. I'm going to set him up for easy lay ups and he's going to screen the offense so I can drive to the basket."

"I'm glad to hear you're learning to compromise."

"Don't get me wrong I still want to punch him in the face until his teeth fall out of his mouth like Chicklets, but I have restraint."

"That sounds like hate."

"Maybe more of a strong dislike. Enough about work. Classes start in a few weeks. Are you excited?"

"No, I feel like I'm in over my head. I registered for my classes and this first semester I'm going to try to continue to work while I'm in school. I don't want to blow through my savings too soon. If I'd just stayed in school, I'd be a lawyer already. Really wish I had a time machine so I could go back and slap the old me."

"Shit, if I had a time machine I would go back and slap so many people. My fifth-grade teacher who told me I wasn't ever going to be shit. Slap. My junior high bully, who made fun of me because I wore off-brand shoes. Slap. Funny enough during the summer before eighth grade, I shot up like a weed and never got bullied again. Anyway, life is filled with shoulda, woulda, coulda's, at least you're doing it now."

"I know you're right. And I'm very excited to start this

new journey. Are you planning to make it home for Christmas?"

"No, I have an away game Christmas Day."

"That sucks."

"Yeah but the team is going to host something, so I'll get my turkey and stuffing fix. What about you?"

"You know my mother puts it down in the kitchen. So I will be wearing sweatpants and going back for seconds."

"That's what's up." I took a bite of the lobster and shiitake salad. "Hey, do you know any good realtors in Philly?"

"Why, are you looking to buy a place out there too?"

"Yeah, not for me, for Duane."

Danessa narrowed her eyes. "I thought he had a place?"

"He does but it's a shoe box. And he wants two bedrooms so my niece has her own space when she visits." Danessa jaw tightened like she was trying to stop herself from speaking her mind. "What Danessa?"

"I think it's great you wanting to provide your brother with a place but …"

"But what?"

"When does it end Aldridge? Are you expected to finance everyone else's life for all of eternity?"

"Duane's had some hard breaks."

"And that's not your doing."

I leaned back into the booth. "So I'm not supposed to look after my family?"

"I didn't say that. I just know you. You've been taking care of your family since high school. You're a giver and people tend to take advantage of that."

"By people you mean my family?"

Her lips stretched into a straight line. "Taking care of

your mother, I totally understand, paying for Tootie to go to college. Acceptable. But Duane is a grown ass man with a child of his own—"

"A grown ass man with a criminal record. It's not like he can apply at a bank and get a nine to five."

"But why does that become your responsibility?"

"What the fuck are you talking about?" I wasn't the kind of man who left my family high and dry when they needed me. I had the funds to provide and as long as I could they would never be without.

"I've seen this play out several times. A talented athlete signs a multi-million-dollar contract and then everyone comes knocking with their hands out. It may seem like a lot of money right now, but shit goes fast when you have four mortgages, utilities, several car payments, and yearly taxes."

"Since when did you become an accountant?"

"I work with people looking to buy homes. I'm well versed on the desirable debt to income ratio needed to achieve that."

"I appreciate the concern, but I'm fully plugged in when it comes to my expenses."

"Tootie, is what, sixteen? And she's smart so she'll probably get into an Ivy League school. That's tuition, boarding, books, and fees. She'll need a car depending on which school she attends. That shit adds up."

"It does. But I've been saving for years for that inevitability. You do remember I majored in business finance for a reason, right?"

"I just want you to be good. I see how hard you work, and I don't want anything to jeopardize that. But it sounds like you have it completely under control, so I'll fall all the way back." She reached for her glass, draining it.

"Danessa—"

"I'm going to go to the ladies room." She didn't meet my eyes, and she didn't wait for me to stand before rushing away from the table. Her stance was nothing new. When we were in college she voiced her concerns about the amount of money I was sending to my folks. It pissed me off then and it pisses me off now. My mother worked long hours to feed and clothe us. Sometimes there wasn't enough to go around for five hungry bellies, and she'd go without. She deserved the world, and I intended to give it to her to show my appreciation.

This wasn't me just blindly spending money. I tracked everything, wrote off what I could. My parents weren't in a mansion, I'd purchased a five-bedroom home in the suburbs just like my mom always dreamed of. I knew Danessa's objections were coming from a genuine place. She wasn't saying this because she wanted me to spend that money on her, she wanted me to think long term.

When Danessa returned it was obvious her bathroom break hadn't helped to thaw the chill that was developing.

"Listen, I appreciate your concern. You have always had my back and my best interest as a priority, but my brother needs a proper place to live, and I can provide it and for that I'm grateful."

"The last thing I meant to do was make a big deal out of this. I'm sorry. I'll find realtors based in Philly for you."

"Thank you."

I didn't receive her words lightly. But there were obligations I couldn't escape, and I was never going to be the guy who forgot where I came from and who supported me along the way just because my bank account has a ton of zeros attached. I grew up struggling and once I made my first million, I vowed to never go back. As a Black athlete, shit as the first person to go to college in my family I was expected to reach back and help pull others up.

When our entrées arrived, it helped to improve our moods. I interrupted our silent enjoyment of the food and Danessa's shoulder shimmy after each bite with a question. "When was the last time you were on a date?"

"That is such a first date question."

"Well, this is a first date."

"I don't know maybe seven months ago."

"How'd that go?"

"I'm here on a date with you so not that great."

"Why?"

"We were just different. He was a nice guy but something was missing. What about you?"

"I went on a date right before I left Kansas City."

"And?"

"It went well. I think because we both knew what it was."

"What was it?" Danessa leaned in.

"So about school."

"No you don't get to throw out a tiny crumb. I want the whole loaf."

"Before I speak, we need to activate the veil of non-judgment over this conversation."

"Agreed."

"Okay, she was a fuck buddy. And I was about to move and knew it would probably be a minute before I got laid again."

"And she was okay with that?"

"You'd be surprised how many women are, when you're upfront and honest about it."

"I guess that's the life of a basketball player. Anyone

you want. Chicks posted up on standby in different area codes."

"I don't have women scattered across the country."

"So no other woman could step forward today and claim you?"

"No, because I'm single."

"I'm single too but my definition of single and an athlete's definition of the word single is often different."

"So, you're telling me there isn't some sorry sack of shit you've been keeping on the line for an ego boost and free meals."

"Yeah. I'm sitting across from him."

I tossed my linen napkin in her direction. "Wow, F you."

"I'm kidding."

"I kind of walked right into that one."

"You made it hella easy."

"Do you still talk to your ex-fiancé?"

"We still wish each other well during the holidays or birthdays. Why is that a problem?"

"Today no, three months from now ... maybe."

"You're not the jealous type."

"No college Aldridge wasn't the jealous type. Me, present Aldridge is a goon about mine and I don't fucking play."

"I don't think it's that serious."

"I bet you a million dollars old boy Marcus is somewhere kicking himself because he lost you. Trust me, I speak from experience."

"What about you and Ashley? Are you still liking her posts with heart eye emojis?"

"First, I don't use heart eyed emojis. And second,

Ashley blocked me. Well first she made a long ass video about knowing her worth and not allowing a man to waste her time, tagged me in it, and then blocked me."

"And were you wasting her time?"

"We were young. I don't know what she expected. It was about having fun."

"So she wanted more and you were looking for a good time?"

"When did you become pro Ashley?"

"I support all women."

"Ashley was great. But I knew pretty early on we weren't going to get married and start a family. And I made that fact very clear."

"You told her you didn't want to marry her?"

"No I said I wasn't looking to settle down anytime soon. And all her influencer friends were switching over to wedding planning content and she felt left out."

"So you no longer talk?"

"That woman wouldn't spit on me if I was on fire."

"Well, that's good to know." We both laughed.

If you didn't get it, you should now. Shit was easy with her. Walking into this restaurant my body was a fist and now I felt completely at ease. Aside from the hiccup about my generosity, this date had gone well. I certainly didn't want this night to end and I hoped she felt the same.

"How was your food?"

"It was great. Everything was delicious."

"Do you want anything else? Because I want you to be satisfied."

"I am full and content. Thank you."

"So what do you wanna do next?"

"I was hoping I could see your hotel room. For real estate purposes of course."

When our waiter returned to check on us, I asked, "Can we get the check? Like we do not need to see a dessert menu. We do not want to go boxes. Just the check."

DANESSA

I'D FUCKED THIS MAN HUNDREDS OF TIMES, BUT NOW I DIDN'T know where to start. Should I just grab his collar and pull him in? Maybe I continue to wait for him to make the first move which he was horrible at doing. Aldridge could anticipate an opponent's next four plays, but when it came to me, he always seemed hesitant.

Our first kiss took him an hour to initiate. He walked me to my dorm and blathered about the most mundane topics because he was too afraid to lean in for a kiss. Not going to lie, I was starting to think he wasn't interested until he said, "Fuck it," and grabbed my face.

"You know if you squint you can see the fountain show at the Bellagio. It should be starting any minute if you're interested." He'd been acting like a tour guide from his hotel balcony, identifying points of interest.

"Are you nervous?"

"Why would I be nervous?"

"Because …"

"You think I'm scared to set things off? Shit I will bend you over this balcony and get to work." His lack of action didn't match the confidence of his words.

"Well, I'm nervous."

"Why?"

"Because I'm older and I have dimples and stretch marks in places I didn't when we were in college."

"Danessa I'm a grown man. I do not care about that shit."

"What if the chemistry is off?"

"You know good and damn well that's never been a problem for us. It doesn't matter what does or doesn't happen tonight. We could just cuddle and knock the fuck out. The night is gonna be perfect because I get to spend it with you."

Fucking my ex after several years filled me with a ton of trepidation. But this wasn't' just any ex, it was Aldridge, and he was right, all that matters is us being together.

"The show's starting." He pointed to a fixed point in the distance. As we stood in silence watching water shoot up into the air to "Viva Las Vegas" by Elvis it felt like the window of opportunity was slipping away. Perhaps we were better suited as friends. Not everything deserved a reboot. Maybe Aldridge and I had already jumped the shark.

The heat from Aldridge's body was like a flame, warm enough to soothe me but also hot enough to burn. His hand was just inches away from mine. I longed to interlock my fingers with his. The hair on my right arm stood on end in an attempt to get nearer. Aldridge was fixated on the sway of the water midair. I don't think he registered I was no longer paying attention to the show.

"Fuck it." Grabbing the collar of his shirt, I pulled him closer while rising to my toes. When Aldridge's lips touched mine, everything sped up and I was weightless, probably because my feet were no longer on the ground as Aldridge was taking long strides to his bedroom. In the bedroom we stumbled over one another in an attempt to remove articles of clothing.

"Normally, I always have something to say but you've got me at a loss for words, you are so damn fine."

"Really?"

"Yes, I love your perfect soft stomach." He planted a kiss on the left side of my belly causing me to giggle. "I love your long, regal neck." His lips were like cushions and his feathery beard tickled my skin. "These violin hips that allow me to grab hold and make beautiful music. This mole right there." He pointed at the mole on my breast. "That is my favorite mole on your body."

I could listen to this man's raspy voice for hours. "Let's hear it for the kneecaps. They're a little wobbly but still strong." Instinctually I swatted in his direction playfully. Aldridge circled my body, his hand sweeping across my stomach. "I love the strength in your back, always straight asserting your confidence." He unhooked my bra and it slipped from my shoulders, landing on the floor.

"God, I wanna taste you." His declaration made me shiver. He wasted no time making my dreams a reality, removing my panties and lowering me to the bed. Taking my right leg, his mouth worked its way up. When he reached my inner thigh my breath hitched. This man was going to have me acting a fool tonight. I just knew I was about to say things that would make me blush and look at myself funny in the light of day.

The warmth of his breath just inches from my core forced me to beg. "Please."

Luckily, he didn't torture me but instead slid his tongue over my most sensitive nerves. My body was electrified with pleasure. Aldridge took to his knees as if settling in for a feast. As he sunk his tongue into my pussy, my soul vacated my body and performed a praise dance. It was the moaning for me as he devoured my pussy. He was acting like he was suffering from dehydration, and my juices were the only thing that could satiate.

My hand grasped at his curls tempted to smother him between my thighs. When Aldridge told me to fuck his face, I showed all the way out, rocking my hips so my clit could connect with his extended tongue. Aldridge ran his hands upward over the length of my body Finding my open mouth, he inserted two of his fingers. Sucking his long digits, I hoped he could imagine what I planned to do to his dick later on.

Saliva was trailing down his hand when he finally removed it and immediately inserted those wet fingers inside of me, forcing my eyes to the back of my head. I was speaking gibberish. Just babbling a string of nonsensical words. Aldridge turned me over onto my stomach and cleared his plate from the rooter to the tooter. No fold was left untouched.

"Is this okay?" He massaged my anus with his thumb.

"Yes." When I tell you I would let this man do the freak nastiest things to me and beg for more.

"What about this?" His thumb inched inside and my normal twenty-twenty vision temporarily went blurry. A French kiss to my clit prompted me to claw at the bedding.

"I think I'm about to come."

"Do it, I dare you. Come for me, baby."

I was a people pleaser, so I did as I was told, writhing across his face until I met a sweet release that forced me to collapse into the mattress. The wake of my orgasm was just as intense, leaving me trembling uncontrollably for almost a full minute.

Aldridge stood licking his lips. "You good?"

"I just …" The English language seemed to escape me.

He headed to the bathroom and returned with a condom he casually rolled over his dick. I'd seen my fair share of penises and Aldridge was the best by far. It was thick, long, and veiny, and his richly hued skin made me want to wrap my lips around it and have him melt in my mouth. Aldridge climbed onto the king-sized bed and hovered over top of me. He slid his finger over my slit to confirm I was still ready. My entire body tensed in anticipation, and I seeped air as he slowly inserted his member until he was snuggly inside. The first few thrusts were daunting.

Aldridge leaned in whispering in my ear. "Nessa, this pussy is so good."

Sometimes I had a tendency to hide out in my head. Thinking about the past or the future and not living in the present. But as Aldridge delivered stroke after stroke, it was impossible for me to be anywhere else but in the moment. My legs were already trembling, a sure sign he was hitting my spot. His hands massaged my skin, from my thighs, to my waist, and my neck. Aldridge buried his face into my chest, sucking my left nipple into his mouth.

He'd always been a multitasker, and he was capable of sparking all of my erogenous zones simultaneously. "Tell me I'm a good boy," he begged.

"Yes, you're the best. You make me feel so good."

He bit down onto my shoulder hard enough that we were straddling the line between pleasure and pain and I loved the danger of it. Aldridge stalled the deep thrust but what came next was far more intense. Precision long strokes rewired my brain sparking joy. "That's it, Princess cream on this dick." A whimper was all I could muster because he felt so good. He grabbed my legs and held them in a wide V and I clawed my nails into his thighs.

This man turned me every which way but loose. Biologically it was impossible, but I would bet money the tip of his dick was connecting with my kidneys. "Aldridge it's too much, it's too deep."

"And you're taking it so well. I'm so proud of you."

"I want it all. Give me all of it." Clearly, I was delusional because each of his thrusts was demolishing this pussy. "Take it, baby." There was a time when I thought my body was molded for his. His hand sat plumb in the curve of my back. My full lips covered his perfectly. His arms would envelop me, and I knew nothing could hurt me when wrapped in his strong embrace. As he rearranged my organs, that belief was affirmed. Given the chance, I would never let this man go again.

Aldridge released my legs and pressed the weight of his body against mine. His face rested in the crook of my neck and he let me know how much he appreciated me. "You are so sexy right now. I love it here inside your tight, wet pussy."

"Am I your little slut?" I groaned.

"Umm … you can be. Do you wanna be my good little slut?"

"Ye … yes, please," I stuttered.

What happened next is difficult to explain but time and space faded away. The planet was silent and all that remained was Aldridge and I fucking in animated suspension. Heavy breathing, deep moans that tumbled up my throat. Aldridge's animalistic growls made me feral. A solar flare permeating in my belly before shooting through my extremities. And the exchange of pure energy as our bodies peaked at the same damn time.

Slowly the world folded in on us. Aldridge's arms were wrapped tight around me as he murmured, "God Nessa. Oh my God." Our hips still in motion not wanting the moment to end. "Oh God. Are you okay?"

"Yeah," I breathed out. "Wow, just wow—"

"Yeah." He planted soft kisses across my face before devouring my lips. His kiss let me know I had minutes until he was ready for round two.

"Good morning, I brought donuts and coffee, and Danishes." I laid the goodies on the breakroom table.

"Aren't you chipper." Jemini smelled the creamer in the fridge, her turned up nose let me know the milk had gone bad.

"It's such a beautiful day, the sun is shining, it's not too cold. It's like a perfect day. It's the most perfect day." I beamed.

Anika entered the breakroom. "You hate Mondays, so why so giddy?"

"I don't hate Mondays. I love them. It's like a new beginning every week. New chances, opportunities, and growth."

"Is this about a man?" Jemini scrolled her phone probably checking her DMs for fresh meat.

"No, no. Why can't I just be genuinely happy?"

Both Jemini and Anika stared at me. Aldridge and I had the best weekend, and I was fucked in places I didn't even think were possible. *I'm talking about physical locations not bodily ones, you pervert.* Anika and my mom were right, though I'd never admit it, I just needed a good fuck. All the tension and stress built up in my shoulders and back was gone. My legs were wobbly, and my pussy was still throbbing and wet. I left his hotel this morning, but not before he fucked me with my face plastered against the window as he spanked me to orgasm.

"I'm gonna go start the day." I shot off fake air guns with my fingers.

"You fucked Aldridge, didn't ya?" Anika said before I could make it to the exit.

Don't be ridiculous. Absolutely not. Damn, can't a girl just be in a good mood? I quickly practiced which denial would sound most convincing. "Nah-uh. I just had a B12 shot, took my vitamins, and drank some orange juice. This is an all-natural high."

"All-natural dick."

"Are you and he back together?" Jemini's voice was optimistic.

"No. I haven't seen Aldi all weekend."

Anika gasped and pointed at me. "You haven't called him Aldi since the breakup. Oh, you two were fucking fucking. His dick reinstalled deleted software."

"Wow this is fanciful. Just making up stories." My brow and upper lip were seconds away from breaking into beads of perspiration. If I had a bag of snakes, I would release them right now, or maybe I could just start a fight to get out of this conversation. I wasn't ready to share, especially with my mother. "I'm going back to law school," I blurted out.

"What? Danessa." Jemini's voice was laced with disappointment. You'd think I'd told her I'd gotten a DUI and not that I was pursuing a degree.

"Why is this shocking? I got into William S. Boyd here in Vegas and I start in January."

Anika grabbed a coffee and two donuts. Walking past

me she whispered, "Nice way to change the subject," before leaving me and Jemini alone.

"What about work?"

"I'll juggle both at first and then I'll figure it out as I go."

"You have clients who rely on you."

"And I will still show up and provide excellent customer service. My hours of availability may be a little different, but it's doable."

"You should be focused on finding a man like your sister."

"At twenty-six a man is the least of my concerns."

"I taught you two life comes at you fast. And before you know it, you're in your forties and the quality of men significantly decrease."

She was right, she taught us our ABCs, 123s and that our value was based on whether we had a man. My mother was what we called male-centered. A man, shit it didn't have to be her man, but any man took priority over her and her daughters. Her pursuit of a husband compromised her judgment allowing her to entertain all types of questionable men, and those men took advantage of her and us.

"Well maybe you should've taken your own advice."

"My DMs are open and active. I can't say the same for you."

As we got older, she saw Anika and I as competition.

"Congratulations, how many thirst traps do you have to post per day to maintain that consistency?"

"You are just like your father. You got the worst parts of him, I swear to God."

"Well at least I didn't get the worst parts of you." Make no mistake this was a regular weekday for me and

Jemini. We'd fight and work hard to push the other's buttons.

"You stay single because you're a constant wet blanket. No wonder Aldridge moved on so quickly."

One thing I did inherit from my mother was her temper. "This from the menopausal woman who is dating a twenty-one-year-old kid?"

"DeMarcus and I have a lot in common."

"Yeah, you both love spending his money."

"I didn't raise you to be so … blah."

"You didn't raise me at all. You left us twenty dollars for pizza while you fucked random men. So because I don't wanna be a whore—" My mother closed the distance between us and slapped me squarely on my face. This wasn't the first time.

"You watch the way you fucking talk to me."

"You just can't …" The lump in my throat made it impossible for words to pass. Tears, however, filled my eyes and fell in streams down my cheeks. Jemini knew how to shut down a conversation when it wasn't going her way. My entire body shook with a mixture of rage and embarrassment. Anika's dainty foot falls hurriedly advanced down the hall. She reentered the breakroom to find me in tears and Jemini's hands balled into fists.

"Maybe you should go back to work Mom," Anika suggested. Jemini complied, I'm sure she was sorry, she always was afterward. With our mother out of the room, Anika pulled me into her arms. "I'm sorry, I shouldn't have left."

"It's okay." I shook my head.

"You know Jemini—"

"Jemini is never gonna change." My lower lip trembled.

Anika rubbed my back. My sister, for all my complaints, was my protector. She'd been my bodyguard our entire lives. Taking the brunt of the beatings and emotional abuse. She'd locked us in our bedroom when strange men spent the night. And she told me I was way more than just a pretty face. "You're right, it's such a beautiful day. Too beautiful for tears."

"I slept with Aldi." My pout turned into a weak smile.

She stepped back and softly clapped her hands in silent celebration. "It's about damn time."

ALDRIDGE

I WAS SORTING THROUGH MY MONTHLY BILLS, SIGNING OFF ON payments and planning for next month while Nori ran through some pending items.

"The rent for Duane's place has cleared and the mortgage on your mother's house has also gone through. The hotel is paid up until the end of the month. Do you think you'll be extending your stay?"

"Don't take that tone with me."

"What tone?"

"You think I'm taking too long to find a place." It had only been a couple of months, but Nori believed I was moving at a snail's pace to settle on home I liked. What she didn't know is I'd been dragging my feet because I needed a reason to keep seeing Danessa. But now that things between me and her had shifted, I imagined house hunting would kick into high gear.

"Yes. Danessa's shown you over three dozen listings and you've passed on all of them."

"When I find the right place trust me, you'll be the first to know."

Nori rolled her eyes. "I hate walking through the casino. I leave smelling like smoke."

"I'm sorry, send me the bill for your dry cleaning.

Speaking of Danessa, can you locate the best bakery in town and send her some cupcakes with a note that reads, 'You bake me crazy'?"

Nori's pen stalled. "Are you serious?"

"Yeah, what you don't like it?"

"It's corny as fuck. Does Danessa go for corny? Because if not, I'd reconsider."

"I think it's kind of cute."

"Oh, you are gone." She tossed her pen into her notebook.

"What do you mean?"

"That woman has got your nose wide open. Out here sending sweet treats with stupid food puns."

"Can you think of something better?"

"Yeah, how about Danessa I had a really good time on our date the other night and I can't wait to see you again."

My face crumpled in disgust. "Nah, I like mine better." I scanned an itemized receipt. "Could you also Cash App her money to get her hair done?"

"How much?"

"I don't know, a thousand, two."

"For her hair?" Nori's eyebrows climbed her forehead. She was an amazing assistant who kept me on track, but she was judging me every step of the way.

"Yeah, whatever it costs her to get a silk press. Because her edges were reverting to their natural state when she left this morning. If you know what I mean." I laughed fiendishly.

"Not you bragging on your dick."

"I'm not bragging. And how many times have I had to listen to you boast about a woman's number you scored?"

"That's because I have game, and the bitches love a cool ass butch fem who can switch it up."

"Can you just allow me to be a tad braggadocious."

"So the date went well?"

"It did."

"Will there be a second date?"

I pushed the paperwork aside. "Do you believe in fate?"

"No."

"I do. I think this was the plan all along, and I couldn't see it back then because I was too hurt. But maybe we needed to live and grow separately so we could come back together better than ever."

"Aldridge, I know you like her, but I don't want you to set yourself up for a letdown."

"What do you mean?"

"If Danessa didn't see how great you were before, what's different now?"

"We were young, she made a mistake."

"Has she even explained why she dumped you in the first place? From where I'm sitting the only thing that's changed is you're a multi-millionaire ball player with money to blow."

"Danessa's not like that."

"How do you know? You haven't talked in years. People change, you have."

"Because I know Danessa." My tone was final. I wouldn't accept any vilification of Nessa. She wasn't a gold digger with dollar signs behind her eyes. Parts of me still felt the heartache, a weekend filled with great sex couldn't erase that. Danessa was my first serious relationship, the first love of my life, and my first heartbreak. Why, was a question I was too scared to ask, because what if she explained only to realize her reasons were still valid?

Worse, what if it was something I did or didn't do that

drove her away? One minute we were eating pie and scrolling through Apartments.com, and the next she was tearfully telling me she needed a break. Not from the apple pie or online screen time, but from me.

"Whatever, I'll send her a grand she looks like she pays a pretty penny for that hair. If there's anything left, she can use it on her nails, brows, or unmentionables."

Nori jotted down notes in silence. She was pissed at me for not at least taking her words into consideration. The line between professional and personal were often blurred between us. Nori was one of my favorite people and although she was on my payroll, I thought of her as a friend ... shit more than a friend, she was family.

"Are we good?" I didn't like it when she was cross with me.

"We'll always be good, Aldridge."

"I'd really like you to get to know Danessa better."

"Yep, I'm down."

"Trust me, you're gonna love her once you know her better. Are we done here?"

"Uhm ... I just have one more piece of business."

"What's up?"

"Your father reached out to me."

Pressure built behind my eyes. I was on cloud nine after my weekend with Danessa and talk about my father would surely drag me down into the pits of hell. "About?"

"He asked for some money. I told him I'd have to check with you, which he didn't like."

"How much?"

"Ten thousand dollars."

"Doesn't he get his monthly five-grand payment in a few days?"

"Yeah, I mentioned that to him and he started ranting

about being an entrepreneur and needing to invest in some amazing opportunity. I don't understand how he goes through it so fast."

"Because he has a gambling addiction, and he likes sex workers. That shit ain't cheap." My father was on an allowance. He received five thousand dollars a month. But that never seemed to be enough. In the past I would bend and give him an extra two grand or a quick five hundred dollars. But I was just feeding the beast. He was lucky to get the five each month. Because if it wasn't for my mom, he wouldn't see a dime from me. As a grown ass man, you'd think he'd feel a way about his son supporting him. The funny thing is he clearly resented me for the financial assistance while steadily begging for funds.

"Do you want me to—"

"No, if he wants more money, he can call me and ask for it." He would more likely scoop out his eyeballs with a rusty spoon before making that request. That's why he had Nori's number on speed dial. On this I was setting boundaries. Danessa was partially right, I was at risk of spreading myself thin by trying to support the village. I needed to start cutting some of these motherfuckers off. Aside from the sperm, my father hadn't done shit for me. "Maybe you should block his number. Nip this shit right in the bud."

"Is that what you want?"

"Yeah. I don't pay you enough to deal with my dad."

"Okay, what's on the agenda for the rest of your day?"

"I'm going to NA in an hour."

"You seem to really like this new group."

"Yeah, it's because of Pete, the facilitator. He gives it to you real, no fluff. I appreciate that."

"Good, I'm glad you found a group you like the first time out. I'm proud of you."

"For what? Not killing myself?"

Nori reached for my hand which let me know she was serious. "It was scary for a while and I'm just happy you're in a better place. You deserve all you've earned. I know you feel guilty, but you worked hard for each and every blessing. And more importantly you keep putting in the work for your sobriety."

"I'm sorry you had to see me like that." Nori witnessed the worst of me. At the height of my addiction, I was abusive and mean. She should've quit over a dozen times, but she didn't give up on me. And for that she would forever have my love and respect.

"I've always got your back, Goofy." She called me that because she claimed I walked like Goofy the cartoon character. Which I didn't by the way. "Can I ask?"

"Hmm?"

"Have you told Danessa?"

"That I'm a drug addict? No, nope I could never find a way to weave it into the conversation."

"But you're going to tell her, right?"

"Eventually. We just went on a first date. There's a ton of catching up we have to do."

"Just promise you'll tell her before shit gets too deep."

I nod in agreement. We were already in too deep.

AFTER A CLOSE GAME AT HOME, THE RAMBLERS WERE ON A mini-winning streak. I couldn't leave the arena fast enough, heading straight to Danessa's place. You know that feeling when you meet someone new, and you want to spend every waking moment with them? That was me right now. When I was at work or the gym, all I could think about was her. And when I was with her, I wished each day was daylight savings so I could have more time in her presence.

Normally, I preferred to play it cool. No declarations of love before the six-month mark. We could discuss the possibility of meeting my mother after a year. It was a pass on matching tattoos or names inked onto my skin. Oddly enough I got Danessa's name tattooed on my chest in college. Something I wouldn't do for any other woman. After we broke up, I'd considered covering it up dozens of times but doing that felt like I was admitting we were a mistake, and it was never that.

From the hall I could detect the sound of footsteps getting closer. When she opened the door her eyes lit up, but then she immediately caught herself as if she didn't want me to know how happy she was to see me. "Hello." Her tone was casual.

"Don't play with me. Acting all formal like I wasn't balls deep in your shit less than twenty-four hours ago."

"Aldridge." She poked her head into the hall to confirm no one overheard me. "Inside now."

When she closed the door, I swooped in. "I missed you." Danessa's body melted into mine as our lips crushed into each other's. All that nonchalant shit she was trying to pull was gone. She framed my face with her hands, moaning softly over my lips. Grabbing her perfect ass I gave it a squeeze.

Danessa scratched at my beard. "I caught the game."

"Did you?"

"You were amazing. Thirty-seven points, twelve rebounds, and ten assists."

"Well, what can I say? I'm true to this not new to this. You know there is a standing ticket in your name if you ever wanna come to a home game." I pulled her body closer to mine.

"I appreciate it. But I hate watching you play in person. It makes my stomach churn, and I can never enjoy the game because I'm always on pins and needles. I'm way better in the comfort of my living room where I can walk away from the TV when needed."

"We are going to work on that because I like seeing your face in the crowd." I brushed her extra-long bangs from her eyes.

"What's in the bag?" She pointed to the paper bag I placed at the front door.

"I'm craving mac and cheese."

"Random."

"I was in the showers after the game and I was like mac and cheese would hit the spot right now."

"And you picked premade mac from Whole Foods? I think you're going to be disappointed."

I imitated the game show buzzer sound. "Nope, I brought stuff to make it myself."

"You're gonna make macaroni and cheese at ten o'clock at night?"

"I know the woman who burns hard boil eggs ain't judging me."

"I only burned them because I forgot and fell asleep."

"The dorm kitchen was filled with smoke because the pot damn near melted on the stovetop. The fire department showed up."

"Okay, we are not going to rehash this. I'm not the best cook, but I'm getting better."

Scooping up the bag, I headed to the kitchen. "Tell me you have butter."

"Of course, what do I look like?"

I licked my lips, prepared to respond.

"Don't answer that." Danessa peeped me checking out the box of cupcakes on the kitchen counter. "They taste just as delicious as they look. Some lanky brother sent them to me. I loved the note. It was cute."

"I knew you'd like it." I gently bumped my forehead into hers. "Nori said it was corny."

"I like a little cornball activity. Brothers are always acting too cool for school. I appreciate a man who isn't afraid to be a bit soft."

I pumped my fist in the air. "Just call me a Squishmallow," I said while planting pecks to her lips. "Why do you always smell so good?" My tongue coasted up the side of her neck. "The women I've hung out with do not smell like you."

"I'm sure they smelled fine."

"Basura, I tell you. All of them."

"If you keep doing that we're not going to get to the mac and cheese."

"True. First let's devour this food and then I'll devour you."

"Promise?"

"Pinky promise." We linked our pinky fingers with a shake. I got down to business pulling out a large pot for the cheese sauce. Danessa was in charge of the vibes, selecting jazzy rap music and pouring me a blackberry ginger ale over ice.

"How was your day?" I asked while mixing the roux.

"I registered for my classes." She presented jazzy hands, giving them a shake.

"Okay, so it's official, official. My baby is fittin' to be an esquire."

Danessa's jaw flinched, and I knew what she was most likely thinking, it was too early for terms of endearment. Just months ago, we were incommunicado, and now I was calling her baby and telling her how good her pussy felt. Even I had to admit it was zero to one hundred in under seven seconds. The last thing I was trying to do was scare her off or give her pause. Danessa probably didn't feel the same, but I was all in. Fuck time to think or test runs. Danessa was mine. I may not be able to pick a place to live, but the love of my life was decided and carved into my skin.

I added carnation milk. "I saw a lady do this online and I was intrigued."

"Carnation milk?"

"Carnation milk and heavy cream. Disclaimer, she was White so if this turns out like crap, I'm going to blame the mayo DNA."

"Is that how you spend your free time, scrolling social media?"

"Yep, those sites have the best thirst traps." I winked playfully.

"I bet your DMs are overflowing with indecent proposals."

"Nope, my DMs are closed."

"Why?"

"Cause that shit's weird. I don't wanna hook up with a fan. The power dynamic would be off."

"How do you distinguish between a fan and someone genuinely interested in you?"

"That's the million-dollar question. Short answer, you don't. So I prefer to meet people organically."

Danessa sat on the other side of the island watching me layer the dish with the remaining cheese, while checking her phone. "Hmm."

"What's up?"

"Why did your assistant send me an email filled with legalese and a non-disclosure agreement attached?" Her tone was lethal as if I was two seconds from getting my ass cussed out.

"Excuse me?" Danessa turned her phone so I could read her screen. "Erm, I don't know but you should disregard."

"Did you ask her to send it?"

"No, it's just standard." I sprinkled the last layer of cheese on the dish.

"What does that mean?" Yep, she was pissed.

"Everybody does it."

"Aldridge if you don't stop fussing with the mac and cheese and answer my question."

I washed my hands, drying them on a dish towel. "Normally when I meet or hang out with someone new and things level up, I have them sign an NDA. All the athletes do it. It's not a big deal."

"Not a big deal?" She scrolled through the agreement on her phone. "It prohibits me from talking about our relationship or acknowledging your existence."

"No, it prevents people from telling tales outside of the bedroom. You'd be surprised how many women are ready to run to TMZ with stories."

Her normally full lips were stretched into a thin line. "I'm not any woman."

"Well according to Whitney, you're every woman."

Danessa slammed her hand on the counter. "Is this a joke to you?"

"Did you hear the part where I said disregard the email?"

"I just want to understand why *your* assistant thought *I* was some random bitch who would sign legal paperwork silencing myself."

"I don't think there was any thinking before she hit send." NDAs were standard practice in my line of business. Nori was just doing what I paid her to do, cover my ass. Do I wish she hadn't sent that email to Danessa? Yes. Because Danessa was clearly the exception to the rule.

Her eyes grew wide, and I could tell her brain was working overtime to connect imaginary dots. "Is that why you Cash Apped over that money? Is this all transactional to you?"

"That money was for your hair."

"I don't want your handouts."

My eyes narrowed as I sized her up. "Not gonna lie, it feels like you're picking a fight."

"Why would I do that?"

"Maybe you're hangry. I know I can be an asshole when I'm hungry."

"Did you just call me an asshole?"

I rounded the kitchen counter and pulled up on her tilting her head until we were eye to eye. "Stop playing with me. I don't expect you to sign an NDA because you, we, are not a secret. If you want, we could go to the roof and I'll shout at the top of my lungs declaring our alliance and my devotion to you and only you." I scanned the room. "Shit, matter fact we don't need a roof. I just ..." Grabbing Danessa's hand, I walked over to the balcony and opened the door. In the still of the evening, I screamed at the top of my lungs. "I, Aldridge Mosley declare in front of God and this snake plant that Danessa Irwin is my person. I knew it when I was nineteen, and I know it now."

Danessa reached for me trying to rein me in. "Aldi, my neighbors are very particular when it comes to noise, and they will slide a strongly worded passive aggressive note under my door."

"Wait are you saying you don't want me to disclose how much I care about you?"

I turned back toward the vast beyond. "We had sex last night and Danessa came five times."

"Aldridge, get your ass back inside." She sounded like a mother whose kid was acting up in the cereal aisle at Kroger.

"When are you going to get that I joke about a lot of things but you … I don't play a single solitary game about you."

Danessa looked up at me with big puppy dog eyes and all her fight seemed to dissolve. God, I loved this crazy woman. "Message received."

Dropping into one of the chairs on the balcony, I pulled Danessa onto my lap. With my hands on either side of her hips, I rocked her overtop of me. "You're not still mad at me, are you?"

"No."

"I hate for you to be mad."

"Aldi," she moaned. "I'm good." Running my hand over her skin, I gave her arm a soft pinch causing her to squeal. "What was that for?"

"I just needed to confirm this was real. You and me here, together after all this time."

"It's kind of trippy, right?"

"I thought you'd thoroughly closed the door. With

multiple locks, a wooden barricade and a firing squad on the other side."

Danessa affectionately stroked the back of my neck. "I'm not the one who closed the door."

Pulling back my face was a puzzle. "You broke up with me and said don't let the doorknob hit you where the good lord split you."

"I said I wanted to remain friends." Her voice was pinched, less ethereal, more restrained.

"And then proceeded to move to Chicago." I stared her dead in her eyes. Because what the fuck? Don't gaslight me.

"What, was I just supposed to traipse to Kansas City with you?"

"No, did I say that?"

Danessa removed herself from my lap, sinking into the chair next to me. "I mean yeah, actually, you said it all the fucking time. You started every sentence with 'When we get to KC,' If you're mad, say so you know I hate apathetic bullshit."

It was less about being mad and more about being confused. She never gave me a real reason why she wanted to go our separate ways. Danessa claimed she needed space and time to think but, in the months leading up to the breakup we were making significant plans for our future. "If I said all the things I wanted to, you'd leave with your feelings hurt."

"There it is. I thought it would take longer to rear its ugly head but you always surprise me."

"What are you talking about?"

"Grudges, you've been holding on to this dry ass bone for years and now you're gonna make sure we're even."

"I'm not fucking holding grudges. You blindsided me, I

was hurt. Don't fucking try to act like … don't fucking do this."

"I did what was best for me and I'm not going to apologize for that."

My hand swept across the open space. "This is what was best for you?"

"Wow, one minute you're telling me I have a great life I should be proud of, and the next minute you're shitting on it."

"I'm not. But don't pretend you didn't choose a two-bedroom condo over a life with me."

"You offered me a life you *thought* I deserved, not the one I wanted."

"So being with me … eventually becoming my wife was something you didn't want?"

"It's difficult to explain because if a man wants to take care of you, most women would let him. But that shit comes with strings. And people never read the fine print. Sure, you drive a fancy car and live in a beautiful house, but none of that shit is in your name. So your boyfriend or husband can take it all away at any moment."

"You're talking about other people's lives, not ours."

"It's always someone else's life until eventually it's you. Famous athletes behave like they can do anything; I've seen it firsthand with the men my mother dealt with. And I didn't want to hold my breath waiting for a call or social media post about you behaving badly with another woman."

"Danessa, I don't even fucking move like that."

"That's what they all say and then slowly over time things shift. I'm sure Colin Pratt's wife didn't sign up to be embarrassed every seven to ten business days. Did you know a woman just came forward claiming he's the father of her unborn child?"

"So, you ended us over what ifs? Because others tried and failed, you decided to cut your losses. Do you hear how dumb that sounds?"

"No, it was more about the fact that we weren't traveling in the same direction."

"And we are now?"

"Somehow our paths crossed after all these years."

"Maybe the reason our paths crossed is to teach me a lesson I still haven't learned."

"Whoa, fuck you." When Danessa was angry, she could be hardcore. It was learned behavior from her mother. They rarely had a conversation that didn't dissolve into a shouting match. "Because us not working out was all my fault? You played your part too."

"How so?"

"You didn't listen. You said you were blindsided but there were signs. I got accepted to a bunch of top law schools. Chicago, California, Texas. And when I told you I was also accepted into the law program at the University of Missouri, it was like that school was my only viable option. It was always Missouri this and Missouri that. You were so excited, and I didn't want to ruin it for you."

"So instead of talking to me about your doubts, you decided to end it and leave me to wonder why all these years? I would be a fool if I didn't entertain the possibility of you ultimately hurting me all over again." Shit, Nori was right. What the fuck was I doing?

"I didn't mean to hurt you."

"I'm not saying leaving me was wrong. I just wish you'd given me the opportunity to make it right."

Her shoulders rounded into a defeated heap. "Walking away was the hardest decision I've ever made."

"Honestly, I don't know if I can ever fucking trust you in the same way," I spat out.

Danessa's face crumbled. And tears fell from her eyes. She was also sensitive, she acted hard but inside she felt everything and took it to heart.

When I reached for her, my hands were trembling. "No, baby please. I didn't mean … I'm just venting. I didn't say it to make you cry. I just … I just really loved you and I didn't see any of that coming. And maybe I should've. And it just fucked me up for a really long time. And I'm not saying that's your fault. Because there were underlying traumas I hadn't dealt with. Like my fear of abandonment and not being good enough. But I just thought you saw me and when you left, I felt all turned around and it was difficult learning how to navigate life alone because you'd always been by my side. I guess I just need to do a better job at protecting myself."

"From me?" Her face was a mess with mascara stained tears.

"You can't make me fall for you all over again if you don't believe in us. I know my persona is bigger than life, and being with me sometimes makes others feel small. But for me you were the reason the sun rose each morning, the moon's sole purpose was to greet you at night. You couldn't tell me flowers didn't grow under your feet. Being loved by you single-handedly altered the way in which I view the world. Loving you isn't something a person just gets over. So, if you have any reservations, maybe we need to take this bitch off cruise control and pump the brakes."

"I don't even know what we're doing. And I can't promise this time will be forever. But I do know two things. That I've never cared for anyone as much as you. And I'm willing to do this life thing with you over and over again until we get it right."

Her kiss hit me like lightning. Our lips urgent and demanding igniting every nerve in my body. Danessa was back in my lap, her hands gripped my shoulders, nails pressing into my skin just enough to send a shiver down my spine, as the heat of her body pressed against mine. I could hear the faint thrum of my heartbeat in my ears accelerating and drowning out everything except the sound of her soft, gasping breaths.

"Take off your fucking clothes," I demanded. We removed several articles of clothing before we made it back in the condo. My need for her was a top priority.

In the bedroom she grabbed my face. "No condom just you. Is that okay?"

"Are you sure?"

"Yeah, I just wanna feel you." If it was anyone other than her that would be a hard no. But let's not pretend I didn't want to perform the backstroke in Lake Nessa.

My dick slid in place like a key entering a lock. A tight, wet, soft lock. She buried her face into my neck licking my skin when her mouth landed on my ear, I almost dropped us. My ears were my spot and having her tongue run across it was sending me. Her soft moans and grunts taking me to auditory heights.

"Fucking look at me." Her eyes landed on my face soft and hazy. "I'm sorry I yelled and made you cry. And I'm sorry for what's about to happen next."

Her eyes turned sober. "What's happening?"

"I'm gonna fuck you so hard I might make you cry again." I braced my back against the wall and dropped into a squat, grabbing her waist I lifted up and brought her down hard so she slammed into my lap. Danessa shuttered and her eyes rolled to the back of her head.

"Whose pussy is this?" I yelled like a drill sergeant.

Danessa groaned. Grabbing her by the back of her neck I tilted her head until our eyes were level. "Answer me. Whose pussy is this?"

"Yours," she breathed out. "It's yours. Ugh, Aldi fuck."

"And you look so pretty riding it." Standing I smacked her ass. "Too hard?"

"No."

"Harder."

"Yes, please." I smacked that phat ass again and her hips hitched picking up the tempo.

I'd clocked forty minutes of game time, but Danessa was working a whole new set of muscles. My arms supported her body which was in a semi state of free fall. She seemed less concerned about her physical safety, all she cared about was working her pussy over my dick. Her legs were loosely hooked around my waist as if she'd placed all her trust in me to support our combined weight. This was the Danessa I liked the most. She was always so routine driven. But when she let herself go, she never cease to amaze me. And right now, she was locked in, twerking on my penis as my hands massaged her skin.

"God your dick is dangerous. It makes me want to do the most deplorable things."

"Use me baby. I'm here for you."

Danessa wrapped her left arm around my neck, her body bouncing up and down on the dick. The sounds our bodies made were reminiscent of the mac and cheese I was stirring minutes earlier. "Dig me out, baby."

Bracing my legs, I pulsated my hips with thrusts that made her scream my name. If her neighbors were pissed earlier, they had to be livid now. The sound of Danessa's screams pinged against the walls. "Fuck me, daddy, I need you so bad."

"Like this?" I took control, grabbing her waist I drove her gushy core up and down my shaft.

"Aldridge," she squealed. "Fuck, baby."

Danessa's body curved into mine. Her head settled into the crook of my neck, and she whispered filthy promises I prayed to God she intended to make good on. Goose pimples pebbled my skin in response to her raspy words.

"Aldi, I'm gonna come. Is that okay?"

"Let go, baby." My approval carried weight of the magical words open sesame, and her body convulsed and trembled while she fucked my tongue with hers.

"You make my body feel so good. No one else ever came close." Danessa grabbed my face. "Come for me. I want you to fill me up." Shit, you ain't got to ask me twice. Danessa stroked the nape of my neck, coercing me to release all this built-up desire. After four quick thrusts my dick jerked and I couldn't hold back a deep moan of pleasure at the thought of painting her walls.

I met her eyes, and her voice was damn near ethereal. "Was it good for you baby?"

"Yes."

"Would you be mad if I begged for more?" My dick was literally still inside her. But with Danessa I stayed on ready.

"You don't have to beg." After back shots that left us both spent, we sat in bed eating the mac and cheese fresh out of the oven.

"I have to admit this mac and cheese slaps." Danessa licked the back of her fork.

"I know right. That random colonizer did her big one with this."

"It hit the spot. Thank you."

"Yep. What is your weekend looking like?"

"I was going to buy my books for class."

"Mind if I tag along?"

"You want to come to a bookstore?"

"I just want to be wherever you are. So if that's a musty school bookstore, then so be it."

"Okay. Friday afternoon I'm booked, dress shopping with Anika. Will Saturday work for you?"

"Yeah. I'll mark it on my calendar. Isn't it a little too early for dress shopping?"

"No shit. I said the same thing. No date or venue yet, but it's Anika. I'm just here for the ride."

"Dante asked me to be his best man?"

"What? I didn't know you two were cool like that."

Hitching a shoulder I agreed. "We're not."

"What did you say?'

"Yes, what the fuck was I supposed to say?"

"Something about being honored but you think it's best he asks someone closer to him."

"You know what I've learned about famous people? Many of us have a ton of acquaintances but few real friends. Like real talk, if I was getting married, I don't know who I'd ask other than my brother. Some people have six dudes in their wedding party. I don't know six dudes I fuck with like that."

"Shit, I could think of at least ten friends who could be part of my bridal party if I choose to go the big wedding route."

Shock furrowed my brow. "Ten? I'm calling bullshit. You have ten close friends?"

"Yes, I'm friends with all my sorority sisters, and my twin cousins, and Antoinette from elementary school."

"What the fuck am I doing wrong?"

"Maybe you should lead with cheese and noodles." She enjoyed another scoop of food.

"You have a little cheese at the corner of your mouth."

Danessa licked both sides of her lips, missing the cheese entirely. "Did I get it?"

"No, I got ya." I steadied her face and kissed the cheese sauce until it was gone. Which morphed into me devouring her full lips with mine. When we finally separated, I couldn't help but stare. Danessa always appeared lightheaded and disjointed after we kissed as if she'd spun in a circle making herself dizzy like I used to do as a kid. The fact my kiss could cause her to unravel made my heart race.

"What?" she asked.

"I don't think I have the words to express what I'm feeling. Sometimes things are better left unsaid. You know."

"Yeah, I do." I retrieved a forkful from the casserole dish, feeding it to Danessa.

DANESSA

DRESS SHOPPING LIKE ANYTHING IN LAS VEGAS WAS AN experience. Crown and Veil Bridal Boutique was the same shop I went to for my wedding that never happened. They offered private suites, unlimited champagne and spirits, and a charcuterie board I couldn't keep my hands off of. As the maid of honor, it was my responsibility to ensure every event leading up to the wedding was giving immaculate vibes. You only get married for the first time once.

"Anika would you hurry up?" my mother called out to my sister who was in the dressing room trying on the first dress.

"These dresses have lots of hooks, buttons, and snaps. Be patient." I popped a fig in my mouth.

"Did you not have lunch?"

"I had to shift my appointments to make the dress fitting, so I skipped lunch."

"Well at the rate you're eating I'll have to pay for another board." Jemini's side eye was vicious. I'd often attempted to replicate it but never quite measured up. It was the arch of her full and perfectly manicured brow.

"You're not paying for any of this. Not the fitting, not the wedding, not the reception party." The cost to reserve the fitting was five hundred dollars. If you purchased a dress here it was applied toward the purchase price, but if you didn't, you were shit out of luck. No dress, no deposit, and no fucks from the upscale Black-owned boutique. This was how you curated the illusion of a luxury in-demand product. We did the same at our real estate firm. It gave off exclusivity and rich people loved to think they were getting an experience no one else could.

"My future son-in-law is wealthy and more than happy to provide." *Do you see how she made it about her?*

"He's happy to provide for Anika, not you."

"What crawled up your butt, hmm? Why are you always looking to pick a fight?"

"Me?"

"Yes, this is a happy time. Anika is getting married. You'd think you'd be happy for her."

Bitch. She would just love to cause a rift between Anika and me. She hated it when we teamed up on her and if she could get Anika to switch sides, the ref would be counting to ten on my ass.

"I *am* happy for her." Honestly, I thought all of this was a joke and in a few months Dante and my sister would go their separate ways. But I had no intention of raining on her parade. She was happy, which I would respect and when it all turned sour, I'd be there to comfort her.

Anika brushed through the arched doorway in a heart-stopping cream dress. "Oh sweetie this is stunning," Jemini gushed.

"I thought I'd start with traditional looks first. Although I'm not sold." Anika stepped on to the circular podium. "What do you think, Nessa?"

The dress was far more conservative than the wearer.

High neckline, lace, full puffy skirt. "It's a beautiful dress for someone else."

"You're right. It's not me. On to the next one." Anika swept out of the room. I may not be onboard with the nuptials, but I wasn't going to have my sister wearing a dress that didn't mesh with her personality. Anika was the life of the party, and her dress should reflect that.

"How's Aldridge?"

"Why?" I eyed Jemini suspiciously.

"Just wondering how he's settled in."

"How would I know?" I'd learned the hard way not to share important information with my mother. She would either find ways to make me doubt myself or hold it close for a future point in time when she could use it against me. When I told her I was getting cold feet, she ran to Marcus betraying my confidence. I had to do damage control for months, which forced me to stay longer because I was a people pleaser, and I didn't want to disappoint Marcus or his family, who'd taken me in as their own.

"He's your client. Don't you two talk about things outside of real estate?"

"No, not really."

"Anika mentioned Aldridge has agreed to be Dante's best man."

"That's news to me." She wasn't getting a crumb of intel from me.

"Don't you think that's a bit fortuitous?"

Jemini and her big fucking words. "I'm not following."

"You're the maid of honor and Aldridge is the best man. Just feels like fate is working overtime to get you two back together."

"Dante and Aldridge are friends. In fact, it was

Aldridge who introduced Dante to Anika. So, him being involved in the wedding makes sense."

"You know Danessa ..." I rolled my eyes, readying myself for a lecture. "I know you think I'm just some gold-digging bitch—"

"I don't." *I did. Not proud of it but if it walks like a duck ...*

"You do. I taught you girls to know your worth. You're smart, beautiful, and personality wise, you do what you can. We work with the tools we are given. Everyone wants to be provided for. It's not a dirty word. Men like Aldridge have the desire to provide coded into their DNA."

Anika entered the suite, saving me from this conversation. "Second dress. What do you think?"

My mother shook her head. "The dress is wearing you. You're not wearing the dress."

Anika looked to me for a varying opinion. "Your body is tea and that dress is hiding all the hours you've spent in the gym."

"Okay, I'll try on a form-fitting one next." We both watched Anika swoosh out of the room.

"That dress was a mess." My mother poured herself another glass of champagne.

"Like seriously what was she thinking?"

"Maybe she's trying to impress his parents. Word on the curb is they're bougie as hell."

"Well, that dress was not screaming welcome to the family."

It wasn't always a fight with my mother. Jemini was funny, and smart as fuck. She'd never gone to college, but she learned quickly and knew a little about a whole lot. She was an avid reader, mostly romance because in the pages of those books she could revel in the type of love that seemed to only exist in happily ever after stories.

"Have you ever heard of the Black Cat Golden Retriever theory?"

"No."

"It's all about opposites attract. Now a golden retriever is loyal, kind, and funny. For the purposes of this conversation that would be Aldridge. Then you have the black cat who is introverted, reserved, not funny."

"That would be me?"

"Yes, in theory. You need to be the black cat so Aldridge can spoil and worship you as God intended."

"So, I'm not a black cat?"

"You're one of those feminist, unhoused black cats who's always talking about equal rights."

"Wait, you're also a feminist."

"While I agree a woman can do anything a man can, why would she want to? Aldridge was ready to turn you into a SAHWNK."

"What the hell is that?"

"A stay-at-home wife with no kids. But no you wanted to be Danessa, attorney at law and you couldn't even do that."

I closed my eyes and inhaled patience and tolerance like my self-help podcast, Girl Hush, taught me. "I made the best choice for me. Besides I don't want to be a stay-at-home anything."

"Aldridge wants to be your golden retriever and you're over there acting like a bird."

"I don't need dating advice from you. Last time I checked we were both still single."

"No, you're single. I have several viable irons in the fire."

And by viable she meant barely legal. "Good for fucking you."

"Alright Danessa, at the end of the day I'm still your mother. Watch your mouth."

I couldn't keep up with her, one minute she wanted to be one of the girls going to clubs with us and hitting on men half her age, and at other times she wanted to be the wise respected matriarchic. "I apologize."

"Part of me thinks you dumped Aldridge just to spite me."

"Why would I do that?"

"Because you didn't want to admit I was right. A man's financial prospects are just as important as being in love. I've fallen in love with pro athletes and brothers who worked in warehouses. And do you know what I learned?" She snapped in my face to confirm she had my attention. "I learned rich or poor they all cheat. But you get to decide where you want to receive the news, in a mansion or a one-bedroom apartment."

"Either way it's gonna suck."

"I'd rather sulk in a Laguna Spa heated Jacuzzi than a bathtub with mold."

"You need to let go of this Aldridge thing." I didn't want to provide any hope. What we were doing beyond fucking was still unclear.

Anika returned for a third time in a form-fitting corseted number that hugged her curves. "This is what I came to see. Anika, you look amazing," I gushed.

"You don't think it's too much cleavage?" Maybe my mother was right about her trying to impress the in-laws. Anika has gone outside with nipple tape and a sheer top. She wasn't modest.

"If you have them, you should flaunt them," Jemini said.

"I agree." My mother gasped, presumably at the fact

she and I were of the same accord. Ignoring her, I continued, "Let's add a veil and get the whole bride effect."

The sales associate left to grab a selection of headpieces while Anika admired herself in the mirror. "Anika?" my mother said. "Didn't you mention that Danessa and Aldridge went on a date?"

"Uhm … I don't know if that ever actually happened." My sister, who was usually a great liar, wasn't convincing anyone.

"We're not dating."

"Okay, hooking up, sneaky links, dicksurfing."

"We're not doing any of those things. And if we were, why would it matter?"

"Because I can't wait to tell you I told you so. I was right five years ago and I'm right now. Aldridge is the one. I'm sorry you decided to implode your love life and future to try to teach me some asinine lesson. You're just lucky he's willing to give you a second chance."

"Give me? Give me! Do you even believe the shit that comes out of your mouth? You tell us to know our worth and that we are the prize, but the minute a man with a little pocket change shows up you want us to bend over backwards to fit into his life. You are such a fucking pick me."

"They also have this dress in a blush, should I try that one on?" Anika was trying to get me to shut up. To stop me from saying things I was bound to regret later.

"You're the queen of the pick mes, and at the end of the day you fuck married men who say they're going to leave their families for you, but they never do. Because you're the woman men fuck, not the one they marry."

"You are such a judgmental bitch. Sometimes I question whether they switched you at birth. Because there is no way this closed-minded prude crawled out of my cooch."

"I wonder the same thing because I know my *real* mother wouldn't have abandoned her kids for a free trip to Cabo."

"There was food in the fridge. All you had to do was warm it up."

"We were taken by CPS. And placed in foster care for three months. But at least you got a tan and your guts dug out. Fucking mother of the year over here."

For once in her miserable life my mother was speechless. No witty comeback, no equally hurtful jab. "I'm going to return some messages." Jemini left the suite, drink in hand.

"You took that shit too far." Anika immediately scolded me. "Did you really have to bring that up? You know that was a tough time for her."

"She doesn't like to talk about it because when you look at it in the light it's real suspect. On a scale of one to ten of motherhood, she was a three point five."

Anika stepped off the pedestal and sat next to me. "What's wrong?"

"I'm not trying to ruin your day."

"It's a little too late for that." She took a sip from my glass of champagne.

"She just needs to keep his name out of her mouth. Jemini acts like he's my golden ticket. Not a fucking day has gone by when I didn't regret the way I handled the breakup. I walked away from a man who loved me, like really fucking loved me. A man who was thoughtful and intentional with his energy and time. And I don't think I appreciated how rare that was."

"Yeah, I could've told you the dating scene was rough. It's the Wild Wild West in this motherfucker."

"He was my first everything. I just got scared because no one gets the love of their life on the first try."

"You were too young to appreciate what you had, but now you have a second chance."

I was so tired of those words, second chance. "What if it's not the same?"

"I can guarantee you it won't be. You're not college kids anymore, but your boobs are still perky and that ass." She made a popping sound. "If we weren't sisters—"

"Don't, don't you dare."

"You don't even know what I was going to say."

"I have a pretty good idea."

"Can I finish?"

I waved my hand giving her the floor. "If we weren't sisters … I would strap on a dildo and fuck you deeply.

"Thank you?"

"Missionary style so I could see your pretty face."

I flashed a glance at the sales attendant who'd returned with several veils, and I was certain she'd heard all of that.

"Hooking up with your ex is a rite of passage. We've all done it." She pointed to the clerk. "Am I right? But I think that's what makes it so exciting, is the chance to fall in love all over again."

"What if he doesn't fall back?"

"Then he's an idiot and we'll TP his house, scratch his car, and post his nudes."

"That's illegal."

"Which one?"

"All of them."

"That man adores you. I'm talking drinking your bathwater after you've run a 10K race. Like you could call him right fucking now and tell him you wanted the Gucci Softbit maxi shoulder bag in green and it would be at your front door in under an hour. Give me your phone, let me text him."

"No." I clutched my phone to my chest.

How about this, after dress shopping, call Aldridge, get fucked and you'll feel better. That post-sex clarity will kick in. Now I'm going to wrangle Mom. You're going to apologize, and we're turning the page." She stood to go in search of our mother.

"Anika."

"Yes."

"You really look amazing. You're going to be the most beautiful bride."

"Thank you, Sissy."

When she exited the suite, I reached for my phone.

> Danessa: Can I come over and let you bury your face in it?

> Aldridge: I was going to wipe down the baseboards but that can wait.

"THE TEAM AGREED TO GIVE COACH JUSTUS A GIFT FOR HIS birthday from all of us. Colin was in charge of purchasing the gift and we all gave him money. So come to find out ..." Aldridge was banging his fist into his palm for emphasis. "Colin had everyone sign the card except me."

"What?" I asked as we traveled from aisle to aisle looking for the legal section.

"Yeah, he deliberately left my name off the card. So

now Coach probably thinks I'm cheap or worse, that I hate him."

"Maybe it was an oversight."

"No this was a blatant power move. So now I have to either bitch slap him in front of everybody or take the L."

"I don't think those are your only options."

"He's trying to son me."

"Okay then just go up to your coach and ask him how he liked the gift the team got him."

"That feels desperate."

"What was the gift anyway?"

"The fuck if I know. Colin's wife handled that."

"Sounds like maybe leaving your name off the card was a good idea," I teased.

"No, this is just how it works. The wives and girl-friends take care of shit like that. They help keep the peace and host the parties and come up with cute dances in the stands." Aldridge broke out into the latest trendy social media dance.

"Sounds horrible."

"What, supporting their husbands?"

"Being a glorified event planner."

"I think athlete's spouses get a bad rep."

"How so?"

"They are the backbone of the family. Without them nothing moves. They make sure the kids are taken care of and their partner's needs are met. And they're forced to take on a lot of the hidden responsibilities of doctor's appointments, little league games, PTA meetings, Ramblers' charity events. And some women have full-time jobs or run small businesses."

"It just sounds like a ton of work with very little reward."

"I guess it just depends on what you prioritize."

"I mean you could just marry your assistant, Nori, if you were looking for someone to organize your life."

"Nori's way out of my league."

"I just don't think everyone is interested in being a tradwife."

"Okay." Aldridge chuckled. "You know the funny thing about relationships is you and your partner can curate a life that works for you both."

"A lot of men say that but—"

Aldridge stepped closer and was now towering over me. "I'm not these other men. So can we stop with the generalizations? If you want to know how I feel about a specific topic, just ask me."

"I wasn't referring to us. We're not even a couple. We're just …" I scanned the vicinity to confirm no one was in earshot. "Fucking."

"Wow, you're really good at making things awkward."

"I wasn't trying to. But let's be real, we don't have titles."

"Right, because we're just fuck buddies."

"Yeah FUBU."

"I don't typically go to bookstores with my fuck buddies."

"Who knows, maybe you have a dark academia fetish."

Aldridge grabbed a random book from the shelf, cracked it open and started to finger fuck it. "I mean I do love the way the pages slide against my skin."

God I'd never wanted to be a piece of literature more in my entire life. There was a summer where I went through a whole cottagecore era and walked around with a well-loved copy of Jane Eyre. "You've gotten to second base with that book, so you're going to have to buy it."

Aldridge slammed the book shut. "The legal section is over there." He was taller than the bookshelves and could survey the entire store with little effort.

"Do you think I'm funny?"

"You make *me* laugh."

"But when you describe me to other people do you say 'You have to meet Danessa, she's hilarious. You're going to love her'?"

"No, I usually lead with how smart you are."

"I can be funny though?"

"I mean you're not a laugh riot, but you have your moments. I think we kind of balance one another out. I'm funny and you're funny to a lesser degree."

"So you think you're the comedic genius that holds everything together?"

"I mean my timing is impeccable, I allow space for the inevitable laugh. People tend to leave conversations with me with a smile on their face."

Pointing to my chest I declared, "I leave people smiling."

"Yes, you leave people smiling because you're warm and thoughtful. You're an amazing listener. You have the ability to read people and say the right thing to make them feel better."

"So I'm not funny?"

"Any fuck buddy dynamic ..." I laughed at his use of the term in relation to us. "has to have a ying and a yang. I'm funny, you're smart. I'm athletic, you can act and sing the entire *Dreamgirls* musical."

My entire body lit up as I enthusiastically delivered my favorite line. "Turn your wigs around. It's sophisticated looking."

"See, balance, symmetry. Who said you're not funny?"

"Jemini."

"Ouch."

"Yeah, we kind of got into a fight at Anika's dress fitting."

"About what?"

"About you."

"How'd I get into it?"

"Jemini has very strong feelings about our ..." I waved my hand searching for the right word.

"Situationship."

"Yeah, thanks."

"Didn't you explain it was a mutually beneficial fuck buddy arrangement? I get to see you naked and you get to ride my dick."

"I think you're getting the short end of the stick."

"That ... that was funny."

"Yeah?"

"Yes." He leaned in placing a soft kiss on my lips. I don't know if it was the campus bookstore or being with my college sweetheart but something about him made me feel soft and girly, like coquette bows and almond-shaped nails. "How do you do that?"

"Do what?"

"Make the world stop and shit."

"Because I only have eyes for you. Everything else, everyone else is just set dressing."

"More kisses. I need more kisses."

He obliged with pecks to my neck, forehead and lips. "You know the only opinions that matter when it comes to you and me are you and me."

"Mhmm?"

"So if we want to keep it casual or transition to something more. Or if we want to go off the grid and make oat milk, that's our business."

"Oat milk?"

"Have you never had ice cream made with oat milk?"

"No."

Aldridge's face lit up. "It's going to change your life. And it's going to ruin you for all other ice creams."

I feel like that could be a metaphor for our relationship. "Really?"

"It's my only vice. I gave up alcohol and all that other stuff and it's just this. My decadent, creamy, little secret."

"I need a man to talk about me the way you do your oat milk ice cream."

"Listen, I have two loves. One is oat milk ice cream."

"What's the other?"

"I can't say because right now she thinks this is a situationship."

I smushed his face playfully, "Shut up." Grabbing a six-hundred-page textbook from the shelf, I handed it to him. I didn't want to hear the love word, this was too new and Aldridge was a serial dater. He was the type who loved being in love and maybe what we had was more about nostalgia than anything else, and he'd quickly lose interest.

It's like Bubble Charm Babies, they were a popular toy when I was growing up. I had like ten of these charms hanging from my backpack. I thought I was so cool. I mean I was because all the popular girls had them. And the more charms you had, the more social credit you earned. But like with all trends, it quickly fizzled out and I wouldn't be caught dead with one of those charms. "I refuse to be a Bubble Charm Baby."

"Not following."

"Bubble Charm Babies, trendy, elusive, flying off the

shelf. My mother punched a woman once to get the last two Twinkle Baby charms."

"I love how you just dropped me into the middle of the story, no background, no foreshadowing, just action."

"I'm not a trend. And I won't be thrown into a dark drawer never to be heard from again." I shoved another book into his hands.

"Okay, I won't put Twinkle Baby in a corner."

"Damnit, you *are* funnier than me."

At the register the clerk scanned my items. "Your total is eight hundred seventy-two dollars and sixty-eight cents."

"Here you go." Aldridge handed the clerk his card.

"Hold up. Aldridge, I'm paying for my own books."

"The hell you are."

"I don't need you to buy my books, that's not why I let you tag along."

"It makes my skin itch having my girl come out of pocket for anything."

We're just going to pin the fact he called me his girl. "I appreciate that but—"

"If you don't let this man buy them expensive ass books for you and be grateful," an older woman holding two thick textbooks with rings on every finger instructed me.

"Yeah, what she said," Aldridge chimed in like a child.

"Cause if you don't, honey I could use some help."

I wasn't trying to be ungrateful, I just didn't want to take advantage.

Aldridge scanned the books in the lady's arm. "I got you."

"What?" she and I said in unison. Aldridge was generous to a fault and that could be a gift and a curse.

Aldridge emptied her arms, "Can you add these to the total?" He asked the clerk.

"I was just joking you don't have to." She was just as shocked as me.

"Don't block your blessing."

"Thank you. That's really very nice of you." She glanced at me and nodded in Aldridge's direction.

"Thank you, Aldridge." I walked into his chest and wrapped my arms around him.

"I got you Danessa. I always got you."

ALDRIDGE

MY PHONE VIBRATED ON THE BEDSIDE TABLE NEXT TO ME. THE display read Lamonte Mosley. Most children saved their father in their phone under "Dad" or "Pops" but in my opinion, those were terms of endearment, and he didn't deserve that type of respect. So, in my phone he was listed under his full government name. I glanced at Danessa, who was fast asleep. It was still dark outside.

"Hello?" I whispered while exiting the bedroom and making my way to the half bath. "Aldridge, it's your father."

"I know who this is. Do you have any idea what time it is?"

"It's six thirty. Don't tell me your lazy ass is still in the bed."

"Six thirty your time. I'm on the West Coast now."

"Well excuse me for calling to check on my son."

"What do you want?"

"The money you deposited into my account was a little light."

"You mean your allowance?" Yes, I intentionally picked that word to chin check him.

My father cleared his throat and, in my mind, probably

fought the urge to call me out my name. "I spoke with your assistant."

"You texted her and you don't get to demand extra money. She doesn't have the authority to approve a request like that."

"I thought she'd run it by you."

"You should've saved us all the trouble."

"Listen I have an opportunity to get in on the ground floor of a very promising business model."

"You can't keep your bank account from being overdrawn, how do you expect to run a business with employees and expenses?"

"I've got a guy who's going to handle the day to day."

"What's the business?"

"It's a strip club slash sportsbook."

"Gambling is illegal in Philadelphia."

"Yeah, well the sportsbook part is silent."

"You woke me out of my sleep to ask for money for an illegal enterprise."

"It's cool, everyone does it."

"I'm sure you know every underground gambling joint in a one-hundred-mile radius."

"Stop acting like I'm asking you for a million dollars. It's just ten grand. That's chump change to you."

"I give you money every month, why didn't you save some of it to fund this dream?"

"Okay then don't give me the money outright, you could be an investor."

"I have no interest in owning a strip club that will most likely get raided for gambling and sex trafficking in less than a year."

"Well, your momma got some money saved up, maybe I'll just ask her."

The way I wanted to reach through the phone and choke his old ass out. Like rockabye baby. Lights out motherfucker. "If you ask my mother for so much as her opinion the checks from me will end. I will freeze your account, and the gravy train will be decommissioned."

"Damn you're strict. You're twenty-four and rich. This should be the best time of your life." I was twenty-six. This motherfucker couldn't even be bothered to remember my date of birth let alone my age. Maybe Danessa was right. Perhaps I'd been too damn generous. The life of an oat milk farmer was looking real good right now.

"I learned from you. Gotta go."

"Aldrid—" I ended the call before he could say another word. As a grown man I wasn't interested in going back and forth with him on this. I didn't mind giving him an allowance, but I wasn't his personal ATM. That's a lie. I hated he got five thousand a month from me for being the most horrible person on the planet. Initially I was only giving my mother money but when my father got wind, he'd bully her to hand over the lion's share.

I weighed my options and killing him wasn't a viable one. Not that I hadn't workshopped the idea of the perfect crime. No DNA or forensic evidence, just my father disappearing, never to be heard from again. At the end of the day, I determined I wasn't a killer and if I had to hire someone it would no longer be the perfect crime. So my father got to walk around Philly breathing fresh air when he should be decaying in a shallow grave somewhere.

My phone dinged with a notification, and I was certain it would be a text from my father telling me he had no son. Instead, it was a message from my brother Duane with a link attached from No Drill, a gossip site that trafficked in rumors and stories loosely based in the truth. There was her side, his side, and then there was No Drill. Clicking the link I opened the post.

NBA SUPERSTAR, ALDRIDGE MOSLEY SPOTTED AT A COLLEGE BOOKSTORE WITH A BARELY LEGAL BEAUTY.

Under the post were two grainy photos of me and Danessa. One was just us talking, the other was me kissing her. Scrolling down, the comments were no better.

@nocaptherealest: That's what's up.

@TiffandStiff: Yet another groomer.

@shakeshaq: Who the fuck is this?

@Polytimestwo: Why is my husband cheating on me?

@Jackieluvs: Shit I don't blame her I'd let this man do unspeakable things to me.

@MEDschool: Men are all the same. At least she's Black.

Sometimes I was able to forget I was famous but shit like this was a stark reminder if you weren't ready to make shit official, don't do official shit. Personally, I didn't care if the world knew about Danessa and me, but I got the sense she didn't feel the same. She agreed when I jokingly called her my fuck buddy. Why would she cosign if it wasn't what she wanted.

Aldridge: Barely legal? That's Danessa.

Duane: Why anyone would be interested in what you do still blows me."

Aldridge: I'm a very important person.

Duane: Yeah, according to you and No Drill.

Aldridge: Have you talked to Lamonte about his latest business venture?

Duane: The last time Lamonte and I were in the same room I punched him ... so no.

Aldridge: I forgot about that. That was good shit.

Duane: Whatever he wants don't give it to him.

Aldridge: ...

Duane: I'm serious, fuck him. He thinks he deserves money because he's your father. But he ain't do shit to raise us. If we're keeping it a hundred his presence only made our lives worse.

Aldridge: I already told him no.

Duane: Good.

Aldridge: How's my niece?

Duane: Shit growing like a weed. She wants to try out for the soccer team.

Aldridge: I'll send you some money to get her started, sports can be expensive.

Duane: I didn't say that looking for a handout.

Aldridge: It's not a handout.

Duane: Aldi, I'd love you if you had nothing. You know that right?

Aldridge: Yeah.

Duane: So Danessa?

Aldridge: Yeah, Danessa.

I made my way back to the bedroom and curled up in Danessa's arms. Her body wrapped around mine. "Are you okay?" she asked, still half asleep.

"I'm just happy you're here." Danessa's fingers played with my curls. "Let's go away for the weekend."

"What?"

"I have a game at noon on Saturday, but after that I'm free until Tuesday. Let's go on a mini trip."

"Really?"

I nodded.

"Okay, I'll Google some places. Do you wanna fly or drive?"

"Nah, I'll get Nori to handle it. You just pack and look pretty."

"Done and already done." She rubbed my chest looking for trouble. "Since we're up …"

"Since we're up, why don't I fucking help you start your day?"

Danessa was already naked, she opened her legs welcoming me. I grabbed her hips pulling her lower on the mattress, so my head didn't hit the headboard. Sweeping the tip over her fold, I located a pool of her juices already dripping and ready. "Why are you always so wet?"

"Because I always want you."

It was getting harder and harder not to tell this woman I loved her. I'd just have to show her. Sliding into place we groaned in unison, her at my girth and me at the tight squeeze. Our bodies fell into a rhythm, stealing kisses in between earth quaking strokes. Danessa stretched her hands overhead, and her body slightly arched. When I tell you this woman was perfect, I wasn't lying. In fact I probably wasn't doing her beauty justice.

"I wanna be on top." She bit down on her bottom lip.

"You can have anything you want." Flipping over, she repositioned herself on my shaft and made good use of her elevated position. I looked on with a curious eye and she hit the hydraulic switches on my dick. Running my hand up the length of her body, I cupped her neck bringing her closer.

"I needed this so bad. Damn Nessa. I'm about to say some shit." I seeped in air practically gasping for breath.

"Tell me you missed this pussy."

"I was lost without it."

Her hips were tyrants the way she floated over top of me damn near bringing me to tears. "Tell me you'd do anything for it."

Sitting up, I locked in on her face. "I would do any and everything for you. Because I lov … I deeply care for you."

Danessa studied my features, her hips slowed but the effect was still the same. Loss of breath, erratic heartbeats, and blurred vision. Her kisses were slow and methodic as if she was attempting to steal my soul. Clutching her waist, I rocked when she rolled. "Aldi."

"Hmm."

"Take all of me." Like a runner at the starting line when the gun fires, I flipped her over and encircled her waist while slipping my erect dick back inside. Her almond-shaped eyes fluttering closed as we both indulged in one another. My dick thrummed as if her pussy was a tuning fork. Each kiss punctuated my deep desire for her. Danessa worked her core over my length, as if we both had the same urgent, unrelenting need. My lips found her perfect breast and I suckled them until they were taunt and slick from my tongue.

Pulling out I teased her clit with the tip of my dick. Both our eyes grew big with lust at the sight of her juices misting my penis. When I slid back into place, Danessa's head lolled back. Her hands landed on her pussy, and she worked her bud while I fucked her like the lyrics to a love song. "That's my girl."

My skin was damp and hot from our increased thrust. I could feel myself unraveling. Danessa's pussy was a dick charmer summoning me to come inside her. When her body shivered and she murmured my name in a low, raspy voice, I knew it was okay to let go. Pressing into her thigh, I lifted her from the bed and stroked her out which spurred on a second orgasm for her as I spiraled into my first.

"THESE COMMENTS ARE CRACKING ME UP."

We were in first class on a quick flight to Arizona. I wanted something low key and Sedona was the perfect place. Normally, Arizona was like sitting on the tip of the Devil's tongue, but in the winter months it was a good time.

"Which ones," I asked.

"@kellyho-land: Why are all the good ones taken.

@Dungeonmaster23768: That motherfucker is tall as hell.

@Beckywithak: When did Aldi and Ash breakup?

@Buzzmightstare: He's so washed.

@MosleyFanatic: Only bad bitches in the building. Do you know this person?"

"No grandma I don't."

"Why I gotta be grandma?"

"Because you act like you don't know how the internet works. I can't control fan sites."

"My bad. I don't have fan sites."

"Enjoy that while it lasts. Fan sites, hate sites. Weird emails. People showing up to your place and breaking in."

"Wait, that's happened?"

"Yeah, a weirdo broke into my house back in KC and climbed into my bed while I was sleeping." My voice got higher with every word.

"Aldi you could have been killed."

"Thank God all she did was grab my dick—"

"What? Who the fuck is she?" Danessa's hands balled into fists ready to fight.

"Calm down."

"How do you fucking know this?"

"Video surveillance."

"That's assault. She assaulted you."

"I pressed charges. Didn't know what happen until the morning when random shit was missing."

"Is she in jail because she should be?" Danessa gasped.

"What?"

"@Anika&Dante: I hope there's a sex tape." She glanced at me. "You don't think it's them, right?"

"No, cause that would be weird."

"I mean we're talking about my sister and your newfound best friend."

"Not too much on the homie," I joked. "I'm sorry again for all this. I should've been smarter about just popping out." The blogs were having a field day with this story; it had been several days of speculation and deep dives into how Danessa was more into me or vice versa. Random strangers acting like they had the inside track into my relationship was laughable.

"It was bound to come out eventually."

"Has Jemini called you about all this?"

"She sent me an 'I told you so' text. I hate the satisfaction she gets from being right."

"Let her have this one."

"I've been avoiding her many calls. Must admit it's weird that everyone thinks we're a couple."

"I wonder what gave them that impression?" Those pictures were giving *Love Jones* vibes.

Danessa ignored my comment, changing the subject. "Why Arizona?"

"Because it's chill and low key. I go there every year for a weekend wellness retreat."

"Wellness retreat. With who?"

"Wanye and—"

"You and Wanye are still tight?"

"That's my ace. The hotel hosts a retreat once a year. No phones. No TVs. Just nature, walking trails, and serenity."

"When did you become so granola?"

"After years of being Pop Rocks, granola is good." I needed to tell Danessa my Pop Rock years included pills and coke. It just never seemed like the right time to bring it up. "Hey Nessa thanks for breakfast, by the way I'm a recovering addict." *You see how awkward that was?* Pete's advice was delaying the inevitable would only make things worse. As much as people swear it to be true, love was never unconditional, and Nessa deserved to know what she was getting herself into.

I was working hard to stay sober and surrounding myself with people who supported me was paramount.

Danessa was down, she always had been, but loving an addict wasn't easy no matter how long they'd been sober. Because every day the only thing preventing me from scoring was a choice. If I woke up one morning and my resolve was tested shit could turn rapidly.

"Hey, come here." The seats laid flat. Danessa joined me in my seat laying her head on my chest. Sinking my hand into her hair I scratched her scalp.

"Mmm, that feels good."

"I'm happy you're here."

"Of course, who doesn't like a weekend getaway."

"I don't mean here in this moment, although that's nice too. I mean here, in my life."

Danessa shifted her head and looked up at me with her doe-like eyes. "Being with you is my happy place. It's always been."

"Come closer I need to tell you a secret." She scootched until my mouth brushed her ear and I whispered three words.

Danessa's lips curved into a knowing smile. "I love you too."

DANESSA

"WHAT'S SO FUNNY?" I ASKED.

"I just think it's wild the way you're bopping around looking at all the vintage stuff when less than two hours ago your legs were shaking while I fucked you raw."

I grabbed his arm and escorted him to a less populated corner of the store. "Stop it. Not appropriate." We were in this cute little area of Sedona with coffee shops and small boutiques.

After checking into our hotel and taking a much-needed rest, we were exploring the town. We dipped into a kitschy home decor shop, with patrons buzzing in and out and Aldridge was speaking in his deep full voice so anyone could overhear.

He imitated my raspy voice from hours ago. "Aldridge … please … baby."

I raised my fist with a shake. "I will assault you in this quaint little shop."

"Like how I beat the pussy back at the hotel." His smile was devilish, and I knew he was trying to get a rise out of me. He was proud of his performance and rightfully so. I was already prepared for an encore.

Crossing my arms, I walked away from him. "I'm not talking to you anymore."

"I'm just saying the faces you made." He contorted his mug into something more similar to pain than pleasure. "Daddy please."

"Aldridge, shut up."

"I'm sorry, don't be mad. I'll stop." He draped his arm over my shoulder and kissed the top of my head.

When he suggested we take a mini vacation, I was thrilled. The holidays flew by, and school was in full swing. I had readings to complete, papers to write and homework that was due, but I also had an unshakable desire to be laid up under this man. So, I powered through the week, staying up late to complete a paper due next Wednesday. All this while showing homes and closing deals.

Aldridge circled the table, picking up a wiener dog napkin holder. "Why?" he mouthed.

Granted this store housed everything but the kitchen sink, but I loved incorporating pops of color or cute kitchen tools into my decor. Not a wiener dog napkin holder but a pink cowboy boot matchbox, yes.

For the next two and a half days I was focused on the Arizona sun, filling my sexual cup, and frothing over items I didn't need but made me smile.

Aldridge's phone was blowing up and he was declining incoming calls. Didn't the world stop for everyone else when we were together? Like in a video game only Aldridge and I mattered and the blonde lady with the bob looking at cookbooks in the corner was just a NPC (Non player character).

I pointed at an item on the table. "This is cute."

"What is it?"

"Measuring cups that look like citrus. I bet they're

hand-painted." I picked up each showing them to him. "You have a grapefruit, an orange, a lemon, and a lime."

"You should get it." He never looked up from his phone to take in the hand crafted wonders.

"I don't need them. They would just be a fleeting serotonin boost."

His eyes were still focused on his phone and not where they should be, locked in on me.

"Hmm."

"Everything okay?"

"Uhm. TMZ reached out to my publicist regarding a breaking story they're working on."

"Not about you and me?" Us dating shouldn't be headline news.

"No, my dad." He scratched the length of his jaw, and his voice was stiff, less relaxed as if he were masking anger or hurt.

"Full sentences, Aldi."

He returned his phone to his pocket and finally looked at me. "Apparently, he's been betting on my games."

The blood drained from my face from the initial shock, but then I went into fix-it mode. After all, I did have a few weeks of law school under my belt. "Okay a parent placing bets on their child's professional NBA games, while some would argue is morally wrong, isn't illegal."

"They want to know if I was in on it." There was a tightness around his eyes and the vein in his forehead was visible.

"That's ridiculous."

"The money he used to place these bets came from a joint account. An account I set up so he'd have a monthly allowance. I knew he was blowing through money quickly, but we barely talk, and I never thought to ask him where the money was going. I knew it was being wasted on dumb shit … but gambling on my games."

"He should've known better. But his inability to identify the conflict is solely on him. Your father is a grown man who, and I can't stress this enough, should've known better."

"You and I both know Lamonte is a piece of shit but when this story breaks people are going to start looking at me and asking questions about the level of my involvement." Aldridge pressed his fist to his mouth. It was clear he was mentally processing this shocking news and all the possible scenarios that could follow, up to and including losing his job. "My publicist is setting up a meeting with my lawyers in thirty minutes. I have to join."

"Okay let's head back to the hotel."

"No, you stay here, buy your measuring cups. I don't wanna ruin your trip."

"Aldridge, I'm not letting you go through this alone." I squeezed his hand. He nodded absentmindedly. "We're in this together."

Back at the hotel, I listened in as Aldridge and his team strategized. The plan was to immediately distance himself from his father and this scandal. He couldn't control the actions of others, and he wasn't responsible for his dad being a major fuck up. After the call I helped Aldi draft a well-crafted statement.

"How does this sound?" Aldridge took a deep breath. "While it is disheartening to think my father would be involved in something like this, I must admit I'm not surprised. Unfortunately, my father has struggled with addiction and gambling for many years. I've paid for treatment facilities and witnessed him navigate twelve-step programs only to fail. Our parents are supposed to be our heroes, but occasionally they're fighting battles that make it difficult to be present for their children in the way most would expect. While I love my father, I don't support his actions and hope he'll be able to get the help he needs."

"I think it's concise and you come off sympathetic but not culpable."

Aldridge hit send on the email to his team for final review. Standing, he straightened his shirt. "Let's go to dinner."

"Dinner? Do you want to talk about this?"

"I'm done with this. There's nothing more to talk about. We're on vacation, and we shouldn't let the fact that my father is an op ruin that."

"It's obvious you're upset, maybe a little hurt."

His shoulders jerked and his mouth wadded into a ball. "I'm not hurt. I expect nothing from him, and he just keeps delivering every single time." The last three words were punctuated by his fist slamming into his palm.

"Maybe you should call him to hear his side."

"Nope. I'm cutting him off. Already texted Nori and asked her to freeze the account."

My gasp telegraphed my surprise. I feared his actions were reactionary and he wasn't taking the time to think things through. We could all agree his dad was a piece of shit, but pretending he didn't exist wasn't going to fix the long-term problems. In my opinion Lamonte should've been cut off years ago. A child shouldn't be expected to support his freeloading father. Aldridge was a good son and Lamonte took advantage of that.

"What? Do you think that was a mistake?"

"Yes … I mean no. If he's going to gamble his money away, then he doesn't need to get it from you. But there's also optics to consider. People could perceive the account being quickly closed as an admission of guilt on your part."

"Bullshit." Aldridge stood, picked up a glass and tossed it at the wall. Shards of glass exploded, falling to the carpet. That wasn't the reaction of a man who was over it.

"Aldi, I know it's upsetting finding out—"

"I'm not upset. You were right, I'm over here taking care of a bunch of people who don't deserve it. What's that saying? New Year, New Me. That's my motto all year long. I'm only helping my mom and you." He sat down on the couch and rubbed his knees. "And Duane, Tootie, my niece. Maybe Nori if she needs anything."

I sat next to him. "You have a big heart. You always have. And that's a quality I appreciate the most in you. I don't want this shit with your father to harden your heart."

"Weren't you the one telling me I was doing too much … giving too much?" He sunk in the space next to me.

"Yes, and I stand by that. But I also heard you say how important it is for you to take care of the people you love."

"And see that's where I messed up with that mother-fucker because he doesn't love me, all he's ever done was use me. As far as I'm concerned, I don't have a father." His expression was pained. It was clear he was taking this betrayal personally, as he should because the choices Lamonte made often felt like a direct attack on his son. But disowning a parent, no matter how horrible they were, was easier said than done.

"Aldi, don't say that."

"Why Nessa it's true. I'm done." Aldi grimaced as if he'd been hit in the gut with a baseball bat. "Why does … Why did he have to be my dad?" His voice was shaky, and he was having trouble meeting my eyes. I didn't have a good answer for that. But I knew what it was like to be disappointed by your family. "All I ever wanted was a dad that would come home after work and ask me how my day was. Ask about what we learned in school. But instead, I came home to my dad passed out drunk on the couch at three thirty in the afternoon. And those were the good days." He seeped in a long breath. "Sometimes he wouldn't come home until well past my bedtime, yelling and banging shit around, waking the whole house up."

"I can't explain why shit happens the way it does, but I do know who your dad is and what he isn't doesn't fall on you. He probably had some bad breaks of his own but at the end of the day he made his choice about who he wanted to be as a man and a father and that's something he'll have to live with for the rest of his life."

Aldridge bit down on his bottom lip, and the first tear fell. He turned his face to the opposite corner of the room trying to hide his pain. "I was always so scared … you know." His voice was heavy with emotion. "He was like a tornado, you say the wrong thing and you got smacked or choked out. You know how kids are like there's a monster in my closet. I never experienced that because the monster was at the kitchen table launching the bowl of peas at my head.

"I'm so fucking tired, Nessa." Aldridge sobbed, bringing his balled fist to his eyes. I just rubbed his knee, allowing him space to vent. "I don't know if I'll ever have kids but if I do, I'm going to be their biggest cheerleader and not their biggest hater. There's this malice laced in every interaction with him. Like how dare I make something of myself. How dare I have the audacity to be better than him. Like that shit's hard. If I'm ever a dad I won't be perfect, but I'm going to try to be the type of father that brings a smile to their faces when they're grown. You know what I mean?"

"Yes." I had vague memories of my father. He was the opposite of Aldridge's dad, he could light up a room and make you feel like the most important person in it. The problem was his visits were few and far between and left me wanting for more. I believed every promise and his affirmations made me love him more, but it was all for show. He was the life of the party but never wanted to make his daughters the center of his world.

"I don't talk about my childhood because so much of it was a shit show. I remember one time my dad pulled up to the house with a new car. Leather interior, big wheels, music bumping, and he told us all to hop in he was taking us out to eat. He took us to a place called Liberty Clucks and I was thrilled because we never ate out. After about fifteen minutes, a police car pulled up and arrested my dad. The car was stolen. We had to take the bus back home."

Resting my head on his shoulder, I said, "Sometimes growing up is realizing our parents didn't do the best they could."

"Why have kids if you're just going to pass down your trauma like a family heirloom? Son, I'm giving you generational baggage. Don't let the small luggage fool you. These suitcases are stuffed with abuse, neglect, addiction, thoughts of self-harm. And then there's the phobias. Fear of vulnerability, love, growth, therapy. What the fuck am I even trying for? Shit is stacked against me."

I hooked his chin, turning his head to face me. "No, you're a cycle breaker. You made it out of poverty, you were the first in your family to go to college, on a scholarship at that. And your sister and niece are going to follow in your footsteps. You have a career you're passionate about. You have money saved, you're buying a house. You are carving a new path for future generations."

"Danessa, I don't want to talk about this shit anymore." He scrubbed his face and any trace of tears. Leaning back into the couch cushions, he seemed to go numb. Eyes closed and silent to indicate this conversation was over. It was as if this news had broken his spirit. I know most of society was hanging on by a thread, walking around with masks to hide the pain, but Aldridge was the type who let shit roll off his back.

"Okay sure. I'll order food and we can watch a movie and laugh the bad parts of this day away."

It was like my words were lost in a void. Aldridge jumped up and headed to the minibar. Opening the fridge, he rummaged around, pulling out ginger ales, soft drinks, and juice. "Shit, I need a drink."

"I thought you didn't drink?"

"Uhm, I don't but it's feeling like a blackout drunk kind of night. You know something to take the edge off." He slammed the fridge door with such force it startled me. "Room service can bring us drinks. Do you want something?" Aldi snapped his fingers, pointing at me.

Aldridge opened the fridge again like mini bottles of tequila and vodka would magically appear. Standing in the middle of the room, he had a silent breakdown. He rubbed his face and examined the room like we were trapped inside, and he was tasked with finding the key to let us out. Aldi's brown eyes were pinging from the door to the coffee table to the wall. He stared at the wall for what seemed like minutes. You'd think the terra-cotta wall had called him a punk ass bitch or something.

"You know what … room service will take too long. I'm just going to ask the guests next door for a taste."

Blocking his path to the door, I cupped his face. "We're not going to beg a stranger for liquor. We don't need alcohol to unwind. All we need is each other." Brushing his cheek, I redirected. "Look at me. It's going to be alright. Right?"

Aldridge's eyes settled on me and it was like being transported into the heart of a storm. Whatever was going on ran far deeper than his backstabbing dad. He pushed out a long sigh. "Yeah, of course. No drinks." Aldi stepped away from me, pacing back and forth, scratching his head. "I need to make a call." He swiped his phone from the table and headed to the bathroom, closing the door in my face.

My heart dried up in my chest and there was a pulsating behind my eyes that would most likely turn into a headache. I didn't like feeling helpless. I'd give anything for the ability to reverse time and make this all go away. At the end of the day, our parents were just like us trying to figure this life shit out. They didn't have all the answers, they no longer had the power to heal boo boos, they were flawed individuals like everyone else. Aldridge deserved peace, and even two thousand miles of space between him and his parents couldn't provide him with solace. I had a mind to call Lamonte and read him for filth my damn self. You knock-kneed, bad built, ashy elbow having, two pack a day smoker smelling, pinky toe missing, sloppy ass drunk.

Outside the bathroom door, I sat anxiously like a loyal puppy. Part of me wanted to ensure Aldi was okay and the other part of me wanted to know who he called. I mean I was right here, who did he need to contact? Why wasn't I enough? I pushed the thoughts from my brain because they were selfish, and this wasn't about me right now. The sound of water running gave me the courage to knock.

"Yeah?" His voice sounded distant behind the other side of the door.

"Can I come in?"

There was a long pause. He cleared his throat and said, "Uhm … sure. Opening the door, I found Aldridge in the shower fully clothed. I placed my hand on the cold glass kind of like you see couples do when one is in prison. Aldridge pressed his hand to mine.

"Baby, can you come out and talk to me?" I kicked off my shoes prepared to join him if he objected. He turned off the water and opened the shower door, walking out dripping wet and cold. I slid my hand over his rib cage. "Let's get you out of these wet clothes." Pulling his shirt over his head I tossed it to the floor. "I don't have the right words … I know that. But you should know your feelings are valid and I just want to be here for you." I stripped him of his slides and sweatpants. My hands trembling the entire time, I'd never seen him like this.

In college his father did some fucked up shit including sending his mother to the hospital, and each call or text he just ate it. Pushing his emotions down. I told him it wasn't healthy, but I guess at that moment his feelings were the only thing he could control. So, he made jokes or deflected to cover up how deeply he was hurt. Grabbing towels from the rack, I shook one out draping it over his shoulders.

Aldridge stalled my hands, capturing them in his. "Danessa, I have to tell you something."

"What?" I surveyed his face hoping to gain clues.

His eyes were bloodshot, and he was shivering from the cold water. "I'm an addict."

My head reared back, caught off guard by his words. I don't know what I expected him to say, but it certainly wasn't that. "Excuse me ... what?"

"I've been sober for almost two years. But at the end of the day, I'm an addict."

My gaze was clouded as if a deep fog just rolled in shrouding the bathroom in a haze. "You're an alcoholic?" That tracked he never drank when we went out. The minibars were only ever stocked with juice and sodas, much like the minibar here.

"No, I mean alcohol wasn't really my vice. Don't get me wrong, I was often drunk when I was high?"

"High?" My voice cracked.

"Yeah cocaine, heroin, pills. I may have tried meth once."

A nervous chuckle spilled from my mouth as I made my way to the other side of the bathroom. What the fuck? He wasn't making any sense. This didn't make any sense. Sure, we partied in college, but nothing hardcore. Just teenage experimental stuff. "I don't understand, you're an athlete."

"Athletes can be the worst offenders when it comes to drugs."

Yeah, that was stupid. I knew that, no one was immune. "How long has this been going on?" My mind recalled all the time we'd spent together. I didn't see any of the signs. Granted, I didn't honestly know what the signs looked like, but if Aldridge had been high any of those times, I would've known. Right? "Are you getting high regularly?"

"There was a time when I couldn't go a day without it.

My addiction started my second season in the league. I was young, partying, making up for lost time. All these people wanted my attention. I was famous and rich. It was harmless at first, pop a pill at a club chase it with a drink. The shit just took the fucking edge off. Evened me out."

"And then?"

"And then I was doing lines in the bathroom. Before long I had my own dealer who made house visits. I could get high whenever I wanted so that's exactly what I did."

I stared at him with my arms pinned across my chest and my mouth hanging open.

Aldridge squinted, examining my tense facial features. "Shit, you're judging me."

"No. But this is a lot of new information, Aldridge. You don't think this is a lot?" My mother was right. I was a judgmental bitch. I'd been that way my whole life. If I didn't agree or understand something, I condemned it. The hardest drugs I'd ever done was edible weed in college. Cocaine, heroin, fucking meth, I felt painfully out of my depth. What's the correct way to respond to news like this?

"I get that. But honestly if I didn't tell you, I'd probably do something stupid tonight. It's who I am. You need to know if we're going to do this … you need to know."

"I love who you are Aldi. I do. I'm just trying to wrap my head around this."

"No, erm … I get it. I totally understand." He encased his arms around his body and took several steps back. The chasm between us growing wider.

"Don't do that, don't withdraw." Making my way back over to him, I rested my hands on his arms. "Please, I'm listening. This doesn't change the way I feel about you. I love you, Aldridge. I just need to understand."

Before tonight, I'd only ever witnessed Aldridge cry

two times. The day his dad came to family weekend on campus drunk and embarrassed himself, calling Aldridge a disappointment and me a gold digger. And the night he was drafted. I think that was the first time he actually breathed all four years, because the pressure placed upon him was so great.

"I felt alone and lost, and the drugs made me feel lost in a different way." He pushed a tear away with his thumb before going silent. It was brief, but if I didn't know better, I'd think he was back in that lonely space. "Anyway, eventually it got bad, and I decided to go to rehab in the off season, and I've been working to stay clean ever since."

"Why didn't you tell me sooner?"

"Because of the way you're looking at me right now." Fresh tears rolled down his cheeks.

I made an attempt to fix my face, plastering on a smile, but that felt wrong. Words escaped me, each answer just spurred a new question. Burying my head into his chest, I let go and sobbed against him. I knew my response was disappointing and that made me cry harder. Aldridge held me tight, and I could feel his body shake against mine.

I blew out a long breath. "Why the shower?"

"I just needed to shock my senses, and it was either punching a wall or hop into a cold shower. Pete said—"

Lifting my head, I looked at him. "I'm sorry who's Pete?"

"He's my sponsor." My brain started making connections. He'd come in here to call his sponsor, that made sense. "Pete helped me process my feelings and accept that using right now would make everything ten times worse. I knew that of course, but sometimes when you're in it it's hard to see the forest for the trees. He also told me if you were going to be a fixture in my life then I'd have to let you in on this part of it."

"I want that. I want you to feel comfortable enough to share that stuff with me. And I'm here to support you in any way you need. You don't have to do this alone." I rubbed his back while he still held me in a secure embrace.

"Yep, I was just afraid of losing you."

"Because of this?"

"Yeah, like you said, it's a lot."

"I did say that, but collectively and independently we've navigated through all types of shit. And will find our way through this too."

"This is not something we get through, baby. This will always be there, and I need you to understand that. Because loving an addict, even a recovering one, is not for the weak of heart. So, if you want to tap out, I totally understand."

"Aldi, I'm not tapping out and I'm not leaving you. Fucking look at me." His eyes reluctantly met mine. "I'm not going anywhere."

"I wouldn't blame you if you needed space to process everything."

"We've had enough space. I hope you'll add me to the roster of people who you can call and vent to when like … you … think—"

"Using. You can say the word."

"I don't want to trigger you or say the wrong thing."

"It helps to be honest. Call it what it is. I'm an addict." Aldridge scrubbed his face. "Be real, how much am I scaring you right now?"

"I'm not scared."

He raised a dubious eyebrow.

"I mean I am but not for the reasons you think. You

being okay is important to me. And sometimes I think you take on too much and I just want to be able to lighten your load. You don't have to always have it all figured out. And when you're struggling, and you feel vulnerable, I want to be your soft place to land. Your judgment free soft place. I want you to know there is nothing you could do or say to make me stop loving you. Because not even time or distance could do that. So no, you're not scary to me. I'm actually really tough. I once fought off a guy who was trying to grab my purse. I kicked him in the nuts and then slammed my palm into his nose, breaking it."

"You are so brave."

"So brave." We both shared a much-needed laugh.

"I'm sorry to dump all this on you."

"I'm just happy you finally let me in. You know if you want, we can find the nearest NA meeting. I mean it's only seven o'clock I'm sure we could find something."

Aldridge nodded. "That would actually be … yeah that would be great."

"Good, great. Thank you for trusting me with this."

Aldridge pulled me closer, his lips trembled against mine, filled with all the words he still wasn't quite ready to say. I never entertained the thought of walking away. If the last few months taught me anything it's that we're stronger together and I wasn't going anywhere.

ALDRIDGE

"Can I ask some follow up questions?" Danessa peppered her eggs.

"Shoot." We were on the veranda of our suite, with sweeping views of the mountains, enjoying breakfast. Admittedly, I was still raw from yesterday. My father hadn't even called or texted in an attempt to render an apology. Saying sorry wasn't going to fix anything but at least it would let me know his reckless actions weren't intentional.

Lamonte rarely thought before making moves. He just jumped into some dumb shit headfirst and only after he started catching flack would he try to backpedal. Most often that looked like him searching for someone else to blame because shit was never Lamonte Mosley's fault. If my mother forgot to bring the gravy to the table, she was a lazy bitch and deserved to be dealt with. And if Duane, Tootie and I laughed too loudly while watching television, we needed to be punished. I stood on what I said last night, fuck him.

"You mentioned you went to rehab. What was that like?"

"It was tough, and I was hardheaded. Even though I knew that was exactly where I needed to be, I was resistant. After a few weeks and listening to other people's stories, I got a little spooked because it was like looking into a crystal ball and seeing what laid ahead for me if I didn't make changes."

"Was it scary, the facility?"

"Nah this was the rich people rehab with cucumber water, massages, and guided meditation. I did a lot of hiking."

Danessa pulled her leg up under her and her robe slipped from her shoulder. "Is that where your love of hiking took shape?"

"Yeah, I see why White folks are into it."

"And then after, how was the transition back to your normal life?"

"I quickly realized I had to cut people off. The first few months were just work, gym, home for me. And then in NA they talked about finding new hobbies, new ways of having fun that didn't include drugs. Apparently being a hermit wasn't sustainable. And then I met Ashley, she was a health nut. I'm talking protein, greens, and powders in her fucking coffee and water. She just made sense because I was trying to adopt a healthy lifestyle, and she was in tune with that world."

"And you told her about your addiction and rehab?"

"Yeah eventually. In Missouri, me going to rehab was like an open secret. My coach shielded me from a lot of it. There was this unspoken rule with the press. In interviews they'd hint at the prior year being difficult for me, but they never came out and said it. The owner of the Pioneers invested too much money in our team and probably threatened to ruin the lives of anyone who crossed him."

"Too many questions?"

"No, I expected questions. This is good."

Danessa pushed her eggs across her plate. Her knowing was a weight lifted off my shoulders. For us to work, she needed to accept the good and the bad. And since we last dated, I'd racked up a ton of bad habits. I loved Danessa but as long as I'd known her, she'd been hypercritical of things she didn't understand. When we first met, life was black and white to her and she struggled to see things from different perspectives. Over time she accepted there were variations of gray mixed in there too.

I knew telling her the truth could potentially end us, so I was more than willing to answer any and every question she had. She needed to be able to trust me. And I needed her to know I had no plans on jeopardizing my sobriety. While yes at times I might struggle, I would never forget the progress I made. I entered rehab for myself and no one else and I had to wake up every morning and choose me. My father was a lifelong addict; Duane had his struggles; I was more than my father's son and the cycle ended with me.

"So tell me how classes are going?" My drama had already occupied too much of this weekend.

"You don't want to hear about that."

"I do? I come over every night and your head is in a book. I wake up and you're on your laptop. But you've been tight-lipped about classes, your professors."

"That's probably because I feel like I'm a bit in over my head. Right now, it's like I'm spinning several plates simultaneously with work, school, wedding planning, and you."

Pulling my face in surprise I asked, "Me?"

"Yeah, I have to make time for you. Something I didn't plan for when I applied."

"Am I a distraction?"

Danessa scratched at my beard. "Yes, in the best way. I just need to find the sweet spot."

I tossed my napkin onto my plate. "You could always put a pause on work."

"Eventually if things get more hectic I may have to, but I just wanna stack my bank account a little bit more so I feel comfortable taking the time off. It's an adjustment but I'm managing. I just have a little less time for me."

"Okay, I'm just going to say the thing. And I know you're going to dismiss it but I'm going to put it out there. I can pay your tuition and other expenses while you're in school."

"You want me to quit my job?"

"Not quit. You own the agency. But you could take a hiatus. Hire another realtor and collect a percentage of their sales. That would be additional income, so you didn't have to deplete your savings. And with your tuition and mortgage covered all you'd have to think about is studying."

"I love that you want to take care of me and that you support me—"

"But?"

"We're not even official yet."

"That's just logistics."

"I have a plan. It's a good plan."

"I respect that you have this law school thing all figured out. I'd expect nothing less. But I'm offering an alternative solution. One that was not available when you crafted your initial plan."

"Look at me." Danessa grabbed my chin. "I only need you. I don't want to be another person you have to take care of. The cute last-minute getaways, fancy cars, and gifts, while all nice, are not a requirement. I do not expect those things. I do expect for you to show up for me, support me, and make me feel safe and listened to."

"Dating me comes with perks." I took a sip of my tea.

"Covering law school and my mortgage is a pretty big perk."

"You know if you wanted the rings around Saturn, I would hire a team of experts to craft a spaceship, go on a one-man mission, and yank that shit out of the galaxy."

"I know."

I pulled her hand from my cheek and gave it a squeeze. "So let me do this for you. Not out of obligation but because I can and want to."

Danessa's soft amber eyes settled on my features. She opened her mouth to speak but quickly shut it.

"Let me take care of you, it's the least I can do. And when you really think about it, for a guy as rich as me, thirty grand is equivalent to a regular guy paying your phone bill. It's light work."

"Well when you put it that way … okay."

"Yeah?" The shock was written all over my face. I expected a hard no.

"All I can hear is Anika calling me a dumb bitch if I told her I'd declined your offer. So yes."

"Consider it done."

"Thank you. I feel extremely guilty, but grateful."

Glancing at my watch, I gulped down the rest of my tea. "We need to head out if we're gonna make our couple's massage."

"Mhmm, massages, well-appointed hotels, free law school a girl could get used to this."

"That's the plan."

After our full-body massages that left me knocked out on the massage table, we headed back to the suite. Danessa was chatty, talking about how great her masseuse was and how she needed to do this more often. All I could offer was occasional uh-huhs because as we got closer to our room, the knot in my stomach tightened. Opening the door, I stood aside so Danessa could enter first. Her loud gasp reached me from the breezeway.

"What have you done?" She called out.

"Wait you didn't do this?" I teased. I entered the room now dimly lit with candles, red rose petals were sprinkled across the floor and over the bed. Various gift bags from some of Danessa's favorite name-brand boutiques were displayed in the center of the bed. Above the bed were heart shaped balloons highlighted by red balloons spelling out, *Will you be my girlfriend?*

"Aldridge." She pushed me playfully but I could still make out the distress on her face.

"Don't even think about telling me this is too much and you don't deserve it."

"No, I definitely deserve this." She picked up a bag from Hermès.

"Danessa being with you is my happy place. I knew the moment I met you there would never be anyone else for me."

"Liar."

"I knew after the first date I wanted another one. And after the second date I knew I didn't want any other man buying you coffee, let alone spending time with you. I think when God created me, he had you in mind. He flipped through his book of creations and landed on your page, and he thought let's create someone for Danessa. He made me tall so I could reach items off the top shelf for you. And he gave me a huge appetite because he knew your eyes were bigger than your stomach. Then right before he closed me all up, he implanted an unwavering devotion to you and only you."

She dipped her chin into her chest. "Baby."

"So asking you to be my girlfriend, *again*, isn't too soon. In fact, I think it's long overdue. When I agreed to come to Vegas I never expected our paths to cross. I didn't even wish for it. Thinking you and I were beyond done."

"But here we are."

"Here we are, and just like that the butterflies are now taking up space in my belly and when I wake up next to you, I say a silent pray of thanks. I love you, Danessa, I always have. Shit, I always will."

"I love you too." The way she fidgeted with the belt of her robe let me know her happiness was mixed with a fretful edge. "Oh my God, something's been missing all these years, and I could never put my finger on it. Or maybe I just didn't want to admit it was you. I was missing you. Because I had all this love for you but nowhere to channel it."

"So will you be my girlfriend … again?"

"Yes, every time you ask the question, the answer is yes."

Leaning in to kiss her, Danessa's laughter bubbled up mid kiss and was muffled by my lips as I cradled her face in my hands. The sound of our laughter intertwined, warm and unguarded, as the kiss deepened with teasing nips and lingering touches. Her hands landed on the waistband of my shorts, and my heart paused before restarting in erratic beats. She pushed me onto the bed, disrupting the gift boxes and petals before taking to her knees.

In record time I was naked. Danessa's eyes were

hooded and filled with carnal desire. She worked her hands over my shaft, her bangles jiggling with each determined twist. The warmth of her breath made my dick stand at attention. Danessa smirked at me, her eyes impressed at my girth. When her mouth found my tip, I couldn't hold back the moan tripping up my throat.

Watching her lips surround me as she attempted to take me all in would never not leave me lightheaded and gasping for air. My body had a visceral reaction to her touch, one that no other woman could produce. Her head bobbed up and down, the slurping sounds echoing through the room drove me insane.

"Danessa …" I grunted

I could feel her mouth curve into a smirk, and she ran her tongue over the side of my penis. Her hand stretched upward, rubbing my chest. "Fuck my throat, baby."

Springing to my feet, I collected Danessa's messy bun, inching my dick toward her mouth until she swallowed me. I moved my hips in and out and Danessa opened her mouth wider to receive me. "Good job, baby. Your mouth feels so good." I untied her hotel robe and found her free hand playing with her pussy. Pulling out I lifted my dick so she could circle her tongue over my balls. My legs shook from the sensation. Bending low I claimed her lips, and Danessa moaned into my throat. Presented once again with my dick, she teased it, slow twirling her tongue over the tip. I gently guided her head forward until my shaft slowly disappeared.

Tilting her back I gave her what she asked for, fucking her open mouth while she gagged and moaned. Her hand pressed against my thighs. I thought she was going to tap out, but she pulled me deeper. My abs constricted and my hands went numb. I was gone. When the first stream entered her mouth, she released a satisfied grunt. Pulling me out she stood feeding me her sticky fingers coated with her juices. Like a good boyfriend I licked her fingers clean, leaving not a trace behind.

Discarding her robe, I knocked all that expensive shit off the bed and Nessa assumed the position face down, ass up. Before sliding inside, I stole a few kisses from her phat lips to hear her appreciative whimpers. When I finally entered, Nessa's loud exhale told me this is what she'd been needing, for daddy to stroke her out. We worked in tandem to fill her up. I knew her body almost as well as mine. I'd spent my formative years at the cusp of her pussy devising new ways to get her to scream my name.

When I said this pussy was mine, I meant that shit. I'd put in the hours. Eagerly participated in extracurricular assignments and felt that pussy throb around my dick. For her part, Danessa was still down to fuck at every conceivable opportunity. Her honeypot always soft, wet and ready to receive me. Grabbing her waist, I picked up the tempo. I wanted to turn those soft moans into screams.

"Oh my God, dig me out, Aldi." She fisted the sheets while coasting over my shaft. Folding into her I trailed kisses down her back. I needed to watch her come. Flipping her over, I sunk into her resting my face against her ear. "I love you so much, baby. You're my everything." My words weren't hollow sex-haze speak. This woman had my heart and everything I did was in hopes of making her happy. I knew I could trust her with every part of me, even the messy unfinished spaces sometimes too scary to share.

She repositioned my head, so we were staring into one another's eyes. "I love you too, baby. I love us." Danessa's body shivered underneath mine. Her undoing spurred on my own orgasm. We clung to each other, riding the wave until our bodies stalled. Planting kisses to her cheek and neck, I released her, rolling onto my back.

"Did you plan this all along?" She motioned toward the balloons and scattered rose petals.

"Yep."

"What if I'd said no?"

I shot her a look that screamed "Be fucking for real."

"You're right. No was never an option."

Breathing in a satisfied inhale I closed my eyes. Danessa Irwin loved me. Even when we were miles apart that love never faded. The knowledge settled in my core, warm and soft until a smile transformed my features.

DANESSA

THIS PAST WEEKEND WAS A ROLLER COASTER, BUT I THINK WE both learned important lessons. My takeaway was to try to be less self-righteous. I was erroneously trotting around on a high horse. Just because I didn't agree or wouldn't make the same decision for myself, it didn't give me the right to voice my differing opinion so loudly. Like MJ said, I need to have an accountability conversation with the woman in the mirror. I snapped along to his song playing over the speakers and when we got to the chorus, I sang along at the top of my lungs. I was so engrossed in my sing-along I didn't hear Anika come in.

"Nah, nah, nah, nah nah nahnah, nah nah, nah" she sang.

I let out a blood-curdling scream. Note to self, get my house key back. "What did I tell you about just barging in?" I reached for my phone, turning the volume down.

"You told me not to. But I'm your sister and those rules don't apply to me."

"That rule was made for you."

"What's with all the liquor? Are you throwing a party?"

"No just doing some winter cleaning."

Anika raised a half-full bottle of Don Julio. "Are you tossing these things out?"

"Yeah, I don't need all this alcohol hanging around." I was ten toes down when I told Aldi I wanted to support him in every way possible, and for me that meant getting rid of the many bottles of alcohol I'd been storing away and changing my bar cart into a coffee station.

"Why?"

"Because I need to focus on school and Aldridge doesn't drink, so what's the purpose?"

"I'll take them off your hands."

"Really?"

"Yes, free liquor is always a yes."

"Great."

"How was Sedona?"

"It was everything I needed and more. I think it brought us closer."

"Well, you're definitely glowing."

I surveyed my sister's face to determine if I should share more about the trip. Aldridge being in rehab and recovering wasn't my business to tell. I'd let him share that information when and with whom he saw fit. But I was itching to share the news about law school because I knew that would make Anika proud. "Aldridge offered to pay my tuition."

Anika clapped her hands. "Good old Aldridge. They don't make men like him anymore. Most men barely have two nickels to rub together, and they hold that shit close, like Gollum's ring. Let me guess, you told him no."

"Wrong, I'm going to let him."

"Who are you and what have you done to my moral high ground taking sister?"

"I think your consistent nagging finally got to me. Plus

you're letting Dante pay for the wedding of your dreams. It just—"

"Actually, about the wedding—"

"Don't tell me you two broke up?" Did I have an I told you so in my back pocket at the ready? Yes. But the new Danessa wouldn't be using it. If things had soured, I'd be supportive ... relieved but supportive.

"No, I just don't want to have a cookie-cutter wedding. I don't think it represents who we are. When we look back on our day, I want to smile because we did exactly what we wanted."

"What does that mean?"

Anika squared her shoulders. "We're going to the Little White Wedding Chappel."

"The place with the drive-up window?" My brows climbed my forehead and I fought the urge to strongly disagree.

"Yes, but we'll be getting married inside." I opened the closest bottle and took a long swig. "Say something."

"Are you sure? Anika, this is your wedding day. You only get one first wedding day."

"I love Dante, and he loves me and honestly that's all that matters."

"What about the wedding dress?"

"I'll still wear a pretty dress, just less traditional and then after we'll have a party with all our friends."

"If that's what you want I support it." Was the best I could muster. I was easy, breezy, and less carping. It wasn't my special day. I just needed to be there for Anika and Dante.

"Yeah, see you get it." I slid the open bottle of Uncle Nearest to her and she took a sip.

"Did you tell your mother?"

"No, I was hoping you could—"

"No, trust me it's not going to soften the blow coming from me. It'll just make things worse."

"But if you're there for moral support. I could tag you in when I need to collect my thoughts."

"Like you had my back at the dress fitting?"

"That was different. The day was supposed to be about me, and you and mom found a way to make it about you."

My head jerked back. "I'm sorry, but that woman ..." I closed my eyes, took a deep breath, and adjusted my tone. "You're right. I'm sorry."

"No hard feelings, but you owe me. You also owe me for helping you and Aldi get back together."

"I don't think you had anything to do with that."

"Bitch, I had to conspire and plot to get you two in the same spaces. If it wasn't for me, you'd both still be in the talking stage and not the fucking stage."

"Okay, I'll help."

"Great. I'm throwing a dinner party at Dante's place this weekend. Feel free to bring your man."

"You want to tell Mom you're forgoing a traditional wedding, something she has been dreaming about since she was a little girl, at a dinner party?"

"It will be intimate, just us. If Dante and Aldridge are there, she can't get as mad as she'd like to."

"You're talking like you've never met Jemini. Do you remember that time she cussed us out in front of that reverend she was dating?"

"That *reverend* was a con man riding around in fancy cars and wearing those ugly ass designer suits. I doubt that was the first time he'd heard that type of language."

"Maybe you're right." All I could remember is I was six and this man of God kept wanting me to sit on his lap. So, whenever he came around, I'd hide out in my room.

"And your newfound puritanical lifestyle is my gain." Anika embraced the many bottles of discarded liquor. When the faint sounds of Michael Jackson's "Don't Stop 'Til You Get Enough" played Anika squealed. "Bitch this is my song, turn it up." I did as told and Anika broke out into a nasty bossa nova.

<hr>

DANTE'S HOUSE WAS EXACTLY WHAT YOU'D EXPECT FROM A twenty-nine-year-old basketball player, all glass situated on top of a hill with views of the city. This neighborhood was filled with celebrities, politicians and families whose wealth could be traced back several decades. Aldridge and I hadn't visited this area during his home search because I knew he'd hate it. He'd call it pretentious and too much home for one person, and he'd complain about the drive.

Even so, when we pulled up, he said, "Gotdamn, now that's a home."

"You like it?"

"Real curb appeal."

"Neighborhoods like this don't have curbs, just miles and miles of tall shrubbery and private gates to keep vagrants out."

"I know there is big money behind these gates. How much does something like this cost?" He pointed to Dante's place with the curved driveway.

"Ten million minimum."

"US currency?"

"Yes."

"How much do you think Dante paid?"

"Are you pocket watching?"

"No, I just … he comes in off the bench, there's no way he could afford something like this."

"I'm not supposed to know this, but he doesn't own the house. It's a long-term rental."

"How do you know that?"

"A simple MLS search can tell you a lot."

"Does Anika know?"

"I don't know that she cares. Not owning doesn't equate to broke. He's paying ten thousand a month in rent and really should just buy at this point. Maybe Anika can help him with that."

"Shit is never what it seems."

"You have to swear to keep that between you and me."

"Cross my heart and hope to die."

Inside Anika took our coats. "Welcome to our home. Aldi, there are drinks and appetizers in the dining room. Dante can mix up whatever you want. You know if he wasn't a star basketball player he'd make one hell of a bartender, just like Tom Cruise in that one movie."

Squeezing Aldi's hand, I asked, "Do you want me to come with you?" I didn't know how this worked and if being around others drinking was approved recovery behavior. The last thing I wanted to do was put him in a precarious situation.

"No, I'm good. Catch up with Anika."

When Aldi walked away to join Jemini and Dante, Anika dug her nails into my arm. "What was that for?"

"I'm just so nervous. You promise to have my back?"

"Yep, remember this is your wedding and you get to call the shots. Jemini can object but she can't do shit to change it."

"What if she gets mad and starts throwing things?"

That was a real possibility. "She won't cause I won't let her. The throwing things part. I can't control her mood."

"Dante thinks I'm making a big deal over nothing, but he doesn't know Mom like we do. When she doesn't get her way, she can be vicious."

"Aldridge and I are in your corner and who knows, maybe we are making a mountain out of a molehill."

After a tour of the house with light refreshments, we sat down to eat, and my mother wasted no time jumping right in. "Have we set a date?" Anika shoved a forkful of food in her mouth. "We need to pick a date so we can start making plans."

"We? Don't you mean they, Anika and Dante?" I asked.

"Yes, the wedding is about Anika and Dante, but it's also about me and our friends and family."

"We do have a date in mind."

"When?" My mother, Aldridge, and I all said in unison.

"The twenty-seventh."

"Of?" Jemini prodded.

"June."

"Right after the finals." Dante smiled.

"If you make it to the finals," Jemini said.

"We're making it to the finals and Dante will be rocking a championship ring alongside his wedding ring." Aldridge's tone was firm.

"June doesn't give us very much time to plan. We need to get the invitations out right away."

I nodded when Anika glanced at me, encouraging her to speak her mind. Even though we were both adults, it was still difficult delivering unexpected news to our mother. "About that. Dante and I want a huge party. Open bar, celebrity DJ, chocolate fountain. But for the ceremony we were thinking something less grandiose."

"Okay, so the vineyard is out."

"How small are you thinking?" I asked, nudging Anika along.

"Pretty much the people in this room and Dante's parents."

"The fuck?" Jemini slammed her glass into the table.

"We want something less traditional."

My mother's outraged gaze settled on me. "Is this your doing? Did you talk her out of the fairy-tale wedding of her dreams?

"Me? No. This is all Anika and Dante's idea."

Turning back to Anika, her tone was less harsh but still tense. "Baby girl, you only get married once."

"We can only hope," Aldridge said in between sampling the scalloped potatoes.

"I know it's once in lifetime and that's why we want to stay true to ourselves."

"Where do you want to have this mini wedding?"

I braced myself for the fallout from Anika's response.

"The Little White Wedding Chapel."

"On the Strip?" She tossed her hands in the air as if signaling she'd heard enough.

"I've actually Googled the place and looked at the pictures. It's really quite lovely." Anika beamed proudly.

"It's so charming," I agreed.

Aldridge leaned in and asked. "Were we looking at the same pictures?"

"Shhh." I pinched his side.

"Is this a joke? Are you two pranking me?"

Dante cleared his throat. "No Mom, Anika and I have made up our minds."

"Don't call me mom. And minds can be changed. What am I supposed to tell everyone?"

"Tell them they're not invited," I said.

"Shut up, Danessa. I just know you had something to do with this."

"Jemini, I know you're disappointed but let's not be rude," Aldridge said.

"Did you push these two bitches out your vagina?"

"No ma'am."

"Then mind your business." Clearly, she was pissed because normally she was uber nice to Aldridge.

"Let's not act like we're not all adults here. Jemini I'm trying to be respectful because you are the *elder* but not too much." I loved how he always had my back. And did you catch the dig at her age?

"I just don't understand you girls. We had a plan, a big traditional wedding with all the extras." She turned to me. "And you and your silly law school dream. You failed the first time and will likely fail again. Law school is a huge waste of time."

Because she couldn't control Anika, she decided to take swipes at me. "I disagree."

"Aldridge, tell her law school would drain her bank account and it's a scam."

"I'm with Danessa on this. She should pursue what she's passionate about. And she'd make one hell of a lawyer."

"Now that you two are doing whatever this is, Aldridge should be your full-time priority. Making sure he's cared for and looked after."

"That's archaic thinking," I protested.

"Women are supposed to be a helpmate to their man. That's from the Bible."

"I know you're not quoting scripture. The Bible also highlights adultery as a sin, but that hasn't seemed to stop you."

"He was separated."

"Which one, Mom?"

"Technically she wouldn't be the adulterer because she was never married," Dante said. "A convenient loophole."

"How about we agree to disagree," I said through gritted teeth. "Better yet. Why not stop meddling in the affairs of your adult children. If Anika wants to get married while Elvis sings Love Me Tender that's her choice."

"You're my daughters, so what you do is very much my business."

"Most parents would be thrilled to have a kid in law school."

"I'm not most parents."

"No shit Sherlock. You had us wearing padded bras at eleven and thong panties at thirteen."

"That was so you wouldn't have panty lines."

"You were always pushing us to grow up way too soon. And don't even get me started on that twenty-year-old you tried to make me date."

"He was nice and willing to buy you anything and you acted like a weirdo."

"I was fourteen, Jemini. I hadn't even had my first kiss, and you wanted me to date a drug dealer."

"You've always been such a baby. Your sister was way more mature than you."

"And you were a pimp."

Aldridge squeezed my knee under the table. "Whoa maybe we should pause. Have you tried the scalloped potatoes, because they are the creamiest if anyone's interested."

"Do you hear that?" Jemini asked.

"What?" Anika said.

"It's the world's smallest violin playing a pity tune just for Danessa. I was a single mother doing the best I could with two ungrateful girls to look after."

"Was the best you could do allowing random men in and out of our apartment?" Biting my tongue was the only option. There were so many skeleton bones I could allow to tumble at our feet. I was convinced my mother was suffering from a mild case of amnesia because she conveniently forgot all the shady parts of the past thirty years. My role was to support Anika, but Jemini knew exactly how to push my buttons, often making me look like the angry Black woman who couldn't let go of the past.

"You turned out fine." Her tone was dismissive.

"Despite you, not because of you. I'm going to law school because I don't want to be an aging video vixen who can't accept that the spotlight has faded along with her beauty."

"Now you're just lying you fucking little bitch."

Aldridge clapped his hands. "Whoa, can we stop with the name calling?"

"Aldridge, you should run. Or at the very least pay so Danessa can get the stick removed from her ass."

"I love dinner parties because they're always so unpredictable," Dante said.

"Oh, this is classic Jemini, never taking accountability, refusing to admit when she's wrong."

"Like mother like daughter, Baby girl. You're an adult and still blaming me for everything that goes wrong in your life."

"I've really gotten into painting," Aldridge chimed in attempting to redirect the conversation. "Very soothing. I'm fucking heavy with watercolors right now."

"Maybe you should teach Danessa. It might make her less uptight."

"Uptight? You'd be uptight too if you had to share the same space with your abuser."

"This is getting dark," Dante whispered.

I stared at Anika who just pushed the garlic parmesan orzo across her plate. What happened to having each other's backs?

"I really can't stand this new generation. They read a couple of books, and they start saying shit about breaking curses and holding space for fuck knows what. When did people turn into such pussies?"

I countered, "Some would say perhaps your generation shoved too much down, never really dealing with the things that hurt you or the people who wronged you. And that crap you hid away still spilled over into your relationship with your kids."

"Hurt people hurt people," Dante added.

"Baby, you're so philosophical." Anika rubbed her nose against his.

I had to close my eyes to prevent them from rolling from my sockets. "Two things can be true, you did the best you could but your children were still affected by the choices you made."

"I didn't come here to be attacked."

I surrendered my hands in the air. "No one's attacking you."

Aldridge scrunched his face. "Mmm."

Leaning in I asked, "What do you mean hmm?"

"I just don't think sniping at one another is beneficial," he whispered.

"She's berating me."

"I don't disagree but arguing with Jemini is like fucking with someone with nothing to lose."

Dante spoke up. "Y'all should probably go to therapy. Everyone is doing it. It's hella trendy right now. It'll give you a chance to unpack all these emotions."

Aldridge nodded. "Dante has a point." We had now entered a surreal realm because Dante was making sense.

"I love therapy. Go religiously every week," Anika said.

"Really?" I asked. Anika's eyes met mine. Bullshit detected. She ain't never a day in her life talked to a licensed professional about anything.

"If that would stop Danessa from blaming me for every goddamn thing, I'm down."

"Exciting, marriage, law school, and group therapy. This year is off to a great start. Danessa and I will be there with bells on. Won't we Nessa?" Anika asked.

"I'll be there, but I'm not wearing any fucking bells."

ALDRIDGE

WHEN YOU CUT OFF A PARENT WITH NO EXPLANATION, THEY will make every attempt to communicate with you. Right now, my father was on a live stream with a sports podcaster giving his account of the gambling debacle.

"I like to gamble for fun. I've been gambling since I was a teenager. I've always had a lucky hand."

"Do you see how placing bets on your son's professional games could be seen as problematic?"

"It's not illegal. Shit, I bet on any and everything. I've placed bets on a coin toss."

"Did you ever bet against Aldridge's team?"

"Occasionally. Not because I don't believe in my kid, but everyone has an off day."

"Have you spoken to your son since the news broke?"

My father removed his baseball cap and looked directly into the camera. "He's trying to ice me out. My bank account is frozen and when I try contacting his assistant, I get sent to voicemail. A son shouldn't treat his father like that. I raised him and taught him everything he knows. That hook shot, he learned that from me. Back in my day, children respected their parents. But Aldridge thinks he's too good for his old man."

"Has he told you that?"

"His silence is doing the speaking. I hope he knows that don't no one love him like his blood. Fuck the fans and the groupies. At the end of the day family is all we've got."

"If Aldridge is watching right now, what would you like to say to him?"

He scratched at his patchy beard. His eyes were sunken, and he looked thinner than I remembered him. "I'd tell him to stop acting all sensitive and give his old man a call. We can work this out."

"Do you regret what you did?"

"Ain't no use in regret. I can't take shit back. It is what it is. I learned that at a young age. We make choices and you need to be a man and stand on that shit."

"You heard it here first folks, Lamonte Mosley, father to basketball star Aldridge Mosley, breaks his silence on the gambling scandal. We reached out to Aldridge's publicist and was referred back to the original statement released when the story was first developing. Tip-in Sports' doors are always open if Aldridge is interested in sitting down with us."

I tossed my phone into my gym bag and shut my locker door. Ramblers' practice ended thirty minutes ago, but I decided to stay behind and get in a quick run on the treadmill. We'd secured a spot in the playoffs which was expected. Next up was the hard part, making it to the finals. To do that, I needed to be in peak physical condition. The Ramblers facility housed every piece of equipment imaginable. A vibration machine, cold plunge room, and a sauna.

The Ramblers gym was empty, another perk, with the exception of Colin Pratt who was using one of the weight machines. Could this day get any worse? Things between us had not improved. We weren't still constantly at one another's throats, preferring to practice the golden rule, "If you don't have anything nice to say then shut the fuck up."

To my surprise Colin acknowledged my presence when I entered the weight room. "Seems like we had the same idea."

"Kinda late for you. Shouldn't you be at home with your family?"

"Haven't you heard, newbie? Charmise kicked me out."

"Damn." Of course I'd heard the rumors about a baby on the way, but I didn't know the rumors were true.

"Are you not going to tell me I'm getting what I deserve?"

"I'm not into kicking people while they're down."

"How about you? Your father's a piece of shit. No disrespect."

"You're not telling me shit I don't already know." I pulled on my lifting gloves.

"You can do everything to rise above your circumstances, but your family will always remind you where you came from for better or worse."

"Before I got drafted my agent at the time told me I needed to distance myself from my family. He called them a liability."

"That's kind of fucked up."

"What's fucked is that he was right."

Colin released a thoughtful breath. "I know we're not friends, but can I offer a piece of advice?"

"Sure."

"They say blood is thicker than water, but sometimes

our friends will be there for us when our family is looking for a handout."

"I don't mind taking care of my family. I just don't like being taken advantage of."

"You have a bastard for a father. Welcome to the club."

My face telegraphed my surprise as I took a seat on one of the benches. "Your dad?"

"I know you think I grew up with a silver spoon in my mouth—"

"Because you did."

"Correct, but that didn't mean I had it made. My father was a taskmaster and nothing I did was good enough."

"I know the feeling. My father can't seem to find it in him to be happy for me."

"It's hard to be happy when you're jealous." To my surprise, it would appear Colin and I had more in common than I initially thought. Having a distant father was tough. The funny thing is from the outside looking in, Colin's suburban childhood was what I'd wished for. Grass isn't always greener. "Sometimes cutting motherfuckers off is the smartest thing you can do."

"So what are you gonna do about Charmise?"

"Focus on work. Hope she agrees to couples therapy and try to keep my nose clean. She's the love of my life, the mother of my kids."

"If she was all that, then why cheat?" I raised my hands to show my intentions were pure. "Not an attack, just a question."

"When you can have anything you want, it's hard to say no."

"My girl gave me hell when that story broke about you and—"

"The baby?"

"Yeah, she seems to think all players are the same."

"Does she know she's dating a born-again choirboy?"

"Not a choirboy by any stretch."

"So, it looks like we're going to the playoffs."

"You sound surprised. Making it to the playoffs was the easy part. Now we're gonna have to hustle for the finals."

"The organization is no doubt patting themselves on the back for signing you on."

"I tried to tell you. I'm the truth and we're gonna win a championship this year."

"And if we don't?"

"If we don't, I'll eat a leather jacket with hot sauce."

Colin clapped his hands, laughing loudly. "I'm going to hold you to it, newbie."

DANESSA GAVE ME A KEY TO HER PLACE SO I COULD COME AND go as needed. I found her in the second bedroom bent over, fussing with the printer.

"Alright Thiccolas Cage."

"Excuse me?"

"The ass is doing a lot of the heavy lifting today." I kissed the top of her head. "What are you doing?"

"I'm trying to print out my color-coded notes for study group tomorrow." She pulled a jammed piece of paper from the machine. "This thing is a piece of shit."

"Move, I'll fix it."

"Now you're a printer repairman?"

"I have many skills." I shooed her away.

"How was NA?"

I seeped in air, gritting my teeth. "One of the members OD over the weekend."

"Shit, are you okay?"

"Yeah, I barely knew her. She was pretty quiet. It just sucks because I've been there and you think it would be a wake-up call but a lot of times it's not."

"Is she going to be okay?"

"Sounds like it, but relapsing is rough. You feel like a failure and that feeling makes you want to use even more. Anyway, the meeting was mostly about recognizing triggers and establishing coping strategies."

"Do you have coping strategies?"

"Yeah, building a support group which I have with you, Pete and Nori. Exercise helps relieve my stress and focus my mind. And avoiding situations that don't support my recovery. That's the part I'm finding the hardest because every party or invitation to hang out often includes drugs. It's a balance you know."

I promised myself I wouldn't shy away from the tough questions. Whatever Danessa needed to know I'd answer. She put her trust in me, and I had to do the same. Because trying to protect her from all this would only make our relationship harder.

"I hope one day I get to meet Pete."

"It's kinda anonymous for a reason." Opening the various printer doors, I located the source of the jam.

"Did you catch the Tip-in interview?"

"How could I miss it with everyone texting and emailing me links?"

"You probably should've asked your father to sign an NDA before you got famous."

"A little too late for legal advice."

"Have you talked to your mother?"

"Yeah, and she's on his side. Let's talk about something else. How'd you do on the torts quiz today?"

"Ninety-seven." Danessa beamed.

"My baby is so damn smart." The printer was jammed with paper, requiring me to remove several crumpled sheets.

"I took your advice and scheduled a family therapy appointment with Jemini and Anika, not that I think it will help."

"If you go into it expecting to fail, then you will. I know Jemini has done a lot to make you distrust her, but I also know you're not ready to cut her off."

"How can I? We're business partners."

"Exactly, it would be in everyone's best interest if you could get to a better place."

"I think we just need to talk about work and only work. When we talk about anything else that's when we bump heads."

"At the end of the day our parents are just trying to figure life out like everyone else. A beautiful woman once told me that."

"You're right. My bad I'm complaining about my mother when you're dealing with the fallout from your dad's actions."

"No, I'm cool. Colin helped me to realize that sometimes when all else fails, limited access is the only thing you can do."

"You and Colin are besties now?"

"No, far from it. But I bumped into him at the gym, and he made some valid points."

"Look at us with our mommy and daddy issues, respectively."

"After the season and the wedding let's go on a vacation."

"I can't, I'm signing up for online summer classes."

"Online means remote. So you can complete your homework just as easily on a beach as you can on that firm ass couch of yours."

"I love my couch."

"Try printing now."

Danessa clicked her mouse and the familiar sound of a machine etching words onto paper kicked on. "You did it."

"Don't sound so surprised."

She came over to where I was seated on the floor and draped her arms over my shoulders. "Thank you, baby. What would I do without you?"

I twisted her onto my lap. "I'm here to make your life easier."

"You're doing a very good job." Danessa's face lit up. "I found a house and I think you're going to love it."

"Tell me more."

"Nope, I have to show you so you can appreciate it with your own eyes. I had Nori pencil me in on your calendar for Saturday morning."

"Sounds good because I'm tired of living out of suitcases."

"I'm not going to say this place is the one, but I have a good feeling."

"I trust you with my heart and my housing."

DANESSA

ON THE DRIVE OVER I DID MY BEST TO CONTAIN MY excitement. I searched far and wide to find a home that met all of Aldi's specifications. And this home in a hidden gem of a neighborhood ticked off most of his boxes. This two-story modern home had curb appeal and was just over five thousand square feet. Which was conservative for an athlete. Most were living in full-out mansions, but Aldridge wanted something a bit more intimate. In Kansas City, he owned a condo so this would be his first single-family home.

When we pulled up to the house, I could hear Aldridge gasp.

"Isn't it stunning?"

"I'm impressed." Aldi shifted the car into park.

"I'm not trying to overhype it, but I think you're really going to like the layout."

Walking toward the house, he asked, "What's the neighborhood like?"

"Mix of young, rich professionals and established families. For entry into this area, you'll need close to two million, and that's for a basic build sans any add ons."

"So expensive."

"Baby this is Vegas. Everything costs. I'd be happy to show you a starter home for five hundred."

"No, I get it, and I'm willing to pay for the right place."

"As you should. You're about to be the NBA's best in show, and that comes with perks like a house to tool around in during the off season."

"I prefer the term NBA champion. But you already know I'm a champion, especially after this morning and that humming thing I did on your clit."

I blushed. "That was a masterclass."

Aldi closed the space between us. "It was my greatest pleasure."

"I'm working."

"You can't flirt at work?"

"No, because I'm a professional."

"Okay, well just know on the drive home I plan on slipping my hand up your skirt."

"Noted." I opened the front door, stepping aside.

Aldridge's face lit up as he took the space in. This home was expertly staged by me, and I left no detail to chance. Aldi was a visual person, and I wanted him to envision himself in this house the moment he walked in. "I did good, right?"

"Calm down. I'm liking what I see, but it's just the entryway."

"An entryway that leads to a formal dining room for dinner with friends or holidays."

"You and I both know this room will be off limits to guest and I might even break out the plastic furniture covers."

"You wouldn't"

"My mom still has them. I bought her a brand-new house with all new furniture, and she specifically requested custom plastic covers for the sofas and all chairs. I said, mom if something gets stained I'll just buy you a new one, but she wasn't trying to hear that."

"I guess old habits die hard. To your left, you have an office. Spacious enough for you to take meetings or invite your entire team to brainstorm."

"Nice."

"Straight ahead leads you to the main living area. But you have several living spaces in this home."

"I can get with the open floor plan."

"Outside we have a smaller structure that was being used as a gym by the previous owner. Equipped with a full bath, a sauna to soothe your muscles after a game, and a mini kitchen where you can make smoothies or after-workout snacks."

"Finally, a place that speaks to my soul."

"The backyard leads to this infinity pool with stunning views of the Las Vegas Strip. Back inside the kitchen is what you would expect from a home in this neighborhood and price tag."

"I could put my culinary skills to the test. Have you ever had vegetarian lasagna? I had it at a restaurant a few months back and didn't miss the meat. I've been dying to try and recreate it."

"Sounds delicious."

Aldi wrapped his arms around me. "I'll make it for you. You can be my sous chef and taste tester."

"I know what I'd like to taste."

Aldridge frowned. "Not very professional," he teased.

"You know what, you're right. Let's head upstairs." Aldridge played grab ass with me as we made our way up.

I stayed in the hall while he walked from room to room. This decision had to be his. I didn't want my bias to get in the way. This place would be almost anybody's dream home. It filled his criteria but the last thing I wanted was him to feel the pressure to buy from me because I'd shown him close to thirty houses with lukewarm reception. It was up to Aldi to choose the type of life he wanted to create in Vegas. Of course, I hoped that life featured me, but I didn't want him buying a multimillion-dollar home because it made me happy and I could see us cuddled up in the living room or sharing a shower in the bathroom with full body shower heads.

When he returned to the upstairs loft space, I asked, "What do you think?"

"I like it. Do you like it?"

"I'm not buying it."

"But I need you to like it."

"Just tell me what you think."

"I think this place is perfect and has damn near everything I'm looking for."

"But?"

"This is a huge purchase. When I bought my mom's house, I didn't really think. She loved it so I bought it. But this is permanent and it's a lot of house for two people."

"Two?"

"You and I equals two."

"No this is going to be your place. So you need to love it whether I'm here or not."

"Not possible, because I can already envision glimpses of you throughout this house. Take this loft for instance, it's nice and spacious but if we're not sprawled on the floor vibing to classic R&B music together it just doesn't work. Walking from room to room all I can think about is you, me, and our future. The room off the primary gets a ton of sunlight and would be great as your office."

We both wanted to make the other happy. But I wasn't buying this house he was, and if I never called this place home he would have to be content with his decision. I reached for his hand, giving it a squeeze. "Do you want to put in an offer?"

"Oh my God. My stomach hurts. This would be the biggest purchase I've ever made."

"You can sleep on it no need to decide now."

"I could always move in with you."

"No."

"What?"

"Absolutely not. I don't move in with men I've only been dating for months. It's one of my rules."

"I'm not just any man."

"You could be Clark Kent and the answer would still be no."

"Well Clark Kent was a flake and living a double life. Says he's going to meet you for dinner and then after hours of waiting, you find out he's halfway across town fighting Lex Luther."

Aldridge leaned against the railing. "Could you see yourself living here someday?"

He was trying to pin me down, get me on record declaring this house was the one to help him feel better. But I wasn't going to take the bait. "It's possible. But this is about you."

"It's important to me that you like it too. I want this to feel like a place you can call home. Because for me home is where you are. So, I could live in a coffin apartment and still be good if you were laying on top of me."

"You'd probably have to fold yourself in half to make it work."

"And I'd gladly endure it with you because I love you

that much. But in this house the possibilities are endless. We could get a green couch right there." He pointed to the living space below.

"What do you know about green couches?"

"I know Black women go up for them. Point out a baddie and I can almost guarantee she has an emerald-colored couch back at the crib. Maybe we could get one with hidden storage to hide the blankets and all the kids' random toys."

"Kids, plural."

"Oh yeah, I'm knocking you up once or twice in this house for sure. I don't even care what we have as long as they have your eyes and my ears."

"Wow the shade. Is this how you talk to the future mother of your long limb children?"

"Just speaking the truth in love. Plus, imagine the parties we can throw. With laidback vibes, dudes playing dominos in the backyard, a heated game of Spades in the formal dining room. The hum of conversations every direction you turn, and me stealing kisses any time you walk past."

"Sounds like you have this all planned out."

"Because this was the plan all along."

"Even after we broke up?"

"Loving you was my best and only plan."

"I'm sorry it took us so long to make it a reality."

"Let's put an offer in."

"Are you sure?"

"Right now this place is just a pretty box, but you and I are going to make it a home."

"Okay."

He leaned in resting his forehead against mine. "Okay, let's buy a house."

ALDRIDGE

Eighty-two regular season games, the NBA playoffs where I vacillated between confident to uncertain and back again, and now the fifth and last game of the NBA Finals. We had home-court advantage which could be a blessing and a curse. If we won, we got to celebrate with the fans who'd never given up on this team and supported the Ramblers through the decade long drought. But if we lost, the silence would be deafening. The disappointment would be great and my place on this team would be scrutinized.

It wasn't enough that I'd brought us all the way to the end, this wasn't a recreational league. This was the NBA and almost didn't count. The only thing that mattered was winning. And everyone from Ramblers' owner Sariah Thornton to the ten-year-old kid with my jersey on in the nosebleed section was hoping we secured a championship. Which was totally understandable, real life was hard. I knew that firsthand. You just lost your job, your kid is being bullied at school, your mother-in-law hates your guts, or you have to decide between paying the light bill or getting your daughter a prom dress. But sports brought people together no matter the circumstance. It was an escape from the harsh realities of life.

I took my part in that very seriously. The Ramblers were the underdogs and fans were rooting for us to prove everybody wrong. If the Ramblers could come out on top, then maybe they could ask for that raise, or tell the nosy neighbor to mind their fucking business.

In the locker room, you could hear a pin drop as Coach Justus gave us one last rallying speech. "You aren't in this room by accident. This is years of planning, trusting the process and creating one of the best NBA teams in history. We've fought hard to get here. We've suffered major losses and devastating injuries. Collectively we've cried real tears and experienced moments of pure elation.

"We're a family. We may not always like one another … shit, look at Pratt and Mosley at the start of the season." The team, me included, chuckled. "But at the end of the day we are a unit. We succeed and fail together. And this year we've been able to come out on top and I'm asking you to do it one last time.

"People have doubted us from the beginning and honestly, we gave them a reason to. Even now after all this winning they're still calling us the underdogs. And that's fine, they can underestimate us. They can say we've only won because other teams didn't show up to play. But after tonight, they'll have to put some respect on our name because we will be NBA champions."

A rumble of feet stomping and hand clapping turned into a roar as we cosigned Coach's words. Standing, we formed a huddle and Deion shouted, "Ramblers!"

"Nation!" the rest of us said in unison."

"Ramblers!"

"Nation!"

"Ramble on, Ramblers, ramble on!" The entire room yelled together.

The arena was packed and if I wasn't nervous before, I was definitely feeling the nerves now. After forty-eight minutes of game play my first season as a Rambler would come to an end. It was up to me whether it would end with a bang or a whimper. The lights dimmed and the Ramblers' starting lineup was announced. When the lights came up, I scanned the crowd in search of Danessa. I located her gleaming face and threw up a half heart matching her bright smile. She returned the gesture, completing the heart and I tried my best not to dissolve into mush.

I took a gamble on a new team and a new city. Vegas wasn't my first choice, but it turned out to be life changing because it brought Danessa back to me. When I say she was the love of my life it wasn't hyperbole. I'd never loved a woman like I loved her. Trust me, I tried but something wouldn't allow me to let go of the ideal of her. Maybe because I knew our ending was abrupt and I felt like we had unfinished business. That unfinished business was loving one another deeply with intention. I was made to fill her cup. We all had a journey in life and mine was to play basketball and love Danessa Irwin.

From the jump ball my team was locked in. We'd worked hard for this moment, and the win was so close we could taste it. Our focused determination had us communicating telepathically so Deion was posted up in three-point range when I blindly passed him the ball. And Colin, who for much of the season had been my rival, could anticipate my next move and was waiting under the basket for an easy layup. As we made our way back up court, we bumped elbows in silent solidarity. Don't get me wrong, Colin was still an asshole, but he was a great ballplayer.

Sometimes during a game everything goes right. You

get several fast breaks with effortless baskets. The referees call almost every foul in your favor. After a shot from three-point territory, the ball circles the rim before sinking into the basket. You couldn't tell me God wasn't a Las Vegas Ramblers fan because on this night everything appeared to align. I'd love to tell you it was a nail-biter, that would make for a better story but actually going into the fourth, I felt really good. All we had to do was continue our full-court press. When Deion passed on the three tossing the ball to me, I was able to secure two points and a foul.

It seemed like the crowd finally let go of the collective breath they were holding and allowed themselves to celebrate the final seconds of the game. When the buzzer blared, I screamed at the top of my lungs. Deion, Colin and Dante made their way to me and we had a mini celebration right there in center court. The fans chanted Ramblers, Ramblers, Ramblers. Some moments are hard to explain like a first kiss, or that feeling on the first day of school. And this was no different. A wave of emotions rushed through me. I wanted to yell, cry, and retreat for silent reflection all at the same time.

Any athlete will tell you winning the ultimate prize in your respective sport is the end goal. None of them pursue a sport to be mediocre. Gold medals, rings, and trophies are always the motivation. Everything that followed was a blur. There was courtside revelry, NBA Championship hats that had been mocked up and purchased months ago in anticipation of this outcome. Reporters formed a gaggle around Coach Justus and the team looking to get a sound bite. One of the courtside reporters pulled me aside and peppered me with questions.

"Aldridge, congratulations. This year you've proven that the Ramblers' gamble on you paid off."

"Well, I like to think of myself as a sure thing. And I trust the abilities of my teammates."

"The team worked hard to secure this win. Looking back, it's as if this was destined."

"I believe in the importance of getting the right players in the correct seats. Once we accomplished that it was hard to stop what I like to call inevitable."

"One thing you don't lack is confidence. Where does that come from?"

"Hard work and dedication to my craft. I've loved basketball since I was a kid and being allowed to play on a professional level is a dream come true."

"You and Colin Prat seemed to put your differences aside during the playoffs and finals. How was it playing alongside him?"

"I'm a fan. Naturally there would be a bumpy transition, but we both had the same objective and that was to win, and we came out here and proved that tonight."

"What does Aldridge Mosley do next?"

"Tonight, I'll celebrate with my girl, who was my support system for much of this season. I was already a winner coming into this game because I had her in my corner."

"Do you want to give her a shout-out now?"

"No because you people are nosy and what she and I have going on is for us. This isn't no Hollywood PR stuff."

"Congratulations again. Enjoy the celebration, you deserve it."

The excitement transitioned to the locker room with bottles of champagne and other manners of carrying on. I never understood the tradition of dousing the coach in liquids like Gatorade or champagne as a form of celebration. It's a waste and everything gets sticky. But when in Rome you do Roman shit. The kinetic energy was so thick you could cut it with a knife.

When Danessa entered the room, she made a beeline toward me. Wrapping her arms around me, she gave me the biggest hug. I leaned into her and lifted her off her feet, planting a soft kiss to her lips.

"Oh my God, baby, congratulations, you deserve this." Danessa whispered affirming words into my ear. "You were so amazing out there. I knew it. I sensed today was going to be a special day."

"You knew we were going to win huh?"

"Never doubted you for a moment."

"Is this the same woman who right before I left held my hands and told me and I quote, 'Just try your best, that's all anyone can ask.' And no matter the outcome, you were proud of me regardless."

"I didn't say that because I didn't believe. I said it to take some of the pressure off of you."

"And I love you for it but you can admit you were split fifty-fifty."

"Maybe just a little bit but once you ran out on that court, I could tell you were locked in. You had that same determined demeanor the afternoon of your NCAA championship."

I planted several pecks to her lips. "I'm just glad you're here to share it with me."

Danessa caressed my cheek. "There is no place on this earth I'd rather be than right here with you, my MVP."

Winning this championship with Danessa by my side

made this moment all the more rewarding. Danessa knew what I had to sacrifice to get here. She would hang out in the stands typing papers while I practiced my free throws at the campus training facility. At the library while she was studying her notes, I was studying my playbook. And at night we'd dream about the life we'd have, me a celebrated NBA player and her a junior lawyer on the thirty under thirty list.

Winning a championship was always an inevitability but winning Danessa's heart was far less certain. My life wasn't perfect, but having her by my side made it easier. Rapping two empty champagne bottles together, I grabbed the attention of the players and their family members who were gathered.

"I just want to take a minute to acknowledge that most of you hated me on my first day. And I don't blame you, I can be a little prickly. But with all sincerity, I am so proud of this team and the opportunity to play alongside each and every one of you. We are forever connected because this is a moment we will remember for a lifetime. Thank you for trusting me."

Teammates patted my back while others cheered or nodded in agreement.

Colin Pratt cleared his throat while raising the half-empty bottle he was holding. "To the newbie."

The locker room erupted with stomping of feet and laughter.

I came to Vegas with nothing and over time I built relationships with these men. When my family let me down this crew had my back. Deion was a no-nonsense mentor who told me what I needed to hear not what I wanted to hear. Dante was my polar opposite, but he taught me not to take myself too seriously. And Colin Pratt taught me basketball was universal and although we might not see eye to eye off the court, he'd always have my back on the hardwood.

"Ramblers Nation, baby!" Deion shouted.

DANESSA

It was three hours before Anika's wedding, and she was as cool as a cucumber. I on the other hand was fussing over every detail. Anika and Dante opted to have a simple wedding at the Little White Wedding Chapel on the Strip. But there were still details to confirm. Like the limo that would be transporting us to the chapel and the makeup artist who should be here any minute to glamify us.

Per usual my sister was on auto-pilot. She trusted I would bring her vision to life. But when I asked her what she wanted, her response was more concepts than concrete plans. It was all about this chill vibe. I didn't know what that looked like, but I did my best to make it happen.

"Don't you just love my wedding nails?" She flashed her long, blush nails adorned with pearls and gems.

"Beautiful." I nodded while typing out a text message to the party planner who was busy preparing the reception site and had questions about the tablescapes.

"We should get pizza," Anika announced.

"What?" My brows curved in surprise.

"Pizza."

"We have to leave in three hours. We don't have time for room service."

"Not room service. Pieola."

"You want me to order pizza from a restaurant over forty minutes away?"

"Yeah, it will be my last meal as a single woman."

"Sweetie—"

"Pieola." Anika flounced away humming a melodic tune.

Danessa: Meet me in the hallway ASAP.

Aldridge: Okay?

We were at opposite ends on the same floor of this luxury hotel. I met Aldridge at the elevator banks.

"How's it going?" I asked.

"Good we're playing Call of Duty."

"Video games … now?"

"Yeah, we still have a few hours to kill."

"And Dante's good, no cold feet?"

"He will be at the altar suited and booted."

"The bride requested pizza from Pieola."

"Yum."

"Not yum that spot is clear across town. It's going to take over an hour to get here and by that time her makeup will be done and she'll ruin her lipstick from the grease."

"Let's take a deep breath. Close your eyes." I followed his instructions. "Breathe in. Breathe out." A deep lungful of air filled my chest followed by an exhale. "Breathe in positive thoughts, breathe in levity. Expel stress and perfectionism. Now open your eyes."

"You think I'm being silly?"

"You're a perfectionist always have been. But Anika is the type of woman who lets the wind determine her next destination. So stop being so hard on yourself it will all come together. And the pizza will be here in an hour."

"How did you do that?"

"It takes a village. Now go back in there and enjoy this moment."

"I love you."

"We got this."

"T-minus three hours until game time." We performed an exploding fist bump before heading back to our respective rooms.

In Anika's suite she was dancing to seventies love songs. "Hi!"

"Hi, the pizza has been ordered. Mom's on her way. And the makeup artist just texted to say she's parking the car."

"I think that's cause for a celebration. Dance with me."

There was so much to do. Like check on the photographer who should be showing up any minute for the get-ready photos. Jemini was minutes away, which would no doubt raise my blood pressure, and I wasn't entirely sure where Anika's wedding shoes were. Despite all that, I reluctantly tossed my phone on the bed and danced with my big sister on her special day.

I WAS ANTI LITTLE WHITE WEDDING CHAPEL BUT NOW THAT we were inside, I had to admit it had its charm. The flowers in the lobby were fake but tasteful and the red carpet added a pop of color when compared to the white walls.

"Welcome to the world renowned Little White Wedding Chapel." A woman with a deep southern accent and hair piled high to the sky announced. "We have presided over the nuptials of everyone from Frank

Sinatra to Britney Spears. Are you two Dante and Anika?"

"Yes, that's us." My sister beamed.

"Alright just need you to sign the paperwork and pay the remaining balance."

Glancing at Aldridge I frowned, this part seemed less about wedded bliss and more about business. Dante handed over his card.

"Alright darling. Last detail is selecting your officiant."

"We've thought long and hard about this, and we are going to go with the Purple Rain package."

Aldridge couldn't contain his chuckle which caused Anika to flash him an icy glare. Aldi was forced to offer a swift apology, "Sorry, who doesn't love the man, the myth, the symbol?"

"Prince … wow. So exciting," I cosigned.

"That's why I'm wearing this purple bedazzled garter." She flashed her leg at me.

"It makes sense. This is all perfectly normal."

"They have tons of options. You know if you two want we could do a bang bang," Dante said.

"Do I want to know what that is?" I whispered to Aldi.

"You and Danessa are all dressed up, you could jump the broom right after me and my soon to be wife."

"I think we're good. This is your day and Nessa and I are happy to be supporting characters."

The lady with the big bouffant returned. "Alright who will be escorting you down the aisle."

Aldridge raised his hand. "That would be me."

"I'm going to ask everyone else to enter the room."

I fussed over the hem of Anika's dress. She settled on a short and flirty blush-toned frock and she looked stunning. "Are you ready to be a Mrs?"

"Yea, I can't wait to be Dante's wife."

Giving her one last hug, I took my place at the altar. Love was so unpredictable you could be with someone for years and not be ready to take the next step. While others could meet and instantly know this person was going to be their life partner. Or in the case of Aldridge and me, you could meet the love of your life, get cold feet and push him away only for Cupid or Eros to manifest other plans. I knew I was ready to spend forever with Aldi, but was in no rush to jump the broom. We still had some catching up to do. And I didn't want to rush through our love story, preferring instead to savor every part.

A slender man dressed in a purple satin suit with hair straightened into a full bouncy updo initiated the ceremony. "All rise for the beautiful one." When the music kicked in from the speakers, I cringed. They went with "Let's Go Crazy" when "Adore" was right there.

As the doors opened, I gasped. Even though I was just with Anika a minute ago, she somehow managed to become more stunning in those sixty seconds. My eyes swept over to Dante and his smile took up half his face. All I asked was that he love my sister and appreciate all the things that made her special.

At the altar I witnessed the man of my dreams usher my sister into her new life. It had been months now and I was still impressed by Aldridge. Each morning, waking up to his face was the best part of my day. *Actually, the morning sex was the best part of my day, but you catch my drift.* When his eyes opened to greet mine, a smile would tug at the corners of his mouth like he was just as surprised to see me as I was to see him. Then came the hug. Aldridge would scoop me up and press my body into his. I'd nestle my face into his neck and breathe deep.

The weight of his large hands rubbing my back would cause me to shiver. Back rubs quickly evolved into back shots that left my legs shaking while begging him to burrow his dick into my soul. *Wait a second. Was this considered a real chapel because my thoughts were not house of God approved. We should focus on the ceremony.*

The officiant was a low-budget Prince look-alike. If you squinted, you could see the vision. "Dearly Beloved today is a joyous day as we bring forth the union of Dante and Anika. This world can be So Dark, that Baby You're a Star when you find your partner. The amount of love in the air makes me Delirious. And on a solemn note ..." Fake Prince dropped the affects, his tone serious as he spoke the next sentence. "Marriage is a sacred bond that should not be entered into lightly, so if anyone has any objections speak now or forever hold your peace."

You could hear a pin drop as slowly all eyes turned to me. "What? I have no objections. Can we please move it along?" A blush took over my cheeks. At one point I had my concerns, but this was Anika's life. And while her choices would not be ones I would make, she was my sister and I was going to stick beside her.

"Excellent. Dante and Anika have written their own vows, which they will exchange now. Dante, you're up first."

"We met in a loud, noisy club but even with hundreds of people surrounding us, I knew you were one of a kind. It took me less than twenty-four hours to know I couldn't live without you. I was not a man who was interested in settling down. But you're the real deal and I just want to be in your orbit for the rest of my life. I promise to fuck you well and often and with me you'll never have to want for a thing. I love you Nica."

My smile faltered at his vows, wanting more declarations of his undying love. Reminder, not your wedding, and not your man.

"Anika, I think Dante is willing to Die For You. Now the bride will say her vows."

"Dante, neither of us were looking for love but it found us. I went to the Enclave to scam some men out of their money, but I ran into you and you instantly stole my heart. I don't take life too seriously but love, that's something I don't play about. So, I vow to love the fuck out of you every day for the rest of our lives. There is no one else on this planet I'd rather huddle through space with. You're stuck with me forever baby."

My man-eating sister had been tamed. Never thought I'd see the day, but Dante clearly had the magic touch because my sister had never been more sincere than in this moment. She loved him. So it didn't matter that she was getting married in a small room which smelled slightly like lemon pepper hot wings by a knock-off Prince impersonator in a ruffled shirt with his chest hair out.

"Nothing compares to the love a bride has for her groom."

The Prince song puns were getting a bit long in the tooth. But I guess that's what you get when you select the Purple Rain package. Our therapist confirmed during the first family session that I was a smidge judgmental. Okay she didn't add a percentage to it, but she did call me out. Don't get me wrong, this is something I already knew about myself, but hearing a medical professional cosign it was a bit jarring.

"This may spark a bit of controversy, but I know all Dante is thinking right now is Do Me Baby. I'm not going to keep you waiting. It's time for you to kiss the bride."

Dante scooped my sister in his arms, kissing her passionately for three full minutes. I'm talking all out tongue, love bites, and audible moaning. At one point, Aldridge covered his eyes because what was on display was clearly bedroom behavior. *Who has a mini make-out session in front of their parents?*

"Ladies and gentlemen, I present to you the Sexy Motherfuckers, Dante and Anika Caldwell."

The newlyweds danced out of the chapel to Prince's Kiss.

IF THE CEREMONY WAS INTIMATE, THE RECEPTION WAS THE complete opposite. A grand hall with all white everything. From the marble dance floor to the flower arrangements with roses, magnolias, peonies, and orchids. When we arrived the cocktail hour was already well underway, filled with friends and family ready to celebrate with the happy couple. Anika even invited some of her frenemies, no doubt to silently brag about her good fortune. Knowing my sister, the thought of her friends secretly envying her life was part of a successful wedding day.

Anika and Dante entered the hall to oohs and aahs from the crowd and immediately spun into their first dance as man and wife. I took my duties as maid of honor seriously and was currently at the bar ordering the couple's first drink. While I waited, massive arms enveloped me. A smile crept over my face as my body melted into Aldridge. Spinning around, I beamed up at the adoring face of the man of my dreams.

"One thing about Dante and Anika they know how to throw a party," he said.

"It's over the top and grand just like their personalities. I kind of love it."

"Well, I have to say you are without a doubt the finest maid of honor I've ever seen."

"You're bias."

"I just have good taste."

"Can you keep a secret?"

"Yes."

"I'm surprised this shit actually happened."

"Not a secret. Sometimes love hits like a freight train."

"The fact that Dante made all my sister's dreams come true tonight makes him brother-in-law of the year in my book."

"Dante is a lot of things. But he seems to be all in with your sister. Literally from their first meeting he had stars in his eyes."

Anika came bounding toward us. "Did you see us out there? We practiced our first dance for weeks."

"It was great. I would've probably omitted the part where you twerked against him but—"

"What, you didn't like that modest display of affection?" Aldridge teased. "That was my favorite part. Well, it's a tie between that and when he hoisted you in the air like Patrick Swayze in that one movie."

"That was actually the best part," I agreed.

"When we practiced the lift I fell a lot. Had to go to the hospital for head trauma but in the end it all came together." I laughed nervously, hoping she was joking.

The bartender knocked on the bar top signaling my drinks were ready. Grabbing both, I handed them to Anika. "For the bride and groom."

"Thank you. I'm gonna get so fucking wasted." She took both drinks to the head. "Alright, I'm going to find my husband." She cackled flashing her wedding rings before walking off.

"Did she say head trauma?"

Anika found Dante in the crowd of people and their faces lit up, elated to be reunited even though they'd only been apart for minutes.

"Are you okay?"

"I feel like a shitty sister for not taking her and Dante seriously. But when I saw how sincere she was during the vow exchange, it all made sense. This hasn't been some massive con she actually loves him."

"He feels the same."

"It's like the end of an era. I never thought my sister would settle down and get married."

"It was a beautiful day."

"It was. And she's a beautiful bride. And the wedding was exactly what she wanted, no compromises and that's what I love about my sister. She's always going to be unapologetically her authentic self."

"That's all anyone can ask for. Now come dance with me."

After toasts, dinner, and cake cutting, it was time for the garter toss. Dante used his teeth to remove the garter and the moans Anika made were obscene. Upon retrieval, he twirled the garter in his hand before handing the garter to Anika and claiming her bouquet. The two cast devilish grins before heading in Aldridge and my direction. Dante made a big show of handing me the bouquet and Anika, well Anika stuffed her garter in Aldi's mouth.

"You're next, my dude," Dante shouted. Aldridge tried his best to conceal his disgust while removing the garter.

"Are you okay?"

He flicked his tongue like a dog. "Am I gonna have to get shots?"

I hit him playfully with the bouquet.

By midnight I was feeling great and was out on the dance floor with Anika and Jemini shaking our asses to Juvenile "Back That Azz Up." Even I had to admit we were some bad bitches. We may not always agree, but my sister and mother knew how to have a good time. And Jemini was in heaven because this reception was a smorgasbord of fine eligible men, and she was making the rounds.

Anika tossed her arms over my shoulder, and we slow danced to a bass-heavy XYZ Baby song. "Sissy, thank you so much for being there for me."

"Of course."

"I know you didn't approve, but you stood by me."

"You deserve the world, and I just needed to make sure Dante was capable of giving that to you."

"He's great, he really is."

"Yep, I'm so very happy for you, and I meant every word in my toast."

"You do know you're so next?"

"What?"

"Aldridge has that look in his eyes. And you know he's a family man."

"I'm cool with where we're at for now."

"I'm calling it, this time next year you'll be a Mrs."

"Hmm."

"And then we'll be two bitching Mrs."

"Oh my God, I love you. You're drunk, but I love you."

"Drunk and horny. I think it's time to wrap this shit up. I'm ready to be stretched out by my husband. I'm talking …" Anika backed her ass up into me. "His dick has a hook in it and my coochie is a pinball machine."

"Remember you were going to work on oversharing?"

"I never promised that."

"I'm gonna make sure your driver is ready to go."

Squeezing her hand, I rushed to the exit. Once Dante and Anika leave, my maid of honor duties would end and I was ready to retire my bouquet. Aldridge helped me gather the guests outside for the farewell with bubbles as "I Wanna Sex You Up" played over the speakers. Dante carried Anika to the car, and they waved as the limousine pulled away from the curb. Anika popped out of the sunroof and screamed, "Bye Nessa, I love you."

I buried my face into Aldridge's chest, hoping to conceal the tears filling my eyes. Anika being happy was all that mattered. She may be my big sister, but I always felt the responsibility to take care of her, mostly because she never thought anything through. But she and Dante seemed to fit.

"You did a really good job supporting your sister."

I dabbed my eyes to prevent additional tears from falling. "I feel like a proud parent. My baby is all grown up."

"Dante has it from here."

"I can't believe I'm related to playboy basketball player Dante Caldwell."

"Playboy no more."

"I'm just glad it's over. This past week has been a lot. Between Jemini and my sister, I'm wiped."

"Two weeks in Greece will fix you right up."

"I can't wait." I squeezed his waist.

"You know this wedding got me thinking."

"Really, about?"

"About our happily ever after."

"Baby, this right here, you and me, *is* our happily ever after."

"I'll accept that for now. But I'm itching to say vows and make things official."

"Oh just you wait, we're gonna make things real official all over that private island you booked."

"I can't wait." He leaned in and I rose to my tiptoes to meet his kiss.

"Since the bride and groom have made their exit can we sneak out and get Fatburger on the way home?"

Aldridge caressed my cheek. "Yes, whatever you want."

"I like how that sounds. I do."

"Don't get used to it."

"Too late." I giggled.

ALDRIDGE

EPILOGUE

THREE MONTHS LATER

THE MOVING TRUCK WOULD BE HERE ANY MINUTE. I'D successfully purchased a home in Vegas. With inspections and a slight delay with the seller, I'd finally been able to close on a Thursday and was moving in. I didn't have much to move seeing how this house was one hundred and twenty percent bigger than my KC condo. But it was nice to have a place of my own and to finally get away from the curtain of smoke and wall of patrons at the casino I'd called home all season.

"ETA?" I asked, entering the kitchen.

"Twenty minutes," Nori said. She was helping Danessa plate pastries and brew coffee for the moving crew.

"You do know that's the third time you've asked that question?" Nessa smirked.

"He's like a kid on a road trip."

"Don't you two start teaming up on me." Danessa and Nori became fast friends. I never had a doubt, knowing they'd vibe instantly upon meeting. "What can I do to help?"

"Can you hand me the box of forks over there?" Danessa pointed to a plastic bag on the counter.

I did as instructed. "You don't have to feed movers you know."

"It's just a nice touch. Plus, this is how I cultivate relationships. You never know when you'll need to call in a favor at the last minute." She placed mini bottles of OJ in a silver bucket filled with ice.

"Are Dante and Anika coming?"

"Anika doesn't move boxes. But she did say they'd stop by with pizza later."

Anika and Dante had been married for one month, which was longer than I'd have placed a bet on. But I could officially add matchmaker to my list of talents because I was responsible for them hooking up. Anika was like a sister to me, and while I wouldn't have picked a playboy like Dante for her to settle down with, he seemed to be reformed, only having eyes for Anika.

"The movers are at the gate. I'll head out front to make sure they don't get lost." Nori set off in the direction of the front door.

"Are you excited?" Danessa asked.

"Yeah., I just want everything to go smoothly."

"It will. These movers are fast and efficient, and you have Nori who will make sure no box is left behind."

"You know we could have the movers swing by your place and box your shit up while we have them for the day."

"I already told you. We are not moving in together."

"Yet. You forgot to add yet." I pulled her into a hug, squeezing her tight.

"Yet." Danessa conceded with a smile.

"Don't act like you're not gonna be here all day every day anyway."

"That may be true but when you get on my nerves, I

need to have a place to go. Even Anika kept her condo and she and Dante are inseparable."

"I don't think we need to base living together around some arbitrary metric."

"Not arbitrary. It hasn't even been a year."

"It's been a year since I've moved to Vegas."

"I'm talking about dating."

"I feel you, but at some point paying two mortgages becomes silly."

"We'll discuss that when the time comes."

"You should know by now I can't get enough of you."

"Well let's see how you feel in a few months."

"Months, years, decades, my answer will always be the same. I love you, Nessa and we have a lot of time to make up for."

She cupped my cheek, her fingers fondling my ears. "I love you too. And this year is all about new beginnings. New house, new semester, new season."

"New beginnings I like that." Moving to Vegas came with the unexpected. I certainly didn't anticipate finding love and for it to be with the woman I couldn't stop thinking about. I'd built new friendships and lost some old ties. Lamonte and I still weren't talking. My mother and I were coolish, no matter what or how many times she took up for him, I'd still always have her back. One of the things I'd learned was if you're not willing to walk away, then you have to meet people where they are.

Vegas also provided new clarity about my sobriety. Change can cause people to stumble and relapse. But I'd pushed through with weekly NA meetings and the support of my friends. I was proud to say I'd now been sober for almost two and a half years, and I didn't take that accomplishment lightly because I fought for this every day.

There was so much to look forward to, the start of a new season, the chance to defend our crown, and my future with this fine woman wrapped in my arms.

Heartbreak taught me there's always love to be had. It might not always be romantic love. It could be love of self, or passion in a hobby, perhaps deep friendships that enrich you and build you up. A broken heart shouldn't stop you from loving and eventually when you're ready, you just might find your soulmate. And if you're really lucky, like me, it will be your first love, the woman who taught you this kind of love was even possible.

Danessa was that for me. My first love, my last love, my forever love.

COMING IN 2026

The final book in the Las Vegas Ramblers series will be releasing in 2026.

One of your favorite side characters is finally getting his book. I can't wait for you to read **Raphael and Anika's** story.

THANK YOU. LET'S CONNECT.

Thank you so much for reading Double Dribble. If you enjoyed Aldridge & Danessa's story, please help a sister out and leave a review or tell a friend. Your feedback is important to me and will help other readers decide whether to read my book too.

Feel free to connect with me virtually. I would love to engage with you.

◯ ♪ @ : @authorkashathompson

𝕏 : @authorkthompson

🌐 : kashathompson.com

HAPPY READING,

Kasha

ABOUT THE AUTHOR

Kasha Thompson is a contemporary romance author. She writes authentic love stories that examine the complexity of falling and staying in love. Her books center black love with relatable characters, humor, and spice.

ALSO BY KASHA THOMPSON

Working Through It
Figure Of Speech
Holding Back The Years
Last Night A DJ Saved My Life
Sight Unseen
Jamaal The IT Guy
Christmas With Kris Kringle

Las Vegas Ramblers Series
Defensive Stance
Jump Ball

The Birch Sibling Series
Love You A Little Bit